The Storm

Clive Cussler is the author or co-author of a great number of international bestsellers, including the famous Dirk Pitt® adventures, most recently *Crescent Dawn*; the NUMA® Files adventures; the *Oregon Files*, such as *The Jungle*; the Isaac Bell thrillers; and the Fargo novels, which began with *Spartan Gold*. His non-fiction works include *The Sea Hunters* and *The Sea Hunters II*; these describe the true adventures of the real NUMA, which, led by Cussler, searches for lost ships of historic significance. With his crew of volunteers, Cussler has discovered more than sixty ships, including the long-lost Confederate submarine *Hunley*. He lives in Arizona.

Graham Brown is the author of *Black Rain* and *Black Sun*. A pilot and an attorney, he lives in Arizona.

Find out more about the world of Clive Cussler by visiting
www.clivecussler.co.uk
Visit the NUMA® website at www.numa.net

D0618783

The Storm

Clive Cussler
and Graham Brown

MICHAEL JOSEPH
an imprint of
PENGUIN BOOKS

MICHAEL JOSEPH

Published by the Penguin Group
Penguin Books Ltd, 80 Strand, London wc2r orl, England
Penguin Group (USA) Inc., 375 Hudson Street, New York, New York 10014, USA
Penguin Group (Canada), 90 Eglinton Avenue East, Suite 700, Toronto, Ontario, Canada m4p 2y3
(a division of Pearson Penguin Canada Inc.)
Penguin Ireland, 25 St Stephen's Green, Dublin 2, Ireland (a division of Penguin Books Ltd)
Penguin Group (Australia), 250 Camberwell Road, Camberwell, Victoria 3124, Australia
(a division of Pearson Australia Group Pty Ltd)
Penguin Books India Pvt Ltd, 11 Community Centre, Panchsheel Park, New Delhi – 110 017, India
Penguin Group (NZ), 67 Apollo Drive, Rosedale, Auckland 0632, New Zealand
(a division of Pearson New Zealand Ltd)
Penguin Books (South Africa) (Pty) Ltd, Block D, Rosebank Office Park, 181 Jan Smuts Avenue,
Parktown North, Gauteng 2193, South Africa

Penguin Books Ltd, Registered Offices: 80 Strand, London wc2r orl, England

www.penguin.com

First published in the United States of America by G. P. Putnam's Sons 2012
First published in Great Britain by Michael Joseph 2012

001

Printed in Great Britain by Clays Ltd, St Ives plc

A CIP catalogue record for this book is available from the British Library

HARDBACK ISBN: 978–0–718–15910–8
TRADE PAPERBACK ISBN: 978–0–718–15911–5

www.greenpenguin.co.uk

MIX
Paper from
responsible sources
FSC
www.fsc.org   FSC™ C018179

Penguin Books is committed to a sustainable
future for our business, our readers and our planet.
This book is made from Forest Stewardship
Council™ certified paper.

ALWAYS LEARNING   **PEARSON**

THE STORM

PROLOGUE

INDIAN OCEAN
SEPTEMBER 1943

THE S.S. *JOHN BURY* SHUDDERED FROM BOW TO STERN AS it plowed through the rolling waters of the Indian Ocean. She was known as a "fast freighter," designed to accompany warships and used to traveling at a decent clip, but with all boilers going full out the *John Bury* was moving at a pace she hadn't seen since her sea trials. Damaged, burning, and trailing smoke, the *John Bury* was running for her life.

The ship crested a ten-foot wave, the deck pitched down and the bow dug into another swell. A wide swath of spray kicked up over the rail and whipped back across the deck, rattling what was left of the shattered bridge.

Topside, the *John Bury* was a mangled wreck. Smoke poured from twisted metal where rockets had pounded the superstructure. Debris littered the deck, and dead crewmen lay everywhere.

But the damage was above the waterline, and the fleeing ship would survive if it avoided any more hits.

On the dark horizon behind, smoke poured from other vessels that had been less fortunate. An orange fireball erupted from one, flashing across the water and briefly illuminating the carnage.

The burning hulks of four ships could be seen, three destroyers and a cruiser, ships that had been the *John Bury*'s escort. A Japanese submarine and a squadron of dive-bombers had found them simultaneously. As dusk approached, oil burned around the sinking vessels in a mile-long slick. It fouled the sky with dense black smoke. None of them would see the dawn.

The warships had been targeted and destroyed quickly, but the *John Bury* had only been strafed, hit with rockets and left to run free. There could be only one reason for that mercy; the Japanese knew of the top secret cargo she carried and they wanted it for themselves.

Captain Alan Pickett was determined not to let that happen, even with half his crew dead and his face gashed by shrapnel. He grabbed the voice tube and shouted down to the engine room.

"More speed!" he demanded.

There was no response. At last report a fire had been raging belowdecks. Pickett had ordered his men to stay and fight it, but now the silence left him gripped with fear.

"Zekes off the port bow!" a lookout called from the bridge wing. "Two thousand feet and dropping."

Pickett glanced through the shattered glass in front of him. In the failing light he saw four black dots wheeling in the gray sky and dropping toward the ship. Flashes lit from their wings.

"Get down!" he shouted.

Too late. Fifty caliber shells stitched a line across the ship, cutting the lookout in half and blasting apart what was left of the bridge. Shards of wood, glass and steel flew about the compartment.

Pickett hit the deck. A wave of heat flashed over the bridge as another rocket hit ahead of it. The impact rocked the ship, peeling back the metal ceiling like a giant can opener.

As the wave of destruction passed, Pickett looked up. The last of his officers lay dead, the bridge was demolished. Even the ship's wheel was gone, with only a stub of metal still attached to the spindle. Yet somehow the vessel chugged on.

As Pickett climbed back up, he spotted something that gave him hope: dark clouds and sweeping bands of rain. A squall line was moving in fast off the starboard bow. If he could get his ship into it, the coming darkness would hide him.

Holding on to the bulkhead for support, he reached for what remained of the wheel. He pushed with all the strength he had left. It moved half a turn, and he fell to the ground holding it.

The ship began to change course.

Pressing against the deck, he pushed the wheel upward and then brought it back down again for another full revolution.

The freighter was leaning into the turn now, drawing a curved white wake on the ocean's surface, coming around toward the squall.

The clouds ahead were thick. The rain falling from them was sweeping the surface like a giant broom. For the first time since the attack began, Pickett felt they had a chance, but as the ship plowed toward the squall the awful sound of the dive-bombers turning and plunging toward him again put that in doubt.

He searched through the ship's gaping wounds for the source of that noise.

Dropping from the sky directly in front of him were two Aichi D3A dive-bombers, Vals, the same type the Japanese had used with deadly effect at Pearl Harbor and months later against the British fleet near Ceylon.

Pickett watched them nose over and listened as the whistling sound of their wings grew louder. He cursed at them and pulled his sidearm.

"Get away from my ship!" he shouted, blasting at them with the Colt .45.

They pulled up at the last minute and roared past, riddling the ship with another spread of .50 caliber shells. Pickett fell back onto the deck, a shell clean through his leg, shattering it. His eyes opened, gazing upward. He was unable to move.

Waves of smoke and gray sky rolled above him. He was finished, he thought. The ship and its secret cargo would soon fall into enemy hands.

Pickett cursed himself for not scuttling the ship. He hoped it would somehow go down on its own before it could be boarded.

As his eyesight began to fail, the sound of more dive-bombers caught his ear. The roar grew louder, the banshee scream from their wings calling out and announcing the terrible inevitability of the end.

And then the sky above darkened. The air turned cold and wet, and the S.S. *John Bury* disappeared into the storm, swallowed up by a wall of mist and rain.

She was last reported by a Japanese pilot as burning but sailing under full power. She was never seen or heard from again.

CHAPTER 1

NORTHERN YEMEN, NEAR THE SAUDI BORDER
AUGUST 1967

TARIQ AL-KHALIF HID HIS FACE BEHIND A CLOTH OF SOFT white cotton. The kaffiyeh covered his head and wrapped around his mouth and nose. It kept the sun, wind and sand from his weather-beaten features as it hid him from the world.

Only Khalif's eyes showed, hard and sharp from sixty years in the desert. They did not blink or turn away as he stared at the dead bodies in the sand before him.

Eight bodies in all. Two men, three women, three children; stripped naked, all clothes and belongings gone. Most had been shot, a few had been stabbed.

As the camel train at Khalif's back waited, a rider moved slowly up toward him. Khalif recognized the strong, young figure in the saddle. A man named Sabah, his most trusted lieutenant. A Russian-made AK-47 lay slung over his shoulder.

"Bandits for certain," Sabah said. "No sign of them now."

Khalif studied the rough sand at his feet. He noticed the tracks disappearing to the west, headed directly toward the only source of water for a hundred miles, an oasis called Abi Quzza—the "silken water."

"No, my friend," he said. "These men are not waiting around to be discovered. They hide their numbers by sticking to the hard ground, where no tracks are left, or they walk on the softest sand, where the marks soon fade. But here I can see the truth, they're heading toward our home."

Abi Quzza had belonged to Khalif's family for generations. It provided life-giving water and a modicum of wealth. Date palms grew in abundance around its fertile springs, along with grass for the sheep and camels.

With the growing number of trucks and other forms of modern transportation, the caravans that paid for its gifts had begun to dwindle, and the role of camel-raising Bedouins like Khalif and his family were fading along with them, but they were not yet gone. For the clan to have any prospects at all, Khalif knew the oasis must be protected.

"Your sons will defend it," Sabah said.

The oasis lay twenty miles to the west. Khalif's sons, two nephews and their families waited there. A half dozen tents, ten men with rifles. It would not be an easy place to attack. And yet Khalif felt a terrible unease.

"We must hurry," he said, climbing back onto his camel.

Sabah nodded. He slid the AK-47 forward to a more aggressive position and nudged his camel forward.

Three hours later they approached the oasis. From a distance they could see nothing but small fires. There were no signs of struggle, no ripped tents or stray animals, no bodies lying in the sand.

Khalif ordered the camel train to a halt and dismounted. He took Sabah and two others, moving forward on foot.

The silence around them was so complete, they could hear the crackle of wood in the fires and their own feet scuffling in the sand. Somewhere in the distance, a jackal began to yelp. It was a long way off, but the noise carried in the desert.

Khalif halted, waiting for the jackal's call to fade. When it died away, a more pleasant sound followed: a small voice singing a traditional Bedouin melody. It came from the main tent and flowed quietly.

Khalif began to relax. It was the voice of his youngest son, Jinn.

"Bring the caravan," Khalif said. "All is well."

As Sabah and the others went back to the camels, Khalif walked forward. He reached his tent, threw open the flap, and froze.

A bandit dressed in rags stood there, holding a curved blade to his son's throat. Another bandit sat beside him, clutching an old rifle.

"One move and I slice his neck," the bandit said.

"Who are you?"

"I am Masiq," the bandit said.

"What do you want?" Khalif asked.

Masiq shrugged. "What don't we want?"

"The camels have value," Khalif said, guessing what they were after. "I will give them to you. Just spare my family."

"Your offer is meaningless to me," Masiq replied, his face twisting into a snarl of contempt. "Because I can take what I want, and because . . ."—he gripped the boy tightly—"except for this one, your family is already dead."

Khalif's heart tightened. Inside his tunic was a Webley-Fosbery automatic revolver. The self-cocking revolver was a sturdy weapon with deadly accuracy. It wouldn't jam even after months in the desert sand. He tried to think of a way to reach it.

"Then I'll give you everything," he said, "just for him. And you can go free."

"You have gold hidden here," Masiq said as if it were a known fact. "Tell us where it is."

Khalif shook his head. "I have no gold."

"Lies," the second bandit said.

Masiq began to laugh, his crooked teeth and decay-filled mouth making a horrific sound. Gripping the boy tightly with one arm, he raised the other as if to slice the boy's neck. But the child slipped loose, lunged for Masiq's fingers with his mouth and bit down hard.

Masiq cursed in pain. His hand snapped back as if he'd been burned.

Khalif's own hand found the revolver and he blasted two shots right through his tunic. The would-be murderer fell backward, two smoking holes in his chest.

The second bandit fired, grazing Khalif's leg, but Khalif's shot hit him square in the face. The man fell without a word, but the battle had only just begun.

Outside the tent, gunfire began to echo through the night. Shots were being traded, volleys flying back and forth. Khalif recognized the sound of heavy bolt-action rifles, like the one in the dead thug's hand, they were answered by the rattling sound of Sabah and his automatic rifle.

Khalif grabbed his son, placing the pistol in the young boy's hand. He picked up the old rifle from beside one of the dead bandits. He plucked the curved knife from the ground as well and moved deeper into the tent.

His older sons lay there as if resting side by side. Their clothes were soaked with dark blood and riddled with holes.

A wave of pain swept over Khalif; pain and bitterness and anger.

With the gunfire raging outside, he stuck the knife into the side of the tent and cut a small hole. Peering through it, he saw the battle.

Sabah and three of the men were firing from behind a shield of dead camels. A group of thugs dressed like the bandits he'd just killed were out in the oasis itself, hiding behind date palms in knee-high water.

There did not seem to be enough of them to have taken the camp by force.

He turned to Jinn. "How did these men get here?"

"They asked to stay," the boy said. "We watered their camels."

That they'd played on the tradition of Bedouin generosity and the kindness of Khalif's sons before killing them enraged Khalif further. He went to the other side of the tent. This time he plunged the knife into the fabric and drew it sharply downward.

"Stay here," he ordered Jinn.

Khalif snuck through the opening and worked his way into the darkness. Moving in a wide arc, he curled in behind his enemies and slipped into the oasis.

Preoccupied with Sabah and his men at their front, the bandits never noticed Khalif flanking them. He came up behind them and opened fire, blasting them in the back from close range.

Three went down quickly and then a fourth. Another tried to run and was killed by a shot from Sabah, but the sixth and final thug turned around in time and fired back.

A slug hit Khalif's shoulder, knocking him backward and

sending a jolt of pain surging though his body. He landed in the water.

The bandit rushed toward him, perhaps thinking him dead or too wounded to fight.

Khalif aimed the old rifle and pulled the trigger. The shell jammed in the breach. He grabbed the bolt and worked to free it, but his wounded arm was not strong enough to break loose the frozen action.

The bandit raised his own weapon, drawing a bead on Khalif's chest. And then the sound of the Webley revolver rang out like thunder.

The bandit fell against a date palm with a puzzled look on his face. He slid down it, the weapon falling from his hands into the water.

Jinn stood behind the dead man, holding the pistol in a shaking grip, his eyes filled with tears.

Khalif looked around for more enemies, but he saw none. The shooting had stopped. He could hear Sabah shouting to the men. The battle was over.

"Come here, Jinn," he ordered.

His son moved toward him, shaking and trembling. Khalif took him under one arm and held him.

"Look at me."

The boy did not respond.

"Look at me, Jinn!"

Finally Jinn turned. Khalif held his shoulder tightly.

"You are too young to understand, my son, but you have done a mighty thing. You have saved your father. You have saved your family."

"But my brothers and mother are dead," Jinn cried.

"No," Khalif said. "They are in paradise, and we will go on, until we meet them one day."

Jinn did not react, he only stared and sobbed.

A sound from the right turned Khalif. One of the bandits was alive and trying to crawl away.

Khalif raised the curved knife, ready to finish the man, but then held himself back. "Kill him, Jinn."

The shaking boy stared blankly. Khalif stared back, firm and unyielding.

"Your brothers are dead, Jinn. The future of the clan rests with you. You must learn to be strong."

Jinn continued to shake, but Khalif was all the more certain now. Kindness and generosity had almost destroyed them. Such weakness had to be banished from his only surviving son.

"You must never have pity," Khalif said. "He is an enemy. If we have not the strength to kill our enemies, they will take the waters from us. And without the waters, we inherit only wandering and death."

Khalif knew he could force Jinn to do it, knew he could order him and the boy would follow the command. But he needed Jinn to choose the act himself.

"Are you afraid?"

Jinn shook his head. Slowly, he turned and raised the pistol.

The bandit glanced back at him, but instead of Jinn buckling, his hand grew steady. He looked the bandit in the face and pulled the trigger.

The gun's report echoed across the water and out into the desert. By the time it faded, tears no longer flowed from the young boy's eyes.

CHAPTER 2

The ninety-foot catamaran lolled its way across calm waters of the Indian Ocean at sunset. It was making three or four knots in a light breeze. A brilliant white sail rose above the wide deck. Five-foot letters in turquoise spelled out NUMA across its central section—the National Underwater and Marine Agency.

Kimo A'kona stood near one of the catamaran's twin bows. He was thirty years old, with jet-black hair, a chiseled body and the swirling designs of a traditional Hawaiian tattoo on his arm and shoulder. He stood on the bow in bare feet, balancing on the very tip as if he were hanging ten on a surfboard.

He held a long pole ahead and to the side, dipping an instrument into the water. Readings on a small display screen told him it was working.

He called out the results. "Oxygen level is a little low, temperature is 21 degrees centigrade, 70.4 Fahrenheit."

Behind Kimo, two others watched. Perry Halverson, the team leader and oldest member of the crew, stood at the helm. He wore khaki shorts, a black T-shirt and an olive drab "boonie" hat he'd owned for years.

Beside him, Thalia Quivaros, who everyone called T, stood on the deck in white shorts and a red bikini top that accented her tan figure enough to distract both men.

"That's the coldest reading yet," Halverson noted. "Three full degrees cooler than it should be this time of year."

"The global warming people aren't going to like that," Kimo noted.

"Maybe not," Thalia said as she typed the readings into a small computer tablet. "But it's definitely a pattern. Twenty-nine of the last thirty readings are off by at least two degrees."

"Could a storm have passed through here?" Kimo asked. "Dumping rain or hail that we aren't accounting for?"

"Nothing for weeks," Halverson replied. "This is an anomaly, not a local distortion."

Thalia nodded. "Deepwater readings from the remote sensors we dropped are confirming it. Temperatures are way off, all the way down to the thermocline. It's like the sun's heat is missing this region somehow."

"I don't think the sun's the problem," Kimo said. The ambient air temperature had reached the high in the nineties a few hours before as the sun had been blazing from a cloudless sky. Even as it set, the last rays were strong and warm.

Kimo reeled in the instrument, checked it and then swung the pole like a fly fisherman. He cast the sensor out forty feet from the boat, letting it sink and drift back. The second reading came back identical to the first.

"At least we've found something to tell the brass back in D.C.," Halverson said. "You know they all think we're on a pleasure cruise out here."

"I'm guessing it's an upwelling," Kimo said. "Something like the El Niño/La Niña effect. Although since this is the Indian Ocean, they will probably call it something in Hindu."

"Maybe they could name it after us," Thalia suggested. "The Quivaros-A'kona-Halverson effect. QAH for short."

"Notice how she put herself up front," Kimo said to Halverson.

"Ladies first," she said with a nod and a smile.

Halverson laughed and adjusted his hat.

"While you guys figure that out, I'll get started on the mess for tonight. Anyone for flying-fish tacos?"

Thalia looked at him suspiciously. "We had those last night."

"Lines are empty," Halverson said. "We didn't catch anything today."

Kimo thought about that. The farther they sailed into the cold zone, the less sea life they'd found. It was like the ocean was turning barren and cold. "Sounds better than canned goods," he said.

Thalia nodded, and Halverson ducked into the cabin to whip them up some dinner. Kimo stood and gazed off to the west.

The sun had finally dropped below the horizon, and the sky was fading to an indigo hue with a line of blazing orange just above the water. The air was soft and humid, the temperature now around eighty-five degrees. It was a perfect evening, made even more perfect by the notion that they'd discovered something unique.

They had no idea what was causing it, but the temperature

anomaly seemed to be wreaking havoc with the weather across the region. So far, there'd been little rain across southern and western India at a time when the monsoons were supposed to be brewing.

Concern was spreading as a billion people were waiting for the seasonal downpours to bring the rice and wheat crops to life. From what he'd heard nerves were fraying. Memories of the previous year's light harvest had sparked talk of famine if something didn't change soon.

While Kimo realized there was little he could do about it, he hoped they were close to determining the cause. The last few days suggested they were on the right track. They would check the readings again in an hour, a few miles to the west. In the meantime, dinner called.

Kimo reeled the sensor back in. As he pulled it from the water, something odd caught his eye. He squinted. A hundred yards off, a strange black sheen was spreading across the ocean surface like a shadow.

"Check this out," he said to Thalia.

"Stop trying to get me up there in close quarters," she joked.

"I'm serious," he said. "There's something on the water."

She put down the computer tablet and came forward, putting a hand on his arm to steady herself on the narrow bowsprit. Kimo pointed to the shadow. It was definitely spreading, moving across the surface like oil or algae, though it had an odd texture to it unlike either of those things.

"Do you see that?"

She followed his gaze and then brought a pair of binoculars to her eyes. After a few seconds, she spoke.

"It's just the light playing tricks on you."

"It's not the light."

She stared through the binoculars a moment longer and then offered them to him. "I'm telling you, there's nothing out there."

Kimo squinted in the failing light. Were his eyes deceiving him? He took the binoculars and scanned the area. He lowered them, brought them up and lowered them again.

Nothing but water. No algae, no oil, no odd texture to the surface of the sea. He scanned to both sides to make sure he wasn't looking in the wrong place, but the sea looked normal again.

"I'm telling you, there was something out there," he said.

"Nice try," she replied. "Let's eat."

Thalia turned and picked her way back toward the catamaran's main deck. Kimo took one final look, saw nothing out of the ordinary, then shook his head and turned to follow her.

A few minutes later they were in the main cabin, chowing down on fish tacos Halverson style while laughing and discussing their thoughts as to the cause of the temperature anomaly.

As they ate, the catamaran continued northwest with the wind. The smooth fiberglass of its twin bows sliced through the calm sea, the water slid past, traveling silently along the hydrodynamic shape.

And then something began to change. The water's viscosity seemed to thicken slightly. The ripples grew larger and they moved a fraction slower. The brilliant white fiberglass of the boat's pontoons began to darken at the waterline as if being tinted by a dye of some kind.

This continued for several seconds as a charcoal-colored stain began spreading across the side of the hull. It began to move upward, defying gravity, as if being drawn by some power.

A texture to the stain resembled graphite or a darker, thinner version of quicksilver. Before long, the leading edge of this stain crested the catamaran's bow, swirling in the very spot where Kimo had stood.

Had someone been watching closely, they would have noticed a pattern appear. For an instant the substance shaped itself like footprints, before becoming smooth once again and slithering backward, headed toward the main cabin.

Inside the cabin, a radio played, picking up a shortwave broadcast of classical music. It was good dinner music, and Kimo found himself enjoying the evening and the company as much as the food. But as Halverson fought against divulging the secret of his taco recipe, Kimo noticed something odd.

Something was beginning to cover the cabin's broad tinted windows, blocking out the fading sky and the illumination from the boat's lights high up on the mast. The substance climbed up the glass the way wind-driven snow or sand might pile up against a flat surface, but much, much faster.

"What in the world . . ."

Thalia looked to the window. Halverson's eyes went the other way, glancing out at the aft deck with alarm on his face.

Kimo swung his head around. Some type of gray substance was flowing through the open door, moving along the deck of the boat but flowing uphill.

Thalia saw it too. Heading straight for her.

She jumped out of her seat, knocking her plate from the table. The last bites of her dinner landed in front of the advancing mass. When it reached the leftovers, the gray substance flowed over the bits of food, covering it completely and swirling around it in a growing mound.

"What is that?" she asked.

"I don't know," Kimo said. "I've never . . ."

He didn't have to finish his sentence. None of them had ever seen anything like it. Except . . .

Kimo's eyes narrowed, the strange substance flowed like a liquid, but it had a grainy texture. It seemed more like metallic powder sliding across itself, like waves of the finest sand shifting in the wind.

"That's what I saw on the water," he said, backing away. "I told you there was something out there."

"What's it doing?"

All of them were standing and easing backward.

"It looks like it's eating the fish," Halverson said.

Kimo stared, vacillating between fear and wonder. He glanced through the open door. The rear deck was covered.

He looked around for a way out. Moving forward would only take them down into the catamaran's berths, trapping them. Going aft would mean stepping on the strange substance.

"Come on," he said, climbing onto the table. "Whatever that stuff is, I'm pretty sure we don't want to touch it."

As Thalia climbed up beside him, Kimo reached toward the skylight and propped it open. He gave her a boost, and she pulled herself up through the opening and onto the cabin's roof.

Halverson climbed onto the table next but slipped. His foot slammed into the metallic dust, splashing it like a puddle. Some of it splattered onto his calf.

Halverson grunted as if he'd been stung. Reaching down, he tried to swipe it off his leg, but half of what he swiped clung to his hand.

He shook his hand rapidly and then rubbed it on his shorts.

"It's burning my skin," he said, his face showing the pain.

"Come on, Perry," Kimo shouted.

Halverson climbed up on the table with a small amount of the silvery residue still clinging to his hand and leg, and the table buckled under the weight of the two men.

Kimo grabbed the edge of the skylight and held on, but Halverson fell. He landed on his back, hitting his head. The impact seemed to stun him. He grunted and rolled over, putting his hands down on the deck to push off with.

The gray substance swarmed over him, covering his hands, his arms and his back. He managed to get up and brace himself against the bulkhead, but some of the residue reached his face. Halverson pawed at his face as if bees were swarming around him. His eyes were shut tight, but the strange particles were forcing themselves under his eyelids and streaming into his nostrils and ears.

He stepped away from the bulkhead and fell to his knees. He began digging at his ears and screaming. Lines of the swarming substance curled over his lips and began flowing down into his throat, turning his screams into the gurgles of a choking man. Halverson fell forward. The spreading mass of particles began to cover him as if he was being consumed by a horde of ants in the jungle.

"Kimo!" Thalia shouted.

Her voice snapped Kimo out of his trance. He pulled himself up and scrambled through the opening onto the roof. He shut the skylight and sealed it hard. From the spotlights high in the mast he could see that the gray swarm had spread across the entire deck, both fore and aft. It was also creeping upward along the sides of the cabin.

Here and there it seemed to be swarming over things as it had done to the fallen dinner items and Halverson.

"It's coming up over here," Thalia shouted.

"Don't touch it!"

On his side the invading swarm had made less progress. Kimo reached over and grabbed for anything that would help. His hand found the deck hose and he turned it on, grabbing the nozzle and spraying high-pressure water at the gray mass.

The jet of liquid swept the particles backward, washing them off the cabin's wall like mud.

"On this side!"

He stepped to her side and blasted away at the muck.

"Get behind me!" he shouted, directing the hose.

The pressurized stream of water helped, but it was a losing battle. The swarm was surrounding them and closing in on all sides. Try as he might, Kimo could not keep up.

"We should jump," Thalia shouted.

Kimo looked to the ocean. The swarm extended out from the boat and onto the sea from which it had come.

"I don't think so," he said.

Desperate for something that would help, he scanned the deck. Two five-gallon cans of gasoline sat near the aft end of the boat. He aimed the hose at full pressure, sweeping it from side to side and blasting a path through the swarm.

He dropped the hose, ran forward, and leapt. He landed on the wet deck, skidded across it and slammed into the transom at the rear of the boat.

A stinging feeling on his hands and legs—like rubbing alcohol had been poured over open skin—told him some of the residue had found him. He ignored the pain, grabbed the first jerry can and began pouring fuel across the deck.

The gray residue recoiled at the flow, curling out of the way and retreating but probing for a new path forward.

Up on the cabin's roof, Thalia was using the hose, blasting the water around her in an ever smaller circle. Suddenly, she cried out and dropped the hose as if she'd been stung. She turned and began to climb the mast, but Kimo could see the swarm had begun covering her legs.

She screamed and fell. "Kimo!" she shouted. "Help me. Help m—"

He splashed the deck with the rest of the gasoline and grabbed for the second can. It was light and almost empty. Fear knifed through Kimo's heart like a spear.

Only gurgling noises and the sound of struggling came from where Thalia had fallen. Her hand was all he could see, writhing where it stuck out from beneath the mass of particles. In front of him, that same mass had resumed its search for a path to his feet.

He looked once again to the surface of the sea. The horde covered it like a sheen of liquid metal all the way out to the limits of the light. Kimo faced the awful truth. There was no escape.

Not wanting to die like Thalia and Halverson had, Kimo made a painful decision.

He dumped the rest of the fuel onto the deck, forcing the swarm back once more, grabbed for a lighter he carried and dropped down to one knee. He held the lighter against the gasoline-soaked deck, steeled himself to act and snapped his finger along the flint.

Sparks snapped and the vapors lit. A flashover whipped forward from the aft end of the catamaran. Flames raced through the approaching swarm all the way to the cabin and then roared back toward Kimo, swirling around him and setting him ablaze.

The agony was too intense to endure even for the brief seconds he had left to live. Engulfed in fire, and unable to scream with his lungs burned out, Kimo A'kona staggered backward and fell into the waiting sea.

CHAPTER 3

KURT AUSTIN STOOD IN A SEMIDARKENED WORK BAY ON THE lower level of his boathouse as the hour crept past midnight.

Broad-shouldered, relatively handsome, Kurt tended more toward rugged than striking. His hair was a steel gray color, slightly out of place on a man who looked to be in his mid-thirties yet perfect for the man all Kurt's friends knew him to be. His jaw was square, his teeth relatively straight but not perfect, his face sun-kissed and lined from years spent on the water and out in the elements.

Sturdy and *solid* were the terms used to describe him. And yet, from that rugged face came a piercing gaze. The directness of Kurt's stare and the brilliance of his coral-blue eyes often caused people to pause as if taken by surprise.

Right now, those eyes were studying a labor of love.

Kurt was building a racing scull. Thoughts of performance ruled his mind. Drag coefficients and leverage factors and the power that could be generated by a human being.

The air around him smelled of varnish, and the floor was littered with shavings, wood chips and other types of debris, the kind that piled up and marked one's progress when crafting a boat by hand.

After months of on-and-off work, Kurt felt he'd achieved something near to perfection. Twenty feet long. Narrow and sleek. The wooden craft's honey blond color shined from beneath nine coats of shellac with a glow that seemed to light up the room.

"A damn fine boat," Kurt said, admiring the finished product.

The boat's glasslike finish made the color seem deep as if you could look into it for miles. A slight change in focus, and the room around him was caught in the reflection.

On one side of the reflection, a new set of tools sat untouched in a bright red box. On the other side, pegged to the backboard of the workbench with meticulous precision, were a set of old hammers, saws and planes, their wooden handles cracked and discolored with age.

The new tools he'd bought himself, the old ones were hand-me-downs from his grandfather—a gift and a message all at the same time. And right in the middle, like a man caught between two worlds, Kurt saw his own reflection.

It seemed appropriate. Kurt spent most of his time working with modern technology, but he loved the old things of this world; old guns, antebellum and Victorian homes and even historical letters and documents. All these things grabbed his attention with equal power. But the boats he owned, including the one he'd just finished, brought out the purest sense of joy.

For now, the sleek craft rested in a cradle, but tomorrow he would lift it off its frame, connect the oars and take it down to the water for its maiden voyage. There, powered by the considerable strength in his legs, arms and back, the scull would slice through the calm surface of the Potomac at a surprising clip.

In the meantime, he told himself, he'd better stop looking at it and admiring his own work or he'd be too tired to row in the morning.

He lowered the bay door and stepped toward the light switch.

Before he could flick it off, an annoying buzz startled him. His cell phone was the culprit, vibrating on the work desk. He grabbed the phone, instantly recognized the name on the screen and pressed ANSWER.

It was Dirk Pitt, the Director of NUMA, Kurt's boss and a good friend. Before he'd taken over as Director, Pitt had spent a couple of decades risking life and limb on special projects for the organization. Occasionally, he still did.

"Sorry to bother you in the middle of the night," Pitt said. "I hope you don't have company."

"Actually," Kurt replied, looking back at his boat, "I'm in the presence of a beautiful blonde. She's graceful and smooth as silk. And I can see myself spending lots of time alone with her."

"I'm afraid you're going to postpone all that and tell her good night," Pitt said.

The serious tone in Pitt's voice came through loud and clear.

"What's happened?"

"You know Kimo A'kona?" Pitt asked.

"I worked with him on the Hawaiian Ecology Project," Kurt replied, realizing that Pitt wouldn't start a conversation that way unless something bad was coming. "He's first-rate. Why do you ask?"

"He was working an assignment for us in the Indian Ocean," Pitt began. "Perry Halverson and Thalia Quivaros were with him. We lost contact with them two days ago."

Kurt didn't like the sound of that, but radios failed, sometimes entire electrical systems did, often the boaters turned up safe and sound.

"What happened?"

"We don't know, but this morning their catamaran was spotted adrift, fifty miles from where it should have been. An aircraft from the Maldives made a low pass this afternoon. The photos showed extensive fire damage on the hull. No sign of the crew."

"What were they working on?"

"Just analyzing water temps, salinity and oxygen levels," Pitt said. "Nothing dangerous. I save those jobs for you and Joe."

Kurt couldn't imagine any reason such a study might offend someone. "And yet you think it was foul play?"

"We don't know what it was," Dirk said firmly. "But something's not right. We can see the life-raft containers from the air. The casings are burned but otherwise untouched. Halverson was a ten-year vet, he was a merchant marine sailor for eight years before that. Kimo and Thalia were younger, but they were well trained. And none of us can come up with a reason for a widespread fire aboard a sailboat to begin with. Even if we could, no one can tell me why three trained sailors would fail to deploy a life raft or get off a distress call under such conditions."

Kurt remained silent. He couldn't think of a reason either, unless they were somehow incapacitated.

"The bottom line is, they're missing," Dirk said. "Perhaps we'll find them. But you and I have been around long enough to know this doesn't look good."

Kurt understood the math. Three members of NUMA were missing and presumed dead. Something both Dirk Pitt and Kurt Austin took personally.

"What do you need me to do?"

"A salvage team from the Maldives is getting set up," Pitt said. "I want you and Joe on-site as soon as possible. That means you're on a plane in four hours."

"Not a problem," Kurt said. "Is anyone still looking for them?"

"Search-and-rescue aircraft out of the Maldives, a pair of Navy P-3s and a long-range squadron from southern India have been crisscrossing the zone since the boat was spotted. Nothing yet."

"So this isn't a rescue mission."

"I only wish it was," Pitt said. "But unless we get some good news that I'm not expecting to receive, your job is to figure out what happened and why."

In the dark bay, unseen by Pitt, Kurt nodded. "Understood."

"I'll let you wake Mr. Zavala," Pitt said. "Keep me posted."

Kurt acknowledged the directive, and Dirk Pitt hung up.

Placing the phone down, Kurt thought about the mission ahead. He hoped against all reason that the three NUMA members would be found bobbing in their life jackets by the time he crossed the Atlantic, but considering the description of the catamaran and the length of time they'd been missing, he doubted it.

He slid the phone into his pocket and took a long look at the gleaming craft he'd built.

Without another second of hesitation, he reached for the light switch, flicked it off and walked out.

His date would have to wait for another morning.

CHAPTER 4

CENTRAL YEMEN

A FIGURE CLOAKED IN WHITE STOOD ON A ROCKY OUT-cropping that jutted above the sand of Yemen's sprawling desert. The wind tugged at his caftan, producing a muted flapping sound as it waved in the breeze.

A gleaming white helicopter sat on the bluff behind him. A green insignia, depicting two date palms shading an oasis, deco-rated its side. Three stories below lay the entrance to a wide cave.

In times past, the cave would have been guarded by a few Bed-ouin men hidden in the crags of the bluff, but on this day there were a dozen men with automatic rifles in plain view, another twenty or so remaining hidden.

Jinn al-Khalif raised a pair of binoculars to his eyes and watched as a trio of Humvees rolled across the desert toward him. They rose and fell on the dunes like small boats crossing the swells of the sea. They traveled in an arrow formation, headed his way.

"They follow the ancient track," he said, speaking to a figure beside and slightly behind him. "In my father's time they would have been spice caravans and traders, Sabah. Now only bankers come to see us."

He lowered the binoculars and looked to the bearded older man who stood beside him. Sabah had been his father's most loyal hand. Sabah was dressed in darker robes and he carried a radio.

"You are wise to understand their motives," Sabah said. "They care nothing for us or our struggle. They come because you promise them wealth. You must deliver before we can do as we choose."

"Is Xhou with them?"

Sabah nodded. "He is. Upon his arrival, all the members of the consortium will be present. We should not keep them waiting."

"And what of General Aziz, the Egyptian?" Jinn asked. "Does he continue to withhold the funds he's promised?"

"He will speak with us three days from now," Sabah said. "When it is a better time for him."

Jinn al-Khalif took a deep breath, inhaling the pure desert air. Aziz had pledged many millions to the consortium on behalf of a cadre of Egyptian businessmen and the military, but he had yet to pay a cent.

"Aziz mocks us," Jinn said.

"We will talk with him and bring him back in line," Sabah insisted.

"No," Jinn said. "He will continue to defy us because he can. Because he feels he is beyond our reach."

Sabah looked at Jinn quizzically.

"It's the answer to the riddle of life," Jinn said. "What matters isn't money or wealth or lust or even love. None of those things were enough to save me when the bandits took our camp. There is only one thing that matters, now just as it did then: power. Raw, overwhelming power. He who has it, rules. He who doesn't, begs. Aziz has us begging, but I will soon turn the tables on him. I will soon attain a kind of power that has never been held by a man before."

Sabah nodded slowly and a smile wrinkled his beard. "You have learned well, Jinn. Even better than I could have hoped. Truly, you surpass your teacher."

Below them, the Humvees were slowing to a stop in front of the cave.

"You have been the pole star that guides me," Jinn said. "That is why my father entrusted me to your care."

Sabah bowed slightly. "I accept your words of kindness. Now, let us greet our guests."

Minutes later they were inside the cavern, four levels below. The interior temperature was eighty-one degrees, a stark contrast to the one-hundred-and-five-degree winds beginning to blow outside.

Despite the primitive setting, the assembled guests sat in comfortable office chairs at a black conference table. The room around them had been engineered and carved from what was once an uneven chamber. It now resembled a great hall filled with modern decor.

Small screens lay recessed in the table in front of them. Computers lined the walls. Hidden rooms beyond this one held sleeping quarters and racks of weapons.

At great expense, Jinn had transformed this old Bedouin meeting place from a dusty fissure to a modern headquarters. It had proven a long and complicated process, much like the evolution of his family from a group of nomads who traded camels and traditional goods to a modern enterprise with its hands in technology, oil and shipping.

Long gone were the camels and the oasis that his family had

claimed for centuries, traded away in exchange for small stakes in modern companies. All that remained were his father's words: *You must never have pity . . . And without the waters, we inherit only wandering and death.*

Jinn had never forgotten this message or the need for utter ruthlessness in obeying it. With Sabah's help and the funds from those who'd gathered in his cave, he was one step from making certain they would control the waters of half the world, like his father had controlled the oasis.

Mr. Xhou walked in along with his aides. Sabah greeted him and showed him to his seat. There were nine men of importance present. Mr. Xhou from China. Mustafa from Pakistan. Sheik Abin da-Alhrama from Saudi Arabia. Suthar had come from Iran, Attakari from Turkey and several lesser guests from North Africa, former Soviet republics and other Arab countries.

They were not government representatives but businessmen, men with an interest in Jinn's plan.

"By the grace of Allah we are together again," Jinn began.

"Please dispense with the religious pronouncements," Mr. Xhou said. "And tell us of your progress. You have called us here to ask for more funding and we have yet to see the effects that you've already promised."

Xhou's bluntness rankled Jinn, but he was the biggest investor, both in funds given to Jinn and in money spent betting on the payoff Jinn had promised. Because of this, Xhou was impatient and had been from the beginning. He seemed most anxious to get past the investing phase and into the profiting phase. And with Aziz stiffing them, Jinn needed Xhou's backing more than ever.

"As you know, General Aziz has been unable to release the assets he promised."

"Perhaps wisely," Xhou said. "So far, we've spent billions, with little to show for it. I now hold two million acres of worthless Mongolian desert. If your boasts do not come true soon, my patience will end."

"I assure you," Jinn responded, "the progress will soon become apparent."

He clicked a remote, and the little screens in front of each guest lit up. A larger screen on the wall showed the same diagram, a color representation of the Arabian Sea and the Indian Ocean. Red, orange and yellow sectors displayed temperature gradients. Circulating arrows showed the direction and speed of the currents.

"This is the standard current pattern of the Indian Ocean based on the averages of the last thirty years," Jinn said. "In winter and spring this pattern is from the east to the west, flowing counterclockwise, driven by cold, high-pressure dry winds from India and China. But in summer the pattern changes. The continent heats up faster than the sea. The air rises, drawing wind onshore. The current changes and flows in a clockwise pattern, and it brings the monsoon to India."

Jinn clicked the remote to show the pattern changing.

"As you know, the temperature and pressure gradients drive the winds. The winds drive the ocean currents, and together they produce either dry air or monsoon rains. In this case, pumping moisture over India and Southeast Asia, creating the monsoon rains that drench those lands, allowing them to feed their massive populations."

New animation on the display showed clouds streaming over India and into Bangladesh, Vietnam, Cambodia and Thailand.

"We know all this," Mustafa of Pakistan said abruptly. "We have seen this demonstration before. While they have abundant crops, our lands remain dry. Your sands are parched. We have come here to see if you are succeeding in changing this for we have invested a fortune in your scheme."

"Yes, that's right," another representative said.

"Would I have called you all together if I had no proof?"

"If you have it, show us," Xhou demanded.

Jinn tapped the remote, and the screen changed once again.

"Three years ago we began to seed the horde into the eastern quadrant of the Indian Ocean."

On screen, a small, irregularly shaped triangle appeared near the equator.

"Each year—with your funds—we have seeded further sections. Each year, the horde, as promised, has grown on its own. Two years ago it covered ten percent of the target area."

The irregular triangle elongated and stretched with the current. A second curving section stretched toward it from the west.

"A year ago it reached thirty percent saturation."

Another click, another diagram. The two dark smears joined and were spreading across the southern loop of the Indian Ocean current.

"We already know that the rains have become less plentiful in India. Last year's crop was the lightest in decades. This year they will be waiting on clouds that do not come."

He clicked the remote one more time. The sparse black swaths had thinned, but a thicker, darker pattern in the central section of the Indian Ocean had grown. Through the natural action of the ocean currents, and Jinn's manipulation, the horde had become highly concentrated in an area known to oceanographers as a gyre, the center of the Great Whirl. Concentrated this way, it would produce a far stronger effect on the water temperature, and the weather that flowed from it.

"Water temperatures are dropping, but the air temperatures

above the sea are increasing, becoming more like the fluctuations one feels over the land," Jinn said. "The weather patterns are changing course. Already it is raining more than ever in the high-lands of Ethiopia and Sudan. After years of drought, Lake Nasser is in danger of exceeding maximum capacity."

The group seemed impressed. All except Xhou.

"The starvation of India will do none of us any good," he said. "Aside, perhaps, from Mustafa, who sees them as an old enemy. Our intent is to have grain to sell them when their silos are bare. Which cannot happen unless there is a corresponding change in the rainfall over our own countries."

"Of course," Jinn agreed. "But you cannot have the second effect without initially accomplishing the first. Your rain will fall, your worthless dry land will sprout with crops and you will make even greater fortunes than you already have by selling rice and grain to a billion starving people."

Xhou settled back with a harrumph and folded his arms. He did not appear satisfied.

"The science is simple," Jinn said. "Six thousand years ago the Middle East, the Arabian peninsula and North Africa were fer-tile, not dry. They were grasslands, savannahs and tree-covered plains. Then the weather pattern changed and turned them to deserts. The cause of this was a change in ocean currents and the temperature gradients of those currents. Almost any scientist you speak to will confirm this as a fact. We are in the process of chang-ing it back. The first sign of progress was last year. This year will be undeniable."

Sheik Alhrama of Saudi Arabia spoke next. "How is it no one has spotted your horde? Surely something this large cannot be missed by satellites."

"The swarm remains below the surface during the day. It

keeps the heat from penetrating into the ocean's lower levels by absorbing it. When night falls, the swarm surfaces and radiates the heat back into the sky. There is nothing to see. A normal satellite picture will show only ocean water. A thermal image will show odd radiation."

"What about water samples?" Xhou asked.

"Unless it, the horde, is placed in its most aggressive setting, even a sample of water will appear to the naked eye as little more than cloudy, perhaps polluted, water. Unless they are viewed under an extremely powerful microscope, the microbots of the horde cannot be seen individually. There is nothing to give us away. But just in case, we keep an eye on the research ships. The horde steers clear of them."

"Not all of them."

Jinn was taken by surprise. He guessed what Xhou was about to say but was surprised he had such information. Then again, one didn't rise to the top as Xhou had without knowing how to dig up information.

"What is he talking about?" Mustafa asked.

"A small research vessel took us by surprise," Jinn said. "Americans. They've been dealt with."

Xhou shook his head. "The Americans you speak of come from an organization known as NUMA. The National Underwater and Marine Agency."

A murmur went through the group, and Jinn sensed he had to control the situation quickly. He needed the next installment of funds or the whole operation would collapse.

"It could not be helped," he said. "We had no reason to suspect a sailboat with a crew of three. They filed no permits, made no announcements. By the time we realized what they were up to, they were on the verge of discovering the horde. They had al-

ready sent data on the temperature gradient back to their headquarters."

"What happened?" the Sheik asked.

"The horde consumed them."

"Consumed them?"

Jinn nodded. "In a foraging mode, the horde can devour anything in its path. It's a part of their program, required for reproduction and self-protection. In this case, it was activated
from here."

Xhou seemed to grow even angrier at hearing this. "You are a
fool, Jinn. For each action taken, there is reaction. In this case,
NUMA will investigate. They will be angered by the loss of their
crew and highly motivated to discover what happened. They have
a reputation for being tenacious. I fear you may have succeeded
only in waking the dogs."

Jinn fumed; he despised being questioned in this manner. "We
had little choice. Now that the horde is concentrated, it is in a
more vulnerable state. If the Americans found it, it's possible—
however unlikely—that action could have been taken before we
initiate the final part of our plan, here and now, in this crucial
growing season. If that had been allowed to happen, all our efforts
would have been for nothing."

"What's to stop that in the future?"

Jinn puffed out his chest. "Once the weather pattern has been
diverted, the horde can be dispersed again. Through its natural
reproduction process it will grow large enough and spread far
enough that even a concerted effort by all the world's nations will
be insufficient to destroy it."

"Where will it go?" Mustafa asked.

"Everywhere," Jinn said. "Eventually it will spread to all the
oceans of the world. We will be able to affect not only the weather

over our continents but across every landmass in the world. The rich countries of the world will pay us tribute to provide what they once received for free."

"And if they attack the horde?" Xhou asked.

"They would have to burn the entire surface of the ocean just to damage it in any significant way. And even if they did, the survivors would reproduce and the horde would come back to life like the forest after a fire."

The members of the consortium looked around and nodded to one another. They seemed to truly understand the power of the weapon Jinn was wielding. A weapon they had a hand in.

"Jinn has done correctly," the Sheik said, supporting his Arab brother.

"Agreed," Mustafa said.

Xhou remained less than satisfied. "We shall see," he said. "It is my understanding that specialists from NUMA are on their way to Malé to begin investigating. If the horde is still vulnerable because of this concentration, I suggest we disperse it."

"Now is not the time for that," Jinn said. "But don't worry, we know who was on the catamaran and we know who they're sending to investigate. I have a plan in place to deal with them."

CHAPTER 5

THE ISLAND OF MALÉ IS THE MOST POPULATED OF THE
twenty-six atolls known as the Maldives. In centuries past Malé
had been the king's private island, the citizens living on the other
islands spread out across two hundred miles of ocean. Now Malé
was the nation's capital. A hundred thousand people lived on it,
packed into less than three square miles.

In contrast to volcanic islands like Hawaii or Tahiti, the Maldives have no peaks or rocky outcroppings. In fact, the highest
natural point on Malé is only seven feet above sea level, though
multistory condos and other buildings sprout in every section of
ground right up to the water's edge.

Flying there from Washington, D.C., was a daylong trip.
Fourteen hours to Doha, Qatar, a three-hour layover, which
seemed short by comparison, and then another five-hour flight
that took great willpower even to board after so much time in the
air already. Finally, after all that, travelers touched down at their
destination. Sort of.

Malé itself was so small and so built up that no room for an airport remained on the circular-shaped island. To reach it meant landing on the neighboring island of Hulhulé, which was shaped something like an aircraft carrier and pretty much covered entirely by the airport's main runway.

Aboard a four-engine A380, Kurt watched other passengers grip the armrests with white knuckles as the plane dropped closer and closer to the water. Just as it seemed like the landing gear would clip the waves, solid ground appeared and the big Airbus planted itself on the concrete runway.

"Whoa," a voice said from beside him.

Kurt looked over. Joe Zavala had been jolted awake by the landing. His short black hair was a little disheveled and his dark brown eyes wide open as if he'd been zapped with a cattle prod. He'd been sound asleep until the wheels hit the ground.

"How about a little warning next time?"

Kurt smiled. "And ruin the surprise? A little adrenaline spike like that will get the day started right."

Joe looked at Kurt suspiciously. "Remind me not to let you choose my ringtones or alarm. You'd probably pick an air horn or something."

Kurt laughed. He and Joe had been through a decade of adventures together. They'd been in endless scrapes and fights and faced dozens of moments that loomed like utter disaster until somehow they'd managed to turn the tide, usually at the last second.

Kurt had risked his life many times to pull Joe out of the fire. Joe had done the same for him. Somehow, that gave them the right to needle each other mercilessly in the downtime.

"The way you snore," Kurt said, "I don't know if an air horn would do the trick."

Thirty minutes later, after a quick run through baggage claim and customs, Kurt and Joe found themselves in an open boat, otherwise known as a water taxi, crossing the narrow straight between Hulhulé and Malé.

Kurt was studying the open water. Joe had his nose in a crossword puzzle he'd been working on for half the flight.

"Five-letter word for African cat?" Joe asked.

Kurt hesitated. "I wouldn't go with tiger," he replied.

"Really?" Joe said. "Are you sure?"

"Pretty sure," Kurt said. "How come you look so tired?"

Joe normally traveled well. In fact, Kurt often wondered if he had some secret handed down from generations of explorers in his family that allowed him to cross a dozen time zones and feel no ill effects of the journey. But right now, there were dark circles under Joe's eyes, and despite his rangy, athletic physique, Joe looked bushed.

"You were in D.C. when the call came in," Joe said. "Ten minutes from the airport. I was in West Virginia, with fifteen kids from the youth program. We've been running cross-country and doing confidence courses all weekend."

In his spare time, Joe ran a program for inner-city kids. Kurt often helped with the outings, though he'd missed out on this one.

"Trying to keep up with the teenagers, huh?"

"It keeps me young," Joe insisted.

Kurt nodded. The fact was they were both athletes. To withstand the rigors of NUMA's Special Projects branch, one had to be. There was literally no telling what would come their way, only a fairly high probability that it would be strenuous, demanding, and likely to exhaust every last bit of mental and physical energy a man or woman had.

To survive such rigors, both men kept themselves in great shape. Kurt was taller and more lean and agile. He rowed the

Potomac or ran nearly every single day. He lifted weights and took tai kwan do, as much for the agility, balance, and discipline as for its value in combat.

Joe was shorter, with broader shoulders and the build of a boxer. He also played soccer in an amateur league and swore he could have gone pro if he'd only been just a little faster. Right now he seemed obsessed with finishing the crossword.

Kurt grabbed the paper out of his hands and tossed it into a basket. "Rest your eyes," he said. "You're going to need them."

Joe stared forlornly at the folded bit of newspaper for a second, shrugged, and then tilted his head back against the headrest. He shut his eyes and began soaking in the warm sun for the ten-minute ride across the strait.

"You come here for vacation?" the water taxi's pilot asked, trying to make conversation.

In a white linen shirt with his sleeves rolled up and his eyes hidden behind dark sunglasses, Kurt looked every bit the tourist arriving at an eagerly awaited destination. The taxi driver couldn't know any different.

"We're here on business," he said.

"That's good," the man replied. "Lots of business on Malé. What kind do you do?"

Kurt thought about that for a second. It was all but impossible to explain exactly what NUMA's Special Projects Team did since they basically did a little bit of everything. The truth came to him, simple and quick.

"We solve problems," he said finally.

"Then you come to the wrong place," the driver said. "Maldives are paradise. No problems here."

Kurt smiled. He only wished the man was right.

The transit continued, slow and easy, until the buildings of Malé began to loom in front of them. The taxi moved through the breakwater and slowed. The turquoise color gave way to clear shallow water with only the slightest hint of blue.

As the boat bumped the dock, the taxi driver cut the throttle and threw a rope to another man onshore.

Kurt stood, tipped the driver and stepped off the small boat. Ahead, on the shore, tourists strolled in the sunlight, moving in and out of the shops of the waterfront. A group of men in bright reflective vests worked on a broken section of concrete, stopping mid-project to lean on their shovels and stare at a rather attractive Polynesian woman who walked by.

Kurt really couldn't blame them. Her lush black hair draped like ink against a sleeveless white top. Her tan face, high cheek-bones and full lips glistened in the sun. And while her legs were covered by conservative gray slacks, Kurt had no doubt they were toned and tan like the rest of her.

She ducked into a jewelry store, and both Kurt and the construction workers went back to their respective tasks.

"You ready?" Kurt said.

"As I'll ever be," Joe replied.

Kurt pulled on his pack, and the two men hiked up the dock. Two other figures waited for them: a man of great height, nearly six foot eight, with a stern, intense look securely plastered on his face; and a woman with a kind yet mischievous look on her face, blue-green eyes and slightly curly hair the color of red wine. She stood about five foot ten, but she looked petite by the man's side.

"Looks like the Trouts beat us here," Kurt said, pointing them out to Joe.

Paul and Gamay Trout were two of their closest friends and

invaluable members of the Special Projects team. Her irrepress-
ible spirit and mischievous nature was the yin to his serious,
sensible yang.

"Welcome to paradise," Gamay said. Originally from Wiscon-
sin, she still spoke with a soft midwestern accent.

"You're the second person to call it that," Kurt said.

"It's in the brochure."

Kurt hugged her and then shook Paul's hand. Joe did the same.

"How in the world did you guys get here so fast?"

Gamay smiled. "We had a head start. We were in Thailand,
sampling some of the most fantastic food I've ever tasted."

"Lucky you," Kurt said.

"Do you want to check into the hotel?" Paul asked.

Kurt shook his head. "I want to get a look at the catamaran.
They bring it in yet?"

"A rescue boat from the Maldives NDF (National Defense
Force) towed it in an hour ago. At our request, they've kept it
quarantined."

That was good news. "Then let's go see what we can find."

A seven-minute walk took them along the harbor to a jetty
manned by a few sailors. Two fast patrol boats were moored just
beyond it, while the burned-out hulk of the NUMA catamaran
was tied to the dock cleats at its side.

At a small kiosk, Kurt filled out some paperwork and handed
over copies of his ID and passport. As they waited for the stamp
of approval, Kurt glanced around the dockside and noticed something odd. He kept it to himself for a moment, took his identifica-
tion back and addressed the man in the uniform.

"Do you speak English?"

"Very much so," the young man said proudly.

"Tell me," Kurt continued, "without staring—is there a beautiful brunette in a white blouse watching us from the walkway?"

The guard began to move his head for a better look.

"Without staring," Kurt reminded him.

He was more cautious this time. "Yes, she's there. Is she a problem?"

"Not if you don't mind being followed by beautiful women," Kurt replied. "Keep an eye on her for us."

The man smiled. "Gladly," he said, then added before Kurt could, "without staring."

"Exactly."

Kurt left the kiosk. And then he, Joe, and the Trouts went aboard the catamaran.

"What a mess," Gamay said, hands on her hips.

That it was. Fire had charred and blackened half the boat, melting the fiberglass near the aft, where it must have burned the hottest. Equipment and supplies were strewn everywhere.

"What are we looking for?" Paul asked.

"Anything that tells us what might have happened," Kurt replied. "Was it an accident or foul play? Were they having continuous problems or did something suddenly go wrong?"

"I'll find the logbook and the GPS unit," Paul said.

"I'll check the cabins," Gamay said.

Joe moved to the driver's seat. He flicked a few switches. Nothing happened. "Power's out."

Kurt glanced around. The catamaran had two solar panels on the roof, which seemed to be intact. In addition, a small windmill high in the mast was spinning freely. The system should have had juice even if there was no one around to use it.

"Check the cables," he said.

Joe climbed on the cabin's roof and found the problem. "Burned through up here," he said. "I think I can splice it."

As Joe went to work, Kurt began poking around near the life-raft canisters. Not only hadn't they been deployed but the casings hadn't even been unlatched.

"Any sign of water below?" he shouted, thinking maybe a rogue wave had hit them and taken them overboard, though that wouldn't explain the fire.

"No," Gamay shouted back. "Dry as dust down here."

Kurt crouched down to examine the marks left by the fire. The residue was odd and thick, more like sludge than soot.

The boat had an auxiliary engine for use in emergencies or when there was no wind; it lay below deck near the aft. He lifted the deck cover to get a look at it.

"No sign of fire in the engine bay," he said, holding the cowling open and glancing over the top of it.

The Polynesian brunette had moved closer to them, standing on the main walk beside a small tree near the edge of the dock. She held a phone oddly as if she was taking pictures of the catamaran with it.

Was she a reporter?

Somehow, this mess didn't strike Kurt as newsworthy unless this woman knew something he didn't at this point.

Gamay returned from below.

"Anything?" Kurt asked.

She held out a handful of items. "Thalia's journal," she said. "Some of Halverson's notes. A laptop."

"Anything out of the ordinary?"

"Nothing major, but the table in the main cabin is broken. And there are dishes and plates smashed in there as well. But the cupboards are latched, so I'm assuming what's broken was out and probably in use at the time. Also, the bulk food in the pantry is gone, everything except the canned goods."

For a second Gamay's words sparked some hope inside Kurt. If a situation had put the catamaran's crew in survival mode, food would be a priority, but they wouldn't have left the canned goods behind. More likely, that's all they would have taken.

Paul made his way back from the bow. He had the GPS unit and the sampling tools. "Nothing out of the ordinary up front, except a deck hose left in the on position."

"Maybe they used it to fight the fire," Gamay said.

Kurt doubted that. A pair of red fire extinguishers sat untouched in their supporting clamps, one on each side of the boat. "Then why didn't they use these?"

With no answers or even guesses, Kurt looked to Gamay. "Dirk tells me you've been taking classes in forensics."

She nodded. "My time last year with Dr. Smith made me realize small things can tell us a lot. Especially when little else makes sense."

"None of this makes any sense to me," Kurt said. "A few containers of missing bulk goods doesn't mean they were pirated, not when the computers and anything of real value was left behind. Broken dishes and a broken table might suggest a struggle, but it isn't enough to make me think they went crazy and killed each other. So the only danger I see is this fire, but if they fought it with the hose, they seemed to forget they had fire extinguishers."

"Maybe the fire disoriented them," Paul suggested. "Maybe it happened at night? Or it released toxic fumes somehow, and they had no choice but to go overboard."

That sounded like a possibility to Kurt. Thin but at least possible. And that might explain the strange residue. Perhaps it was an accelerant or gel of some kind. But if so, how did it get there?

"Let's start with that," he said. "The fire didn't come from the engine bay, so something else had to cause it. Let's get samples of the sludge, and anything else that seems odd."

"I'll do that," Gamay said.

"And I'll help Joe get the power back up," Paul added.

"Good," Kurt said smiling. "Leaves nothing for me to do except introduce myself to an attractive young woman."

CHAPTER 6

GAMAY STARED AT HIM AS IF HE WAS JOKING. "OF COURSE you will," she said. "You're Kurt Austin, what else would you do?"

Despite her gibe, and suspicious glances from the others, Kurt said nothing more. He crossed the gangway onto the jetty but kept his eyes on the guard at the kiosk as if the guard was heading back inside.

At the last second he turned, locked his gaze on the woman by the tree, and began to march toward her.

He moved briskly, with long strides. She stared at him for a second and then began to back up. Kurt kept going.

The woman moved faster, backing toward the street. As she did so, a delivery van came racing down it. A partner coming to whisk her away, Kurt guessed.

But the woman stopped in her tracks, appearing confused. She stared at the approaching van and then looked at Kurt and then back at the van as it screeched to a stop several feet away.

The door flew open and two men jumped out. She tried to run, but they grabbed her.

Kurt didn't know what the hell was going on, but he knew that wasn't a good sign. He broke into a run, shouting at the men.

"Hey!"

The woman screamed as they dragged her backward. She struggled, but they flung her through the open door and piled in behind her. By the time Kurt reached the street, they were speeding off. The guard from the kiosk raced up behind him, blowing a whistle.

A whistle wasn't going to cut it.

"Do you have a car?"

"Just a scooter," the guard said, pulling out a key and pointing to a little orange Vespa.

Kurt snatched the key and ran for the scooter. It would have to do.

He threw a leg over the seat, stuck the key in the ignition, and turned it. The 50cc engine came to life with all the power of a bathroom fan.

"Who doesn't have a car?" he shouted as he popped the kickstand, twisted the throttle.

"The whole island is only two miles across," the guard yelled back to him. "Who needs a car?"

Kurt couldn't argue with that logic, and even if he could have, he didn't have time. He twisted the throttle wide open, and the Vespa accelerated, buzzing like a weed whacker, chasing after the fleeing van.

A minute ago he'd wondered if the woman was a reporter, then became suspicious that she might be something more dangerous. Now he was trying to save her from kidnappers. It was making for a very interesting morning.

The van rumbled down the street two hundred yards ahead of him. Its brake lights came on and it turned left, moving inland.

Kurt followed, nearly taking out a bicyclist and a street vendor selling fish. He swerved and went up onto the sidewalk, nearly dumping the scooter in the process. A moment later he was back on the street.

The van had widened its lead substantially, and Kurt was afraid he might not be able to catch it on his underpowered ride.

"Great," he mumbled to himself as bugs began hitting him in the face. "All those years listening to Dirk tell stories about the Duesenbergs and Packards he borrowed, and I end up on a thirty-horsepower scooter."

He ducked down, trying to make himself more aerodynamic, and decided to count himself lucky that the scooter didn't have tassels on the handlebars or a basket for Toto on the front.

A group of pedestrians lay ahead, moving along the crosswalk. Kurt's thumb found the horn.

Meep-meep.

The annoying, high-pitched buzz was just enough to part the line of people. Kurt zipped through the gap like a madman and focused in on the van.

They were racing inland now, traveling along a road with so many letters and vowels in the name Kurt didn't bother trying to read or remember it. All that mattered was keeping the delivery van in sight.

He wasn't sure how fast other scooters went, but this little Vespa topped out at about forty miles per hour. Just as he began thinking his task was impossible, his luck began to change for the better.

Despite the guard's rhetorical question as to who needed a car, plenty of people seemed to have them. The narrow streets were filled with cars—not to East Coast rush-hour standards perhaps—but enough to make the road into an obstacle course.

As Kurt swerved around one sedan and then cut between two others traveling side by side, he found himself gaining on the van. He could see it up ahead, trying to bull its way through a busy intersection.

As he whizzed around another slow car, he could hear the van's horn blowing loudly. It made it to the corner and turned right.

Kurt negotiated the turn easily, knifing between a pair of stopped cars and hoping no one decided to open a door.

They were headed west now, and Kurt was closing in on the van, suddenly thrilled with his little orange steed. He saw the water approaching. Somehow, they'd reached the other side of the island already.

The van broke out into the open, zoomed along past the containers and equipment of the commercial harbor. It skidded to a stop across from a waiting speedboat, and the door opened.

The two men who'd thrown the mystery woman inside dragged her out. The van itself raced off.

Kurt ignored it and bore down on the Polynesian woman and her captors. He sped toward them and jumped off the scooter.

Without a rider, the Vespa went down and slid across the concrete. Kurt flew through the air and tackled the two men and the woman all at once.

The four of them tumbled and rolled across the concrete. Kurt felt his knee and hip scraping on the street, the familiar pain of road rash shooting through him. But he hopped up and charged the assailants.

One of them ran for the boat. The other stood, drawing out a knife. He faced Kurt for a second, backed up a few steps and then threw the knife.

Kurt dodged it, but the effort gave the man a precious second or two. He followed his friend to the boat and jumped in. The outboard engine roared and the utility boat moved off in rapid fashion. Kurt saw no identifying numbers or marks on it.

He shook his head. The match was a draw. The thugs had been denied their captive, but they'd made a clean getaway.

He turned his attention to the woman. She was crouched on the ground, holding a bloody elbow and looking as if she were in great pain.

He walked toward her.

"You all right?" he asked gruffly.

She looked up, her face streaked with tears, her mascara running. She nodded but continued to cradle her arm. "I think my arm is broken," she said, speaking English.

Kurt's natural protective instincts kicked in, but he reminded himself that, moments before, this woman had been spying on him and his friends and even taking pictures of the catamaran. He figured she owed him a few answers.

"I'll get you to a hospital," he said, helping her up, "but first you need to tell me who you are, why you're following me, and what you find so interesting about a derelict catamaran?"

"You're Kurt Austin," she said in a tone of determined certainty. "You work for NUMA."

"That's right," he said. "And just how do you know that?"

"I'm Leilani Tanner," she said.

The name rang a bell. She explained before he could place it.

"Kimo A'kona was my brother. My half brother. He was on that boat."

CHAPTER 7

SEVERAL THOUSAND MILES FROM MALÉ, IN SHANGHAI Province, Mr. Xhou of China and Mr. Mustafa of Pakistan rode in a private car on a bullet train, rushing to Beijing. Xhou wore a suit, Mustafa wore Pashtun tribal dress. A half dozen others riding with them could easily be identified as belonging to one side or the other.

The speed and smoothness of the ride were undeniably impressive, as was the decor. Recessed lighting lit the car in a soft mix of white and lavender. Supportive leather seating cushioned the bones of the passengers while air purifiers and conditioners kept the cabin feeling fresh at a perfect temperature of seventy-four degrees.

Chinese and Pakistani delicacies sat in trays tended by a pair of chefs. Out of respect for Mustafa's religion, there was no alcohol present, but herbal teas quenched the thirst and refreshed the palate.

Despite the opulence, this was a business meeting.

Xhou spoke firmly. "You must understand the position we're in," he said.

"The position *you're* in," Mustafa corrected.

"No," Xhou insisted. "All of us. We have made the gravest of mistakes. And only now does the full scope of reality become plain to us. The technology Jinn controls will be one of the most powerful ever developed. It will remake the world, but our stake in it is limited. We have invested in an outcome without any claim to the machinery that will produce that outcome. We are nothing more than end users of what Jinn is selling. Like those who buy power from a utility instead of building a power plant of their own."

Mustafa shook his head. "We have no use for the Jinn's technology," he said. "There are none in my country who would be able to use it. All we want is for the Jinn to keep his promises, divert the monsoon from India to Pakistan. Change the weather in our favor. Weather can build an empire or destroy it. My people hope it will do both."

A condescending look appeared on Xhou's face for a moment. He knew Mustafa as a shrewd but simple man. Simple desires, revenge against an enemy. Simple thoughts, not the kind that extended beyond short-term gain.

"Yes," he said. "But you must understand, the weather change is not once and for all. It is not permanent. In this form, it is a gift from Jinn, revocable at his will. Once the rains begin falling on our lands, we become as dependent on them as those in India who are now desperately watching the skies. There is little to stop Jinn from changing his mind and sending the rains back."

Xhou paused to let this sink in, and then added, "If he wishes, Jinn will become the rainmaker, selling to the highest bidder year in and year out."

Mustafa lifted his cup of tea but did not take a sip. The truth hit him, and he placed it back on the saucer.

"India is more wealthy than my country," he said.

Xhou nodded. "You will not be successful bidding against them."

Mustafa seemed to brood. "Jinn is Arab, he is Muslim, he would not chose the Sikhs and Hindus of India over us."

"Can you be sure of that?" Xhou asked. "You told me that Jinn's family have long been called foxes of the desert. How else to explain their rise to wealth? He will choose what is right for his clan."

Still considering Xhou's point, Mustafa placed the cup and saucer back on the table. He glanced at the food and then turned away disgustedly. It seemed his appetite was gone.

"I fear you might be right," he said. "And what's more, I now suspect this has occurred to Jinn long before it occurred to any of us. Why else would he insist on keeping the production facilities in his tiny country?"

"So we agree," Xhou said. "With only the Jinn's promises and no way to enforce them, we are all in a precarious situation."

"None as precarious as mine," Mustafa said. "I do not enjoy the luxuries you have here. We have no bullet trains in my country or new cities with gleaming buildings and untraveled roads. We have little in the way of foreign reserves to cushion our fall if it should come."

"But you have something we do not," Xhou said. "You have people with long memories and a history of dealing with Jinn. He is far more likely to trust you than an envoy of mine."

"Jinn will never let us near his technology," Mustafa said.

Xhou grinned. "We do not need it immediately."

"I don't understand," Mustafa said. "I thought—"

"We need only eliminate Jinn's ability to direct it. Or better yet, eliminate him and direct it ourselves. Without Jinn to countermand the existing orders, the horde would do what he has already promised. The rains will come to us permanently."

Mustafa's mustache turned slowly upward as a sinister smile came over his face. He seemed to grasp what Xhou was getting at. "What are your terms," he said. "And be advised I cannot promise success. Only the attempt."

Xhou nodded. There was no way anyone could guarantee what was being asked.

"Twenty million dollars upon confirmation of Jinn's death, eighty million more if you can deliver the command codes."

Mustafa almost began drooling, but then a chill seemed to take him, strong enough to cool the fires of his greed.

"Jinn is not a man to be trifled with," he said. "The desert is littered with the bones of those who've crossed him."

Xhou sat back. He had Mustafa and he knew it. A little prod to his pride would seal it. "There is no reward without risk, Mustafa. If you are willing to be more than Jinn's puppet, you must understand this."

Mustafa took a breath, steeled himself against the fate. "We will act," he said firmly, "upon receipt of ten million in advance."

Xhou nodded and waved one of his men over. A suitcase was dropped to the floor. Mustafa reached for it. As he touched the handle, Xhou spoke again.

"Remember, Mustafa, there are places in my country littered with bones as well. Betray me, and no one will care if a few Pakistani carcasses are added to the pile."

CHAPTER 8

AFTER A BRIEF SESSION WITH THE MALDIVE POLICE, KURT took Leilani to the island's main hospital, a modern building dedicated to Indira Gandhi. As they waited for X-rays to come back, he sent a text to Joe, letting his partners know where he was and how the chase had ended. Then he turned his attention back to Leilani.

"I don't mean to be blunt, but what in the world are you doing here?"

Her arm was in a sling. A scrape above her eye had been stitched and dabbed with iodine. "I came to find out what happened to my brother."

Understandable, Kurt thought, except he knew for certain that Dirk Pitt hadn't contacted any family members yet. "How did you know something was wrong?"

"My brother studied currents," she said, looking at him sadly. "I studied the things that swim around in them. We spoke or e-mailed every single day. In his last few e-mails he mentioned that he and the others were beginning to find some very strange temperature and oxygen readings. He wanted to know what effects these changes could have on local sea life. He said they were finding drastically reduced krill and plankton counts and far less fish. He said it was like the sea had begun turning cold and barren."

Kurt knew this to be true from Halverson's last report.

"When he stopped e-mailing, I got worried," she added. "When he didn't answer the satellite calls, I contacted NUMA. And when no one there would tell me what was going on, I flew here and sought out the harbormaster. He told me about the salvage. Told me people from NUMA were coming to check it out. I thought maybe you were here as a search party, but then I saw the boat and . . ."

She grew quiet, looking down at the floor. Kurt expected tears, and a few of them seemed to be coming, but she kept herself under control.

"What happened to my brother?" she asked finally.

Kurt remained silent.

"Our parents are gone, Mr. Austin. He's all I have . . . all I had."

Kurt understood. "I don't know," he said. "That's what we're trying to find out. Any idea who those men were?"

"No," she said. "You?"

"No," Kurt admitted, though any doubts he had about the catamaran's troubles being accidental were fast disappearing. "When did Kimo last contact you?"

She looked back at the floor. "Three days ago, in the morning."

"Anything unusual in the message?"

"No," she said. "Just what I already told you. Why?"

Kurt glanced around the small alcove of an emergency room:

staff members were busy, patients waited, there was the occasional electronic chirp or pinging bell. Calm, quiet, orderly. And yet Kurt sensed danger lurking somewhere.

"Because I'm trying to figure out what those men might have gained from kidnapping you. To begin with, we only suspected foul play before. Now we can almost be certain of it. And if you don't know any more than we do . . ."

"All Kimo sent me was the base data. I'm sure you have it too. Even if you didn't, taking me wouldn't hide it."

She was right. But that meant there was even less reason for someone to stage such an attack.

"Are you going to look for them?"

"The police are looking for them," Kurt said, "though I'm sure they're long gone. My job is to figure out what happened to the catamaran and its crew. I'm guessing they found something out there that someone didn't want them to find. Something more than temperature anomalies. If that leads us to the men who attacked you, we'll deal with them then."

"Let me help you," she said.

He'd been expecting her to say that. He shook his head. "It's not a science project. And in case you couldn't tell, it's likely to be dangerous."

She pursed her lips as if stung by the comment, but instead of lashing out she spoke calmly: "My brother's gone, Mr. Austin. You and I both know that. Growing up in Hawaii, you learn the power of the ocean. It's beautiful. It's dangerous. We've lost friends before, surfing, sailing and diving. If the sea has Kimo in its arms, that's one thing. If some men put him there because of what he found, that's far worse to me. And I'm not the kind to just let it be."

"You're going through a lot," he said. "And it's probably going to get worse before it gets better."

"That's why I have to do something," she pleaded. "To take my mind off it."

Kurt had no choice but to be blunt. "In my experience, you're going to be unstable whether you have something to do or not. That can have an effect on the whole team. I'm sorry, but I can't have someone like that tagging along for the ride."

"Fine," she said. "But plan on seeing me out there anyway because I'm not going to sit around and grieve."

"What are you saying?"

This time she was blunt. "If you won't let me help, I'll continue to investigate on my own. If my search messes yours up, I guess that's just too bad."

Kurt exhaled. It was hard to be angry with someone who'd lost a family member, but she was pushing him toward it. He guessed she meant every word. The problem was, she had no idea what she was getting into.

The doctor walked in carrying the X-ray films. "You are going to be okay, Ms. Tanner. Your arm is only bruised, not broken."

"You see," she said to Kurt, "I'm tough."

"And lucky," he replied.

"Nothing wrong with having luck on your side."

The doctor stared blankly, confused at the conversation he'd walked in on. "I also think luck is a good thing."

"You're not helping," Kurt mumbled.

He was trapped. He could hardly dump her off on her own after what just happened. Nor could he have her locked up for her own good or deported back to Hawaii, where she might be safe. It left him only one choice.

"Fine," he said.

"I won't cause any trouble," she said.

He smiled at her through gritted teeth. "But you already are," he assured her.

Twenty minutes later—to the horror of the medical staff—Kurt helped Leilani climb onto the damaged Vespa. With far more caution than his first trip on the machine, he rode her back to the other side of the island.

They arrived intact. Kurt promised the stricken guard that his scooter would be repaired or replaced by NUMA and offered his watch as collateral.

The guard eyed it suspiciously. Kurt wondered if he realized the watch was worth twice what a new scooter would cost.

With Leilani at his side, Kurt stepped back on board the catamaran and introduced her to the Trouts.

"And this is Joe Zavala," he added as Joe came up from below the deck. "Your new best friend and chaperone."

They shook hands.

"Not that I'm complaining," Joe said, "but why am I her new best friend?"

"You're going to make sure nothing happens to her," Kurt said. "And, more important, that she doesn't cause any problems for the rest of us."

"I've never been the chaperone before," Joe said.

"First time for everything," Kurt said. "Now, how are we doing?"

"Power's back up," Joe said. "Battery is pretty low, but the solar panels and the wind turbine are carrying the load."

"Did we find anything?"

Paul spoke first. "Once Joe got the power back on, I was able to access the tracking mode on the GPS. They kept to a westerly course until a little after eight p.m. on the last night they reported in. Then the course and speed become erratic."

"Any idea why?"

"We think that's when the incident occurred," Paul said. "The sail was partially burned in the fire. Losing its shape would change the boat's profile and speed. Looks like it began to drift."

"Where were they when this happened?"

"About four hundred miles west-southwest of here."

"What else?"

"Nothing out of the ordinary on the ship's log or in any of their notes or computer files," Paul said. "But Gamay found something of interest, as usual."

Kurt turned to Gamay.

She held up a glass beaker with an inch of charcoal-colored water in it.

"This is the residue left behind by the fire. I mixed it with distilled water. In most cases, soot is primarily carbon. And while there's plenty of that in this sludge, it's also carrying a strange mix of metals: tin, iron, silver, even trace amounts of gold. And a strange speckling that's quite hard to see."

Kurt looked closely at the water in the beaker, there was an odd, almost iridescent shimmer to it.

"What's causing it?"

Gamay shook her head. "None of my equipment was strong enough to tell us. But they had a microscope on board. Once Joe got its power on, we photographed the samples. Whatever it is, it's moving."

"Moving?" Kurt repeated. "What do you mean moving?"

"It's not inert," she said. "The carbon and the residue are still, but something on or within the residue is still active. Whatever it is, it's so small, we can't make it out under a microscope."

The news seemed to make Leilani uncomfortable. Kurt thought about tabling the discussion for later, but this was the deal: it was going to be uncomfortable, and if she couldn't handle it, now was the time to realize that.

"Are we talking about a bacteria or some other microorganism?" Kurt asked.

"Could be," Gamay said. "But until we get a closer look, all we can do is guess."

Kurt considered this. It was strange, but it didn't really tell them anything. For all they knew, whatever they'd found in this residue had been deposited on the boat after the fire.

"Could this strange discovery, whatever it is, have caused the fire?" he asked.

"I tried to burn it," Gamay said. "The residue isn't flammable. It's oxidized carbon and metals."

"If that's not the cause, then what was?"

Gamay looked to Paul, who looked at Joe. No one wanted to deliver the bad news.

Joe finally spoke up. "Gasoline fire," he said somberly. "And we can't find either of the five-gallon tanks they had listed on the manifest."

Kurt's mind put the facts together quickly. "The crew set the fire."

Joe nodded. "That's our guess."

Gamay turned toward Leilani as if to make sure she was okay. "I'm so sorry," she said.

"It's okay," Leilani replied. "I'm okay."

"Why would anyone light a fire on their own boat?" Kurt asked.

"Only two reasons we can come up with," Gamay said. "Either

it was an accident or something on the boat seemed more dangerous than setting a fire."

"The residue," Kurt guessed, "and whatever's inside it. You
guys think they were fighting that?"

"I'm not really sure what to think," Gamay insisted. "I honestly don't see how it could have presented such a danger, but Paul
and I have an appointment with a professor at the university here
in an hour to get a better look at whatever's in this sample. Maybe
that'll tell us more."

"All right," Kurt said. He looked to his wrist to check the time
and then remembered his watch was in hock.

"What time you got?"

"Four-thirty," Gamay said.

"Okay," he said, "Joe and I will take Leilani back to the hotel.
We'll check in with Dirk and wait for you guys. Go see your
professor, but be careful."

CHAPTER 9

PAUL AND GAMAY TOOK A BUS FROM THE WATERFRONT TO the Maldives National University. It pulled to a halt at Billabong Station, and the two Americans stepped off the bus with a group of students as if they were attending night school.

"Ever want to go back to the university?" Gamay asked.

"Only if you go with me and let me carry your books," he replied.

She smiled. "Might have to consider that."

They made their way inside. The National University courses ran the gamut from traditional Sharia law to engineering, construction and health care. Its maritime engineering curriculum was widely known to be excellent, perhaps spurred on by the low-lying nation's desire to prevent the rising seas from drowning it.

A colleague at the maritime school, who was familiar with NUMA, received Paul and Gamay. He introduced them to a female faculty member in a purple sari, Dr. Alyiha Ibrahim, a member of the sciences department.

"Thank you for seeing us," Gamay said.

She took Gamay's hand in both of hers. "In the ocean, like in the desert, travelers in need are not turned away," she said. "And if there is a danger to Malé in what you have found, I would not only be selfish to ignore you, I would be a fool."

"We don't know if there's any danger," Gamay insisted, "just that something has gone wrong, and this may help us determine the cause."

Dr. Ibrahim smiled, the mauve color of her wrapping highlighting the green tone in her eyes. "Then let's not waste any time."

She led them to a laboratory room. The scanning microscope was set up and ready to operate. A panel showed all systems green.

"May I?" Dr. Ibrahim asked.

Gamay handed her the vial and she drew out a sample. With great precision she placed it on a special tray and slid it into the scanning compartment.

A few minutes later the first photos came up on the screen.

The image was so strange, it caused each of them to pause. Gamay squinted, Paul stood with his mouth slightly open, and Dr. Ibrahim adjusted her glasses and leaned closer.

"What is that?" Paul asked, staring at the monitor.

"They look like dust mites," Gamay said.

"I'm not sure what they are," Dr. Ibrahim said. "Let me try increasing the magnification."

The bulky electron microscope whirred and took another scan. As the second picture emerged on the screen, their surprise only deepened.

Dr. Ibrahim turned to Paul and Gamay. "I don't know what to tell you," she said. "I've never seen anything like this in my life."

*   *   *

WITH PAUL AND GAMAY at the university and Joe watching over Leilani, Kurt went through the personal effects of the missing crewmen. It felt wrong somehow, like picking over the bones of the dead, but it had to be done if just on the chance there was some clue hidden in them.

After an hour of working that thankless task, he was ready for it to be over. He found nothing to help him but at least one item that might be helpful to Leilani: a printed photo of the crew, her brother front and center, filled with joy, as if the world were his oyster.

He put the crew's effects away and stepped out into the hall with the photo in hand. One door down he found the suite he'd booked for Joe and Leilani. It was divided into two adjoining rooms, but to reach the second room one had to make it past the first.

He knocked, heard nothing, and knocked again.

Finally the handle turned. Leilani's face appeared, framed by the door, and it hit him just how strikingly beautiful she really was.

"Where's your bodyguard?"

She opened the door wider. Joe was sound asleep on his bed, snoring softly, still in his clothes and even his shoes.

"Top-notch security," she said. "Nothing gets past him."

Kurt tried not to laugh. It had been a thirty-hour day for Joe. Even if his animal magnetism didn't have an off switch, apparently the rest of Joe did.

Kurt slipped inside. Leilani closed the door gently and padded silently across the carpet in bare feet, black yoga pants, and a green T-shirt.

Kurt followed her to the adjoining room, which had the shades drawn and the lights dimmed.

"I was meditating," she said. "I feel so out of touch with any kind of balance right now. One minute I'm angry, one minute I want to cry. You were right, I'm unstable."

Funny thing, she seemed okay to him. "I don't know, you seem to be hanging in there."

"I have something to put my mind to now," she said. "Finding out what happened. I have you to thank for that, however grudgingly you agreed. Any leads?"

"Not yet," he said. "So far, all we've found are inconsistencies."

"What kind of inconsistencies?"

"Kimo and the others were looking for temperature anomalies," he said. "They found them, but not the way they expected. Ocean temperatures are rising all over the world, but they discovered reduced temperatures in a tropical zone. That's the first odd data point."

"What else?"

"Strangely enough, reduced ocean temperatures are normally a welcome thing. Cooler temps lead to higher oxygen content in the water and more abundant life. That's why warm, shallow seas like the Caribbean are relatively barren while the dark, cold sections of the North Atlantic are where the fishing fleets congregate."

She nodded. And Kurt realized he was going over basic data and conclusions that she would be easily able to make for herself, but they knew so little it seemed best to leave nothing out.

She seemed baffled. "But Kimo told me they were finding lower levels of dissolved oxygen, less krill, less plankton and less fish in the water even as the temperature dropped."

"Exactly," Kurt said. "It's backward. Unless something was absorbing the heat and using up the oxygen as well."

"What could do that?" she asked. "Toxic waste? Some type of anaerobic compound?"

Ever since he double-checked the numbers, Kurt had been racking his brain for a possible cause. Volcanic activity, red tides, algae blooms—all types of things could result in dead zones and deoxygenated waters, but none of them explained the temperature drop. Upwelling of deep cold water might, but that usually brought abundant nutrients and higher levels of oxygen to the surface, causing an explosion of sea life in the local vicinity.

It was a problem, perhaps even a problem Kimo and the others had been killed for discovering. But it didn't tell them anything directly.

"I don't know," he said. "We've gone over everything they sent off, including Kimo's e-mails to you, just to see if we missed anything. So far, we've come up blank."

A flash of concern appeared on her face. "You looked over his e-mails to me?"

"We had to," Kurt said. "On the chance he'd inadvertently sent you some vital piece of data."

"Did you find anything?"

"No," he said. "I didn't really expect to. But we can't leave any stone unturned."

She sighed, and her shoulders slumped. "Maybe this is too big for us. Maybe we should leave it up to some international organization to investigate."

"What happened to all that determination from a few hours ago?"

"I was angry. My adrenaline was pumping. Now I'm trying to be more rational. Maybe the UN or the Maldives National Defense Force can handle the investigation. Maybe we should just go home. Now that I've met you and your friends, I can't bear the thought of anyone else being hurt."

"That isn't going to happen," Kurt said. "We're not leaving this to some agency that has no real interest at stake."

She nodded her agreement as Kurt's phone chirped.

He pulled it from a pocket and clicked ANSWER.

It was Gamay.

"Making any progress?" he asked.

"Sort of," she said.

"What do you have?"

"I've sent you a photo," she said. "A snapshot from the microscope. Pull it up."

Kurt switched into the message mode on his phone and pulled up Gamay's photo. In black-and-white but crystal clear, a shape that looked both insectlike and strangely mechanical. The edges of the subject were sharp, the angles perfect.

Kurt squinted, studying the photo. It resembled a spider with six long arms extending forward and two legs at the rear that fanned out into flat paddles shaped like a whale's tail. Each set of arms ended in different types of claws, while a ridge running down the center of the thing's back was marked with various protrusions that looked less like spines or barbs and more like the printed wires of a microchip.

In fact, the whole thing looked positively machinelike.

"What is it?"

"It's a micronic robot," Gamay said.

"A what?"

"That thing you're looking at is the size of a dust mite," she said. "But it's not organic, it's a machine. A micromachine. And if the sample I took is any indication, these same machines are seared into the residue from the fire in great numbers."

He looked at the photo, thinking about what Gamay had just

said. He tilted the phone so Leilani could see. "Four and twenty blackbirds baked in a pie," he mumbled.

"Try four and twenty million," Gamay said.

Kurt thought about their earlier conversation and the theory that the crew had set fire to the boat to rid themselves of something more dangerous.

"So these things got on the boat, and the crew tried to burn them off," he said, thinking aloud. "But how'd they get aboard in the first place?"

"No idea," Gamay said.

"What are they for?" he asked. "What do they do?"

"No idea on that either," she repeated.

"Well, if they're machines, someone had to make them."

"Exactly our thinking," Gamay said. "And we believe we know who that might be."

Kurt's phone pinged again, and another photo came up. This time it was a page from a magazine article. A photo in the corner showed a businessman stepping out of a gaudy orange Rolls-Royce. His mahogany hair was pulled back into a long pony-tail, and bushy beard covered most of his face. His suit looked like a navy blue Armani or some other double-breasted Italian cut.

"Who is he?" Kurt asked.

"Elwood Marchetti," Gamay said. "Billionaire, electronics ge-nius. Years ago he designed a process for printing circuits onto microchips that everyone uses today. He's also a huge proponent of nanotechnology. He once claimed nanobots will do everything in the future, from cleaning cholesterol out of our arteries to min-ing gold from seawater."

"And these things are nanobots?" Kurt asked.

"Actually they're larger," she said. "If you think of a nanobot as a Tonka truck, these things are earthmovers. A similar concept, still microscopic, but about a thousand times bigger."

Leilani was studying the photo. "So this guy Marchetti is the problem," she said firmly.

Kurt reserved judgment. "How do we connect these microbots to him?"

This time Paul answered. "According to an international patent on file, this is very close to one of his designs."

Kurt's own sense of righteous anger was building, he noticed Leilani wringing her hands.

"Is he using them for something?" Kurt asked. "Experimenting?"

"Not that we know of."

"Then how'd they end up in the sea?" he asked. "And more important, how'd they end up on the catamaran?"

Paul's guess came through. "Either they escaped from the lab like the killer bees forty years ago or Marchetti is using them for something without letting the rest of the world know."

Kurt clenched his jaw, grinding his teeth. "We need to pay this guy a visit."

"I'm afraid he lives on a private island," Paul replied.

"That's not going to stop me from knocking on his door. Where do I find it?"

"That's a rather good question," Gamay said.

There was an odd tone in Gamay's voice, and Kurt wasn't sure he followed. "Are you saying no one knows what island he lives on?"

"No," she told him. "Just that no one knows exactly where it is right now."

Kurt felt as if he and the Trouts were having two different conversations. "What are you guys talking about?"

"Marchetti is building an artificial island," Paul explained. "He calls it Aqua-Terra. He launched the core last year and has been outfitting it ever since. But because it's mobile, and because he chooses to stay in international waters, no one's quite sure where he is at any given time."

Suddenly, Kurt remembered hearing about it. "I thought that was just a publicity stunt."

Leilani spoke up. "No," she said, "it's real. I read something about it. Six months ago it was anchored off Malé. Kimo said he wanted to see it if he got the chance."

"Okay," Kurt said. "You guys find out whatever you can about these microbots. I'm putting a call in to Dirk. As soon as we track down Marchetti, I'm going to pay him a visit. I'm sure a floating island isn't too hard to find."

CHAPTER 10

JINN AL-KHALIF WALKED ACROSS THE DESERT UNDER A moonlit sky with Sabah close beside him. The sands he'd known since childhood shimmered like silver beneath his feet. They reminded him of the night his family had been attacked in the oasis more than forty years ago. A night when predators disguised as friends had slinked out of the desert and murdered his brothers and mother. It was a lesson in deception he had never forgotten. And one that seemed to be repeating itself.

"No word from Aziz?" he asked, speaking of the Egyptian general who had promised support for his plan.

Sabah was calm and stern in the cool night air. "Like you suspected, Aziz has reneged on his promises. He no longer has any interest in supporting us."

A flicker of light reached them from the distance. Out on the horizon, near the coast, a line of thunderstorms had begun to form. The rains had not yet pressed inland, but soon the desert would begin to feel the relief of unexpected showers; the final proof of his brilliance. And yet things were threatening to fall apart on the very cusp of victory.

"Aziz is a traitor," Jinn said, his face expressionless.

"He is a man with his own interests," Sabah counseled. "Like all men, he follows those that profit him. You would do well not to take offense personally."

"Those who break their vows offend me personally," Jinn said. "What excuse does he give?"

"The politics of Egypt," Sabah said. "The military has controlled everything there for fifty years, including the most profitable businesses. But things are still in turmoil. The Muslim Brotherhood is consolidating power, and it's dangerous for the military to support anything secular these days. Especially an outsider."

"But our program will help them," Jinn insisted. "It will bring life to their deserts as well as ours."

"Yes," Sabah said. "But they have the dam at Aswan, and the water in Lake Nasser behind it. They don't need what we offer as much as the others do. Besides, Aziz is not a simple man. He knows the truth. You can bring the rain or you can withhold it. But if you bring it for the others who pay, it will fall on his country just the same."

Jinn considered this. It was unavoidable. "I am more than he suspects," Jinn insisted. "I will force his hand."

"I warn you, Jinn, he will not turn."

"Then I will take my revenge."

Sabah did not seem pleased by this. "Perhaps this is not the time to make new enemies. At least until we have dealt with the Americans. You know they've found evidence of the horde on the damaged sailboat."

"Yes," Jinn said, displeased with the news. "They are now hunting for Marchetti. He is their prime suspect."

"They will find him easily," Sabah said. "These people from NUMA are determined. They will not hesitate to confront him."

"Of what concern is that to us?" Jinn said. His words dripped with arrogance and self-assuredness.

Sabah did not seem pleased. "Do not underestimate them."

Jinn tried to reassure him. "I promise you, my good and faithful servant, suspicions will not be cast our way. When they find Marchetti, they will find their end and whatever lies beyond for infidels like them. Now, on to harsher business."

Up ahead a group of Jinn's men stood guard around two of their own. The two sat on the ground, tied back to back, directly beside an old abandoned well. Its cavernous mouth waited, dark and gaping, surrounded by only a mud brick wall that rose less than a foot and burnished with A-frames of iron on either side that might once have supported a crossbar from which a bucket was lowered on a rope.

Their eyes looked to Jinn, filled with fear, as they should be.

"Have they admitted their failure?"

The captain of the guard shook his head. "They insist they did only as ordered."

"You told us to attack the woman," one of the men said. "We did as you commanded."

"You were supposed to attack her only as a diversion to lure the man away. He was the target, you were supposed to take him if you could, not run like cowards when he chased you. And, above all else, you were not supposed to be seen. There are now descriptions of you circulating, even a photograph from a dockside security camera. Because of that, you are no good to me anymore."

"The island is so small, we had nowhere to hide. We had to escape."

"You admit it," Jinn said. "You took the path of cowards, the way of ease."

"No," the man replied. "I swear, this was not the case. The trap did not work. The man overpowered us. We had no guns."

"Neither did he."

Jinn turned to Sabah. "What do you suggest?"

Sabah looked at the men, and the small crowd of Jinn's other loyalists that had gathered around.

"They should be lashed," Sabah said. "Covered in honey and staked to the ground. If they survive till the noon hour, they should be forgiven."

Jinn considered this for a moment. It would please the other men, but it might send the wrong message. One of weakness.

"No," he said. "We must not have pity. They have failed us due to a lack of will. Such thoughts cannot be allowed to spread to the others."

He stepped closer to the men. "I will take care of your families. May they live to be more noble than you."

He stepped back and sent a powerful kick into the first of the men. The man fell sideways, dropping over the edge of the abandoned well. For a second he hung there, suspended and held in place by the weight of the other prisoner, whom he was tied to.

"No, Jinn," the second man shouted. "Please! Have mercy!"

Jinn kicked the second prisoner even harder than the first. Teeth flew along with blood and saliva. He fell backward, and both men tumbled into the well, their cries echoing as they dropped. A second or two later a sickening crunch silenced them both. Not even cries of anguish followed.

Jinn turned to the other men. Fury lined his face.

"They have forced me to do this," he shouted. "Let it be a lesson for all of you. Do not fall short in your tasks. The next to fail me will die slowly and more painfully, I assure you."

The men shrank back from him, reminded of his wrath and power.

He stared at them and then began to walk off. Sabah fell in beside him, keeping up with his stride.

"I'm not sure that was—"

"Don't question me, Sabah!"

"I only advise you," Sabah insisted calmly. "And my advice would be, mercy to your own and wrath to your enemies."

Jinn fumed as he walked. "Those who fail me are my enemies. As are those who betray me and break their promises like Aziz. The funds he's withheld have us teetering on the brink. They have us pleading with the Chinese and the Saudis for more. I want that changed. I want Aziz groveling before us and begging for our help."

"And just how do you propose to do that?"

"The dam at Aswan gives him power," Jinn said. "Without it, Egypt could not feed itself, and Aziz would need us more than all the rest. Find me a way to bring it down."

Sabah paused. If Jinn was right, he was calculating the possibilities. His eyebrows rose. "There may be a way."

"See to it," Jinn said. "I want that dam in ruins."

As Jinn spoke, the sound of thunder rumbled across the desert toward them. Lightning flashed across the sky in the distance. To Jinn, it seemed like a sign from above.

Sabah noticed it too, but his eyes showed only concern.

"Many will die," he said. "Perhaps hundreds of thousands. Most of Egypt's population lives near the banks of the Nile."

"Payment for Aziz's betrayal," Jinn said. "Their blood is on his hands."

Sabah nodded. "As you wish."

CHAPTER 11

"Is there any food service on this flight?" Joe Zavala asked.

Kurt chuckled as Joe complained. The two of them sat with Leilani in the passenger compartment of a Bell JetRanger. Five thousand feet below, the shimmering surface of the Indian Ocean passed. They could make out the pattern of waves, but there was no sense of movement. It was like staring at a glittering picture.

"Seriously," Joe added, "I'm starving."

The pilot, a Brit named Nigel, glanced back at Joe. "What do you think this is, mate, bloody British Airways?"

Joe turned his attention to Kurt. "I'd like to lodge a complaint with the leader of this expedition."

"You shouldn't have missed breakfast," Kurt replied.

"No one woke me up."

"Believe me, we tried," Kurt said. "Maybe you should have let me set your alarm to steam whistle mode. Or brought along a real one."

Joe sat back. "This is terrible. I've gone from sleep-deprived to forced starvation. What's next? Chinese water torture?"

Kurt knew Joe's complaining was more a way to pass the time, though from years spent traveling with him he also knew Joe could eat like a champ and never gain a pound. With such a metabolism it was entirely possible that he might whither and fade away after a single day without food.

He turned his attention forward. "Well, feast your eyes on this," he said. "Aqua-Terra two o'clock low."

From five miles out the island was easy to see, like a giant oversize oil platform. As they flew closer, it became obvious that there was some real genius to Marchetti's design.

Five hundred feet wide and nearly two thousand feet long, Aqua-Terra was truly a sight to behold. To begin with, the island itself wasn't round—like so many floating cities envisioned by futuristic architects—it was teardrop-shaped, narrowing to a point in one direction while sporting a wide, curving border on the back end.

"Amazing," Leilani whispered.

"Bloody huge," the pilot said.

"I just hope they have a food court down there," Joe replied.

Kurt laughed and glanced toward Leilani. "Are you okay?"

She looked pensive and determined, like she was about to go into combat. She nodded yes but seemed as if she'd rather be somewhere else. He decided to distract her by talking about the island.

"See that ring around the outside of the island?" he asked.

"Yes," she said.

"That's a breakwater made up of steel-and-concrete barriers. They sit on powerful hydraulic pistons, and, from what I've read, when a big wave hits, they're driven back, taking the brunt of the force like shock absorbers. When the wave disperses, they spring back into position."

"What's all that stuff over on the far side?" she asked, pointing.

Kurt gazed in the direction she indicated. An artificial beach sat next to a half-circular cutout in the hull. In this section the breakwaters overlapped but didn't line up. Several small boats and a twin-engine seaplane were docked against a jetty.

"Looks like an inlet," he said.

"Every island has to have a harbor," Joe added. "Maybe they have a few restaurants on the waterfront."

"No one could ever accuse you of lacking focus," Kurt said.

The helicopter turned and began to descend. Kurt heard Nigel talking with an air controller over the radio. He looked back toward the island.

Large sections were obviously still under construction, exposed steel and scaffolding confirmed that. Other sections seemed closer to completion, and the rear of the island looked all but finished, including a pair of ten-story structures shaped like pyramids with a helipad suspended dramatically between them like a bridge.

"Could someone like this really have been involved in what happened to my brother?"

"The leads point this way," Kurt said.

"But this Marchetti has everything," she said, "why would he do something so horrible?"

"We're going to do our best to find out."

She nodded, and Kurt looked back out the window. As the helicopter began to turn, he focused on a row of soaring white structures that sprouted along each side of the teardrop-shaped island. They were widest at ground level, narrowing with a gentle rake toward the top.

They reminded him of oversize tails plucked from mothballed

747s. He quickly realized why. They were airfoils, mechanical sails, designed to catch the wind. He watched as they changed their angle slightly, turning in unison.

In the center of the island he saw a rectangular swath of green, complete with trees, grass and hills. It reminded him of New York's Central Park. On either side were long, wide strips of land on which wheat seemed to be growing.

At the forward end, banks of solar panels reflected the sun while a group of large windmills turned with gentle grace.

Nigel turned to Kurt. "They're denying us permission to land."

Kurt had expected that. He reached over and flipped a switch. A canister he'd rigged up to the tail boom began to emit black smoke. He doubted it would fool anybody for long, but it couldn't hurt.

"Looks like we're having an emergency," he said. "Tell them we have no choice but to set down safely or crash."

As the pilot relayed the message, Kurt grinned at Leilani. "Have to let us land now."

"Are you always so incorrigible?" she asked.

Joe replied, "From what I've heard Kurt here was the type to skip school and sign his own notes and have all the teachers fawning over him when he came back from his 'illness.'"

Leilani smiled. "I call that resourceful."

With a line of smoke trailing from it, the JetRanger angled for the helipad that bridged the gap between the roof of the pyramid-like buildings. The descent was smooth, almost too smooth.

"Make it look good," Kurt said.

The pilot nodded, he waggled the stick, shaking the copter to simulate some type of trouble, then stabilized as they got closer and safely touched down on top of the big yellow H.

Kurt pulled off his headset, popped open the door, and stepped out. Stretching his legs, he gazed at the sights around him. It was like being on a rooftop restaurant and getting the best view in the house.

The sails he'd seen were at least a hundred feet tall, all marked with a bright blue stripe and the name AQUA-TERRA. A scent lingered in the air, but it was so out of place, it took a moment for Kurt to recognize it: fresh-cut grass.

Another sight heading his way appeared similarly out of place. Wearing orange slacks, a gray shirt and a flowing purple robe decorated with green-and-blue paisley was a man who looked a lot like Elwood Marchetti, and a little like a peacock.

A thick brown beard on his face and circular red sunglasses completed his dizzying ensemble.

A thin man with strawlike blond hair trailed behind him. He wore a business suit and appeared to be upset.

"Mr. Marchetti, you shouldn't be greeting these people," the man said. "They have no right to land here."

Kurt looked past Marchetti to the suit. "We had engine trouble."

"A convenient time to get it."

Kurt smiled. "I'll say. Fortunately for us, your island was right here."

"It's a lie," the man said. "They're obviously here as spies or to attempt an audit."

Marchetti shook his head and turned to the aide. He put his hands on the man's arms and gripped him like an old-time revival preacher, healing someone from the crowd.

"It grieves me," Marchetti began. "Truly grieves me. To think I've made you so paranoid and yet not given you the wisdom you need to see clearly."

"Blake Matson," he said, directing the aide's attention back to

Kurt. "This isn't *the man*. This fellow doesn't even resemble *the man*. *The man* comes in boats and ships, he brings guns and lawyers and accountants. He doesn't wear boots and bring beautiful young women with him."

Marchetti was taking in Leilani as he spoke.

"Excuse me," Kurt said. "But what on earth are you babbling about?"

"Tax man, my friend," Marchetti said. "The IRS, the various European equivalents and members of one particularly irksome South American country that seem to think I owe them something."

"Internal Revenue Service," Kurt said. "Why would you be worried about them?"

"Because they don't seem to get the idea that I have now become *external* to their world and thus am not part of their *revenue* stream or in any way, shape or form interested in any of their so-called *service*."

Marchetti put a hand on Kurt's shoulder and ushered him forward.

"This is my domain. A billion dollars' worth of effort so far. Terra firma of my own. Only it's not firma," he said, stumbling over his words, "it's aqua. Terra-aqua. Or Aqua-Terra, actually. But you understand what I'm saying."

"Barely," Kurt deadpanned.

"Tax man calls it *a ship*. They say I have to pay tariffs and registration fees and insurance. Comply with OSHA rules and inspections. They tell me that's the bow. I tell them this is an island, and that right there is land's end."

Kurt stared at Marchetti. "You can call it the planet Mars, for all I care. I'm not with the IRS or anyone else who wants to tax you or question your sovereignty—or your sanity, for that matter. But I am a man with a problem and good reason to believe you're the cause."

Marchetti looked stunned. "Me? Problem? Those two words don't often go together."

Kurt stared until Marchetti stopped fidgeting.

"What kind of problem?" the billionaire asked.

Kurt pulled a capped vial from his breast pocket. It contained the slushy mix of soot, water and microbots that Gamay had given him.

"Tiny little machines," he said. "Designed by you, meant to do God knows what, and found on a burned-up boat that's missing three crew members."

Marchetti took the vial and lowered the rose-colored glasses. "Machines?"

"Microbots," Kurt replied.

"In this vial?"

Kurt nodded. "Your design. Unless someone's been filing patents in your name."

"But it can't be."

Marchetti seemed positively baffled. Kurt could see he would have to prove it.

"You have equipment on board that can look at this?"

Marchetti nodded.

"Then let's go for a reality check and remove any doubt."

Five minutes later Kurt, Joe and Leilani had taken an elevator down to the main deck, which Marchetti called the zero deck because the decks beneath it had negative numbers and those above it had positive ones. They walked to a line of parked golf carts, climbed into an extended six-seater and drove off toward the front tip of the island. Matson was left behind, and Nigel remained on the helipad, pretending to work on the helicopter.

Their travels took them across the island, an island that seemed almost deserted.

"What's your compliment?" Kurt asked.

"Usually fifty, but this month we have only ten on board."

"Fifty?" Kurt had expected him to say a thousand. He looked around. The sounds of construction reached them from various spots, but Kurt did not see a single worker or even hear voices.

"Who's doing all the work?"

"Total automation," Marchetti said.

He pulled to a stop beside a recessed section. He pointed.

Kurt saw sparks jump where things were being welded, heard the sound of rivets being hammered and high-powered screwdrivers turning, but he saw no one. After a few more welding sparks, something moved. An object the size of a vacuum cleaner, with three arms and an arc welder on a fourth appendage, scurried to a ladder.

The machine made the same sudden awkward movements as the robots on an assembly line, jerky but exacting. Robots might be precise, Kurt thought, but they still had no sense of style.

As the machine finished the welds, it retracted two arms and attached itself to one post of the ladder. Gripping on with a motorized clamp, it began to rise. When it reached the deck a few feet from Kurt, it released itself and scurried on down the road.

A smaller machine followed it.

"My workers," Marchetti said. "I have seventeen hundred robots of different sizes and designs doing most of the construction."

"Free-range robots," Kurt noted.

"Oh yes, they can go anywhere on the island," Marchetti boasted.

Halfway down the path, the robots were joined by several others, forming a little convoy heading somewhere.

"Must be break time," Joe said, chuckling.

"Actually, it is," Marchetti said. "Not like a person's break, but they're programmed to watch their own power levels. When they run low, they return to the power nodes and plug themselves in. Once they're charged up, they go back to work. It's pretty much a twenty-four/seven operation."

"What if they have an accident?" Joe asked.

"If they break down, they send out a distress signal, and other robots come and get them. They take them to the repair shop, where they get fixed and sent back on the line."

"Who tells them what to do?" Kurt asked.

"A master program runs them all. They get instructions downloaded through Wi-Fi. They report progress to the central computer, which holds all of Aqua-Terra's specs and drawings. It also tracks progress and makes adjustments. A second set of smaller robots check on the quality level."

"Supervisor robots," Kurt said, almost unable to contain a chuckle.

"Yeah," Marchetti said, "in a way, but without all that labor/management strife."

Marchetti restarted the golf cart, and moments later they were back on foot, three decks down, and entering his lab. The sprawling space was a mixture of plush couches covered in brightly colored patent leather, steel walls showing a bit of condensation, and blinking computers and screens. Everywhere screens.

Soft blue light bathed the room, filtering in from a huge circular window, front and center. On the other side of that window, fish swam and the light danced.

"We're below the waterline," Kurt noted, gazing at the huge aquarium-like view port.

"Twenty feet," Marchetti said. "I find the light soothing and very conducive to the thinking process."

"Apparently not conducive to neatness," Kurt noted, seeing how the place was a mess.

Junk lay piled everywhere, along with clothes and food trays. A couple dozen books were spread about a table, some opened, some closed and stacked precariously like the Leaning Tower of Pisa. In a far corner a trio of the welding robots sat dormant.

"A clean desk signals an unhealthy mind," Marchetti said as he carefully extracted a drop of water from the vial, placed it on a slide and took the slide over to a large square machine that sucked the slide in and began to hum.

"That would make you one of the healthiest people around," Kurt mumbled, moving a stack of papers from a chair and sitting down.

Marchetti ignored him and turned back to the machine. Seconds later a representation of the water drop appeared on a flat screen above Marchetti's desk.

"Increase magnification," Marchetti said, apparently talking to the machine.

The image changed repeatedly until it looked like a satellite view of an island chain.

"Again," Marchetti told the computer. "Focus on section 142. Magnification eleven hundred."

The machine hummed, and a new picture appeared, this time it showed four of the little spiderlike things clustered around something.

Marchetti's mouth gaped.

"Go in closer," Kurt said.

Looking concerned, Marchetti took a seat at the terminal. Using the mouse and the keyboard, he zoomed in. One of the spiders appeared to be moving.

"This just can't be," Marchetti mumbled.

"Look familiar?"

"Like long-lost children," Marchetti said. "Identical to my design, except . . ."

"Except what?"

"Except they can't be mine."

"Here we go," Kurt said, waiting for all the denials and talk of preventative measures that should have worked. "Why not?" he asked. "Why can't they be yours?"

"Because I never made any."

Kurt hadn't expected that.

"They're moving," Leilani noted, pointing to the screen.

Marchetti turned and magnified the screen again. "They're feeding."

"What do you mean they're feeding? Feeding on what?"

Marchetti scratched his head, then zoomed in again. "Small organic proteins," he said.

"Why would a tiny robot want to eat an organic molecule?"

"Because it's hungry," Marchetti said. He turned from the machine.

"Forgive me for asking, but why would a robot be hungry?" Kurt added.

"Here, on my island," Marchetti explained, "the larger robots get to plug in. But if you're going to make bots that are independent, they have to be able to power up one way or another. These little guys have several options. Those lines on their backs that look like microchips are actually tiny solar collectors. But because the independent bot has other needs, they have to be able to get sustenance from the surrounding environment. If these microbots follow my design, they should be able to absorb organic nutrients from the seawater and break them down. They should also be able to process dissolved metals and plastics and other things found in the sea, both to sustain themselves and reproduce."

"This conversation is going from bad to worse," Kurt said. "Explain how they reproduce. And I don't need a lesson on the birds and the bees. I've just never heard of it in regards to a machine."

"Procreation of the bot is a fundamental need if you want it to do anything useful."

Kurt took a deep breath. At least they were getting answers even if he didn't like the details. "And just what useful purpose did you design these things for?"

"My original concept was to use them as a weapon against seaborne pollution," Marchetti began.

"They eat pollution," Kurt guessed.

"Not just eat it," Marchetti said, "they turn it into a resource. Look at it this way. There's so much pollution out there, the sea is literally choking on it. The problem is, even in places like the Pacific Garbage Patch, the stuff is too spread out to be economically cleared up. Unless the instrument that's doing the clearing feeds off what it clears, turning the garbage itself into a power source that enables the cleanup."

He waved toward the screen. "To accomplish that, I designed a self-sustaining, self-replicating microbot that could live in the seawater, float around until it found some plastic or other garbage and chow down once it did. As soon as these things find a food source, they use the by-products and the metals in the sea-water to copy themselves. Voilà!—reproduction—without all the fun parts."

Kurt had always been baffled by the world's collective unwill-ingness to do anything about the pollution being poured into the marine environment. The world's oceans created three-quarters of its oxygen, a third of its food. Yet the polluters acted as if this was a trifle. And until there was nothing left to fish, or no one could breathe, it was doubtful anyone would do anything about it because it just wasn't economical.

In a bizarre way, there was a certain elegance to Marchetti's solution. Since no one wanted to do anything about the problem, he'd proposed a way to fix it without anyone actually having to lift a finger.

Joe seemed to agree. "There's some brilliance in that."

"There's also insanity," Kurt said.

"You'd be surprised how often those traits coincide," Marchetti said. "But the real insanity is doing nothing. Or dumping billions of tons of plastic and trash into the thing that feeds half the planet. Could you imagine the vociferous outcry, the wailing of epic pro-portions, if the amber waves of grain were choked with cigarette lighters, plastic bottles, monofilament line and broken bits of chil-dren's toys? That's what we're doing to the oceans. And it's only getting worse."

"I don't disagree," Kurt said. "But turning some self-replicating machine loose in the sea and just hoping it all works out isn't exactly a rational response."

Marchetti sat back down, he seemed to agree. "No one else thought so either. So like I said, we didn't produce any."

"Then how did these things get on my brother's boat?" Leilani asked bluntly.

Kurt watched Marchetti, waiting for an answer, but he didn't reply. His gaze was locked onto Leilani. Fear flickered in his eyes. Kurt turned and he saw why.

Leilani held a compact snub-nosed automatic in her hands. The muzzle was pointed directly at the center of Marchetti's chest.

CHAPTER 12

"I swear," Marchetti said, putting his hands up instinctively, "I don't know how they got on your brother's boat."

Kurt stepped in between Leilani and the billionaire. "Put the gun down."

"Why?" she asked.

"Because he's our only link to the truth," Kurt said. "You kill him, you'll never know what happened. And as sad as it sounds, I'll make sure you end up in prison for it."

"But he built these machines," she said. "He admitted it. We don't need to go any further."

Kurt looked her in the eyes. He hoped to see fear, doubt, and nerves, but he saw only coldness and anger.

"Get out of the way, Kurt."

"Tired of being alone," he said, repeating her words from the night at the hotel. "You pull that trigger, you'll be more alone than you can possibly imagine."

"He killed my brother, and if he's not going to tell us why,

I'm going to even the score," she said. "Now please, get out of my way."

Kurt didn't budge.

"Listen," Marchetti said nervously, "I didn't have anything to do with your brother's death. But maybe I can help you find out who did."

"How?" Kurt asked.

"By tracking down those with knowledge, those with an understanding of the process," Marchetti offered. "Obviously you don't just pick up a screwdriver and a soldering gun and put these things together, it's an extremely complicated endeavor. Someone connected with the initial design had to be involved."

As Marchetti spoke, Joe began circling in behind Leilani as quiet as a cat. "Keep talking, Marchetti," Kurt said.

"There might be nine or ten people who know major parts of the system," he stammered, "but only one guy knows as much as I do. His name is Otero—and he's right here on the island."

"He's lying!" Leilani said. "He's just trying to blame someone else."

As Leilani ranted, Joe pounced. He knocked the gun away and grabbed her arm, twisting it up behind her back in a half nelson.

A loud bang rang out, and for a second Kurt thought the pistol had discharged. "Everyone all right?"

Marchetti nodded, Joe did the same, Leilani appeared upset but unharmed.

"What was that noise?" Kurt asked.

No one knew, but when another clanking sound reached them Kurt caught sight of movement in the back of the darkened lab. The acrid smell of electrical discharges came next. The welding robots had become active. They were standing up on their feet, knocking items out of their way and discharging blue arcs of plasma from their appendages.

Kurt turned to Marchetti. "Let me guess," he said, "Otero's your master programmer."

Marchetti nodded.

"I have a feeling he's been watching."

The welding robots began moving toward the humans. Two of them had small tracks like a tank's to roll on. A third had claw-like feet that were scraping on the metal deck.

Joe released Leilani. She turned to Kurt, apologizing.

"I'm so sorry, I just—"

"Save it," Kurt said, his eyes on the menacing machines.

Marchetti raced for the bulkhead door. He twisted and pulled the handle, but it wouldn't budge.

"Watch out," Joe shouted.

One of the machines had begun to zero in on Marchetti. It charged forward on its tracks with one appendage reaching for him and a second arm spouting blazing white plasma.

Marchetti ducked and scampered to a new spot. The machine tracked him and began to close in again.

Kurt looked for the gun and spotted it across the room. Before he could move, a fourth machine came alive and stepped in his path.

He backed up, putting the couch between him and the walking machine. Joe and Leilani retreated as well.

"How do they operate?" Kurt shouted as one of the robots reached the table and carved it in two with a circular saw.

"Either autonomously or guided from a remote site," Marchetti said. "They have pinhole cameras for eyes."

The machines lumbered toward them like sleepy animals.

Each time they reached something solid, their actuators spun and their claws extended. A chair was flung out of the way, a couch set on fire with the welding torches.

Kurt noticed that their movements were odd, only one machine at a time seemed to do anything out of the ordinary. "Could Otero be at that remote site right now?"

Marchetti nodded. Kurt turned to Joe. "Now would be a good time for a suggestion."

"I'd say, let's pull the plug," Joe replied, "but I'm guessing they have batteries."

With that, he grabbed a chair and hurled it at the closest robot. It caromed off the lumbering machine, rocking it backward a bit, but other than that it seemed to have no effect.

By now Kurt had been forced closer to where Marchetti stood. Joe and Leilani held a different spot. But the machines, or Otero, seemed intent on herding them together.

Kurt made a break to the right, but a blast from a welding torch stopped him. He went the other way, relying on his quickness.

The machine pivoted and released another blinding flash of plasma, but Kurt was already inside the machine's reach. He felt the heat singe his back but not directly. He grabbed the first thing he could get his hands on and yanked until it broke off. Then he found another protrusion that looked like a camera and bashed it sideways.

The welding torch flared out over his shoulder again, and some other arm began to move.

"Do these things have an off switch?" he shouted.

"No," Marchetti said. "I couldn't imagine wanting to shut them off manually."

"I'm guessing you can imagine it now."

Kurt reached for what looked like a trio of hydraulic lines only to receive a blow to the chest that sent him flying off the machine. Some type of hammer used to drive rivets had extended and struck him in the ribs.

He landed on his back, only to see a saw blade dropping toward him from a second machine. He rolled out of the way and ended up against the huge circular window, beyond which the turquoise hue of the sea loomed.

Marchetti was there as well, and Joe and Leilani had been successfully herded into the same general vicinity.

"I have an idea," Kurt said.

He lunged for the same machine he'd just been on, careful to avoid the appendages. The torch flashed again, almost blinding him. The hydraulic hammer came out again, but Kurt twisted his body to avoid it.

The machine lumbered forward with Kurt clinging to it. It pushed him back, banging him against the window like the captain of a football team might bang a geeky freshmen against a locker. The torch flashed again, carving a line in the acrylic window. A second swipe left another scar.

Kurt tried to push the machine back, but it shoved him against the window. He felt like his ribs were cracking from the pressure.

"I hope . . . these things . . . aren't waterproof," he managed.

He reached for the hydraulic lines again. Right on schedule, the battering ram of a hammer fired just as it had before. But with Kurt's body twisted out of the way, it slammed into the huge oval window.

The eerie sound of cracks traveling through the acrylic caught everyone's attention. They turned just as the window, designed convexly with all its strength focused outwards, failed from the inside.

The water blasted in like a crashing wave, hitting everyone and everything at once. It swept the people, the furniture, and the machines across the room, slamming all into the far wall.

Kurt felt several jarring collisions and struggled to free himself from the welder. Even as he got loose, the swirling water pinned him against the wall and held him down like a vicious wave might trap a surfer. He pushed off the floor with one foot and broke the surface.

Foam and debris were being blasted about by the gushing water. Kurt felt himself being pushed up by the rising flood as the room filled with liquid. As he neared the ceiling, the trapped air slowed the process, but it must have been leaking out somewhere because the space was collapsing.

Kurt looked around. Joe was there, holding Marchetti with one hand and clinging to the wall with the other.

Leilani popped up and grabbed ahold of a pipe that ran along the ceiling, which was now easily within reach.

"Any sign of the robots?"

"I never taught them to swim," Marchetti said.

"First thing you've done right," Kurt told him. "How far down are we?"

"Twenty feet."

"We have to swim out."

"I can make it," Marchetti said, coughing as if he'd swallowed half a gallon of water.

"Leilani?"

"Of course," she said.

"Okay. Get rid of your shoes," he said, then, turning to Marchetti, added, "and lose that stupid robe. Not only will it drown you, it's been giving me a headache since the moment I got here."

They undid their shoes and pulled them off, Marchetti shed

the wet robe, and they swam to the gaping hole where the window had been.

Before they went under to swim out, Kurt looked Marchetti in the eye. "Where do I find this Otero character?"

"The control center, in the main building, back near the helipad."

"Can you override his access so I don't get welded, nail-gunned or otherwise screwed by your robots along the way?"

Marchetti tapped the side of his head as if the idea resonated with him. "That's the first thing I'm going to do."

"Good," Kurt said. He glanced at Joe, determination in his eyes accompanied by the energy surge that came with going on the offensive.

"I hope you're rested," he said, "because now it's our turn."

CHAPTER 13

IN A DARKENED CONTROL ROOM NEAR THE PEAK OF AQUA-Terra's highest completed structure, Martin Otero looked from one screen to the next. Three large monitors sat in front of him. Two had gone blank, a third showed something moving and then pixilated out. In a few seconds it was blank like the others.

"What happened?"

Otero ignored the question. Blake Matson, Marchetti's attorney leaned in closer. "What happened? Did the old man get it or not?"

Otero gestured to the blank screens. "You tell me. Obviously I can see only what you see. So how would I know?"

While Matson stared, Otero ran through the reboot program, hoping to get a signal from the construction robots. At the same time an alarm began flashing on the island's schematic display.

"Water in the forward lab," Otero said. Suddenly, he understood what happened. "The compartment's flooded. Marchetti's picture window must have fractured."

"What does that mean for us?"

Otero swiveled in his chair, feeling better, more confident. "It means we're in luck. They're as good as dead. And now it looks like an industrial accident."

"As good as dead won't cut it," Matson explained. "Only dead for certain works. We need bodies."

"They're twenty feet beneath the surface," Otero insisted. "The pressure of the water rushing in will probably crush them, and if it doesn't, they'll drown trying to fight against it."

"Listen," Matson said, "you and I have made millions getting Marchetti's design to Jinn and his people. But if we don't make sure these meddlers are finished, we won't live long enough to spend it. So get some more robots over there and find their drowned carcasses and haul them up like dead fish."

Otero went back to his keyboard. He punched up a list of active robots and scrolled down to the section labeled *Hydro*. He tapped the down arrow until he found two submersibles currently deployed near Marchetti's lab.

"What are those?"

"Hull cleaners," Otero said. "They roam around the hull, clearing the algae and barnacles."

"Are they lethal?"

"Only if you're a barnacle," Otero replied. "But they can give us a look."

Otero switched the hull cleaner to manual control and directed it to section 171A: Marchetti's lab. The machine wasn't built for speed, but it only needed to travel a short distance.

"There's the observation deck," Otero said as it passed a long rectangular window. "Marchetti's lab should be just ahead."

A moment later the exterior of the lab was front and center.

The damage was obvious. What had once been a majestic portal often beaming with light now looked like a dark cave. The circular window was shattered. A few pieces of the thick acrylic clung to the frame like broken teeth in some giant mouth. No light came forth.

"Take it inside," Matson ordered.

Otero had already planned to, but movement on the right side of the screen caught his eye. He turned one of the cleaners that way. Its camera was locked on a group of swimmers, headed topside.

"Grab them!"

Otero extended the cleaner's grasping claws and accelerated toward the last pair of bare feet. It was the woman.

The hull cleaner clamped onto the woman's feet. A struggle began. The camera shook, bubbles rose when the girl had exhaled. Otero pushed the joystick on his panel downward, ordering the hull cleaner to dive.

The machine nosed over but went nowhere. Suddenly, a face capped with silvery hair came into the frame. The machine went sideways. The sound of an actuator arm snapping off came through the headset.

The screen cleared. The woman wriggled free and the man's face appeared once again. He was holding on to the hull cleaner, staring into the camera. Otero felt the weight of that gaze through the water and into the control room. The man pointed a finger directly at the camera, directly at Otero, and then he made a slashing motion across his throat, before smashing the camera and rendering the hull cleaner useless.

The message was clear. The men from NUMA were coming for them, and it wasn't going to be pretty.

Otero tapped a few keys and hit ENTER on the keyboard— setting up one last trick to cover his back—and then he stood and grabbed a small briefcase filled with cash. His final payment.

"What are you doing?" Matson asked.

"I'm getting out of here," Otero said. "You can stay if you like."

Otero pulled a revolver from his desk drawer and hustled out the door into the hall. Seconds later he heard Matson racing to catch up.

At the starboard section of Aqua-Terra, Kurt found a ladder running up the side of the hull. He and Joe hustled up first and took cover behind a small oak tree on a pile of woodchips. He stared across the wheat field as Leilani hauled herself up the ladder and slumped beside them, looking exhausted.

"Now what?" Joe asked.

"We need to find the best way to that control center," Kurt said, thinking it'd be nice to have some input from the man who designed the island.

He glanced over his shoulder. Down the ladder, Marchetti was climbing at a snail's pace. One rung, then a rest, then another rung, another rest. He coughed, spat water.

"Come on, Marchetti," Kurt said in a harsh whisper, "we don't have all day."

"I fear I can go no farther," the billionaire said. "This is where it ends, right here on this ladder. You should go on without me."

"I'd love to," Kurt mumbled, "but I need you to turn off the machines."

"Right," Marchetti said as if he'd forgotten. "I'm coming."

Marchetti began to climb once again. In the meantime, Kurt spotted a pair of figures exiting the second floor of the starboard pyramid and scrambling down a stairwell. He thought he recognized one of them as Marchetti's arrogant aide. The other was unfamiliar.

"What's Otero look like?" he asked.

Marchetti poked his head over the top of the ladder. "Average-sized man," he said, "dark complexion, close-buzzed hair on a very small, very round head."

The figures were too far away for Kurt to be certain, but that description fit the man he spotted. A moment later the two figures began a fast jog down one of Aqua-Terra's roads. The occasional glance back was enough to tell Kurt they were on the run.

"Anyway off this boat," Kurt said, "er—I mean island?"

"By helicopter," Marchetti said. "Or via the marina, by boat or seaplane."

The marina. If Kurt guessed correctly, that was their goal.

"I think Otero and your lawyer friend are headed that way," he said. "Leilani, help Marchetti find a computer terminal and try not to kill him in the process. As annoying as he is, I think we've cleared him of anything more than crimes of fashion."

"I'm sorry," she said. "I promise."

Kurt turned to Joe. "Ready?"

Joe nodded, and an instant later they took off running, sprinting into the wheat field and cutting their way through the neck-high stalks of grain. They reached the other side and began to cut across the park. Halfway there, Kurt heard the sound of an engine starting up.

"That sound like a boat to you?"

"More like an air-cooled Lycoming," Joe said. "They're going for the seaplane."

"Then we'd better hurry."

As Kurt and Joe raced to the other side of the artificial island, Leilani and Marchetti scampered forward, eventually ducking into a maintenance building. The sight of fifty machines plugged in and charging gave her chills, but none of them moved.

Marchetti found the programming terminal and quickly logged on.

"I'm sorry I tried to scare you," Leilani said, hoping it had some effect on Marchetti's judgment.

"Me too," Marchetti said, typing furiously. "But I can't blame you for being angry."

She nodded.

"I'm in," Marchetti said. For a second he seemed elated, and then he paused with his mouth open as if surprised by what he saw. His eyes narrowed, focusing on one particular part of the screen. "Otero," he mumbled, "what have you done?"

Suddenly, the machines around them began powering up. Motors whirring, LEDs going from orange to green.

"What's happening?" Leilani asked.

"He changed the code," Marchetti said. "When I logged on, it triggered a response. He's set the robots on intruder mode."

"Intruder mode? What exactly is intruder mode?"

"They go after everyone on the island not wearing an ID badge with an RFID chip in it. It's my defense against pirates."

Leilani realized instantly she didn't have a badge, but as the machines began to disconnect from their plugs she wondered about him.

"Where's your badge?"

"In the pocket of my robe," he said, "the one Kurt made me get rid of."

Kurt and Joe made it through the park and into the second strip of wheat on the far side. The sound of a different kind of motor rumbled to life, and far to their right, at the end of the field, a small combine sprung to life. It straightened and began moving toward them, its blades whipping through the wheat.

"A little early for harvesttime," Joe said.

"Unless they're trying to harvest us."

Kurt picked up the pace and rushed out the other side onto the narrow path that led toward the marina. Running at full speed, with Joe right beside him, he noticed other machines coming out of the woodwork and tracking toward him.

"Apparently Marchetti hasn't finished reprogramming things yet," Kurt said.

"Let's hope he remembers his password."

Speed and agility were still in their favor, and after racing a hundred feet down the path and hopping a wall they cut away from the machines. A few seconds later Kurt and Joe were bounding down the stairs to the marina. Ahead of them the seaplane was taxiing out past the breakwater.

They had to hurry.

Kurt ran to the fastest-looking boat he could find: a twenty-two-foot Donzi. He jumped in and went to the control panel as Joe untied the lines. Pressing a start button, Kurt smiled as the V-8 inboard roared to life.

"Bogies coming up the dock," Joe said.

"Nothing to worry about," Kurt said, glanced at the collection of machines scrambling toward them. He gunned the throttle and spun the wheel.

The boat shot forward, curving and accelerating across the marina. As soon as they were on track, Kurt straightened out and pointed the bow toward the gap in the breakwater. The seaplane was already taxiing through it.

Kurt hoped to catch them, maybe tip them over, but that plan had a low margin for success.

He pointed to a radio on the dash. "Get Nigel on the horn," he said. "Tell him to scramble. I don't want to lose these guys."

Joe switched the radio unit on, dialed up the right frequency, and began to transmit. "Nigel!" he shouted. "This is Joe. Come in."

Nigel's British voice came back with everything but a *cheerio*. "Hello, Joe, what's the word?"

"Get that bird airborne," Joe shouted. "We're chasing a seaplane in a boat, and that's not going to work for long."

"Awfully sorry," Nigel replied. "Wish I could help, but I took the engine apart."

"What?" Kurt shouted, overhearing.

"Why?" Joe asked.

"Kurt told me to make it look good. The cowling off, a few parts on the ground, and a befuddled look on my face seemed the best way to me."

"I didn't need him to make it look that good," Kurt mumbled.

"So much for that plan," Joe said.

All they could do now was a little bump and run with the plane, hoping to damage it or flip it without getting themselves killed in the process.

The Donzi zipped through the gap in the breakwater. The seaplane was two hundred yards ahead, turning downwind to line up for its take-off run.

Kurt held the throttle all the way forward and slashed in front of the seaplane. The pilot turned away instinctively but the aircraft remained upright.

Kurt wheeled around to port and came back. The plane was accelerating now. Kurt charged toward it, riding in its wake.

"Come on," Kurt said, coaxing every last bit of speed out of the boat.

Skipping across the waves, he pulled out to the left, passed the plane, and then cut in front of it again.

Joe ducked and shouted a warning. The plane leapt off the water, its metal prop roaring past and the pontoon rudders clipping part of the boat as it leapfrogged them and came back down.

Kurt looked up. "Glad to see no one lost their head."

"Let's not try that again," Joe said. "I have no desire to find out what a margarita feels like inside the blender."

Kurt had actually expected the plane to turn, not leap over them. But the effort had done them some good. The plane had landed awkwardly, and the pilot had slowed it down to stabilize it. When the plane began accelerating away again, it was headed in a bad direction.

"They're headed downwind," Joe said. "It'll be a lot harder for them to take off with a tailwind than heading into this breeze."

"Harder but not impossible," Kurt replied. He guided the speedboat with an expert touch, sweeping back in behind the plane, dropping into the trough of the wake and ramming one of the pontoons. The plane lurched and twisted as the pilot fought for control, but it was quickly back on track.

"Look out!" Joe shouted.

A spread of bullets punched a line of holes in the prow of their boat as one of the fugitives unloaded the contents of a submachine gun in their general direction. Kurt and Joe were forced to turn away, and the plane slowed and turned, pointing itself into the wind once again.

In the maintenance room, Leilani stared at the army of machines, watching in horror as they stood up and began moving forward. Three of the things attacking down below had been enough to scare her, but fifty of them was an absolute nightmare. Anger flashed through her mind, along with the distinct impression that she'd gotten more than she had bargained for.

"Do something!" she shouted to Marchetti.

"I'm trying," Marchetti said. "Tricky little man, that Otero. If I'd have known he was this smart, I'd have paid him more."

Leilani looked around for help. All she saw were the machines and a bank of lockers.

"What's in the lockers?"

"Work uniforms."

"With IDs?"

"Yes," Marchetti said excitedly. "Exactly. Yes, go!"

Leilani raced across the floor, slid under the swinging arm of one of the robots and slammed into the lockers like a baseball player stealing home. She popped up, threw one locker door open and yanked out a work uniform. A white ID badge came with it, and she held it tight.

The approaching machines stopped and turned away from her, and then all of them zeroed in on Marchetti, who was pounding the keyboard to no avail.

"I can't break the code!" he shouted. The machines were on him now, one of them knocked him to the ground. Another brought a powered screwdriver down toward him, the Phillips head bit spinning furiously.

Leilani ran forward, pushed through the machines, and dove on top of Marchetti. Hugging him tight, she hoped the robots would see their combined heat source as one person and read the ID tag at the same time.

The drill bit spun and whined. She gripped Marchetti and closed her eyes.

Suddenly, the noise ceased. The screwdriver wound down and retracted. The other robot released Marchetti, and the small army of machines began to move away, looking for some other victim.

She watched them go, still holding Marchetti down.

As the machines filed out of the maintenance building, she looked down at him, her eyes hard and cold. She needed him to understand something.

"You owe me," she said.

He nodded, and she eased off him. Neither of them took their eyes off the door.

A HALF MILE from the floating island, Kurt and Joe were taking direct fire from the seaplane. It was angling around, heading back downwind and accelerating. When it surged forward, Kurt dropped in behind it once again.

"Now or never, Joe."

"I have an idea," Joe said. He climbed forward onto the bow, grabbing the anchor.

"A friend of mine in Colorado taught me how to rope," he shouted. He began whirling the twenty-pound anchor on its cord like a one-sided bolo.

Kurt guessed at his intentions and firewalled the throttle one last time. They began closing the gap. The gunfire returned, but Kurt swung the boat to the pilot's side and ran it up under the seaplane.

Joe spun and released the anchor like an Olympic hammer thrower just as the plane came off the water. It flew forward and wrapped around the pontoon struts and pulled taut.

The plane's nose came up, yanking the front end of the speedboat out of the water. The weight and drag were too much. The left wing dropped, hit the water, and the seaplane tumbled in a cartwheel, shedding pieces in all directions.

The speedboat was yanked sideways, the anchor cleat ripped

free, but Kurt managed to keep the boat from flipping. He turned to port, backed off the throttle and wheeled around to see the carnage behind them.

The seaplane had come to rest with one pontoon missing, its wings bent and folded and part of the tail ripped off. It was being swamped by the water pouring in and looked to be going down.

"Yes!" Joe shouted, firing a fist pump into the air.

"We have to get you in the rodeo," Kurt said, bringing the boat back around toward the shattered airplane.

He pulled up beside it. The plane was sinking fast, the two occupants trying desperately to get free. Matson got out first and was soon clinging to the speedboat. Otero made it over next.

They began to climb in, but each time they did Kurt bumped the throttles.

"Please," Otero shouted, "I can't swim well."

"Maybe you shouldn't live on a floating island then," Kurt said, goosing the throttle until they dropped off the side and then chopping it again. They dog-paddled back to the boat, grabbing at the handrail.

Kurt scraped them off again.

"It was all his idea," Otero said, trying to tread water.

"What was?" Kurt asked.

"To steal the microbots," Otero said.

"Shut up," Matson said.

"Who'd you give them to?" Joe asked.

The half-drowned duo latched onto the boat, and Otero clammed up once again.

"Mr. Austin," Joe said, "I believe we have a policy against boarders and hangers-on."

Kurt nodded and smiled. "That we do, Mr. Zavala. That we do."

He pushed the throttle a little more this time. The two strag-glers tried to hold on, but they were soon pulled free. This time Kurt continued to idle away from them.

"Wait!" Otero shouted, splashing around furiously. "I'll tell you."

Kurt put a hand to his ear. "Before we get too far away," he shouted.

"His name is Jinn," Otero sputtered. "Jinn al-Khalif."

Kurt cut the throttle, and the boat settled.

"And where do I find this Jinn?" he shouted.

Otero looked at Matson, who was shaking his head.

"He lives in Yemen," Otero blurted out. "That's all I know."

CHAPTER 14

In the courtyard of a Moroccan-style house, a stone's throw from the Gulf of Aden, the man known as Sabah enjoyed the evening. As dusk draped a cloak over the world, he savored a dinner of lamb with fresh-made flatbread and sliced tomatoes. Around him gauzy drapes wafted in the soft breeze while the sound of waves crashing against the nearby cliffs played its soothing, repetitive song.

A servant arrived and whispered in his ear.

Sabah listened and nodded. A slight wrinkle of aggravation crossed his forehead at the news.

The servant took his plate, and Sabah reclined with a glass of black tea. The sound of approaching footsteps halted beneath the archway.

"I request an audience with you," a figure in the shadows reported.

"I would say you already have one," Sabah replied, "since you are in my presence, invited or otherwise."

"I do not mean to disturb you," the man said. "I waited while you dined."

Sabah motioned to a seat. "Come sit with me, Mustafa. We are old friends, ever since the first war with Israel. The weapons you provided did not help us to win, but they allowed me to bolster al-Khalif and his family. My good fortune has followed."

Mustafa walked over and sat down across from Sabah, who noticed a sense of trepidation in his steps. As Mustafa was normally the boldest of men, arrogant, feisty, Sabah wondered what could be shaking him.

"Good fortune is what I've come to discuss," Mustafa said, "both yours and mine. And that of others who take the lion's share for themselves."

Sabah took another sip of the tea and then set the glass down. On a small plate beside it were freshly cut leaves of qat, or khat, a plant with stimulant-like properties. It was similar to a mild amphetamine. Sabah took one of the leaves, folded it and placed it in his mouth. He began chewing slowly, sucking on the juices of the leaf.

"Lions take the largest share because they are lions," Sabah explained. "No one can challenge them."

"But what if the lion is weak and arrogant?" Mustafa asked. "Or if it is blind to the needs of the pride? Then another will rise up and take its place."

"Come now," Sabah said, "there's no need to speak in metaphors. You're talking of Jinn and the project. You believe he's failing us somehow."

Mustafa hesitated, wringing his hands as if in great turmoil.

Sabah slid the plate of leaves toward him. "Take one. It will free your tongue."

Mustafa plucked one of the leaves and folded it between his fingers, much as Sabah had. He placed it in his mouth.

"What actions of Jinn seem wrong in your eyes?" Sabah asked.

"Three years of promises," Mustafa said, "not one new drop of rain."

"The changes take time. You were warned of this."

"We're running out of time," Mustafa said, "as are you. Yemen is dying. People are being forced from the cities at gunpoint because there is not enough water for all of them."

Sabah spat green saliva and the remnants of the qat leaf into a small bowl. He took a sip of tea to refresh his palate. Mustafa was correct. It was strongly believed the nation's capital would run so low on water in the next year that no amount of rationing would save it. Forced migration was the only option, forcing people to other regions, but the rest of the country was in little better shape.

"It's rained here three times in the last week," Sabah said, "rains we normally don't see. Even now, clouds linger over the mountains to the north. The change is coming. Jinn's promises will be kept."

"Perhaps," Mustafa said, "but what prevents him from reversing those promises?"

From the gleam in Mustafa's eyes Sabah sensed he was coming to the point.

"Honor," Sabah said.

"Jinn has no honor," Mustafa said. "For proof, I point to you yourself. It's well known that you, Sabah, are the reason for Jinn's success. His wealth and power have been built on your wisdom. His family fortune has been made from your efforts, your labor, your loyalty. Many millions Jinn has: companies, palaces, wives.

And what has he given you?" Mustafa looked around. "You have a nice home, a few servants. Fine foods to dine on. Is that all you get for a lifetime of dedication? No, it's a trifle, and surely you deserve more. You should be a prince in your own right."

"I am a loyal servant," Sabah replied.

"Even servants share in the master's rewards," Mustafa said. "In the courts of old, even a slave could become a trusted adviser."

Sabah had heard enough. "Perhaps your tongue has been loosened too much, Mustafa."

"No," his guest replied excitedly, "just enough. I know the truth. Jinn uses you just as he uses us. He takes much and gives only what he has to. We are at his beck and call. If he stops the project, we shall perish. If he asks for more, we have no choice but to give it."

"So it's the money that disturbs you."

"No," Mustafa said, "it's the power. Jinn will soon pass beyond our ability to control or even bargain with him. He's created magic like the genies of ancient times. But if he alone wields it, the rest of us are no longer necessary. There's good reason why the Jinns of old were cursed. They were magicians who could not be trusted. If not held down, they make themselves into gods. This is Jinn's goal."

Sabah took the measure of his old friend, trying to sense how far he would go. So far, Mustafa had stopped short of advocating betrayal, but that was clearly his purpose. If Sabah was right, he'd been put up to it.

"So a council has been taken among the investors," he guessed. "Tell me who had the will to call it?"

"It doesn't matter," Mustafa said.

"It matters to me."

"What should matter is your position," Mustafa insisted. "I ask you to consider why are you here in Aden instead of with Jinn at his genie's cave in the desert?"

"Because he doesn't need me at this time."

"More and more, that seems to happen," Mustafa suggested. "And what will you—the loyal servant—do when Jinn doesn't need you at all?"

Sabah was taken aback, but the words struck him as honest and not merely posturing.

Mustafa continued, pressing, "When he was young, you controlled him with strength. As he aged, you controlled him with wisdom. What do you have left? You've given him everything, Sabah. Now is the time to take. To take what you have earned."

"A palace coup of some type, is that it? Is that what you seek?"

"You built this empire," Mustafa whispered, "you more than him. You should possess its keys, not stand outside the walls like the second-class member of the clan you've always been."

Mustafa's words hit the one emotional trigger Sabah had buried the deepest. He wasn't part of the Khalif clan. No matter how loyal or hardworking or ruthless, he would never be anything more than a trusted hand.

Indeed, as Jinn's sons and daughters grew, what had become a partnership would fade. The clan and the family bonds would become dominant. Sabah would be pushed to the side, his own offspring unable to reap what he had sown.

In a sense, it had already begun. In the past year or two, Jinn had spent less and less time in Sabah's presence. His habits had changed. He seemed tired of listening to Sabah's advice where he used to savor it.

But that alone was not reason for betrayal. Sabah reached for the qat, folded another leaf between his fingers and stuck it in his mouth. There was much to consider before making such a decision.

As he chewed, the stimulants released by the plant sent a surge of energy through his body.

He knew Mustafa would not change his mind, not after he'd voiced his plan. If Sabah did not agree in principle, there would be trouble right here and now. Perhaps Mustafa had men waiting nearby. Perhaps he believed he could kill Sabah on his own.

Sabah would not give him that chance. "You have a strategy?"

Mustafa nodded. "We must see the horde in action even if it's on a small scale."

"By 'we,' you mean the others as well?"

"I will be the witness, along with Alhrama from Saudi Arabia. Jinn trusts us the most. We will report to the others."

"I see. And how should I arrange this?"

"Jinn must grant us an inspection of the control room and the production facilities. He must give us access to the programming and the codes."

Sabah pondered what they were asking for. He stroked his beard. "And when you have seen this?"

"Then I will signal you," Mustafa said. "And you will kill Jinn and take over the operation as a full partner in the endeavor and the head of the Oasis consortium."

CHAPTER 15

KURT AUSTIN WAS HEADED FOR MARCHETTI'S HIGH-TECH office atop one of Aqua-Terra's two completed buildings. In the twenty-four hours since he and Joe had caught the seaplane, preventing Matson and Otero from escaping, much had occurred.

Back in Washington, Dirk Pitt and the NUMA brass had gone into high gear, gathering intelligence on Jinn al-Khalif.

Nigel, the pilot, had finished putting the helicopter back together and, at Marchetti's invitation, had picked up Paul and Gamay Trout.

Marchetti himself had spent fifteen hours debugging the computer code, trying to be sure Otero had left no additional traps for them. He found none, but there were hundreds of programs running on his automated island. He insisted he couldn't be sure that all of them were unaffected. At Kurt's urging he'd concentrated on the more critical ones and completely deactivated the construction robots, just in case.

With a report due in from NUMA HQ, everyone was gathering in Marchetti's office to await the transmission and discuss their next move.

Kurt opened the door and stepped inside. Joe and the Trouts were already there. Marchetti sat across from them. Leilani sat next to him.

"That's a mighty fine brig you have down there," Kurt said to Marchetti. "I've stayed in worse five-star hotels."

Marchetti beamed. "When Aqua-Terra is ready, we expect to have millionaires and billionaires on board. If I have to put some of them in jail, I don't want to ruin the Aqua-Terra experience for them."

Kurt chuckled.

"Any luck getting them to talk?" Leilani asked.

"No, they've clammed up tight," Kurt said, glancing at Joe and then turning back to Marchetti. "Don't suppose you have a hungry python around here anywhere?"

Marchetti looked shocked by the request. "Um . . . no. Why?"

"Never mind."

Kurt sat down just as the satellite feed locked in. A moment later Dirk Pitt's rugged face appeared on the screen.

After a quick round of introductions, Pitt spoke.

"We've developed some information for you on this Jinn character. The bulk of the data will be sent to you in an encrypted file, but here's the gist of what we know.

"Thirty years ago Jinn al-Khalif was a nineteen-year-old Bedouin camel herder; twenty years ago he entered the arms trade for a brief, profitable spurt, and shortly thereafter he used those funds to get a toehold in several legitimate businesses. Shipping and construction, infrastructure work. Nothing huge, but he did okay.

"Five years ago he forms a company called Oasis. It's an oddly designed international consortium, heavy into technology and funded from murky sources. Interpol has been watching it from the get-go. Their big concern was the vast amount of money and technology flowing into Yemen without any type of control."

"Can't imagine Yemen is a magnet for attracting foreign capital," Kurt said.

"Not in the least," Pitt replied. "Because of that, Interpol thought Oasis might be a terrorist front or a money-laundering operation, but Jinn has not been political, not even within his own struggling country. And they've seen no transactions that would suggest laundering. It seems the technology transfers and the high-tech investments were legitimate."

Pitt tapped something on the keyboard in front of him. A satellite photo came up, showing the stark beauty of Yemen's northern desert region. The display sharpened and zoomed in as if they were dropping in from space. When the resolution locked, it was focused on a rocky outcropping that jutted above the sand and cast a long shadow. It reminded Kurt of Shiprock, New Mexico.

Leading up to the outcropping, and stretching out behind it, were vehicle tracks and swaths of discolored sand.

"What are we looking at?" Kurt asked.

"Our intelligence agencies have tracked some of Jinn's activities to this area of the desert."

"It doesn't look like much," Paul noted.

"It's not supposed to," Dirk replied. "See all that darker sand and soil? It's spread out over a hundred acres."

"It looks like it's been washed down from somewhere," Gamay said. "Erosion or flash flooding."

"Except it's in the driest part of the desert," Dirk said, "and the grade runs off kilter to the pattern we see."

"So it's camouflage," Kurt said. "What are they hiding?"

"Our experts think they've moved a lot of earth," Pitt said, "suggesting an underground compound of massive proportions. Infrared scans have detected an inordinate amount of heat coming from vents in the sand. All of which suggests manufacturing, though until now no one could guess what they were up to."

"Stealing my design," Marchetti said, "and going into production."

Pitt nodded. "So it would seem. The question is, why?"

Marchetti considered this for a second. "I'm not sure," he said. "I intended them to eat garbage, but from what we saw the design has been modified. Obviously that would imply a different purpose. At this point all we know for sure is that they attacked your catamaran, but unless I've missed something no other vessels have been attacked or gone missing. That would suggest it's not their main purpose."

"Then why use them for it?" Kurt asked.

Marchetti glanced at Leilani for a second and then spoke. "Under normal circumstances the boat would have been picked clean. Not a speck of organic matter would have remained. And the bots would have disappeared back into the sea."

Kurt understood. "No evidence. No witnesses. The boat would have been found in perfect working order like the *Mary Celeste*. Only they didn't count on the crew setting a fire to fight them off."

"Exactly," Marchetti said. "Without the residue you found, there would have been nothing to tell us what had happened. Even if another vessel had been watching from a distance, they would have seen nothing."

Pitt returned the conversation to the original track. "So they can be a danger to shipping," he noted, "but if that's not their main function, what is? Could they be causing the temperature anomalies our team discovered?"

"Possibly," Marchetti said. "I'm not sure how, but to some extent what they're capable of depends on how many of them are out there."

"Can you explain that?" Pitt asked.

"Think of them as insects. One isn't a big problem—one wasp, one ant, one termite—not much of a threat. But if you get enough of them in the same place, they can cause all kinds of trouble. My design was capable of reproducing autonomously and spreading ad infinitum. That was the only way to make them effective. No reason to think these aren't doing the same thing. Millions of them can cause problems for a small vessel, billions could pose a threat to a large vessel or oil platform or even something the size of Aqua-Terra, but trillions of them—or trillions of trillions— that could threaten the entire sea."

"The entire sea?" Joe asked.

Marchetti nodded. "In a way, the microbots are a pollutant in their own right. Almost like a toxin. But because they're active in feeding, reproducing and protecting themselves, it's better to think of them as a nonnative species invading a new habitat. They all tend to follow the same trajectory. Without natural enemies, they start off as a curiosity, quickly become a nuisance and shortly thereafter become an ecosystem-threatening epidemic. Unchecked, the microbots could do the same thing."

"I remember when the gypsy moths came to New England," Paul said. "Nonnative. Arrived from China with no natural enemies. One year there were a few furry caterpillars. The next year they were abundant, and by the third year they were absolutely everywhere, by the billions, covering every tree, stripping every leaf and practically decimating the forests. Is that the kind of effect you're talking about?"

Marchetti nodded glumly.

Quiet followed as the group pondered what Marchetti had said. Kurt imagined the microbots spreading through the Indian Ocean and around the world. He wondered if the thought was rational or paranoid and why someone would want that to occur or how they could profit from it.

"Whatever they're doing, I think we can assume it's not a good thing," Pitt said. "Therefore we need to find out what it is and get on top of it. Any suggestions how we can do that?"

All eyes focused on Marchetti again.

"Two ways," he said. "Either catch the microbots in the act, for which I offer my services and the island, or go to the source and see what their orders are."

"Go to Yemen," Pitt clarified.

Marchetti nodded. "I hate to say it, and I certainly wouldn't want to ride along, but if these things are being manufactured in this underground compound in Yemen, your best chance of discovering what they're being created for is to go to the factory and check out the specs."

Pitt nodded thoughtfully but said nothing for the moment. He looked over the assembled team one by one.

"All right," he said finally. "Our original goal was to find out what happened to the crew, but I think we can all agree that we've discovered a greater threat here. One they were probably killed for. We need to follow this up from both angles. Paul and Gamay will take advantage of Mr. Marchetti's hospitality and head up the waterborne search, using Aqua-Terra as home base. Kurt, you and Joe get ready. Unless you have any objections, I'm going find a way to sneak you into Yemen."

Kurt looked at Joe, who nodded. "We'll be ready."

Pitt signed off. The meeting adjourned, and everyone began to file out.

Leilani came up to Kurt. "I want to go with you," she said.

Kurt continued gathering up his things. "Not a chance."

"Why?" she asked. "If this Jinn is the guy that caused all this, I want to be there when you get him."

Kurt cut his eyes at her. "You jeopardized us once, I'm not going to let you do that again. Nor am I going to take you into danger. Nor are we going to *get* this guy. Unlike you, we're not some kind of hit squad. We want to find out what he's up to and why, that's it. The best thing you could do is go home to Hawaii."

"I don't have anyone to go home to," she said.

"I'm sorry," Kurt said, "but that isn't going to work on me this time."

Gamay came over to intercede. "We could use a marine biologist if we're going to analyze what's going on with the food chain. Why don't you stay here with us?"

Leilani didn't seem to like that idea, but it was clear she had no other option. Finally she nodded.

Kurt stepped out through the door without another word. He felt badly for her, but he had a job to do.

CHAPTER 16

GULF OF ADEN, OFF THE COAST OF YEMEN

THIRTY-SEVEN HOURS AFTER THE MEETING IN MARCHETTI'S conference room, Kurt and Joe found themselves sitting in a wooden fishing boat in the dark of night a mile or so off the coast of Aden.

Clad in black wet suits, with fins, and small oxygen tanks on their backs, they waited patiently for a signal.

Kurt rubbed a light coat of baby shampoo on the inside glass of his mask before rinsing it to keep it from fogging up. Joe checked his air one last time and secured a diving knife in a sheath on his leg.

"You ready?" Kurt asked.

"As ready as I'm going to be," Joe said. "You see anything?"

"Not yet."

"What if this guy got held up?"

"He'll make it," Kurt said. "Dirk swears this guy has helped him out a few times before."

"Did he give you a name?"

Kurt shook his head and smiled. "He said we wouldn't need it."

Joe chuckled. "Dirk has his secrets, that's for sure."

It was a moonless night with a light wind from the northwest. Kurt could smell the desert on that breeze, but he could see nothing. They were anchored off a desolate stretch of the coast, bobbing up and down on the swells and waiting to hit the water. But they couldn't go until they were sure someone had arrived to pick them up.

Finally a pair of lights flashed in their direction. On-off. On-off. And then back on again for a few seconds before going permanently dark.

"That's our man," Kurt said, pulling his mask into place.

Joe did the same, pausing for a second. "One question," he said. "What if those bots are in the water here, waiting to chow down on us?"

Kurt hadn't thought about that and, quite frankly, wished Joe hadn't either. "Then you better hope they're not hungry," he said.

With that, he pushed back over the side and dropped into the inky black water.

A few seconds later Joe hit the water behind him, the muted sound of his plunge reverberating through the dark.

Without delay, Kurt got his bearings and began to kick with smooth, powerful strokes, the thrust from his fins moving him swiftly through the water. It was a quiet, slow-motion approach to the beach.

As he closed in on the shore, he could hear the sound of the waves pounding, he could feel the pull of the ebb tide trying to drag him to the east. He angled slightly into it, but rather than wear himself out fighting it, he mostly rode with it.

Closer in, he focused on the swells, trying to get a rough sense of timing for the set of waves. One big swell pushed him upward, threatening to dump him face-first, but it passed, broke and sent white foam racing up onto the sand fifteen yards in front of him.

The undertow caught him as the water flowed back, but Kurt powered through it, caught the next wave and bodysurfed right up onto the beach.

Thirty feet ahead boulders offered shelter. He pulled off his fins and dashed forward, taking shelter between them. Once he was there, he pulled his mask off, unzipped the wet suit a few inches and drew out a small night vision scope. He scanned the beach and the road above it. He saw no movement, no sign of anything living.

Seventy yards to the west, an old VW bus sat parked on the road. That was their transportation.

He turned his head in time to see Joe coming up onto the beach. After a short delay, Joe sprinted to the rocks.

Kurt pointed to the van. "Not bad," he said. "We only missed it by a football field."

"Easier to walk that distance than to swim head-on into the current," Joe replied.

"My thoughts exactly," Kurt said. "Besides, on the off chance our friend has been watched or tailed, probably best not to come out of the water right in front of the getaway vehicle."

The two men stripped out of their diving gear to reveal plain clothes. Watching for trouble, they moved down the beach in spurts until they reached the VW.

The thirty-year-old vehicle was a tawny brown color, pitted and scratched from years of flying sand. Its tires looked bald, and the VW emblem on the front was broken, missing half of the W.

"Maybe it's a knockoff," Kurt said.

"Yeah," Joe replied, "a Volks Vagon."

"Not much style to it," Kurt said, and then, thinking of the Vespa, he added, "but at least it has four wheels."

"You must be moving up in the world," Joe said.

Kurt chuckled as he slid the door open. Whatever it lost on style points, the van had other attributes, including ample room for supplies, an air-cooled engine that would be more reliable crossing the desert than a water-cooled power plant, and authentic Yemen plates that Kurt hoped were current.

It was also unoccupied. Whoever Dirk Pitt had found to drop the van off had vanished. A second set of tire tracks on the soft shoulder by the road suggested the driver had been ferried off in another vehicle.

They piled into the van. Kurt made his way to the driver's seat as Joe checked the supplies in the back.

"We've got boots and caftans back here," Joe said. "Food, water and some equipment. The guy set us up well."

Kurt looked for the key. He flipped the visor down and it dropped into his hand, along with a note.

He stuck the key in the ignition and unfolded the note as Joe made his way up front and took the passenger seat.

"It says take the coast road northeast for seven miles. Turn northwest on the paved road that marks the Eastern Highway. It will be paved for thirty miles and then become a dirt track. Continue on for exactly forty-five miles. Hide the van and hike northwest on a course of 290 for 5.2 miles. You'll cut the corner and come upon the compound you seek. Good luck."

"Any signature?"

"Anonymous," Kurt said. He folded the note and tucked it away. "Whoever he is, let's not disappoint him."

After a quick look around, Kurt turned the key, and the engine came to life with that sound that only old VWs ever seemed to make. The gears made a grinding noise as Kurt put the van in first and released the clutch, but at least they were off and running.

He hoped to make the compound before daybreak. They had four hours.

CHAPTER 17

GAMAY TROUT WAS FILLED WITH GLEE AS SHE RODE ALONG at twenty knots, a mere thirty feet above the waves, in a small airship of Elwood Marchetti's design.

To call it a blimp would have been a disservice to the sleek craft. The crew compartment sat between and slightly below what Marchetti called air pods. Filled with helium, the pods resembled pontoons, although much larger and longer. They were flat on the bottom and curved on the top to provide lift as the craft moved forward. They were attached to the passenger compartment by a series of struts that ran up and out at a forty-five-degree angle. A second raft of struts ran between them, bracing them and keeping them apart. The design allowed a view upward to the sky, something no other airship had.

The passenger compartment was shaped like that of an upscale cabin cruiser, raked backward as it dropped away from the inflated sections. A platform to the rear allowed open-air cruising, sunbathing and a way to enter and exit the airship. Twin ducted fans, placed well forward of the cabin, pulled the craft along like a pair of sled dogs. A stubby set of wings acted as a canard while a pair of vertical tails, one on each pod, acted as the airship's rudders.

"This is amazing," Gamay said, leaning over the side and staring at a trio of dolphins they'd found and begun following.

With Marchetti at the controls, Paul, Gamay and Leilani were free to enjoy the moment. They soaked it in, feeling the breeze, gazing at the dolphins flying through the clear waters below.

The bottle-nosed mammals easily kept pace with the airship, accelerating with powerful strokes of their flat tails. Occasionally, one would break the surface and propel itself through the air, leaping toward them and then arcing back down to the water.

"It's like they're trying to reach us," Leilani said.

"Maybe they think we're the mother ship," Paul replied.

Gamay laughed. She could only imagine what the dolphins would think of such a vessel. Clearly they weren't afraid of it, though. "Marchetti, I think this will work."

Leilani nodded, seeming to be in better spirits. Paul smiled.

"You look like the cat who ate the canary," Gamay said.

"I was just thinking how lucky I am to be up here with two beautiful women," Paul said, grinning, "instead of hiking through the desert with Kurt and Joe."

Gamay laughed.

"And it's not just the company," he added. "For once we've got the multimillion-dollar toys to work with. Kurt and Joe are probably wrestling with a few smelly camels right about now."

"Have to agree," Gamay said, then turned to Marchetti. "How much farther can we go?"

"We can stay aloft for days if we need to," he said. "But my suggestion is to put another hour on this leg and then head home to the island. My crew will have the other two airships put together and ready for action tomorrow, and we can take all three up and cover more ground—er, water."

"Do you have pilots?" Paul asked.

"Pilots?" Marchetti replied. *"We don't need no stinking pilots."*

"Who's going to fly them?"

"Any of you can," Marchetti said. "You drive this thing like you drive a car or boat."

Gamay found Marchetti a welcome addition to the team. Certainly he'd been true to his word so far, putting his full backing behind the expedition. He'd already turned the floating island of Aqua-Terra toward the northwest and brought it up to the blazing speed of four and a half knots and turned over all specs of the microbots to NUMA. He'd even brought back another dozen members of his crew to keep the island running sans robots.

"Give us a few lessons before you send us out," Paul asked.

"Sounds fair."

Gamay turned her attention back to the sea. The dolphins continued to race along with them, staying just ahead of the airship's floating shadow. Another one looked as if it were about to jump, when suddenly they scattered, darting in opposite directions and vanishing in the blink of an eye.

"You see that?" she asked.

"They're quick," Paul said.

"Must have gotten tired of us," Leilani said.

Still gazing at the water, Gamay sensed something different. The sea was growing darker. A murky gray hue had begun to replace the clear deep blue they'd seen only moments before.

She guessed the dolphins had sensed the change, processed it as danger and fled in the other direction.

The happiness left her. "Slow us down," she said to Marchetti. "I think we've found them."

CHAPTER 18

"Riding in this thing makes me feel like i'm headed to Woodstock in the desert," Joe said, talking over the VW's engine noise and peering into the dark.

"Let's hope it's not quite as crowded," Kurt replied.

He and Joe drove through the night. When they reached the waypoint, they pulled off the desert track and parked the VW behind the curved slope of a sand dune.

While Joe brushed away the tire tracks, Kurt pulled out a tarp. He peeled a thin film off the topside of the tarp, exposing an adhesive layer. Laying the tarp facedown and dragging it across the ground caused the adhesive to pick up a fine layer of sand as grains stuck to its surface.

Satisfied, Kurt flung the tarp over the top of the VW, staked it in the ground and dumped several small bucket loads of sand on the top.

Joe returned just as Kurt finished. Joe blinked as if his eyes were deceiving him.

"What happened to the VV?"

"I made it invisible," Kurt said, heaving a small backpack over his shoulders. "No one's going to spot it."

"Yeah," Joe said, "probably not even us. I lose my car in the parking lot, this I might never find."

Kurt hadn't really considered that. He looked around for landmarks, but the desert offered only endless dunes in every direction. He pulled out a GPS receiver and dropped a pin, marking the location of the hiding spot. He hoped that would help.

As Joe pulled on his own backpack, Kurt slid a pair of snowshoes on his feet. They were modern carbon fiber design, not the tennis rackets of old, but they would do the same thing: spread his weight out over a wider area and allow him to walk on top of the sand instead of sinking in and trudging through it with every step.

Joe donned a similar pair, and the two men began hiking.

Ninety minutes later they crested the latest in a series of endless dunes. As they reached the top, they caught wind of a helicopter approaching from the south.

Scanning around for the source of the noise, Kurt spotted a flashing red beacon in the sky. It looked to be no more than two or three miles away, cruising at five hundred feet and headed straight for them.

"Get down," Kurt said, dropping flat to the ground and trying to burrow in the sand like a sidewinder.

Joe did the same, and in a moment they were just about covered up to their necks. Despite this camouflage, the helicopter continued toward them, never deviating or changing course.

"This looks bad," Joe whispered.

Kurt's hand found the holster on his hip and the .50 caliber Bowen revolver inside it. The gun was a cannon, though it wouldn't do much good against a helicopter unless he made a couple of perfectly lucky shots.

He locked onto the red light. A dimmer green light glowed on the other side. If it came to it, Kurt would aim right between the two and empty the cylinder in hopes of hitting something vital.

He heard Joe unlatch his own pistol, likely planning to do the same, when a thought occurred to him: if they'd been spotted and the copter sent out to hunt them down, why wasn't it blacked out?

"Nice of them to leave their nav lights on for us to aim at," he said.

"You think they made a mistake?"

The helicopter continued toward them, now only a quarter mile away and still descending but also changing course.

"I guess we're about to find out."

The helicopter thundered past, two hundred feet above them and a couple hundred yards to the west.

Kurt watched it pass and tracked its course. Seeing no other aircraft trailing it, he pulled out of the sand and raced after it. He made it to the bottom of the dune and clambered up the top of the next one, throwing himself flat against the sand as he reached the peak.

Joe hit the ground next to him. Ahead of them the helicopter slowed to a hover, descending toward a dark shape that rose from the desert floor like a ship on the sea.

A band of low-intensity lights came on, marking a circle on the top of the "ship." The helicopter adjusted, pivoting slowly and then settling onto the rocky bluff.

"Looks like we've found the compound," Kurt said.

"We're not the only ones," Joe replied.

Lights could be seen approaching from the southwest. It looked like a small convoy, maybe eight or nine vehicles. It was hard to count the headlights with all the dust they were kicking up.

"I thought Dirk said this place didn't get much traffic?"

"Apparently it's rush hour," Kurt replied. "Let's hope they're not here on our account."

As the vehicles pulled up in front of the bluff, the quiet desert filled with commotion. The headlights blazed and the dust swirled and voices rose through it, not arguing but discussing something tersely in Arabic. Armed men appeared from the mouth of a cave and walked out to greet the newcomers.

On the bluff above, the helicopter was shutting down. Two men climbed out and made their way toward the side of the cliff, disappearing into what looked like a hole cut out of the rock. Kurt guessed it was some kind of tunnel or hidden entrance.

"Come on," he said, "while the valet's busy with all those cars."

Kurt backed down the sand dune for a few paces and began to scamper along it. Joe followed, trying to catch up.

"What are we going to do?" Joe asked. "Walk right in and pretend we're with the band?"

"No," Kurt said. "We make our way around the back by that landing pad. I saw the passengers from that chopper disappear without climbing down. Somewhere on top there must be a way in. All we have to do is find it."

CHAPTER 19

OUT OVER THE INDIAN OCEAN, MARCHETTI HAD PUT THE airship into a slight climb, brought it up to an altitude of a hundred feet and slowed it considerably. To make the design as sleek as it was required some compromises, one of which meant the craft didn't have quite enough buoyancy to float without some forward motion providing lift.

As the engine cut out and they started drifting, the passengers grew nervous.

"We're still sinking," Gamay said. Seventy feet below the sea was calm and dark. If she was right and that darkness was related to the microbots swarming beneath the surface, she had no desire to land on it.

"Just a second," Marchetti said.

He threw a lever, and compartments at either end of the airship sprang open like he'd popped the trunk and hood of his car at the same moment. The hissing of high-pressure gas followed, and two additional balloons sprang forth from the hatches. They floated upward, quickly filling to capacity with helium and snapping their tether lines taut. As they inflated, the sinking slowed and then stopped.

"I call them air anchors," Marchetti said proudly. "We'll deflate them once we get moving again. But in the meantime, they keep us from ending up in the drink."

Gamay was relieved to hear that. Around her, Leilani and Paul both exhaled.

"I guess we should break out the sampling kit," Paul said.

The airship stabilized at forty feet. By releasing small amounts of helium, Marchetti coaxed it down to five feet and then set its buoyancy at neutral.

"Close enough?" he asked.

Paul nodded as he climbed toward the aft platform with the telescoping sample collector.

"Be careful," Leilani said, looking as if she didn't want to go anywhere near the edge.

"I second that," Gamay added. "It's taken me years to train you. I'd hate to start over with a new husband."

Paul chuckled. "And chances are, you'd never find one as handsome and debonair as me."

Gamay smiled. She'd never find one she loved as much as him, that was for sure.

As Paul reached the edge, Gamay moved up beside him. Knowing what lay below, she wanted to strap him in like a lookout at the top of the crow's nest, but there was no way to do it, and no real need.

They were in the gyre of the Indian Ocean, near its center, a spot sort of like the eye of a hurricane. Under normal conditions it was "the doldrums," with no wind or waves to speak of.

The sea below looked oily and flat, the sun blazed down from behind them. It was remarkably calm. Only the slightest of breezes could even be felt, not enough to worry about as they drifted a few feet above the water.

Paul extended the pole and dipped the vial in the water, scooping up a sample. He pulled the vial free and held it over the water, allowing the excess to drip off before reeling it in.

Wearing thick plastic gloves, Gamay took the sample and wiped the outside of the vial with a specially charged microfiber towel that Marchetti said would attract and trap any microbots that might be present.

She didn't see any residue, but the little suckers were small. A hundred could fit on the head of a pin.

She glanced at the water in the vial.

"It looks clear," she said.

She capped the vial and placed it in a stainless steel box with a rubber seal, which she wrenched down tight. She put the towel in a matching container.

Gamay and Paul gazed into the waters down below the way people might look over the edge of a dock. A few feet out the water looked normal. But they'd flown over two miles of discolored ocean since the dolphins scattered. It made no sense.

"They're not on the surface," Gamay said, realizing the truth. "We can see them, looking straight down, but at any kind of an angle all we can make out is seawater."

From the cockpit Marchetti agreed. "They're floating just below. You'll have to get a deeper sample. If you want, I can take us right down to the—"

"Let's not do that," Leilani said. "Please. What if we hit the water or something goes wrong?"

She was in the main part of the cabin, watching over the side but protected by the wall. She looked rather green.

"I'm pretty sure I can get them from here," Paul said, being his usual accommodating self.

He laid down flat on the deck, his head and shoulders over the edge. He stretched out, using his long arms to great advantage and dipping a second sample vial in as far as he could.

Marchetti edged closer. Gamay did the same.

Paul pulled the sample out. It also looked clear. He dumped it out and tried to stretch even farther.

Leilani began protesting. "I don't know about this," she mumbled, sounding terrified. "Do we really want to bring those things on board?"

Kurt had said she was unstable. Now Gamay saw why. Gung ho to come with them and suddenly filled with fear.

"Somebody's got to do it," Gamay said.

"Maybe we could just call the Navy or the Coast Guard or something."

"Hold my legs down," Paul asked, "I have to take a deeper sample."

Gamay crouched down and put her hands on the back of Paul's legs, pressing down with all her weight. She heard Leilani muttering something and backing farther away as if the bots were going to leap out of the water like a crocodile and snatch Paul up.

Paul extended the pole and stretched as far as he could. He dipped it in maybe seven or eight feet. As he raised it above the surface, Gamay could feel the strain on his body. The sample looked dark.

"I think you got some."

As Paul started to reel in the pole, Leilani started to tremble. She backed up another step.

"It's okay," Marchetti said, trying to comfort her.

Just then a loud bang shook the craft. It tilted to the side, and the back end dropped like a covered wagon that had lost a wheel.

Paul slid, hit the sidewall of the deck and almost went overboard. Gamay slid with him, grabbed his belt and wrapped her arm around a strut protruding from the deck.

Leilani screamed and fell but held on to the door of the cabin while Marchetti clung to the steering console.

"Hang on!" Gamay shouted.

"You hang on," Paul called back. "I have nothing to grab."

Another bang, and the airship leveled out, but with the back end down even farther, like a dump truck spilling its contents. Gamay held on with all her might. She was physically strong, but keeping Paul's six-foot-eight, two-hundred-and-forty-pound body from sliding off the platform and dropping into the water was quickly taking its toll. She felt his belt cutting into her fingers.

Behind her, Leilani and Marchetti were trying to help.

"The balloon," Leilani shouted, pointing to the sky.

Gamay glanced upward. The rear air anchor had come loose and was drifting up toward the heavens like a kid's balloon lost at the fair. As a result, the airship was sinking toward the water tail first.

"Get us moving!" Gamay shouted.

"On it," Marchetti said, rushing to the cockpit.

"Leilani, I need help."

As Marchetti scrambled into the cabin, Leilani crouched beside Gamay and grabbed onto Paul's leg. The ducted fans up front began to spin, and the airship began to crawl forward. As it did, the strain of holding on to Paul increased.

Gamay felt as if she were going to be ripped loose. She saw Leilani trying to get a better grip.

The airship began to pick up speed, but it was still dropping, the tail end only a foot or so from the water. Paul arched his body in a reverse sit-up to keep his face from hitting the sea.

As the speed picked up, the airship began to level off.

"Now!" Gamay shouted. She pulled with all her might, and, with Leilani's help, they managed to slide Paul back up to where he'd begun, head and shoulders over the edge. She realized he was still holding the sample pole.

"Drop that thing!" she yelled.

"After going through all this?" Paul said. "I don't think so."

By now the speed of the craft was coming on, providing enough lift that Marchetti could level off completely.

As the ship climbed and then flattened, Gamay reeled Paul in and held him tight.

"Paul Trout, if you ever do something like that again, it will be the death of me," she said.

"And me," he replied.

"What happened?" he said, looking to Marchetti.

"I have no idea," he said. "The anchor released somehow. It must have been a glitch or a malfunction of some kind."

Gamay looked at Paul, thankful to have him with her instead of in the water with those things. It seemed they'd found a horrible bit of bad luck. Or had they?

She began to wonder about Marchetti's crew. Otero and Matson had been bought. What was to stop any of the others from selling out? She kept the thought to herself, looked at the dark sample they'd recovered and tried to remind herself that aside from Paul there was no one she could trust implicitly.

CHAPTER 20

JINN AL-KHALIF STRODE THROUGH THE HALLS OF HIS CAVE in a state of fury. He kicked the door to his sprawling office open and threw a chair aside that blocked the path to his desk. Sabah entered behind him, shutting the door with more care.

"I will not be summoned like a schoolboy!" Jinn bellowed.

"You have not been summoned," Sabah insisted.

"They contact you unannounced, tell you they're coming here, and that they expect to see me!" Jinn shouted. "How is that not being summoned?"

Jinn stood beside an impressively large desk. Behind him, visible through a glass partition that acted as the rear wall to the office, the production floor of his factory could be seen twenty feet below.

Here and there in the "clean room," men in protective hazmat-like suits were calibrating the machines, preparing to produce the next version of Jinn's microbots. The lethally redesigned batch was destined for Egypt and the dam.

"They made a request," Sabah said. "Considering their tone and actions of late, I thought it necessary to promise your presence."

"That is an act of insolence!" Jinn shouted. "You do not promise for me."

Many times in his life had Jinn felt the type of rage that filled him now, never before had it been directed at Sabah.

"Why, as we get closer and closer to the goal, do all my servants seem to be losing their minds and forgetting their places?"

Sabah seemed on the verge of speaking but held back.

"You've already said enough," Jinn told him with a dismissive wave. "Leave me."

Instead of bowing and departing, Sabah stood taller.

"No," he said plainly. "I have taught you from a young age, ever since your father died. And I have sworn to protect you, even from yourself. So I will speak and you will listen and then you decide what to do when I am through."

Jinn looked up in shock, enough so that his instinct to kill Sabah for disobeying him was checked.

"This consortium," Sabah began, "they've given billions of dollars to your effort. And they are powerful men in their own right, bound to flex their muscle every now and then."

Jinn gazed at Sabah as if mesmerized, listening as he often had during the years.

"The fact that they come as one suggests danger," Sabah continued. "They're unified."

Jinn looked around his office. There was little in the way of decor. But weapons of the past were displayed on one wall, a curved scimitar caught his eye.

"Then I will kill them all," Jinn said. "I will cut them to pieces with my own two hands."

"And what would that get us?" Sabah asked. "They have not come alone. Each brings a squad of armed men. In total numbers they are almost equal to our own. It would bring only war. And even if we won, others would undoubtedly investigate, perhaps even seek revenge."

For the first time in a great while, Jinn felt vulnerable, cornered. If they had known what they were stirring in him, they would not have pressed the issue.

"This could not have come at a worse time," he said. "We have other guests to prepare for."

"They will be dealt with," Sabah insisted.

"Fine," Jinn said. "What do you suggest?"

"We must send a message that does not start a war. I suggest we show them what they want to see. One to see it closely, the other to observe from a distance."

A sinister look came over Sabah's face, and Jinn began to understand. He had to discount Sabah as old and out of touch, but no more.

"Order the test bay flooded," Jinn said.

"It has been configured to simulate the attack on Aswan."

A smile crept onto Jinn's face. "Perfect. Proceed with the demonstration. Give them a front-row seat. It would make me very happy for them to see more than they bargained for."

A flash of understanding appeared on Sabah's face.

"I will do as you command," he said.

Jinn looked back through the glass partition to his workers below. They moved here and there. The machines were operating again, running at full capacity. At the end of the production line a trickle of silver sand had begun to fill a yellow plastic drum. Beyond it, fifty-nine other drums waited. They would carry the latest batch of his horde. And if Jinn was right, they would break the will of Aziz and force Egypt's military leaders and their wealth back into his hands.

CHAPTER 21

KURT REACHED THE TOP OF THE BLUFF A FEW SECONDS ahead of Joe. He studied the layout.

The landing pad was set up three-quarters of the way to the front edge. A Russian-made helicopter sat in the center of the pad. The cargo door was rolled back, and a pair of men dressed like guards sat in the open doorway, sharing a cigarette and talking.

Glancing around, Kurt saw no one else. "Can you get them both?"

Joe nodded. "Two birds with one stone," he said. "Or, in this case, multiple wires."

Kurt was glad to hear that. He pointed to the far side of the copter. Joe moved that way, clinging to the side of the bluff like a rock climber.

When Joe reached a covered spot beside the gray machine, Kurt pulled the cloth of the caftan across his face. He stepped from his own hiding spot and walked toward the men, holding his hands out and muttering something about a lost camel.

The men snapped to attention and moved toward him. One

put a hand on his sidearm but didn't draw it out, perhaps because Kurt looked like a local, perhaps because he had his hands up as he spoke.

"*Nāqah, nāqah,*" he said, using the Arabic word for female camel.

The men seemed utterly baffled. They continued toward him looking angry, never seeing Joe move in behind them.

"*Nāqah,*" Kurt said once again, and then watched as the men stiffened and dropped to their knees.

They fell forward silently. Reveling Joe grinning and holding a Taser, which he'd fired into the two men.

"Oh where, oh where has my little *nāqah* gone?" Kurt finished.

"Great thing about Tasers," Joe said, "they work so quick, people can't even yell out."

The coiled wires were still attached, and when the men began to move, Joe zapped them again.

"I think they've had enough, Dr. Frankenstein."

Joe switched the power off, and the tension left the two men instantly. Kurt was on them, jabbing a tranquilizer dart into each and watching their eyes roll up in their heads. As the men went limp, Joe pulled out the Taser wires and helped Kurt carry the two back to the helicopter.

They piled the men inside, climbed in after them, and then slid the door shut.

A few moments later the door opened. Kurt and Joe came out dressed in the guards' dark blue clothing, complete with kaffiyehs that covered their faces and hair. While Joe pretended to watch the helicopter, Kurt looked around for the tunnel he'd seen.

He discovered a cut in the stone and followed it to a ladder that dropped straight down. At the bottom he found a door made of steel with an electronic sensor lock above the handle. It looked familiar, like the locks in any hotel.

"Let's just hope we have a reservation," he said to himself as he rummaged through the guard's pockets. Finding a card key in one, he slipped it in the card reader and pulled it out. When the light went green, he turned the handle.

"Easy as pie," he whispered.

Propping the door open with a small rock, he climbed back up the ladder and whistled to Joe. A moment later they were in the tunnel and taking a steep set of stairs downward.

"Into the rabbit hole," Kurt said. "Just keep an eye out for the Jabberwocky."

"What exactly is a Jabberwocky again?" Joe asked. "I was never quite sure."

"It's something bad and scary," Kurt said. "You'll know it when you see it."

They descended the stairs and came to a warren of tunnels. They took one that angled downward and came to another crossroads.

"I feel like I'm in an ant farm," Joe whispered.

"Yeah," Kurt said. "I can just imagine giant people watching us through the glass."

They moved down the tunnel to another intersection.

"Which way?" Joe asked.

"No idea," Kurt said.

"We either need a guide or a map."

Kurt's brow wrinkled. "If you see a lighted display that says 'You are here,' be sure to let me know."

They found no such thing, but then Kurt noticed something else.

Up above, a series of pipes ran through the tunnel. Power conduits and possibly water or natural gas. All the things a production center needed.

"We need to find the factory," he said. "I'm thinking we follow the power lines."

They moved along a tunnel, tracking the conduits. It led them to a larger hallway, wide enough to drive a car through. A pair of men dressed like them walked toward them, coming from the opposite direction. Kurt forced himself to remain relaxed as they approached. Nevertheless, he was ready for a fight. But they passed without a word, and he breathed a little easier.

At the end of the tunnel they came to an open section of the cave. Concrete flooring had been put in, and a dozen tables surrounded by chairs filled the space. It was lit up brightly. A far wall had refrigerators and sinks stacked against it.

"Congratulations," Kurt said. "We've found the mess hall."

"And I'm finally not hungry," Joe said.

Groups of men sat at three of the tables. Strangely, they looked nothing like Jinn's men.

"All kinds of people here," Kurt whispered. "We better keep going."

They moved on, following the pipes and conduits until they reached a glass wall. It looked down into a cavernous space. The lighting was low, but from what they could see it looked like an Olympic-sized pool sat down below. A large shape took up the middle.

"What is this, a health spa?" Joe whispered.

"It won't be if we get discovered."

"That's a big tank," Joe said. "Reminds me of our simulation tank back in D.C."

"Curiouser and curiouser," Kurt said, quoting Alice from the

Lewis Carroll classic. "These guys must be modeling something. Currents or waves or something."

"What's with the setup in the middle?"

"No idea," Kurt said. "But let's get a closer look."

They found a door and slipped through it. Stairs led down to a locker room of sorts. White hazmat-style uniforms hung in stalls.

"Time for a wardrobe change," Kurt said.

"You think these are necessary?"

"For camouflage," Kurt said. "And if there are any of those microbots down here, it might be good to have a protective layer on."

In a minute, Kurt and Joe had each donned hazmat suits, pulling them on over the uniforms they'd stolen from the guards.

They moved out onto the pool deck and stood at the surface level. Kurt noticed the object in the center was not a model ship or even the depiction of some coastline but a wide curving object wedged between the two sides. The water level was high on one side of it but far lower on the other side and constricted to a narrow, irregular channel.

He and Joe descended one more flight of stairs and opened a door. They now stood below the water level, looking into the tank and the cross section of the obstruction through the tank's clear acrylic side.

"I've seen this before," Kurt said. "It's an embankment dam. The top layer is crushed rock and sand. The gray core in the center is most likely waterproof clay. The bottom liner is known as a cutoff curtain. It's usually made of concrete, designed to keep the water from seeping under the dam."

He pointed to the high water behind the dam. "They're even filling the high side like it's a reservoir."

"Why would these guys be modeling a dam?" Joe asked.

"I'm not sure, but I have a feeling we're not going to like the answer."

The sound of a generator starting up caught their attention. A moment later the main overhead lights came on and the room brightened. Through the water Kurt saw the distorted shapes of other men in white hazmat suits on the far side of the pool.

"We better look busy," Kurt said.

Joe grinned. "I'm pretty sure there's an exit sign I need to inspect."

"That sounds like a job for two."

They climbed back up the stairs and slipped out of the observation dugout. Back on the pool deck, they waved to the men across from them in identical suits, received a wave in return and then entered the locker room once again.

"What now?" Joe asked.

Through a window Kurt saw another group entering the room. These men were dressed sharply in fine Arab clothing. Another man dressed in white was pointing out this and that to them. A bearded man in a plain gray caftan trailed behind them.

"That's Jinn," Kurt said, basing his guess on a surveillance photo he'd seen.

"Who are these other guys?" Joe asked.

"They look like dignitaries on a tour," Kurt said.

Jinn led the Arab men around the pool and over to the very stairway Kurt and Joe had just ascended. They went down to the underwater viewing area.

"They're here for a demonstration of some kind," Kurt whispered.

"I hate to sound like the reasonable one," Joe began, "but maybe we should beat a hasty retreat while they're otherwise occupied."

Kurt shook his head. "Sage advice, my friend. Except we now have a front-row seat, and they're about to show us what they're planning. I think it behooves us to stick around, keep the suits on and try to blend in."

"*Behooves* us?"

"It was the word of the day on my calendar last week. Never thought I'd get a chance to use it."

"Glad to hear you're expanding your vocabulary. But what if something behooves one of them to ask us what we're doing here? Or to perform some task we don't know how to do, like turn some big machine on?"

"We'll just press a lot of buttons, throw some switches, and pretend we're incompetent," Kurt said.

"Go with our strengths, then."

"Exactly."

Kurt would have tried to reassure Joe further, but additional machinery starting up dragged his attention back to the window.

He saw Jinn gesturing and speaking, but he couldn't make out the words through the glass.

"This is like watching TV with the mute button on," Joe said.

At the far end of the pool, a large yellow drum was being secured to a hoist and lifted by an overhead crane. By the caution they showed, and the fact that only the white-suited men got anywhere near it, Kurt figured he knew what was in that drum.

"Sound or no sound," he said, "I think we're about to see a show."

CHAPTER 22

IN THE CAVERNOUS BAY SURROUNDING THE TANK, JINN'S words to Mustafa of Pakistan and Alhrama of Saudi Arabia echoed with a strange dissonance. He'd managed to be gracious and munificent—at least in his own mind—despite wanting to choke them with his bare hands. But he was ready to send them a message. In fact, he'd decided to send two.

Sabah leaned closer. "Separate them," he whispered and then stepped back, remaining behind Jinn and out of sight.

Jinn did not react to the words. He had agreed to this show on Sabah's request. But he would decide what must occur now.

"You see in the tank before you a mock-up of the Aswan High Dam," he said. "It will soon be the focal point in a demonstration of my powers."

"I don't understand," Alhrama said.

"General Aziz has emboldened you with his refusal to pay what he promised. He has his reasons, but prime among them is the dam. As long as it exists, Egypt has a five-year supply of water stored up. But Aziz has little understanding of either my power or my wrath."

Jinn lifted a radio to his mouth and pressed the talk switch. "Begin."

The machinery spooled up again. The crane shifted and moved the barrel out over the water and into its final position. A cable attached to the bottom half of the yellow drum was reeled in and the drum began to tip.

The silver sand began to pour out; millions upon millions of Jinn's microbots, pouring into the tank and dispersing like sugar in tea. The water began turning murky and gray.

"Give the command," Jinn said.

In a control room high above, someone pressed a button and sent out a coded command.

The murky water began to stir. The gray cloud coalesced into a tighter pattern and then moved toward the edge of the dam like a dark spirit drifting through the water.

"What's happening?" Mustafa asked.

"The dam is made of aggregate," Jinn said. "Easy to put together and held in place by its great weight, but not completely impervious."

As he spoke, the silver sand adhered to the edge of the dam in two separate places: one spot near the top of the dam and a second about one-third the way down the sloping wall. After a minute or so, the progress of the tiny machines became noticeable in the cross section of the dam.

"Remarkable," Alharma said, "the speed with which they penetrate."

"The actual dam is much thicker of course," Jinn pointed out.

"But the effect will be the same, it will only take longer. A matter of hours, I should think."

Within minutes the leading fingers of the horde had reached the central core of the dam. Progress slowed dramatically, but the etching continued until a pinprick had been bored through to the other side.

In another minute or two the sand had reached the right edge of the aggregate and broken through. A trickle of water began, quickly accelerating. Soon the weight of the water behind the dam was forcing out a jet of liquid through the tiny gap.

"This effect will be heightened in the real event," Jinn said. "The weight of the water behind Aswan numbers in the trillions of tons."

Even in the scale model, the breach was quickly being scoured and enlarged. Soon the gap was two inches in diameter and then four. Moments later a section of the top dropped in, taking the miniature road and cars along with it. The water from the high side of the tank flowed through the gap, pouring over the far side like a waterfall. But it was the lower tunnel through the dam that made things interesting.

As the water surged over the top, it reached a point of equilibrium, scouring downward far less rapidly where the waterproof clay core resisted the erosion.

"The dam is not falling," Mustafa pointed out.

"Watch the lower tunnel," Jinn insisted.

The lower tunnel finally made it through to the far side, and in minutes the higher-pressure water from the deeper part of the tank had widened the lower tunnel from a pinprick to a few inches in diameter.

Water blasted out the far side in a fine spray. After another minute, the core collapsed in the center, creating a deep V-shaped groove as the material above it caved in.

A huge wave surged through and crashed into the narrow channel that represented the Nile. It flooded the miniature embankments, sweeping away dirt, sand and small boxes that represented structures.

The test was successful, the dam was breached, the Nile was flooded. Mustafa and Alhrama stared in shock at the devastation.

Jinn smiled to himself and took a step back. It was the perfect moment. Sabah held the door behind him.

Mustafa turned and looked at them, grinning and expectant. He nodded to Sabah. The look on his face reminded Jinn of a thief with stolen treasures in hand. When Sabah took no action, the look changed, first to confusion, then to anger and fear. He must have now realized that Sabah would not kill his master.

The thief with the stolen goods had been caught and his face showed it. He reached for a weapon, but Sabah pulled Jinn aside and slammed the door.

In a blink, the hatch was locked tight. And the hammering of gunfire up against it did nothing but ring in their ears.

Mustafa began shouting from behind the door. "What are you doing? What is the meaning of this?"

From outside the room Jinn pressed an intercom switch. "The meaning is simple. You tried to turn my servant against me and he has passed the test. Now you will suffer the consequences."

The sound of fists banging followed and then several more shots rang out, and Jinn was in wonder that the ricochets didn't kill either Mustafa or Alhrama.

Alhrama began shouting. "Jinn, be reasonable! I have nothing to do with this."

Jinn ignored them. He brought the radio up to his mouth once again. "Begin the frenzy."

Up in the control room the operator punched another button, and the yellow drum was tilted farther, dumping more of the metallic sand into the pool. The murky gray color returned and deepened, and the water changed complexion once again. From outside the tank where Jinn and Sabah stood, it seemed as if the water had begun to boil.

Inside the viewing chamber, the effect was enhanced. Mustafa stared at the acrylic wall. A dark, viscous shape, thick like octopus ink, surged forward. It flowed onto the clear surface and spread across it like some kind of film.

Mustafa froze. Alhrama pushed past him and yanked on the locked door handle. "Let me out!" he shouted. "It was Mustafa. I was not part of this!"

A strange scratching sound began to resonate, and the film darkened and thickened in a pattern that Mustafa recognized as fissures. The fissures spread across the acrylic in a branching pattern, growing deeper in two small areas.

The etching noise grew louder and sharper, almost like fingers on a chalkboard. The noise seemed to penetrate Mustafa's brain. He could see the acrylic vibrating, the water shuddering around it.

The clear wall creaked ominously. Behind him Alhrama continued to yank on the door handle and plead with Jinn to let him free. Mustafa began to shake and fell to his knees.

"No!" he shouted. "No!"

The acrylic wall fractured. It caved in, and water flooded the bay. Mustafa tried to swim through it, but the swarm of silver sand enveloped him, soaking into his clothes, burrowing into his skin, and dragging him down to the bottom of the tank like a fifty-pound anvil.

For a minute he struggled like a speared fish, jerking in spasms, but very quickly he was still, and shortly afterward his blood began to stain the water red. Behind him, drowning in the bay, Alhrama fared no better.

CHAPTER 23

KURT STARED AT THE CARNAGE IN THE TEST ROOM. "Suddenly, I wish we'd left when you suggested it," he said to Joe.

From inside the locker room he and Joe had watched the whole thing, and with the water turning crimson, it seemed they'd outstayed their welcome.

They shed their hazmat suits, moved to the rear door, left the locker room via the stairs.

"Hope you left a trail of bread crumbs," Joe said.

"Just keep moving upward and away from here," Kurt replied.

They reached the main hall, overlooking the tank room, but neither of them looked back. Halfway down the hall, the sound of gunfire broke out. The first wave sounded deliberate and calm, but then it became sporadic and peppered with shouting. What sounded like return fire was mixed in.

"The mess hall," Kurt said. "Those other guys we saw must have been working for the two guys who just became microbot food."

The gunfire continued, growing more intense. "Sounds like

a major battle," Joe said. "Maybe they didn't all get taken by surprise."

"Too bad for us," Kurt said. "Unless we want to join up with the blue team, we need to lay low for a bit."

Kurt found a door, cracked it open, and looked inside. He saw computers, printers and drafting tables. None of them occupied.

"In here," he whispered.

They ducked inside. Kurt spun and closed the door. He pressed himself to the wall and found he could see part of the hallway through a narrow crack between the doorjamb and the edge of the door itself.

"See if there's a back way out," he said, "or a closet or somewhere else to hide in if we need to."

Joe began to look around, and Kurt squinted through the narrow fissure. Whatever plan had been arranged to deal with the outsiders seemed to be falling apart. Some of Jinn's men ran down the hall, wounded. Moments later reinforcements charged up it, and the noise of the battle grew louder, including explosions from stun grenades.

"Nowhere to hide back here," Joe said. "No back door either."

Kurt kept his eye on the gap. "Just our luck to show up in time for the family feud."

"A minute earlier, and we'd have been caught in the fight," Joe countered.

"But two minutes earlier, and we'd have been through the battle zone and on our way up to the roof, with them fighting behind us to give us cover."

"You have a point," Joe said.

Kurt wedged his foot against the base of the door, widening the gap just a bit and allowing him to see more of the hall. The sound of footsteps reached him well before he could see who or what was approaching.

"Company coming," he whispered.

Joe held still.

A group passed by, two guards prodding a young woman along. Her face showed fear, but more of something else. Kurt settled on acceptance or resignation.

She passed by in a blink, but a strange feeling rushed over Kurt as he considered her appearance. She was short, with dark spiky hair, a tan complexion and sad eyes. She looked like a prisoner, and, what's more, she looked like . . .

Kurt leaned back against the wall. "We have a problem," he announced.

"You mean beyond being trapped in a maze in the middle of the desert surrounded by ruthless thugs?"

"Yeah," Kurt said, "beyond that. You've met Kimo, right?"

"A couple of times," Joe said. "Why?"

"Describe him for me."

"Great guy," Joe said. "Built like a running back. Stocky, broad-shouldered. He was only about five foot seven, but he was strong as an ox and probably one hundred and eighty pounds."

"Now, describe his sister."

"Sad and a little unstable, but with good reason."

"This isn't the time get deep on me," Kurt prodded. "What does she look like?"

"Beautiful," Joe said. "High cheekbones, fine features, long tan legs."

"Right," Kurt said. "Tall and thin, with long limbs and fine silky hair."

"What are you getting at?"

"I just saw a woman in the hall who looked a lot more like Kimo than the woman we left back on Aqua-Terra."

"You've really got to be kidding me. Was she a prisoner?"

"Looked that way."

"You don't think . . ."

"I do."

Joe grasped the seriousness of the situation instantly. "So if Leilani is here, then who's back there on Marchetti's island?"

"I'm not sure," Kurt said. "But considering how quick she pulled the gun on Marchetti and then somehow found a way to make up with him afterward, I'm guessing she's a professional."

"You called her a hit squad," Joe reminded him.

"I was joking, but she didn't bat an eye."

"No, she didn't," Joe said. He took a deep breath. "Paul, Gamay and Marchetti are in danger."

Kurt nodded. "We have to warn them. Whoever she is, she has to be working for Jinn."

Before Joe could add anything the door burst open, kicked in by a heavy boot. Men carrying Uzis piled through the gap, swarming over them before they could respond. They were knocked to the ground, subdued and disarmed without a fight.

Two men searched them while others held them down.

"Jabberwocky," Joe grunted.

"Thanks," Kurt grunted back sarcastically, the weight of three men holding him down, "I didn't realize."

When they'd been relieved of all the tools and weapons, they were lifted to their feet and held in place as another figure entered the room: Jinn al-Khalif, with a rifle in his hand.

He strode up to Kurt. "We've been waiting for you," he said.

"No doubt your spy told you we were coming."

Jinn smiled like a jackal. "Yes, as a matter of fact, she did."

With that, he slammed the butt of his rifle into Kurt's gut, knocking the wind out of him and dropping him back to the floor.

"Her name is Zarrina. She sends her regards."

CHAPTER 24

BACK ON BOARD THE FLOATING ISLAND OF AQUA-TERRA,
Paul and Gamay had spent most of the day with Marchetti, studying the sample of "wild" microbots they'd captured.

A makeshift lab had been set up to replace the flooded forward
compartment. Marchetti's computers, a small radio transmitter,
and other equipment now lay scattered about the room.

Without the electron microscope, they couldn't see the in-
dividual microbots, but under a pair of medical-grade optical
scopes Paul and Gamay were studying two separate samples
that had grouped together in little clusters almost like algae or
bacteria.

Marchetti sat at his computer console, tapping away. Leilani
sat nearby, fidgeting nervously. After spending the morning
calling up the original design specs, they'd begun testing and attempting to signal the bots with the standard commands Marchetti had programmed into the prototypes years before.

"They're not doing anything," Paul said for the tenth time.

"Are you sure?" Marchetti said, still transmitting command

protocols. "I mean they're awfully small, maybe you're missing something."

"We're looking at them through the microscopes," Paul said, "and they're just sitting there. Like lazy relatives after a Thanksgiving feast."

Gamay shot him a look. "You're not talking about my relatives, are you?"

"Just Cousin Willie, for the most part."

She appeared hurt for an instant and then shrugged. "You're right, he flops on that couch Thursday afternoon and doesn't get up until Sunday."

Marchetti coughed loudly to get their attention. "Assuming the microbots haven't been taken over by the spirit of Cousin Willie, I can only conclude that Otero has changed the command codes."

"So how's this going to help us, then?" Leilani asked.

Before Marchetti could reply Gamay asked a more practical question. "Is there any way we can extract the codes from the bots themselves? Maybe reverse engineer them and read their programming?"

Marchetti shook his head. "Not with the equipment I have here."

"What about extracting it from Otero himself?" Leilani added. "Or from his friend? We have them down there in those cells. Let's grab the keys and go talk to them. And by talk, I mean force them to talk."

Gamay glanced at Paul. They were worried about Leilani. As the days wore on, she seemed only to grow angrier and more frustrated, especially since the incident on the airship.

"I'm pretty firmly in the anti-coercion camp," Marchetti said.

"He tried to kill you," Leilani said.

"Good point," Marchetti noted. "Let's go beat it out of him. I'll see if I can find a rubber hose or something."

"That was a quick turnabout," Gamay said.

"I'm a flip-flopper," Marchetti replied, "what can I tell you?"

"Maybe there's another way?"

"Like what?"

"If the bots in open ocean are being given directives, shouldn't we be able to intercept those signals?"

"Theoretically," Marchetti said. "But we'd have to move closer to them."

"Closer?" Leilani said.

That didn't sound great to Paul either. "How close would we have to go?"

"Depends on the type of transmission," Marchetti said. "It could be a low-frequency signal or a shortwave burst. Those would cover a wide area and could be sent from almost anywhere. It could be a high-frequency or line-of-sight transmission from an aircraft, ship or satellite. It's even possible that the signal is sent to one part of the floating swarm and then they transmit it to one another like a game of telephone. In which case we'd have to be in the right place at the right time even to pick it up."

"It sounds easier to force the information out of Otero," Leilani said.

"All things being equal, the simplest solution is usually the best," Paul said. "What type of transmission would you use?"

Marchetti paused for a moment. "Short-range coded broadcast," he said eventually. "High-frequency."

"Then that's what we'll look for."

"It will likely be an extremely short broadcast," Marchetti warned. "On the order of milliseconds. Perhaps repeating at intervals, but very fleeting. Without knowing what we're looking for, it might be impossible to pick it out from the background noise of the atmosphere. Static, other radio transmissions, ionization, all those things could be a problem."

"You're a wet blanket," Paul said, feeling as if every solution came with its own roadblock.

"We don't have to pick it out," Gamay said, "we have something here that will do it for us." She waved a hand over the samples. "All we have to do is record the chatter, watch for the little bots to wake up and then dissect the transmission after the fact."

Marchetti appeared impressed. "That should work," he said. "That should work perfectly. I'll direct the island toward the edge of the swarm. Based on the last plotted location, we should reach it in thirty-six hours."

CHAPTER 25

KURT AND JOE HAD BEEN IN CAPTIVITY FOR SEVERAL HOURS. No food, no water, no light and no company. They hadn't been beaten or interrogated or threatened, just left in the dark in a small room, chained to the same heavy pipes they'd followed on their journey to the test tank.

Joe's voice came out of the dark in a raspy tone. "Can't say much for the accommodations."

Kurt's own throat was getting dry. He'd done what he could to keep his mouth shut and breathe only through his nose. "Didn't we call for turndown service an hour ago?"

"I believe we did," Joe said. "I wonder if the delay has something to do with the firefight?"

"It didn't sound like that went into overtime, but they might have a big mess to clean up or others to deal with. More likely, they don't need to question us if this Zarrina is still reporting."

"One thing I don't get," Joe said. "Why'd they attack her at the dock if she was on their side?"

Kurt thought about that. "Any number of reasons. Maybe she's under deep cover, and the thugs didn't know. Maybe it was a diversion. One thing for certain, it made us want to protect her. Took away any sense of suspicion. The best con jobs never come from the con artist, always from the mark. We saw what we wanted to see: a friend in need. We were already in a defensive mode because Kimo and the others were gone. After rescuing her, our natural instinct to circle the wagons took over."

"It didn't hurt that she had Leilani's passport and e-mails. Or that she knew Leilani had been calling NUMA for updates on her brother."

"I'm guessing they got those from the real Leilani," Kurt said.

"They must have grabbed her and replaced her the moment she hit Malé."

Joe was undoubtedly right, which made it all the more imperative that they escape. "We have to figure out a way to get free," Kurt said. "I've run my hands all along this pipe. I can't find a weak spot."

"Nothing over here either. I tried rocking it loose, but it's bolted into the stone, I can't get any play in it."

As Joe finished speaking, the door to their cell opened. The overhead lights snapped on, blinding Kurt and Joe for a second.

In walked Jinn and the bearded man, Sabah, who always seemed to be with him. Several armed guards accompanied them.

"I don't see any towels or mints in their hands," Joe said.

"Silence!" Sabah shouted.

Jinn raised a hand as if to say it was all right.

"It has been an interesting day," Jinn said, "more so for you than for me."

His English was good, tinged with an accent, but he'd definitely been schooled, perhaps in the UK.

"It's going to get a lot more interesting when we don't turn up at our extraction point," Kurt said. "A lot of people have their eyes on you, Jinn. And getting rid of us will only make the scrutiny more intense."

"Resigned to your fate, then?"

"Unless you're here to let us go," Kurt said.

"Not afraid to die?"

"It's not on our to-do list, but we're not kidding ourselves. The question is, are you?"

Jinn looked puzzled, a good thing in Kurt's eyes. Though he had no idea where he was going with this, anything that put their host off balance would be helpful at this point.

"I do not kid, as you say," Jinn replied.

"Sure you do," Kurt said. "You build toys in your basement and blow them up. You're playing some kind of game and you're oblivious to how rapidly it's coming to an end. NUMA is onto you. That means the CIA, Interpol, Mossad will soon be onto you as well. Especially when we don't turn up safe and sound. Kill us and you'll have nowhere left to run."

"What makes you think we are running, Mr. Austin?"

"If you're not, you should be. Trouble's coming at you from all sides. Your attack on our catamaran proves that you're desperate. The firefight tonight and the two guys you killed prove your vulnerability."

A soft, rumbling laugh bubbled up from somewhere inside Jinn. "I would say your position is far more vulnerable than mine."

"And I'd tell you we have a way out for you."

Joe glanced at Kurt from the corner of his eye as if to say *"We do?"*

Kurt was grasping at straws, making up a story as he went along. It was the only card he had left to play. He needed to sow a little seed of doubt in Jinn's mind and make him believe, however preposterous it sounded, that Kurt and Joe and NUMA could help Jinn avoid the trouble that was surrounding him.

Jinn moved to Kurt's left.

"I neither want nor need whatever it is you're attempting to offer me," Jinn said. "I simply came here to tell you that you were going to die."

"No surprise there," Kurt said without batting an eye. "But let me ask you this: Why do you think my government sent us instead of a squadron of predator drones or Stealth fighters carrying bunker-busting bombs? Come on. You might be safe here from some of your enemies but not from the U.S. government. You know that. You're on the A-list now. Like the reactor and enrichment facilities the Iranians are building. And you're no different than dozens of other threats they've eliminated over the last few years. There are no borders for a guy like you to hide behind anymore. But you have something the Bin Laden's of this world don't. You have something to barter with. Technology."

Jinn held his place. Clearly he was thinking about Kurt's words, a fact almost too good to be true. Now Kurt had to push him. If he could just buy some time and some freedom, he and Joe might have a chance.

"You expect me to believe what you're saying?"

"Let me be clear," Kurt said. "I wouldn't give you the time of day. You're a killer and a thug. But I work for Uncle Sam, I do as I'm told. Our orders were to come here, infiltrate and report back. To make contact with you later if possible through third-party channels. They want what you have."

"Do I look like a fool to you?" Jinn asked, growing angry.

"I wouldn't answer that," Joe said.

"Your government doesn't make deals."

"You're wrong about that," Kurt said. "We've been making

deals for two hundred years. You ever hear of Werner von Braun? He was a Nazi, a German scientist who built rockets that killed thousands. We took him under our wing after the war because he had knowledge we needed. Viktor Belenko was a Russian pilot who brought us a MiG-25. We take baseball players, ballet dancers, computer programmers, anyone with something to offer. That might be unfair to the poor farmers and peasants who want to come, but it's good for you. It gives you an out."

"Enough of this." He turned.

"This country is falling apart," Kurt shouted. "Even your money and power won't keep you safe if anarchy strikes. And I'm guessing you have other problems in the outside world or you wouldn't have to kill off your guests and hide down here in the first place. I'm offering you a way out. Release us and let us report what we saw, and my government will contact you in a more professional manner."

Jinn didn't even consider the offer, despite Kurt's well-played deception. He turned and smiled. "Before long, men from your government, among others, will be begging me to contact them. And your bleached bones lying in the sand won't make a bit of difference."

Jinn waved to the guards. "Teach this one a lesson, and then take them to the well. I will meet you there."

Jinn walked out, Sabah followed, and the four men who remained moved forward.

A few punches landed first to soften them up and then another series of blows from extendable metal batons. The strikes were heavy, but Kurt had taken worse and he managed to twist and bend so they landed in a more glancing fashion.

Joe did the same, ducking and moving like the boxer he was.

One baton caught Kurt above his eye, splitting the skin and

leaving a bleeding gash. Kurt pretended it had knocked him woozy. He slumped in the chains, and the men around him seemed to lose their enthusiasm. A halfhearted kick hit him in the back, and the men laughed among themselves.

One of them said something in Arabic, and then they reached down and hauled Kurt up to his feet. They undid his cuffs and dragged him out. Through eyelids intentionally at half-mast he saw Joe being forced to march next to him.

They were out of the frying pan. The question was, where would they land?

The first part of that answer arrived as they reached the main entrance to the cave. Sunlight beamed through in orange shafts. It was late afternoon, the hottest part of the day. They were marched outside and led to the tail end of an SUV. While the other guards held their arms, a rather vicious-looking man tied their hands to a hitch with two-foot lengths of rope.

"This can't be good," Joe said.

"I think we're about to get keelhauled, desert style," Kurt replied.

The vicious-looking man laughed, climbed into the SUV and began to rev the engine repeatedly. Kurt tried to come up with a way out. His only thought was to climb onto the SUV before it took off, but the outside of the vehicle was smooth, and with their hands tied there was no way to hang on to it.

The engine revved again.

Joe looked over at him.

"I got nothing."

"Great."

The SUV lurched forward, Kurt and Joe were yanked along, they stumbled and nearly fell, but they got their feet going and managed to stay up with the vehicle by running. To Kurt's surprise the driver didn't accelerate beyond that. He merely rolled along at an idling speed, dragging the two prisoners at the pace of a fast jog.

The guards behind them laughed as Kurt and Joe struggled to keep up.

The SUV moved out past the entrance to the cave and onto a track that crossed the sand.

"What about now?" Joe asked. "Anything come to you?"

Kurt was jogging hard, his feet sinking into the soft sand. "No," he said.

"Come on, Kurt," Joe said.

"Why don't you come up with something?"

"You're the brains of this team, I'm the good looks," Joe said.

"Not after you get dragged face-first through the sand, you won't be."

Joe didn't reply. They'd begun to climb a low hill and it was even harder to keep up. The rear tires of the SUV were kicking sand into their faces. They topped the hill and came down the other side. Kurt was glad to see another flat section.

The desert sun was beating down on them, the air temperature close to a hundred degrees. After two or three minutes of running in the heat, both of them were drenched with sweat, more water their bodies couldn't afford to lose. In the far distance, Kurt saw another rock formation. It had to be at least a mile off, but it seemed to be in their line of travel.

Joe caught his foot on something, tripping and almost falling.

"Stay up," Kurt yelled, looking ahead.

Joe managed to keep running. Kurt tried to think.

If they made it to the rocky section coming up, he would look for a stone to scoop up. It would be risky to try to grab something off the ground, but there was no way he and Joe could keep running much longer.

Before either of those things happened, the SUV turned south and approached a group of parked vehicles. It rolled to a stop, and both Kurt and Joe fell to the ground.

Lying on the sand, trying to catch his breath, Kurt saw Jinn and several of his men standing beside what looked like an old abandoned well.

Jinn walked over. He must have seen Kurt's eyes lingering on the well. "Thirsty?" he asked.

Kurt said nothing.

Jinn leaned close. "You don't know the meaning of thirst until you've crossed a desert in search of the smallest oasis. Your throat closes up. Your eyes feel like they're boiling dry inside your head. Your body can't sweat because it has no more water left to give. That is the life of a Bedouin. And he would not fall after a mile or two in the desert."

"I'm pretty sure he'd be riding a camel and not getting dragged by a truck," Kurt rasped.

Jinn turned to his men. "Our guests would like some refreshment," he said. "Bring them to the well."

The guards untied Kurt and Joe and hauled them up, pushing and shoving them toward the well. As they reached the opening, Kurt realized they wouldn't be getting a drink. The smell of death rose up from below.

He turned and kicked one of the guards, shattering the man's ankle and lunging for his weapon. Joe sprang into action at almost the same instant, ripping his arm free and coldcocking the man to his left.

The speed of the assault seemed to take the guards by surprise. These men had been denied food and water for the entire day. They'd been beaten and dragged through the desert. They'd looked all but dead lying on the sand only moments before.

Four of Jinn's men rushed in to help their comrades, but the Americans fought like spinning whirlwinds. For each man who landed a punch, another took a blow to the face, a kick to the knee or an elbow to the gut.

One guard tried to tackle Kurt, but Kurt dodged and tripped him, sending him into another guard. As those two crashed into the sand, Kurt jumped to his feet. He saw a pistol on the ground and lunged for it. But like a football player diving for a fumble, he was immediately covered by three of Jinn's men, also grabbing for the gun.

It discharged, and one of Jinn's men cried out in pain, his fingers blown off. But before Kurt could fire it again, a heavy blow hit the back of his head, and the gun was ripped from his grasp.

Beside him, Joe had been tackled as well.

"Pick them up!" Jinn shouted. "Throw them in!"

Kurt struggled mightily, but Jinn's men had him by his arms and legs. They carried him toward the well like a spectator crowd surfing at a rock concert.

Joe was faring no better. One guard had him in a half nelson, pushing him forward, about to shove him over the edge.

As Kurt reached the well, he shook a leg free and kicked one of the men in the face. The man fell back, caught his ankle on the low adobe wall and tumbled backward, headfirst, into the well. His scream echoed for a second and then abruptly stopped.

The group holding Kurt wobbled like a table on three legs and then heaved him toward the opening.

As they released Kurt, he twisted, saw the low wall and the small A-frames made of iron jutting up from it. He threw his arms out, caught it and held on.

A second later Joe was shoved into the pit. He grabbed Kurt's legs, perhaps instinctively.

The added weight pulled Kurt down until only a death grip on the scalding-hot bars held them up.

A shadow moved in front of the setting sun.

Jinn held a baton in his hand. He swung it back and whipped it forward toward Kurt's fingers. Before it hit, Kurt let go.

He and Joe dropped straight down. They fell twenty feet, crashed into a pile of sloping sand and slid another ten feet to the bottom.

The impact jarred Kurt, but the slope of the sand and a pair of decaying bodies acted like an air bag of sorts, absorbing much of the impact. He ended up in an awkward position, facedown against the floor.

Stunned and all but knocked cold, Kurt forced his eyes open. Joe lay a foot to the left, piled up against the wall like a rag doll thrown in the corner. His arms were under him, one leg was bent up at an odd angle. He wasn't moving.

A sound above caught his ear, Kurt didn't dare move, but from the corner of his eye he saw Jinn leaning over the edge of the well. A group of shots rang out, and dirt and chinks of rock flew around the bottom of the well. Something sharp cut Kurt's leg, and a bullet or rock fragment hit inches in front of his face, kicking dirt into the air.

Kurt held still, not flinching, not moving, not even breathing.

He heard shouting in Arabic and distorted words from far above. A flashlight came on, pointed down the well. The beam danced around them almost hypnotically. Kurt remained still. He wanted them to see him as nothing more than another dead body at the bottom of the well.

More words were exchanged. The light snapped off and the faces disappeared.

A minute later the sound of engines starting up echoed down the gullet of the well. Kurt listened to the vehicles driving off until he could no longer hear them. He and Joe had been left for dead. At least for the moment they weren't, but if they didn't get out of the well, it was just a matter of time.

CHAPTER 26

GAMAY WALKED INTO THE MAKESHIFT LAB TO CHECK ON Marchetti. She found him hunched over an experiment that involved a heat lamp, several temperature probes and a tall, narrow beaker full of water, the top layer of which looked murky.

"Am I right to assume there are microbots in that beaker?"

Marchetti sat straight up. "Oh, Mrs. Trout," he said, holding his chest. "You snuck up on me."

"Not really. You're just very into your work."

"Yes," he said, tinkering with one of the probes and checking a display.

"Care to tell me what it is?"

"I'm just trying to figure something out," he said, sounding as if he'd rather not talk about it.

She sat across from him and stared into his eyes. "Why is it men don't like to share their hunches?" she asked. "Are you so afraid to be wrong?"

"I've been wrong a million times," Marchetti said. "I'm more afraid to be right, actually."

"About what?"

"I have a hunch as to what might be occurring out there."

"And yet you're keeping it a secret," she said. "Like most men I've known, you want proof before you speak, or at least a reasonable amount of corroborating evidence."

She waved her hand over the setup. "This looks like an attempt to get that to me."

"You really have a marvelous sense of intuition, Mrs. Trout. I bet Paul can't get away with anything."

"He's learned not to try."

"A wise man," Marchetti said, offering a sheepish grin. "You're right of course. I have a hunch that the microbots are indeed responsible for the temperature anomaly. I remember hearing of a plan to stop global warming. It involved years of continuous rocket launches and the dispersal of millions upon millions of reflective discs in orbit around the planet or perhaps only over the poles, I really can't recall for certain. These reflective discs would block a portion of the sunlight, reflecting it back into space. A small percentage. Just enough to counteract the effect we've begun feeling."

She remembered hearing something about it.

"Obviously there were huge problems with the idea," Marchetti continued, "but the concept intrigued me. I've often wondered if it would really work."

"There are precedents," Gamay said. "After large volcanic eruptions, the ash in the air spreads around the globe, doing much the same thing as these discs you're talking about. Famines in the sixth century have been blamed on ash dimming the sun's output and causing crop yields to fall. Eighteen fifteen has been called the year without a summer because the average temperatures around the globe were surprisingly low. The eruption of Mount Tambora in Indonesia is the prime suspect."

"I feel a similar principle may be at work here," Marchetti said. "Not in the atmosphere but in the sea."

He pointed to the experiment. "I've attempted to re-create a solar warming-and-cooling cycle in this water sample. But there's a problem with my theory. Even with the murky layer of bots at the top, it behaves almost like regular salt water."

"Meaning?"

"The microbots absorb some of the heat, but nowhere close to what would be required to cool the water in the manner we've seen."

"How large is the difference?"

"Very substantial," he said. "Close to ninety percent deviation. And that's a lot in anyone's book."

"You mean in your experiment you found—"

"Only ten percent of the cooling we've recorded out there in the open ocean. Yes, that's exactly what I mean."

She looked around. She didn't have to ask if he'd done the experiment right or if he wanted to try it again. He'd been secluded up here for hours, and he'd been an engineer before becoming a computer programmer. She guessed he knew what he was doing. Besides, she saw six other setups that looked identical to the one in front of them. She assumed they were controls.

"So what does that mean?" she asked. "And this time pretend you're a woman and share."

"There are two possibilities," he said. "Either something else is responsible for the majority of the cooling or the microbots are cooling the ocean through some other process or mechanism that we've yet to observe or discover."

"All the more reason to keep sailing toward them," she said.

"I'm afraid so," he replied.

Before Gamay could say anything more, an alarm began to

sound throughout the lab. It was sharp, piercing, and accompanied by flashing strobes.

"What's happening?"

"Fire alarm," Marchetti said. He reached for an intercom switch and pressed it. "What's happening, chief?"

"We have multiple heat signals," the chief replied, sounding as if he was still checking. "We have confirmation," he added. "There's a fire in the engine room."

CHAPTER 27

PAUL TROUT HEARD THE ALARMS AND RACED DOWN THE hall until he reached the makeshift lab. Marchetti was on the intercom in a rapid-fire discussion with his chief of engineering. Gamay stood next to him with a concerned look on her face.

"Fire," she said.

"I figured that," Paul replied.

He began to smell smoke and the distinctive odor of diesel fuel burning. "Engine room?"

She nodded.

Marchetti asked into the microphone. "Can you get the robots back online?"

"They're not responding."

"What about the fire-suppression system?"

"Also not responding."

Marchetti looked ill. "Keep working on it," he said, pressing the intercom button again. "We'll have to fight it by hand. Have Kostis and Cristatos meet me there. Have the others stand by."

Marchetti looked over to Paul and Gamay. "Either of you have firefighting experience?"

"I do," Paul said. "I'll go with you."

Now Gamay looked ill. "Paul, please," she said.

"I'll be okay," he replied. "I've had plenty of training. Get yourself to somewhere safe."

"The control room," Marchetti said. "My chief is there."

Gamay nodded. "Be careful."

Paul raced out the door with Marchetti and they took a stairwell down toward the main deck. From there a second stairwell took them into the hull and then along a hall that led to the engine room. The smoke thickened as they neared the aft end of the island.

"This is the fire station," Marchetti said, reaching a storage area with several tall doors.

They were fifty feet from the engine room. The smell of fuel was sickening, and the heat of the fire could be felt and heard.

Marchetti opened the panel marked FIRE. Inside on pegs were bright yellow firefighting suits made of Nomex and accented with reflective stripes of orange. On a shelf above each suit, the familiar air tanks and masks rested. Each SCBA, or Self-Contained Breathing Apparatus, included a fire- and heat-resistant mask with an integrated regulator, a communications system and a heads-up display. A harness supported flashlights and other tools, along with low-pressure air cylinders that would mount on men's backs.

Marchetti grabbed a fire suit, Paul did also. As they pulled them on, Kostis and Cristatos arrived and did the same.

Pulling his mask into place, Paul opened the regulator valve. He gave a thumbs-up. The air was good.

Marchetti reached over and flicked a switch on the side of Paul's mask. Paul heard static for a second and then the sound of Marchetti's voice came through headphones.

"Can you hear me?"

"Loud and clear," Paul said.

"Good. The respirators are equipped with radios."

Paul was ready. The two crewmen were almost ready. Marchetti moved to the stanchion on the wall and began unfurling the hose.

Paul slotted in behind him, and they began to move forward.

As they approached the open bulkhead door to the engine room, Paul asked, "What's the plan?"

"While the chief tries to get the robots back online, we do the best we can to fight the fire."

"Why not just seal it off?"

"One of my men is in there," Marchetti said.

Paul took a look at the burning engine room. He could barely imagine anyone surviving what was fast becoming a conflagration, but if there was a chance, they had to search.

"Is there anywhere he could shelter?"

"There's a small office near the back of the engine room, a control room. If he was in there when it started, he might be alive."

Two lines were now laid out. The hose Paul and Marchetti held and a second one for Kostis and Cristatos.

"Open the tap," Marchetti shouted.

One of the crewman turned the valve, and the hoses came to life as they swelled with water. Marchetti opened the nozzle, and the high-pressure stream burst forth like a jet. Even with Marchetti also holding tight, Paul felt himself fighting the recoil.

He tightened his grip and flexed his knees, pushing forward as he and Marchetti forced their way into the engine room.

Passing the bulkhead felt like crossing the threshold into hell. Black smoke swirled around him so dark and thick that at times all he could see of Marchetti was the beacon on his respirator. Waves of heat baked him through the Nomex suit, and his eyes stung from smoke seeping beneath the seal of the mask. Here and there orange flames cut through the dark. They raced up and down and around, occasionally shooting over the top of the men like demons dancing to perdition. A series of small explosions shook the room from its farthest recesses.

Marchetti sprayed the water back and forth and adjusted the nozzle to widen the pattern. The second hose was brought in by Marchetti's crewmen. Attacking with the two jets of water, they fanned the blaze, adding waves of superheated steam to the cauldron.

"Can you see the source?" Marchetti asked.

"No," Paul said, trying to peer through the smoke.

"In that case, we have to move forward."

Until now, Marchetti had seemed weak to Paul, sort of a bumbler, but he admired the man's guts in defending his island and fighting for his crewman's life.

"Over here!" the lead man on the other hose shouted.

Paul turned to see them laying down a wave of suppressing water, clearing a path for Marchetti and him to move through.

Paul steeled himself and moved in unison with Marchetti as they pressed into the heart of the conflagration.

By now Paul could feel the heat from the deck like he was standing on top of glowing lava rocks. A new wave of fire spewed to the left of them, and a blast knocked Marchetti to the ground.

Paul pulled him back up. "This is no good!" Paul shouted. "We have to get back."

"I told you, one of my men is down here!"

Another small explosion buffeted them, and a wall of flame rose up, only to be forced back by the water from the two hoses.

The engine room was three stories tall, four times that in length and filled with equipment pipes, hoses and catwalks. The flames were reaching the roof in places, everything was obscured. If they weren't losing the battle, it was at least a stalemate.

"We have to flood the compartment," Paul said. "It's the only way."

"We tried," Marchetti said. "The fire-suppression system is not responding. It should have kicked on at one hundred and seventy-five degrees but didn't. We tried to trigger it from the bridge but nothing happened."

"There has to be an override," Paul said, "a manual trigger down here somewhere."

Marchetti began looking around. "There are four," he said. "The closest should be that way. By the generator stack."

"We need to activate it."

Marchetti hesitated. "The doors will auto-seal as soon as we trigger it," he explained. "Whoever does it will be trapped inside."

"How long?"

"Until the fire goes out and the temperature drops."

"Then let's not waste any more time."

Marchetti looked back down the mangled path that led to the possible safe haven of the office. The walkway was twisted and bent as if an explosion had gone off halfway across. Flames and smoke and boiling water dropping from above made it obvious: there was no way they were going to fight through that.

"Okay," he shouted, turning toward the far wall. "This way."

CHAPTER 28

GAMAY FOUND A STATE OF CHAOS IN THE CONTROL ROOM. Two of Marchetti's men were working the computers with all due haste, trying to bring the robots or the firefighting system back online.

The chief, a short but burly Greek man, was monitoring the fire. In the background Gamay could hear the radio conversations between the two firefighting teams. It didn't sound like they were winning.

"How bad is it?" she asked, thinking it hadn't seemed quite as overwhelming down below.

"It's grown quickly," the chief said. "The whole engine room is burning. Fuel leak of some kind. Has to be."

"Is it spreading?" Gamay asked, fearful that Paul would end up trapped.

"Not yet," the chief said.

As Gamay tried not to focus on the words *Not yet*, Leilani came in looking scared and bewildered.

"What's happening?"

"Engine room fire," Gamay said. "One of the crew is trapped inside. And the automatic systems are down."

Leilani sat down and began to shake. It seemed like she might break down, but Gamay couldn't worry about that right now.

"What if it does spread?" Gamay asked. "My husband and Marchetti and your other men will be cut off."

"Not if they contain it first," the chief said. "They have to beat it back."

"You need more men down there." The words came from Leilani.

Gamay and the chief looked over.

"If the robots aren't working, you need to send more men," she repeated.

"She's right," Gamay realized, surprised by her suddenly strong stand.

"We're trying to get the robots back online," the chief insisted.

"Forget the damn robots," Gamay said. "Four men can't fight this fire."

"We have only twenty crewmen on board," the chief said.

That had always seemed like a mistake to Gamay, suddenly she saw why. "Anyone trained to fight fires should be down there," she urged, "or Paul and the others should pull back."

The chief looked over at the two men working on the computers. "Anything?"

They shook their heads. "It's a looped code. Every time we break through the outer layer, it resets and we have to start over."

Gamay didn't know exactly what that meant, but it sounded like there wasn't much point in continuing.

The chief exhaled. "The robots are down for the count," he

said, admitting the obvious. "Go," he said to the men at the computer terminals. "I'll have the others meet you at the engine room."

The two men at the computer stations headed for the door.

"Thank you," Gamay said, glad to know backup was headed Paul's way.

Marchetti's voice came over the radio: *"Any luck, chief?"*

"Negative," the chief said into a microphone. "We're locked out, sending you help."

"Understood," Marchetti said. *"We're going for the override."*

"What does that mean?" Gamay asked.

"They're going to flood the compartment with Halon," the chief said. "It'll suppress the fire and put it out."

"What's the drawback?"

"Halon's toxic. And it requires a closed room to be effective. Once they activate it, the doors will shut and lock automatically. They'll be trapped in there until the sensors determine that the fire is out and the room temperature has dropped below the reignition point."

Gamay felt sick. She knew what that meant.

"It shouldn't be a big problem," the chief said. "Once the compartment is flooded, the fire should burn out in thirty seconds. The temp in there is two hundred and fifty-five now. By my calculations the cooldown time should take about ten minutes if everything goes according to plan."

Ten minutes with Paul sitting behind a locked door in a cauldron of heat. She could barely stand the thought. But another thought was worse.

"If everything goes according to plan," she repeated. "The way things are going, that's an awfully big assumption. What if the doors don't shut? Worse yet, what if they don't open?"

The chief said nothing, but she guessed from his body language that he had already thought of that.

DOWN IN THE ENGINE ROOM, Paul and Marchetti had begun fighting toward the far wall. It seemed to take forever to cross the cavernous space. In one section debris and burning fuel blocked their path. In another, steam was blasting from a broken waterline.

With Marchetti's crewmen at their backs to keep them from getting cut off, they forged onward one yard at a time, beating the fire back as they went. Eventually they saw a path through.

"Hold the line," Marchetti said. "Keep the fire back while I run through. I'll signal you when I get there."

Paul slid forward and grabbed the nozzle. "Okay, go!"

Marchetti let go, and it took all of Paul's strength to keep the hose on target. As Marchetti lumbered forward, Paul washed down the flames to the left and then back to the right on a wide-pattern setting, drenching Marchetti purposefully in the process.

He watched as Marchetti made it through the first wave of flame and continued forward only to be suddenly obscured by a sideways blast of fire and smoke. Paul directed the hose into the blast and forced the flames back, but he still couldn't see through.

"Marchetti?"

He heard nothing.

"Marchetti?!"

The smoke was so thick, Paul could barely see a thing. He was sweating inside the fire suit, and his eyes were stinging badly from the fumes and the salt of his own perspiration. He washed the walkway back and forth with the spray until he saw a dim light through the darkness. It was down low, close to the ground. Marchetti's beacon.

"Marchetti's down!" Paul shouted. "I'm going to get him."

He shut off the nozzle, dropped the hose and ran forward. The crewmen swept in behind him, washing him down as he went.

He made it past the blast furnace of the open flame and reached Marchetti. Marchetti's hood was blackened, his mask half off. It looked like he'd run smack into a protruding beam. Paul pressed the mask back onto Marchetti's face and Marchetti coughed and came around.

"Help me up," he said.

An explosion shook the engine room, and debris rained down on them from above. Paul lifted Marchetti to his feet, but he immediately stumbled back down to his knees. He put a hand out.

"No balance," he said.

Paul heaved him up and kept him vertical. They trudged forward like two men in a three-legged potato-sack race. They reached the wall. The manual override beckoned.

"We've made it," Paul shouted into the microphone. "Get out. We're going to trigger the Halon."

Paul reached for the handle, flipped the safety aside and put his hand on the override. He waited what seemed like forever. Another explosion rocked the engine room.

"We're clear of the bulkhead," one of the crewmen finally reported.

"Now," Marchetti said.

Paul yanked the handle down hard.

From eighty points around the room Halon 1301 blasted into the compartment at an incredible rate, hissing from the nozzles and flowing in from every direction. It quickly filled the room, smothering the fire. In places the flames jumped and flickered and seemed to cower in a desperate quest for survival. And then, as if by magic, they went out all at once.

Stunning silence followed.

It seemed unearthly to Paul. The raging flames, the explosions, the buffeting currents brought on as the fire sucked air in and expelled heat, all were gone. Only the thick smoke lingered, accompanied by the continued hissing from the Halon nozzles, the sound of dripping water and the creak and groan of super-heated metal.

The absence of flame seemed almost too good to be true, and neither Paul nor Marchetti moved a muscle as if doing so might break the spell. Finally Marchetti turned toward Paul. A smile crept over his face, though Paul could barely see it through the smudged, soot-covered face mask.

"Well done, Mr. Trout. Well done."

Paul smiled too, proud and relieved at the same time.

And then a shrill electronic beeping began, accompanied by the strobe light on the back of Marchetti's SCBA. Seconds later Paul's own strobe began flashing and chirping. The two alarms combined into an annoying cacophony.

"What's happening?" Paul asked.

"Rescue beacons," Marchetti said.

"Why are they going off now?"

Marchetti looked glum. "Because," he said, "we're running out of air."

CHAPTER 29

KURT AUSTIN HELD THE AWKWARD POSITION HE'D LANDED in as long as he possibly could. Even after the vehicles drove off, even after the rumbling of their engines had faded and he was left with only the sound of flies buzzing in the dark, he remained still.

They zipped here and there, settled for a moment and then buzzed around again. Even when they landed on him and crawled on his face, Kurt did all he could not to flinch in case someone was watching. But eventually he had to move.

With a glance up to the circular opening high above, he slid one arm to the side, rolled over slowly and then propped himself up. From there he managed a sitting position and eased back until he was leaning against the wall. Every movement brought new levels of pain, and once he'd settled against the wall he decided to stay there for a minute or two.

He checked his leg. Something hit it during the shooting, but he found no bullet hole and figured it was a piece of the wall blasted off when a shell ricocheted. His shoulder hurt like crazy, but it seemed to move okay.

He reached over and checked Joe, shaking him gently.

Joe opened his eyes halfway like a man coming out of a deep sleep. He moved a few inches, grunted and generally appeared confused. Looking around at their surroundings didn't seem to bring any clarity.

"Where are we?" he asked.

"You don't remember?"

"Last I remember, we were being dragged by a truck," he said.

"That was the high point of our journey," Kurt said, looking up. "Literally."

Joe forced himself to sit up, an act that seemed to cause as much pain for him as it had for Kurt.

"Are we dead?" Joe asked. "'Cause if not, this is the worst I've ever felt while still alive."

Kurt shook his head. "We're alive all right, at least for now. We're just stuck at the bottom of a well without a rope or a ladder or any other way out."

"That's good," Joe said. "For a second I thought we were in trouble."

Kurt looked around, taking note of the other bodies in the sand. Two of them seemed to have been there for a while. The stench emanating from them was horrendous, almost enough to make him gag. The third was the guy he'd shoved over the edge just prior to being tossed in himself. A large gash split the man's forehead. His neck was bent at a grotesque angle. He wasn't moving.

Kurt was surprised to be alive. "I guess the sloping pile of sand and dropping feet first helped. It looks like this guy hit his head."

"Plus we dropped from a little lower," Joe said. "Or, at least, I did. What about those other two?"

"No idea," Kurt said, looking at the bodies half covered with flies. "Must have made the boss angry."

"If we ever leave NUMA," Joe said, "remind me not to work for an egomaniacal dictator, madman or other type of thug. They don't seem to have adequate channels for working out grievances."

Kurt laughed, and it felt like he was being stabbed. "Oh, that hurts," he said, trying to stop. "No more jokes."

He looked up at the narrow opening above. A small circle of blazing orange sky lay beyond.

"We've got to figure a way out of here or we'll be next on the flies' menu. Think you can stand?"

Joe stretched his legs. "My ankle is pretty stiff," he said. "But I think I'll be all right."

Using the wall for balance, Kurt got to his feet. He felt light-headed for a second, but it cleared quickly. He offered a hand and helped Joe up. In the five-foot-wide circle of the well they stretched and flexed their legs.

It seemed like the well had been dug in sections. The top part was lined with adobe bricks to a depth of about twenty feet. Below that it was raw dirt all the way down.

"Think we can climb out?" Joe asked.

Kurt put his hand on a protruding stone and put some weight on it to test its strength. It crumbled in a disappointing shower of dust and rubble.

"Nope."

"Maybe we can wedge ourselves up?" Joe said. "Use our hands and feet and sort of force ourselves upward."

Kurt stretched his arms out. He could just barely touch both walls. "We'll never generate enough force to go up like that."

He looked around. In addition to the three bodies, the well

seemed to be a repository of junk and trash. Tin cans, plastic bottles, even a thin bald tire sat piled and strewn about. Small bones were everywhere. Kurt guessed they were from animals that had fallen in or someone's dinner tossed down here when they were finished with the edible parts.

Kurt looked at the tire, then at the walls, then at the dead men.

"I have an idea," he said.

He searched the thug he'd shoved over the edge, pulling a knife, a Luger-style pistol and a set of compact binoculars from the man's kit.

He found a canteen on his belt. It was three-quarters empty. He took a swig, no more than a mouthful really, and handed it to Joe.

"To your health."

Joe drank the other mouthful as Kurt pushed the junk aside and dug the old tire out of the sand.

"Tidying up?" Joe asked.

"Very funny."

He dropped down beside the other dead men, holding his breath and sending the flies swarming. He untied the rope that bound them together. "We're gonna need this."

"Don't suppose they have a grappling hook on them?"

"No," Kurt said. "But we don't need one."

He piled the bodies up in the center of the well, stacking them one on top of the other.

"Sit down," Kurt said.

"On the dead guys?"

"I put the fresh guy on top," Kurt said.

Joe hesitated.

"They're dead," Kurt said. "What do they care?"

Finally Joe sat down. Kurt lifted the narrow tire and set it vertically against Joe's back like he was hanging a wreath. Next he sat down with his back to the tire and to Joe.

"Put your feet on the wall and push."

As Joe complied, Kurt felt the rubber tire pressing into his back. He put his own feet against the wall on his side and pushed. He felt the tire between them compress slightly. He felt plenty of pressure on his back and feet, pressure that would allow them to wedge themselves up the shaft of the well, and he still had six to eight inches of flex in his knees.

"Flex those abs, and let's see if we can do this," he said.

As Joe flexed and pressed harder, Kurt did the same. He felt the pressure in his back, both upper and lower, where the tire was being pressed into him. With a minimum of effort, they rose up off the pile of dead men.

"This might actually work," Joe said.

"You, then me," Kurt told him. "One foot at a time."

The first time Joe moved his foot they almost fell, tipping to one side. They steadied themselves, and Kurt pressed hard with his left foot and forced them upward about nine inches. He quickly moved his right foot to a new position.

Joe's next move was steadier, and soon they were inching their way up, making steady if unspectacular progress.

"I forgot to tell you," Joe said, grunting with the effort but apparently unable to keep himself from talking, "before we got bounced in that drafting room I saw a chart with currents and such. It covered the Persian Gulf, the Arabian Sea and half of the Indian Ocean."

He and Kurt pushed off in unison, raised themselves six inches and repositioned their feet one at a time.

"Anything unusual on it?" Kurt asked, his own words sounding strained as they came out through a clenched diaphragm.

"Didn't . . . exactly . . . have time to study it," Joe said. "But it makes me . . . wonder about something."

They moved again.

"What?" Kurt asked, keeping his responses short.

"If Jinn's using his little beasties . . . to erode some dam . . . why did we . . . find them in the Indian Ocean . . . a thousand miles from land?"

Kurt allowed a portion of his mind to consider the question, keeping most of his concentration on the task at hand. "Good question," he said. "Dams block rivers . . . Rivers run to the sea . . . Maybe the little bots were swept down to the ocean accidentally, after all."

He tried to think of dams that emptied into the Indian Ocean or the Persian Gulf, but nothing major came to mind.

They paused with their legs in a semilocked position.

"Either way," Kurt added, "we've got to get out of here. Whatever this lunatic's goals are, they're not good for anyone but him."

By this point they'd reached the second section. The joking and laughing stopped because the climb was getting harder.

Kurt felt his back and abs and legs beginning to burn. He gritted his teeth and kept moving.

"You okay?" he asked.

"Yeah," Joe grunted. "Wouldn't want to start over, though."

Kurt looked down. His foot slipped a fraction, but he caught it by locking his knee and wedging his heal. He could see his leg quivering and feel his calf cramping up.

"Five more feet," he said, breathing hard. "Then part two of the plan . . . can be activated."

"What if the bad guys are still up there?" Joe asked.

"I haven't heard a sound since the cars drove off."

"And if they left a guard?"

"That's what the gun is for."

They pushed up another foot, and Kurt's face was bathed in the late-afternoon sunlight.

A foot from the top the well's mouth caught a strange sound: a high-pitched whistling that echoed off the adobe walls.

"Do you hear that?" Joe asked.

"Trying to place it," Kurt said.

The whistling grew louder with each passing second, and then, directly above them, a giant shadow passed. Kurt saw the belly of a large gray-and-white aircraft race overhead, flaps and slats fanned out like feathers, its six-wheeled main undercarriage stretched forth like an eagle's claws grasping for a branch to land on.

"What was that?" Joe said.

"Jet of some kind," Kurt said.

It couldn't have been at more than a hundred feet as it flashed above the mouth of the well. The view lasted only a second or two, but in that brief instant Kurt realized there was something odd about its shape.

"Didn't realize we were at the end of the runway," Joe said. "I'd hate to pop out at the wrong moment and get run over by a 747."

Stifling the laughter that tried to bubble up, Kurt pushed harder until they were just below the lip of the well.

He could feel the buildup of lactic acid growing in his calves and thighs, and though he was in little danger of having them cramp or give out, he felt they needed to hurry. His abs burned from keeping his back pressed hard into the tire. It felt like he'd done a hundred crunches with a fifteen-pound medicine ball clutched to his chest.

He pulled the 9mm pistol from his pocket and switched off the safety.

"Easy, now," he whispered.

Joe adjusted his feet. Kurt went next, and they slowly moved up through the last six inches. Kurt raised the gun and stretched his neck so he could just peer over the edge. He saw no one guarding the well.

"Clear," he said.

"Clear on this side," Joe said. "Now what?"

Kurt tossed the gun over the edge and drew the rope out from beneath his shirt. He passed it through his hands until he had the length he needed.

With one hand on each end of the rope he let out a half loop approximately four feet in length. With a flip of the wrist and an extension of his arms he sent a wave of energy through the rope. The middle sailed out away from him in a big U shape and dropped over the top of one A-frame neat as could be.

Kurt slid it taut and pulled it downward so it wouldn't ride up the metal bars.

Making sure not to twist, he passed one end of the rope back to Joe. "Hold on to that with both hands and hold on tight."

Kurt pulled his section taut and wrapped a loop under his arm, around his triceps and then around his hand twice. Joe followed suit.

"You holding that rope tight?"

"Like it's a winning lottery ticket," Joe said.

"Good," Kurt replied, "because you know what's going to happen once we give our poor legs a rest, right?"

"Yeah," Joe said. "Like everything else connected with you, it's going to be painful."

"No pain, no gain," Kurt said. "This time the gain is our freedom. Ready?"

"Ready."

Kurt tensed his arms, locking them in place.

"Three . . . two . . . one . . . go!"

At almost the same instant both men pulled on the rope and relaxed their legs and abs. The rope snapped taut around the A-frame. The tire fell from between them and they swung forward, slamming into the wall and dangling there a few feet below the top.

The tire hit bottom with a noisy clunk, but Kurt and Joe held on tight high above it.

"We have to do this part at the same time," Kurt said, "otherwise someone's going back down."

They pulled themselves up side by side, arm over arm, until they were able to grasp the metal of the A-frame. It burned their hands as it had Kurt's earlier, but they held on, pulled themselves up and clambered over the low wall.

Kurt hit the sand face-first and was damn glad of it. Joe crashed down beside him.

Breathing hard and resting for a moment, Kurt could feel his legs shaking. It seemed like they'd been in that well for days. He looked to his wrist. His watch was still with the guard in Malé.

He held a hand toward the setting sun.

"What are you doing?" Joe asked.

"Trying to make a sundial." He gave up. "What time do you have?"

"Six forty-five," Joe announced. "It must be a new record. Left for dead and back to the action in less than an hour."

Another jet approaching began to whistle across the desert as they sat there, catching their breath. It came in on the same path, dropping closer and growing louder as it neared.

Out of natural fugitive instinct, both men hunkered down and pressed themselves against the low wall of the well.

They needn't have bothered. A jet aircraft on final approach at one hundred and fifty knots required the pilot's eyes to be well ahead of the plane and focused on the landing zone. The chances of a pilot allowing his attention to be drawn to irrelevant objects on the ground was slim to none.

Then again, there was no accounting for passengers.

The jet roared over the top of them just as the first one had, a little higher this time. Kurt noticed the same odd features: a weirdly shaped underbelly, two big engines set high above the fuselage near the tail, a thick boxy wing section. It looked something like a DC-9 or a Super 80 or a Gulfstream G5 on steroids and put together with the wrong instruction booklet and a bunch of extra parts.

"Same type," Kurt said. "Looks Russian to me."

"It does," Joe agreed. "Might even be the same plane making another pass."

The gray-and-white jet dropped lower and lower, sinking toward the ground as if it were headed in for a landing. They lost it behind a sand dune before they heard it touch down.

The sound of its engines faded for a moment and then a deep howl rose up, booming across the desert for fifteen seconds or so before dissipating.

"Sound like thrust reversers to you?"

"Yep," Joe said. "I guess the eagle has landed."

"I think we just found our escape route," Kurt said.

Joe looked at him sideways.

"None of the satellite photos showed any aircraft parked out here," Kurt explained, "which means that plane isn't going to sit around baking in the desert sun all day. It's going to drop off whatever cargo it's bringing in and then turn and burn at some point before sunup."

"Sure," Joe said. "But that's not Terminal One at Dulles over there. We can't just walk up to the counter and buy a ticket."

"No," Kurt said, "but we can sneak in under cover of darkness. They can't possibly be expecting us."

"That's because we'd be crazy to attempt what you're suggesting."

"We have no water," Kurt said. "No GPS. And no idea how to find the VV without it. So unless you want to go wandering through the desert trusting in dumb luck, we have to go back into the lion's den."

Joe appeared conflicted, though he seemed to be coming around. "You're confusing me with these animal metaphors," he said. "I thought it was a rabbit hole?"

"It changed when we got caught," Kurt said. "These guys are a lot tougher than any rabbit."

"Except for the one in that Monty Python movie," Joe said.
"Monty Python and the Holy Grail."

"That's the one."

"Right," Kurt said, remembering the movie and trying not to laugh since it hurt his ribs and parched throat.

"The way I see it, we have a choice," he said. "We can either *run away* like Sir Robin. Or we can sneak back into their base and tuck ourselves into a hidden corner on one of those jets and depart this land before we dehydrate to nothing more than dust and bone."

Joe cleared his throat. "I *am* kind of thirsty."

"So am I," Kurt said.

Joe took a deep breath. He reached over, plucked the gun out of the sand and handed it to Kurt. "Lead on, Sir Knight," he said. "Doubt we're going to find the Holy Grail down there, but I'll settle for a way out of here, or at least a well-stocked beverage stand."

CHAPTER 30

PAUL SAT BESIDE MARCHETTI, GATHERING HIS STRENGTH for the moment. The mental and physical toll of fighting the fire had drained him. The stinging smoke, the sickly odor of fuel and the broiling heat left over from the blaze assaulted his senses. But even with all that, his only real concern centered on the flashing lights and chirping alarms connected to their breathing gear.

"How much time do we have?"

"Ten minutes," Marchetti said. "Give or take."

A sweeter voice came over the speakers in his headgear. "Paul, can you hear me?"

"I hear you Gamay," he said.

"What's going on?"

"The fire's out," he said. "The Halon did its job. But we're low on air. How soon can you open the doors?"

"Hold on," she said.

A few seconds of silence lingered and then she came back. "Chief says you guys dumped enough water down there to keep

the temps reasonable. We'll be safely below reignition temp in
about seven minutes."

"That's good news," Paul said. He helped Marchetti up. "Let's
go find your crewman."

"This way," Marchetti said, moving stiffly toward the rear of
the huge room.

They began to make their way back through the debris field.
The series of explosions had destroyed half the engine room. They
picked their way past ruined machinery and across the metal
deck. Steam rose from it in ghostly boiling sheets as the water
they'd used to fight the fire evaporated. The smell of fuel was
everywhere.

"Here," Marchetti said, moving to a sealed door.

It wasn't a watertight bulkhead, but the scorched steel door
was formidable looking, and the edges appeared to be tight. Hope
rose in Paul's heart.

"It's designed as a shelter," Marchetti said, "though I wasn't
sure it would survive something like this." He grabbed the locking bar and then pulled back.

"A little hot?" Paul asked.

Marchetti nodded, got himself ready and grabbed it again. He
grunted, trying to force the bar down. It wouldn't budge and he
let go again.

"The heat might have expanded the door," Marchetti said.

"Let me help," Paul said. He moved into position, and together
the two of them grabbed the bar and put all their weight on it. It
snapped downward. Paul shouldered the door and it swung open.
He let go of the bar instantly, though his hands felt as if they'd
been burned through the Nomex gloves.

Air from the compartment streamed out, mixing with the
steam and smoke in the engine room. It was pitch-black in the

control room. The only illumination came from the lights on their masks and the flashing strobes on their gear.

They split up. Near the back wall, Paul spotted a man in mechanic's coveralls lying on the ground. "Over here."

UP IN THE COMMAND CENTER, all eyes were on the central monitor and the flashing red number indicating the temperature in the engine room. It was slowly dropping, winding down until eventually it changed from red to yellow.

"Almost there," the chief said. "I'm going to arm the doors."

Gamay liked the sound of that. She checked the clock. Six minutes had elapsed since Paul's and Marchetti's oxygen supply warnings had gone off. For once it felt like they had a margin of error, but she wouldn't feel safe until her husband was out of that room and back in her arms.

The chief pressed a couple of switches and then checked his board. Whatever he saw aggravated him. He cycled the switches and began flipping a toggle back and forth.

"What's wrong?"

"The doors aren't responding," he said. "I just armed them to open, but they're remaining in lock-down mode."

"Could the fire have damaged them?"

"Doubt it," he said. "They're designed for this."

He fiddled with the switches a few more times and then checked something else. "It's the computer. It's blocking the directive."

"Why?"

To her right, Gamay saw Leilani stand. "I know why," she said. "Otero messed with it."

"Otero is in the brig," the chief said.

"Marchetti told me he was a genius with computers," she said. "He could have planted something ahead of time in case he was caught, in case he needed to cause some trouble and keep Marchetti off balance. Just like he did with the robots."

The chief continued to try to bypass whatever was blocking him. "It's definitely the computer," he said. "Everything else is operating correctly."

Gamay felt as if she was spinning. How this guy could reach out from the brig and torment them, she didn't know.

"We need to go down there and force him to deactivate whatever he's done," Leilani said. "Put a gun to his head if we have to."

Gamay's mind raced. Her balance and convictions against coercion were suddenly fading when she thought of her husband trapped in an engine room filled with toxic fumes and running out of air.

"Gamay," Leilani pleaded. "I've already lost someone to these people. You don't have to."

On the monitor, the temperature gauge dropped into the green and the clock ticked into the seventh minute. Paul had three minutes of air.

"Fine," Gamay said. "But no guns."

The chief turned to one of his men. "Rocco, take over, I'm going with them."

Leilani grabbed the door and opened it. Gamay went through, headed for the elevator and the brig with no idea what she was going to do when she got there.

DOWN IN THE ENGINE ROOM, Paul had reached the missing crewman. He crouched beside the man and rolled him over. The man didn't respond. Paul removed his gloves and checked for a pulse as Marchetti arrived at his side.

"Anything?"

Paul held his hand in place, hoping to sense something he'd missed. "I'm sorry."

"Damn," Marchetti said. "All this for nothing."

Paul felt the same. And then in the flashing of his strobe he noticed something on the side of the man's neck. He rolled the crewman a half turn and brushed his dark brown hair out of the way.

"Not totally for nothing," Paul said, aiming his light at a dark bruise on the back of the man's neck. He felt for the vertebrae, there was no rigidity.

"What's wrong?"

Paul reached over and switched Marchetti's radio off and then did the same to his own. Marchetti seemed confused.

With no one else listening Paul felt he could speak freely. He was not normally given to such leaps, preferring to be the calm, rational one while others shouted conspiracy theories and insisted the sky was falling, but he could see no other reason for all that had happened.

He looked Marchetti in the eyes and spoke loud enough for him to hear through the masks. "This man didn't die from smoke inhalation or the heat. His neck's broken."

"Broken?"

Paul nodded. "This man was murdered, Mr. Marchetti. You have a saboteur on board."

Marchetti looked stunned.

"It's the only explanation for the fire and systems failures. Since you're in here with me, I'm assuming it's not you. But it could be anyone else. One of the skeleton crew or even a stowaway. Probably someone with hidden ties to Otero or Matson. I suggest we keep it to ourselves until we can figure out who it might be."

Marchetti looked at the dead crewman and then back at Paul. He nodded.

Paul switched his radio on and scooped up the dead man. Marchetti turned his own radio back on. "We're headed for the main door," he said, informing the bridge.

DOWN ON THE LOWER DECK, Gamay, Leilani and the chief made it to the brig. The chief used his keys to unlock the cell door. Gamay stepped in. Otero looked up at her from his seat. His sullen eyes were dark.

"We know you've messed up the computer system," she said. "My husband is trapped in the engine room after fighting a fire. You need to enable the doors so he can get out."

"Why would I do that?"

"Because if he dies, it's murder, and that's a lot worse for you than what you've already done."

Otero's head bobbed slightly back and forth as if he were weighing the pros and cons of her request.

"Damn you!" Gamay shouted, stepping forward and slapping him. "There are people here who would kill you for what you've already done. I told them it wasn't necessary, it wasn't right."

She grabbed a Wi-Fi-enabled laptop from the chief and shoved it toward him.

Otero looked at it but did nothing.

"I told you he was worthless," Leilani said.

Looking angry, the chief stepped past Leilani and moved up beside Gamay. "You've tried it your way, now I'll try mine."

He loomed over Otero. "Open the damn doors or I'll beat you until you can't remember your name."

Otero pulled back a bit, but he seemed less afraid to Gamay than he should have, considering the build of Marchetti's chief. It took a second to realize why.

The unmistakable sound of a pistol cocking came from behind them, and Gamay's heart froze.

"No one's going to get beaten today," Leilani said from behind them.

Cautiously Gamay turned. Leilani held another gun, different than the one Kurt had taken from her.

"Thanks for moving past me," she said. "I was wondering how to get the drop on both of you at the same time."

PAUL AND MARCHETTI WAITED at the main door in the engine room. Time was running out.

"Thirty seconds," Marchetti said. "Give or take."

Paul tried to control his breathing. No doubt he'd sucked a lot of oxygen while fighting the fire, he hoped remaining calm at this point would counteract that.

"Anytime now," Marchetti said loudly.

It concerned Paul that they hadn't heard from the bridge in several minutes. His last few breaths had been awfully stale. His instincts urged him to take off the mask as if it was smothering him. He knew better of course, the toxic fumes from the fire were far worse than stale air. But any second that air would become no air at all.

"Are you guys out there?" Marchetti shouted. He began banging on the door.

"Save your air," Paul warned.

"Something's wrong," Marchetti said. He pounded on the door with his fist until the warning light on the side panel went from red to yellow. Around them the sound of fans spooling up and the bang of exhaust vents flipping from closed to open rang out.

"Or maybe not," Marchetti said, looking pleased.

The smoke and steam and fumes began to drift upward, sucked out of the compartment by the system, and the indicator beside the door turned green.

An instant later the door handle spun and the hatch cracked open with a hiss as the heated air from the engine room forced its way out.

An instant of exaltation was followed by a blow of crushing defeat. Outside the door, Gamay and seven of the crewmen, including the chief, were down on their knees with their hands behind their heads. Just beyond them, holding a mix of rifles and short-barreled machine guns that looked like Uzis, were two other crewmen, along with Otero, Matson and, of all people, Leilani Tanner.

"I guess we know who the saboteur is," Paul said. "You're not Kimo's sister, are you?"

"My name is Zarrina," she said. "Do as I order and I won't have to kill you."

CHAPTER 31

Lying flat in the sand once again, Kurt peered through the gathering dusk to a dry lake bed on the desert floor. A half mile from them sat the two odd-looking jets that had flown over them and a third aircraft of the same type, which they hadn't seen approach. All three sat quietly up against the right side of what passed as the runway.

From a breast pocket he pulled the compact set of binoculars he'd liberated from Jinn's dead guard at the bottom of the well. Brushing sand from the lenses, he lifted them to his eyes.

"You were right," he said. "Not exactly JFK. More like Edwards Air Force Base out in California."

"Dry lake bed for a runway," Joe replied, "but what on earth are they doing down there?"

Kurt watched as Jinn's men poured from holes in the ground like angry ants. They scurried around the three aircraft in a haphazard way. Nearby, a set of trucks idled with black diesel smoke drifting from their exhaust stacks. A trio of forklifts seemed to be staging huge loads of equipment, and a tanker truck was easing out of a tunnel in the rock wall, moving at a snail's pace.

Joe's concept of an ant farm seemed more accurate every minute.

"They must have ramps and tunnels everywhere," Kurt said, watching as men appeared from out of nowhere and then disappeared just as quickly.

"Can you see what they're bringing in?" Joe asked.

Kurt saw wide cargo doors at the tail ends of the aircraft opening up, but nothing was coming out.

"They're not here to drop off," Kurt said. "They're picking up. Pilots are talking with some sort of loadmaster."

"So this is moving day."

"Or D-day," Kurt said.

"Can you catch the tail numbers off the jets?" Joe asked. "That might help us down the road."

With the sun down and the light fading fast, Kurt zoomed in on the closest aircraft and squinted.

"White tails," he said. "No markings of any kind. But I'm pretty sure they're Russian-built."

"Can you make out the type?"

"They look modified to me. They have the six-wheeled main landing gear of an An-70, a large tail ramp like a C-130 or other military transport but the shape of something else, they almost look like . . ."

It hit Kurt all of a sudden. He'd seen the odd-shaped plane two summers ago, fighting fires in Portugal. "They're modified Altairs," he said. "Beriev Be-200s. They're jet-powered flying boats. They land on the water, scoop up a thousand gallons of the stuff, fly off and dump it out over a blaze."

Joe seemed all the more baffled by this news. "What would Jinn want with a firefighting plane that lands on water? There's not a lot out here that can catch on fire, and there isn't much water to scoop up and fight fires with if there was."

As Kurt watched the tanker truck sidle up to the first of the jets, he thought he understood. "This is how they're getting the microbots to the sea," he said.

"In the water reservoirs," Joe said.

Kurt nodded. "There's a tanker truck hooked up to one of the jets right now, but unless someone put the fuel port in the wrong place it's not Jet A or JP-4 they're pumping."

"So they're not washing down from here or escaping," Joe said. "What about the model of the dam?"

He handed the binoculars to Joe. "Take a look beside that line of trucks."

Joe put the binoculars to his face. "I see yellow drums on pallets," he said.

"Look familiar?"

Joe nodded. He scanned back toward the aircraft. "I don't see any of those going onto the planes. Looks like they're loading weapons and ammunition onto the closest one, and I think I see a couple of ribbed Zodiacs like the SEAL teams use set up in the staging area."

"Sounds like our friends are headed somewhere a little wetter than here," Kurt said. "Which really isn't a bad idea."

Joe handed the binoculars back to Kurt. "See if you can spot a water fountain down there somewhere."

"Sorry, partner," Kurt said. "I think we just escaped from the only water fountain in this vicinity. And it's out of order."

"Just like in the mall," Joe said, trying to clear his throat of the dust and sand they'd breathed in. Kurt did his best not to think about the thirst he'd built up or the dry, caked feeling in the back of his own throat.

"I wonder," Kurt said. "Maybe we're trying to connect the wrong dots. Maybe the model dam they wrecked has nothing to do with the current diagram you spotted in the drafting room and what's going on in the Indian Ocean."

"Two targets?"

Kurt nodded. "Two modes of transportation. Two different ways of carrying those microbots. Maybe they have two distinct operations going here."

"Have we underestimated our maniacal little friend?"

"We might have," Kurt replied.

"What do you want to do?"

"My original idea was to catch a flight out of here," Kurt said, "but now that we appear to have a choice in our mode of transport. What do you suggest, trucks or planes?"

"Trucks," Joe said.

"Really?" Kurt said, surprised. "Planes are faster. And we both know something about flying."

"Not those things."

"They're all the same," Kurt insisted.

Joe pursed his lips. "Have you ever calculated how much trouble your endless optimism gets us in?" Joe asked. "They're NOT all the same. And even if they were, where are you going to go once you have control of the plane? This is the Middle East. Planes crossing borders without permission don't last long around here. The Saudis, the Israelis, the Seventh Fleet, any one of them might shoot us out of the sky before we could explain why we violated their no-fly zone."

Kurt hated to admit it but Joe had a point.

"Besides," Joe added, "those planes might end up in a worse place than this. But trucks have to stay on the beaten path and stick close to civilization. There are only so many roads and so many places a truck can go from here. I say we climb aboard."

"In the back?" Kurt said. "With ten billion little eating machines?"

Joe took the binoculars from Kurt and trained them on the drums beside the line of covered flatbeds. "From the way Jinn's men are keeping their distance I'm gonna guess they have some idea what's in those drums. That plays in our favor. It'll keep 'em away and reduce the chances of our being discovered and redeposited in that well."

Kurt remained quiet.

"And," Joe added, perhaps sensing victory was near, "if we are discovered in the trucks, we can jump and run. Kind of hard to do that from thirty thousand feet."

Kurt could not remember a time when Joe had made such a forceful argument. "You've talked me into it."

"Really?"

"When you're right, you're right," he said, brushing some dust off his uniform and straightening it. "And in this case you are right on, my friend."

Joe handed the binoculars back to Kurt, looking very pleased with himself. He tried to make his own uniform look more presentable.

"Shall we?"

Kurt tucked the binoculars into his breast pocket. "We shall."

As darkness fell and the moonless night spread across the

desert, the loading and servicing of the Russian-built jets continued. To provide some light a few temporary spotlights and the
high beams of several parked Jeeps and Humvees were moved
into place.

The strange setup made it easy for Kurt and Joe to sneak up
on the staging area as the men in the lighted zone were all but
blind to the darkness of the desert beyond.

Upon reaching the operations area, Kurt and Joe pulled up
their kaffiyehs to cover their faces and heads. Aside from looking
dirty and scruffy, their uniforms matched those of the men han-
dling the loading.

"Grab something," Joe whispered, picking up a small crate of
equipment. "Everyone looks official if they're carrying something
and walking briskly."

Kurt followed suit, and the two of them walked right into the
main staging area without receiving a second glance. They began
to get their bearings, trying not to look conspicuous.

Kurt spotted the row of yellow drums. Only a dozen of perhaps sixty remained.

He pointed, and the two of them moved that way. As they
closed in, someone began to shout at them in Arabic.

Kurt turned and saw the bearded man named Sabah standing
by the row of trucks. Kurt recognized some of the words, something about lazy workers.

Sabah pointed and shouted again and waved his hands in ear-
nest. He seemed to be indicating an idle forklift.

Kurt raised a hand in acknowledgment and began walking
toward it.

"I think he wants us to drive it."

Joe followed him. "Do you know how to drive one of these
things?"

"I've seen it done once or twice," Kurt said. "How hard could it be?"

Joe cringed but followed Kurt to the gray-and-orange forklift. He stood by as Kurt climbed on the four-wheeled machine and tried to familiarize himself with the controls.

Sabah began shouting again.

"You better at least start the engine," Joe whispered.

Kurt found the key and twisted it, the motor rumbled to life.

"Climb on," he said.

Joe scrambled up onto the side of the forklift and held fast something like a fireman on the ladder trucks of old.

Kurt found the clutch and the gearshift. The rig had three gears: low, high and reverse. Kurt pressed the clutch down, forced the shift into low and added some gas.

Nothing happened.

"We're not moving," Joe whispered.

"I realize that."

Kurt let out the clutch a little more and pressed the accelerator a little harder. The engine revved, the gears meshed and the big machine lurched forward like a driver's ed car in the hands of a three-time dropout.

"Easy," Joe said.

"I thought that was easy," Kurt replied.

Sabah waved impatiently, pointing them toward the stack of yellow drums, each of which sat on its own pallet.

Kurt turned that way. Up ahead one of the other forklifts was raising a pallet that held one of the yellow drums. As it lifted the load, a second workman lashed it to the apron with a metal cable. Apparently no one wanted to spill the contents of these barrels.

The forklift reversed and headed off with the worker still hanging on to the front.

"That's your job," Kurt said.

"Great."

"You'd better find us a cable."

Joe discovered one hooked to the forklift's roof guard. He disconnected it and hopped down to the desert floor.

As Joe edged toward the yellow drums, Kurt struggled to guide the big machine. He lined up and moved forward. He grabbed the fork control and went to lower the forks, but they moved opposite to what he remembered. The forks came up, threatening to puncture the drum.

He slammed on the brake, and the forklift stopped short.

As he lowered the fork, Kurt caught sight of Joe. His eyes were wide. Kurt couldn't really blame him. When the forks were at the correct height and angle, Kurt inched the rig forward and picked up the pallet.

Joe stepped up and lashed the drum tight and gave Kurt the thumbs-up.

With a great degree of caution, Kurt backed up and turned. Going forward once again, he found the rig far better balanced with Joe and the yellow drum weighing down the nose.

He moved slowly toward the line of trucks, following in the tracks of the other forklift.

There were five trucks in all. They were flatbeds with treated canvas tarps stretched over the top of metal ribs. It looked like the lead truck was filled and being buttoned up. The others were still being loaded.

Sabah pointed toward the last truck in the line, and Kurt moved toward it. He lined up with the rear bumper and raised the forks. When it was even with the bed of the truck, Joe unlashed the drum and eased it forward, sliding the entire pallet onto a set of rollers on the bed of the truck.

Moving it like that, he slid it into place and lashed it down like the other barrels. With the job done, Joe climbed back onto the side of the forklift.

"You realize this could be considered aiding and abetting the enemy," he said as Kurt turned the forklift back toward the staging area.

"We can leave this off the report," Kurt said. "A simple omission."

"Great idea. It could happen to anyone."

"Exactly," Kurt said. "When we load the final barrel, you stay in the truck bed. I'll park this thing and join you when no one's looking."

It sounded like a good plan and it seemed to be working. All the way up until they were almost ready to put it into action.

As they waited to grab the last barrel, Jinn and several of his men came out of the tunnel.

Sabah held up a hand like a traffic cop, and all activity stopped as he went to talk with his master.

Kurt cut the engine, hoping to overhear.

Another group of men joined Jinn. The young woman Kurt suspected to be the real Leilani was with them.

"You're bringing her with us?" Sabah asked.

"I am," Jinn said. "This complex is no longer secure."

"I'll contact Xhou," Sabah said. "The Chinese are treacherous, but they always prefer to save face. That is why he sent Mustafa. He will redouble his efforts and release more funds. He will not be a problem until the sting of this failure has gone away. And that will be long enough for us to gain full control."

"I'm not worried about the Chinese," Jinn said. "That American was right. His government will move aggressively. They no longer care about borders. We're not safe here."

"We shall see," Sabah said.

"I need a new headquarters," Jinn insisted, "one they will not suspect. And I must do more to ensure our plan goes into effect, efforts I cannot make from here."

He pointed to the woman. "Keep her out of the way until the loading is done. Then put her in the third plane, away from the men. I don't want them near her."

"She should be guarded," Sabah said.

"Her will is broken," Jinn said. "She will soon do as I demand, but if you must have her watched, send two guards, no more. And warn them, Sabah, if they touch her, I will stake them to the ground and set them on fire."

Sabah nodded. He picked two men and they took Leilani toward one of the waiting transports. As she was dragged away, Kurt and Joe exchanged glances.

Kurt started the engine again and turned in silence toward the last of the yellow drums. He picked it up deftly, an old hand by now. Joe secured it and came back aboard the forklift.

"I know what you're thinking," Joe said.

"Don't try to talk me out of it."

"Wouldn't if I could," Joe replied. "Do you want some help?"

"I'd love some," Kurt said. "But someone's got to figure out where these drums are going and warn whoever they're meant for. This way, we're not putting all our eggs in one basket."

They'd reached the truck. Kurt grabbed the lift lever and began to raise the drum.

"As soon as you can get to civilization, contact Dirk. We have to let Paul and Gamay know they have a mole in their midst."

Joe nodded. "Once you grab that girl, get out of the hornet's nest. Don't take on more than you can chew."

The drum had reached an even level with the truck bed and

the rollers. "Hornet's nest? I thought we established that this was a lion's den?"

"Lions don't fly," Joe said. "Once you're up in the air, it's a hornet's nest."

"Now you're getting the hang of this."

The two men stared at each other for a moment, friends who'd bailed each other out of countless scrapes. Splitting up went against every instinct in their hearts. *Fight together, survive together,* they'd often said. But in this case it would mean abandoning a young woman to a terrible fate or cutting in half their chances to alert the world and their friends of pending danger. The stakes were too high for that.

"You sure about this?" Joe asked.

"You take the low road and I'll take the high road," Kurt said, "and I'll be in civilization before you."

"Define civilization?" Joe said, unlashing the barrel and sliding it forward.

"Somewhere that no one's trying to kill us and where you can get an ice-cold Coke if you want one. Last one to reach it buys dinner at Citronelle for the whole team."

Joe nodded, probably thinking of the menu and the ambience of the well-regarded D.C. area restaurant. "You're on," he said, lashing the drum into place.

Kurt watched, feeling a mixed sense of concern and relief. The trucks were not meant for cross-country desert travel, they had to go where the roads went. And even in a country like Yemen, that would soon lead to some area of civilization. With luck, Joe would be quenching his thirst and on the phone to NUMA before dawn. Kurt knew his own prospects were less certain.

Joe grabbed a tarp that would cover the back of the truck. He glanced at Kurt. "*Vaya con Dios,* my friend."

"You too," Kurt said.

The tarp dropped, Joe vanished and Kurt backed the forklift away, turning toward the staging area without another glance behind him.

All he had to do now was find out which plane Leilani was on and sneak aboard without being discovered.

CHAPTER 32

JOE ZAVALA HAD HUNKERED DOWN IN THE MOST FORWARD section of the flatbed, between the yellow drums and the front wall. No one had seen him there. Beyond taking a cursory glance from the back end of the truck to count the barrels, no one had even checked. With all accounted for, the tarp had been tied down tight. The doors up front opened and then slammed shut, and the big truck had gone into gear. Soon they were rumbling across the desert.

At periodic intervals, Joe had stealthily checked the surroundings. He'd seen only darkness and sand and the other trucks in the convoy. He wondered where they were headed.

After four hours, they finally began to slow.

"I hope we're about to hit a rest stop," Joe muttered to himself. He snuck a peek from under the canvas but saw no sign of civilization. Eventually the truck coasted to a stop, though the engine continued to idle.

Joe wondered whether to make a break for it. He hadn't really considered jumping from the truck while it crossed the desert because he had no idea where they were and without water he didn't want to go back into walking mode. At least not until there was somewhere to walk to.

He considered making a break for it now, but a second problem had compounded the first. Somehow, his truck had ended up in the front of the convoy. The other trucks sat behind him with their lights blazing away in the dark. To move now would be like going over the prison wall in broad daylight. He had to wait and hope for a better opportunity up ahead.

Shouting and orders came out of the dark. The big rig lurched as it went back into gear and began to inch forward again. It went over something that felt like a curb, and the flatbed trailer twisted and flexed as each set of wheels crossed whatever it was. The yellow drums shook from side to side. Joe put a hand out to steady the closest one.

"Take it easy on those speed bumps," he whispered.

Then the nose of the truck angled down as if descending a ramp. The drums strained forward against their lashes, sliding his way. Joe's sense of anxiety grew.

They leveled out after going no more than fifty feet and then continued forward on much smoother ground. Finally they stopped again. The driver and passenger climbed out, slamming their doors behind them. The lights of the second truck crept closer, penetrating the tarp as they came.

As Joe listened to the sound of the engine and the sound of the shouting voices, he detected an echo. He noticed the smooth ground beneath them after bouncing so long on the desert road and the fact that the truck's engine had been shut off for the first time.

I'm in a warehouse.

That meant civilization: computers, phone lines and running

water. Maybe even a Coke machine in a break room somewhere. A smile crept over his face.

When the lights of the next truck inched up tight and then shut off, Joe was certain of it. He only had to wait until all the trucks were parked and shut down for the night and then he could probably slip out unnoticed.

The smell of diesel fumes grew thick as the other trucks maneuvered back and forth in what must have been a fairly tight space. Finally the last engine shut off. He heard more talking.

"Come on," he whispered, "everyone out. It's got to be Miller time by now."

Voices echoed through the dark for a while longer, but they were slowly growing more distant. The sound of heavy doors sliding shut rang out, and the silence that followed told Joe he was probably alone.

Choosing to be extra cautious, Joe waited in the silence. After a few minutes, he felt it was safe to move. If there were guards, they were probably posted where they could keep people from getting into the warehouse, not out.

Joe made his way past the other barrels and toward the rear of the flatbed.

Kurt really should have come with me, Joe thought. In a few minutes he'd be free of trouble and dialing up NUMA. From there a description of the Be-200s could be relayed to the military, a satellite sweep could identify the traveling planes and Special Forces could be called in. Leilani Tanner would stand a much better chance of being rescued by them than she did with just Kurt and the stolen 9mm pistol he'd taken from the guard.

But this way Joe would be responsible for saving both of them. He was glad for the chance and he looked forward to the satisfaction of having Kurt foot the bill at Citronelle and admitting that he had rescued him.

He reached the tailgate of the flatbed. He pulled the tarp up a fraction and peered out. It was pitch-black in the warehouse. All he could see was the nose of the other truck pressed right up against the rear bumper of his.

Nice parking job.

He listened again for any signs of trouble. He could hear something. It sounded like a distant rumbling. Almost like another truck beyond the walls. Or even the diesel engine of a freight train in the distance. Trains meant rails and rails led places. He found himself growing more excited by the moment.

He untied the rear flap, slid his legs over the edge and lowered himself down. As he turned sideways to fit between the two trucks, an odd sensation came over him, like dizziness or vertigo. Perhaps he'd been sitting too long. Perhaps the lack of water had begun to affect his balance.

He put a hand on the hood of the second truck, steadied himself and let go. He edged out into the space between the two rows of vehicles. The rigs were parked so tightly, they'd had to fold in their mirrors to stop them from breaking off.

With just enough room to walk between the rows, Joe headed toward the end of the rows of trucks and what he assumed was the door through which they'd come in.

The vertigo hit him again and he felt his knees almost buckle. He began to fear some of the microbots had gotten out of the barrels and into his ears. That was the problem with things too small to see: one never knew where they were.

"A Q-Tip," he mumbled, rubbing his ear, "my kingdom for a Q-Tip."

His balance came back and he moved another step. This time

the sensation came quicker, more pronounced and smoother some-how. Joe felt it in his legs and felt it in his neck as if he was be-ing pushed back and forth. He heard a creaking sound.

He held as still as possible. The sensation repeated itself yet again. It wasn't his imagination. It wasn't vertigo. It wasn't even the bots, throwing off his balance. The feeling was real and ex-tremely familiar.

His heart began to pump. He moved faster, slipping between the trucks, his feet sliding across the metal floor. By the time he reached the steel door at the end of the rows he could feel the floor moving beneath his feet in a slowly repeating pattern, smooth and steady, up and down.

The sound of a foghorn far above confirmed what Joe al-ready knew.

He was on a ship of some kind, not parked in a warehouse. The odd sensation beneath his feet was the deck moving on what he could only assume to be a freighter of some kind riding out past a breakwater and into the swells at an angle.

The deck rose and fell and also pitched and twisted. The movements weren't pronounced, just enough to throw him off in the darkness, but they were unmistakable now.

Joe found the latch to the rear door. It was bolted heavy and tight.

He recalled his boast to Kurt. *There are only so many roads and so many places a truck can go from here.*

Yeah, he thought. Unless you put the truck on a ship. Then it can pretty much go anywhere.

CHAPTER 33

KURT AUSTIN WAS TRAPPED IN THE LAVATORY. HE'D SNUCK aboard the plane with the most equipment and the fewest of Jinn's men milling around and had hidden himself in the small facility near the front of the cargo compartment. After drinking a dozen cupped handfuls of water from the small faucet, he'd stepped up on the toilet so no one could see his feet.

With the curtain drawn, he waited and listened. Crates and big stacks of equipment were loaded aboard and lashed down. He heard swearing as something heavy was dropped and then the voices of the pilots as they climbed up a small ladder and entered the flight deck.

Eventually he'd heard the sound of harsher voices ordering someone around. In response, a woman's voice said in American English; "Okay, okay. Stop pushing me."

Kurt felt certain it was the woman from the hall, who he believed to be Kimo's sister. At least he'd chosen the right plane.

A few minutes later the aircraft had sprung to life. With Kurt holding on and trying desperately not to slip from his perch, the

Russian transport/flying boat taxied onto the runway, ran its engines up to full power and accelerated down the surprisingly rough lake bed. The takeoff seemed to last forever, and Kurt was glad when the plane finally clawed its way into the air.

Based on the slow pace of the climb and the length of the roll out, they had to be fully loaded and heavy with fuel. That meant a long journey.

In a way, that played into his hands. Sooner or later someone would have to go to the bathroom. If it was Leilani, he would get a chance to talk with her. If it was one of the pilots, he would stick the pistol in the man's face and take over the plane. If it was one of Leilani's guards, it would be the last thing the man ever did.

As it turned out, one of Jinn's guards was the first to feel the call.

Two hours into the flight, Kurt heard the man's boots clunking toward him from the rear of the aircraft. He put the pistol away, pulled out the knife and pressed himself as far to the side as possible in the closet-sized space.

The man grabbed the curtain, yanked it aside but didn't step in.

Kurt had the knife out ready to strike, but the guy was looking back down the aisle of the plane, shouting some joke to his comrade and laughing at his own words even as he spoke.

Finally he turned and stepped in. Kurt grabbed him, wrapped a hand around his face, clamping it over his mouth, as he drove the knife into his back just below the nape of his neck.

With the spinal column severed, the man went limp. Kurt held him up and turned him, keeping his mouth covered until he sensed no breath coming forth. Gently, he sat the man down on the toilet seat and stared into his eyes. The light was gone from them.

He pulled the knife out. No reaction.

Kurt hated killing, but there was no grounds for mercy here. Only one side would get off the plane alive: either Jinn's men or he and Leilani.

Recognizing the thug as the one who'd driven the truck that dragged him and Joe across the desert, Kurt felt a little less remorse. The next stage in the plan was more complicated. To begin with, blood was everywhere. Kurt used the man's head covering to staunch the flow and eased him back against the bulkhead, wedging him into the space.

He gauged the man as roughly similar to him in size and shape, and they wore similar uniforms, but there was one glaring difference: the thug had thin black hair, Kurt's hair was thick and steel gray.

With few other options, Kurt chose to wet his hair down and press it flat to his head. It was dark and cold and tremendously noisy in the plane. *And who would suspect trouble at thirty thousand feet anyway?*

He figured the other guy had seen his friend walk to the head. He would have to look really closely *not* to see his friend coming back a few minutes later.

Kurt pulled the curtain and prepared to play his gambit. Just in case, he held the knife concealed in his hand.

He stepped out of the lavatory and marched confidently back toward Leilani and the remaining guard. It was easier than he thought. The hold was filled with equipment. At least two of the rigid inflatable boats he'd seen and, more ominously, racks of what looked like handheld ground-to-air missiles.

But the clutter left only a small space for the passengers. Leilani and the guard were sitting across from each other in foldout seats that attached to the aircraft's walls.

The most cursory of glances was all the guard gave him. He then leaned his head back against the headrest on the side of the plane and shut his eyes.

Even Leilani had her eyes closed.

After all, it was the middle of the night, and even with the pressurization of the cargo hold the air was still thin and dry, most likely set to an altitude nine thousand feet or so. That kind of air had a way of making people drowsy even if it was all but impossible to really sleep in such conditions.

Kurt sat down a foot from the guard, right across from Leilani. He switched from the knife to the gun once again and stretched his foot out to tap her.

She opened her eyes and saw him with a finger to his lips.

The one thing Kurt had remembered Kimo saying about his sister was that she worked with deaf kids. Kurt knew American sign language. Or at least he once did.

With great effort he signed *I . . . am . . . a . . . friend*, hoping he hadn't misspelled the last word and told her he was a *fiend*.

She seemed puzzled but her eyes were hopeful. On the chance he'd messed up the whole sentence, he signed something she would have to understand: *N . . . U . . . M . . . A . . .*

Her eyes grew wide and he held a finger to his lips again.

He nodded toward the guard, pulled the pistol from his pocket and cocked it. The man's eyes opened at the sound.

"Don't move," Kurt said.

He held the pistol with his right hand and grabbed the man's own pistol. The guy didn't flinch.

Kurt pointed toward the back of the plane. When the guard looked that way, Kurt whammed him on the side of the head with the pistol. The guard dropped like a sack of flour, but he didn't go out. A second blow did the trick.

By the time he woke up, he was bound and gagged and tied to the floorboards of one of the boats near the tail end of the aircraft.

As Kurt finished tying him down, Leilani spoke. "Who are you?" she asked.

Kurt smiled. "Can't tell you how glad I am that you don't know."

Of course she had no idea what he was talking about, but Kurt was making a mental note that from now on he'd be suspicious of anyone who knew who he was before he'd introduced himself.

"My name's Kurt Austin," he said. "I knew your brother. I'm with NUMA. We've been trying to figure out what happened to him."

"Did you find him?"

Kurt shook his head. "No," he said. "I'm sorry."

She gulped back a wave of emotion and took a slow, deep breath. "I didn't think anyone would," she said quietly. "I could almost feel that he was gone."

"But the search led us to Jinn and by accident to you," he said.

She glanced nervously toward the cockpit door.

"Don't worry," Kurt said, "they're not likely to come back here anytime soon. And if they did, all they'd see is you and one of your guards."

She seemed to accept that.

"When did these guys grab you?" he asked.

"In Malé. As soon as I checked into the hotel," she said.

It seemed as if a tremor of fear swept over her as she thought back to the incident, but she stiffened. "I kicked one of them in the teeth," she said proudly. "The guy will be eating soup for weeks. But the others threw me down."

She was feisty, but far different from the way Zarrina had portrayed her. She was less worldly, more like a twenty-five-year-old should be. Kurt wished he'd seen her before.

"I woke up in the desert," she added. "I couldn't escape. I don't even know where I was. They interrogated me and got everything—passwords, phone numbers, bank accounts. They took my passport and driver's license."

All of which explained how the impostor knew so much and why the American Embassy confirmed for NUMA that Leilani Tanner was in Malé.

"You don't have to feel bad about that," he said. "You're not some hardened operative who would be expected to resist interrogation. Besides, you must have done something right, you're still alive."

She looked ill. "I think that Jinn looks at me like some type of horse to break," she said. "He's always touching me, telling me how I'll enjoy being with him."

"He's never going to find out how wrong he is," Kurt said. "I'm getting you out of here."

"Off the plane?"

"Not exactly," he said, then switched subjects. "Any idea where we're going?"

"I figured you might know that better than me," she said. "I'm a prisoner, remember?"

"And I'm a stowaway. We make a fine pair."

Kurt moved to one of the tiny circular windows in the side of the plane. It was still dark outside, but as he looked down below he could see a smooth gray surface with a slight shimmer.

"We're out over water," he said. "The moon's come up."

He glanced toward his wrist to check his watch. Never again

would he trade his watch in as collateral. A kidney maybe, the deed to his boathouse perhaps, but not his watch. At least not without grabbing another one along the way.

"You don't happen to have the time do you?"

She shook her head.

He and Joe had made their way to the staging area around eight p.m. As near as he could tell, loading the trucks and then the aircraft had taken a total of three hours. The plane had sat on the ground for another couple of hours after that, which put take-off sometime around one a.m.

He went to the starboard window to see if he could see anything out that side. The view was the same: nothing but water.

It was slightly possible that they were over the Mediterranean, a couple of hours' flying time would have crossed Saudi Arabia, but with everything else that had been going on Kurt guessed they were headed south, out over the Indian Ocean, with a cargo of microbots in the tanks beneath his feet. Two and a half hours from Yemen in a jet aircraft would put them all but smack-dab in the middle of it.

He wondered where they were headed. He wondered if Jinn had a secret base hidden on a deserted island somewhere. Staring out the window again, he strained to see forward as far as he could but saw only more waves.

Leilani watched him go back and forth. "What do we do next?" she asked. "Look for parachutes? I heard them talking about some."

Kurt had already spotted the chutes she was referring to. "They're not for people," he said. "They're attached to the boats so they can fly low and dump them out the back without having to land. They call it LAPES, Low Altitude Parachute Extraction System."

She looked confused.

"You ever see a drag race?"

She nodded.

He pointed toward the two nylon packs that sat beside each ribbed boat. "They're drogue chutes," he said. "They pop out the back like the ones that slow down drag racers or the space shuttle after it lands. Not exactly made for jumping."

"Okay," she said. "You got any other plans?"

He smiled. "You sound just like someone else I know. A good friend of mine, actually."

"Is he on the plane?" she asked hopefully.

"No," Kurt said. "He's probably sitting in the first-class lounge at Doha by now. Looking over the menu from Citronelle and getting hungrier by the minute."

She tilted her head like a child or cocker spaniel might. "It could be me," she said. "But you don't make a lot of sense."

"I'll be more clear," he promised. "We're not jumping out of this plane, we're taking it over. We're going to force our way into the cockpit, order the pilots to fly us somewhere safe and make a dinner reservation under the name Zavala at a place called Citronelle as soon as we touch down."

"Can you fly it?"

"Not really."

"So we make them fly it," she said, smiling, "like *we're* the hijackers."

"Exactly."

She looked toward the front of the plane. "I didn't see any kind of armored door," she said. "Just a ladder. Breaking in should be easy."

"The trouble comes on the other side," Kurt said. "We're at high altitude. The plane is pressurized, and that cockpit's draped in acres of glass. A struggle and an errant shot through one of the panes and we end up with rapid decompression."

"Which is?"

"A controlled outward explosion," Kurt said. "Basically, a giant sucking sound that ends with us flying out through the shattered window and free-falling toward the ocean for approximately ten minutes. Which will seem rather pleasant when compared to the sudden stop at the bottom."

"Don't want to do that," she said.

"Neither do I," he replied. "If we're going to take over the plane without a struggle, we need to upgrade our weapon status."

With Leilani trailing him, he walked toward the cargo pallets, hoping to find something more lethal.

As he dug into the first pallet, the high-pitched whine of the engines slowed and dropped an octave or two. The odd, slightly weightless feeling of an aircraft nosing over from cruise to descent came next. It was far more pronounced than on your average airliner.

"We're descending," Leilani said.

"Must be getting close," Kurt said. "We'd better hurry."

CHAPTER 34

THE FLOATING ISLAND OF AQUA-TERRA WAS UNDER NEW management. As Zarrina gave orders on the bridge, even Otero and Matson were feeling the heat.

Many decks below, Paul Trout walked the confines of Marchetti's five-star brig, taking inventory of the surroundings. It came with floor-to-ceiling windows, soft recessed lighting and comfortable pillow-top mattresses. It even had a massage chair and a juice dispenser.

"A juice dispenser," Paul said incredulously.

"Good idea," Marchetti said, calling to him from the massage chair. "I'll take a guava-pineapple while you're up."

Paul looked over at their host. He was arching his back like a cat rubbing on the furniture as the chair's shiatsu tumblers moved up and down his spine.

"Oh, that feels good," he mumbled. "Yeah, right there."

On the one hand, it struck Paul as the height of absurdity; on the other hand, he couldn't wait for Marchetti to get done so he could have a turn. Fighting the fire had knotted up his back something fierce.

He poured three cups of the guava-pineapple mixture and brought them back to the other side of the room. He placed them down between Marchetti, who was still making strange sounds of pleasure, and Gamay, who was scowling like an assistant principal ready to put everyone in detention.

Paul offered her one of the cups. She shook her head in disgust.

"When you two are done enjoying your spa day, maybe we could try and figure out a way to escape?"

"I tried the windows," Paul said.

"Oh, you'll never get through those," Marchetti promised. "They're designed to withstand a Force 10 gale."

"What about doors?"

"Key-coded from the outside," he said, shifting his position in the chair. "No way to access the control box from in here. If you notice, we don't even have a handle."

"I noticed," Gamay said.

Marchetti pushed back into the seat a little farther, and the tumblers began to vibrate, shaking him and giving his voice a strange staccato sound like someone pounding on his own chest as he spoke. "I . . . think . . . we . . . should . . . just . . . sit . . . tight . . ." he said. "Conserve . . . our . . . energy . . ."

Paul saw the fires of fury rise up in Gamay's eyes. He got out of the way quickly as she lunged toward Marchetti and his chair. She grabbed the plug and yanked it out of the wall. The massage ended abruptly.

Marchetti looked stunned. Paul guessed his own session was now on permanent hold.

"You'd better get serious," she growled. "These people aren't playing a game. That wench Zarrina killed one of your crewmen, and who knows how many others in her time. And if we don't get ourselves out of here, they're going to kill us before this is over."

Marchetti looked to Paul for help, got none and turned back to Gamay.

"Sorry," he said finally. "Denial is my favorite coping mechanism. When you have a billion dollars, problems have a way of disappearing if you ignore them long enough."

"This one isn't going away," Gamay said.

Marchetti nodded.

"Do you have any security protocols?" Paul asked. "Any emergency codes or scheduled check-ins that will cause you to be missed?"

Marchetti scratched his head. "Not really," he said, sounding as if he hated to disappoint them. "Being too accessible kind of messes up the whole reclusive billionaire persona I've been trying to cultivate."

"How do you run your companies?" Paul asked.

"They kind of run themselves."

"What if you need to give an order?" Gamay said. "What if one of them has to make a big purchase or close a deal or a merger that only you can sign off on?"

"I'd have Matson do it."

That was a problem.

"So," Paul said, summing things up, "as long as Matson keeps communicating with the outside world, no one will ever know you're missing."

Marchetti nodded. "I'm afraid so."

Gamay looked as glum as Paul felt. "At least until they come up with a nice story about your disappearance during some expedition or other stunt."

"Yes," Marchetti said. "I'm starting to realize there are drawbacks to being a recluse."

"All kinds," Gamay insisted. "There were rumors that Howard Hughes died years before his official date of death. Probably false, but the thing is he became so isolated no one knew for sure. You're in the same boat. And if you call it an island, I'll slap you."

"Boat," he agreed. "And assuming we survive, I promise to be far more public from here on out."

That's great, Paul thought, but it wasn't going to help them now. "What do you think they've done with the rest of the crew?"

"A couple of them seemed to be on Zarrina's side," Gamay said.

"The others are probably locked up like we are," Marchetti added. "There are five cells down here."

"Keeping us spread out," Paul said, "prevents us from plotting against them."

"What about your people?" Marchetti asked. "The ones back in Washington. You're expected to report and check in. Surely you'll be missed."

Paul exchanged a knowing glance with his wife, after years together their minds melding in some way. "Not quickly enough."

"What do you mean?"

Paul explained. "We send them data every twenty-four hours. But it won't be too hard for Zarrina and Otero to fake it. She knows what we've been sending and what we're after. I imagine it'll be quite some time before anyone becomes suspicious."

"Maybe Dirk will call us," Gamay said hopefully. "They can't fake a video linkup."

"No," Paul said. "But they can threaten all kinds of dire consequences should we try to broadcast the truth. Which we shall of course attempt to do regardless of their threats."

Gamay looked at him. "How do we tell Dirk, or anyone else who calls in, that we're in trouble without our captors knowing about it?"

"We're hostages," Paul said. "Dirk has been in this situation a few times. Maybe we slip in the name of one of those places or one of the thugs who held him. That ought to get his wheels turning."

"That's brilliant, Mr. Trout," Marchetti said. "A secret code."

"The *Lady Flamborough*," Gamay said.

"The what?"

"The *Lady Flamborough*," she repeated. "It was a cruise ship. Dirk's father, the Senator, was held hostage on it in Antarctica. Dirk had to rescue him. If any of us get a chance to talk to Dirk, we play our part and keep up appearances for Zarrina and her thugs. We say what they want us to say. At some point Dirk will fire off a general question about our well-being or what the weather's like or something along those lines. We just have to smile nonchalantly and say things are going great, like taking a cruise on the *Lady Flamborough*."

"That's a bit vague," Marchetti said. "What if he doesn't get it?"

"You don't know Dirk Pitt," Paul insisted. "He'll get it."

"Okay, that's good," Marchetti said excitedly. "So we have a plan, assuming they cooperate and ask you to speak with him. What if they don't?"

Marchetti looked Paul's way. All Paul could offer in return

was a blank stare. He flicked his eyes toward Gamay and got nothing from her either. It seemed none of them had a plan B yet.

With frowns settling deeper on their faces, Gamay reached over and plugged the chair back in. The massage began anew.

Marchetti looked surprised.

Gamay threw up her hands. "Maybe it'll help you think."

CHAPTER 35

KURT AUSTIN HAD SPENT SEVERAL MINUTES RUMMAGING around in the cargo bay of the plane. He'd bypassed guns and ammunition and the rockets he'd spotted earlier, much to Leilani Tanner's bewilderment.

"What are you doing?" she asked.

"A wise general forages from his enemy," Kurt said.

"Again," she said. "I really have trouble following you."

"Sun Tzu," Kurt explained. *The Art of War."*

"Oh," she said. "Him, I've heard of."

He pulled a set of zip ties from one crate, the kind used to bind the hands of prisoners.

Leilani stared at the thick plastic loops. "Seen those before."

"Our friends are planning on taking more hostages," he said, wondering once again where they were headed.

He slid a handful of the ties into his pocket and dug into the next crates.

"So what else are we looking for?"

"There are probably two or three guys on the flight deck.

Two pilots and an engineer, if they have one. Maybe even a fourth in the bunk up top."

"But we can't shoot them," she said. "So how do we fight them?"

"We don't," he said.

She pointed. "See, that's what I mean, the confusion thing. I was with you and then . . . poof."

Kurt couldn't help but smile. He held up a single finger, the way he remembered the master doing it on old reruns of the show *Kung Fu*.

"To fight and conquer is not excellence," he said. "But breaking the enemy's resistance without fighting is supreme."

"Sun Tzu again?"

He nodded.

"Can you translate for me?"

"Make them too afraid to move and they won't do anything stupid," he said. "But to do that, we need something more deadly than a knife and more lethal than a gun, something so scary the pilots will do what we tell them to do and not even think about resisting."

He pulled the lid off another crate and smiled. A look of fear came across Leilani's face.

"I don't know about this," she said.

"Trust me," he said, "this is exactly what we're looking for."

They heard the flaps extending, and the turbulent air began to buffet the plane.

"We're coming in for a landing," Leilani said.

Kurt looked out the window. The horizon was beginning to glow, the sky changing hue. He saw no sign of land. "Depends on your definition of landing."

"What do you mean?"

"This is a seaplane," he said, "more accurately called a flying boat. It lands on the water."

Kurt was torn. One part of him was anxious to make his move before they got too close to whatever rendezvous they were heading for, the rest of him was curious as to where they were headed.

He remembered Jinn saying he needed to move to a more secure location. It would be grand if Kurt could report back and give that location to the powers that be.

But then he thought about the water tanks in the belly of the plane and the load of microbots he suspected they were carrying. He decided it would be better to move sooner rather than later.

He went to the seating area, pulled out his knife and began working on the item he'd liberated from the crate.

"I'm not even going to ask," Leilani said, looking away.

When he was finished, he slid the knife back into his boot and covered it with the leg of his pants. Next he took one of the 9mm Lugers and popped the clip out. He quickly unloaded all the shells, including the one in the chamber, and then jammed the clip back in.

He handed it to Leilani with the safety off.

"I don't like guns," she said.

"Don't think of it as a gun."

"But it *is* a gun," she insisted.

He was already moving toward the front of the plane. "Not without the bullets, it's not. It's just a big, crazy bluff, and you better wield it like Dirty Harry"—he saw the blank look appearing on her young face and changed references—"like Angelina Jolie, if you want them to believe you're going to shoot it."

"But I'm not going to shoot," she said.

As he approached the ladder that led up to the flight deck,

Kurt hoped his own bluff would be sufficient because he didn't think Leilani quite had the concept down.

"Just stay behind me and to my right, and point the gun at them," he said.

"Anything else?"

"Yeah. Try to look mean."

Kurt climbed the ladder, which was canted sideways to the flight deck.

The pilots snapped their heads around at the commotion and saw Kurt. The captain shouted. The copilot reached for his seat belt release. And Kurt showed them what he was carrying.

They stopped in their tracks, staring at a pineapple grenade in Kurt's hand. He pulled the pin in an exaggerated manner and held the safety lever, or spoon, down tight.

Leilani came up beside him, aiming the empty gun nicely. "Everybody freeze!" she growled.

The pilots had already frozen, but he appreciated the effort.

"That's right," he said. "Let's just assume that the seat belt sign is on and you're *not* free to move about the cabin."

The captain turned back to the controls, the copilot stared. "What are you talking about?"

"Hands on the yoke," Kurt ordered. "Eyes forward."

The copilot complied, but also mumbled something in Arabic to the captain.

"Are you trying to take her?" the captain asked. "To rescue her? You're a fool to throw your life away for this puny woman."

"Shut up, jerk!" Leilani growled. "Or, so help me, I'll fill you full of lead!"

She looked at Kurt, smiling proudly. "How's that?"

"We need to work on your dialogue a bit, but not bad."

Kurt glanced out the window. The horizon to the east was

starting to sharpen, but the sky was still inky purple, and for the most part it was hard to tell where it ended and the sea began.

He could see the other two jets ahead of them, but only because of their navigation lights. The closest plane looked to be a mile away and maybe a thousand feet lower. The lead plane might have been three miles out and a thousand feet below the other one. The whole squadron was descending. He heard no transmissions and assumed they were operating under radio silence.

"Where are you taking us?" he asked.

"Don't say anything," the captain ordered.

Kurt figured that was a dead end, he could hardly threaten to blow up the plane if they didn't tell him. He checked the altimeter and saw they were dropping through eight thousand feet. Another ten minutes like that and they'd be in the drink. He strained his eyes forward but still couldn't see a speck of land.

He decided they'd waited long enough. "Here's the deal," he said. "If you two want to live, you're going to do what I say."

"What if we don't?" the copilot spat.

"Then I'll blow up the plane," Kurt said.

"It's a bluff," the copilot said. "He's a weak American. He'll never have the—"

Before the man finished his sentence, Kurt backhanded him across the temple. The man's head snapped sideways, and he put a hand to the fuselage wall to steady himself.

"You think I want to end up back in Jinn's hands," Kurt said, "would you?"

The guy held the side of his face and looked back at Kurt like a scolded animal. The two pilots exchanged a look. Kurt was counting on the fact that both men knew what kind of a lunatic Jinn was. He guessed the bodies at the bottom of the well weren't the only employees he had dispensed of in his day.

An argument broke out between them in Arabic.

Kurt backhanded the copilot again. "English!"

The man glared at him and slowly began to reach for his seat belt lock once again. "You're right," he said. "Jinn will make you beg for death if he catches you. But if we let you go, it will be worse for us."

The seat belt clicked loose, and the man turned in his seat and stood, looming taller in the small cockpit.

"So blow us up," he said. "Take us all to paradise."

Kurt looked at the man, trying to stare him down. The man didn't blink, and while Kurt didn't blink either it was a standoff he couldn't win.

"So be it," Kurt said.

He let go of the spoon and flung the grenade at the copilot. It hit him in the center of his suddenly shocked face. He grabbed for it like a man in a shower trying to catch a wet bar of soap. He knocked it toward the captain.

With eyes as wide as saucers, he lunged for it, only to be intercepted by a mighty right cross from Kurt.

Kurt had put his whole body into the swing, pivoting from the hip and shoulder, pushing off with his right foot and firing his arm forward with every ounce of muscle fiber in his body.

The man went limp and fell backward on the captain and the control yoke he held, sending the aircraft into a steep dive.

Weightless for a second, Kurt collided with the ceiling. When he crashed to the floor, he lunged forward, grabbing the unconscious copilot by the belt and yanking him backward. As he pulled the dead weight off of the captain, the dive flattened out a bit, but a small pistol appeared in the captain's hand.

With a swing of his left arm, Kurt knocked the captain's hand sideways and the gun discharged. The bullet plugged the copilot in the side. A second shot hit the seat.

Kurt tried to hold the captain's arm away, but the leverage wasn't with him. The captain yanked his arm back, pulling it free and aiming at Kurt again.

Kurt ducked and shoved the yoke with his palm, pushing it over. The aircraft rolled hard as the captain fired again.

The shot missed, hitting the panel above them. It exploded in a shower of sparks. A group of warning lights came on accompanied by alarms sounding.

The plane went into a rolling dive, dropping toward the sea. It became difficult to do anything but hold on. Kurt managed to slug the captain once before being thrown back by the centrifugal force of the turning aircraft.

Kurt reached for his boot. The pistol swung his way as the captain lined up the kill shot.

Kurt thrust his arm forward and the captain stopped in mid-motion with Kurt's knife in his heart. His face went blank, the small gun dropped and his eyes drifted backward.

The plane began to roll over once again, and Kurt grabbed the control stick, fighting to counter the spin. Slowly the aircraft wings leveled. But by now the ground-proximity warning was going off and the computer voice was chirping, *Pull up. Pull up. Pull up.*

Kurt was pulling up, but he didn't want to rip the wings off. The nose came up slowly even as the altimeter continued to unwind. Finally Kurt saw the horizon again, and a second or two later the nose of the aircraft pointed above it.

As the speed bled off and they began to climb, some of the warning lights and alarms shut down. As they passed a thousand feet on the way back up, the computer stopped telling Kurt what to do.

With the plane stable and level, Kurt looked around the cockpit. He was sharing a seat with the dead captain. The copilot lay on the floor between the two seats, looking just as dead. Someone else was missing.

"Leilani?" Kurt shouted.

"I'm here," she said, poking her head back into the flight deck from below.

"What happened to you?"

"I fell down the ladder," she said, coming forward and looking a little groggy. She bent and picked something up off the floor. It was the grenade. "Why didn't we blow up?"

"I took the fuse out," Kurt said. "It's still got explosives inside, but they can't go off without the fuse."

She placed it gently in a cup holder.

"Should I tie these guys up?"

"It's a little late for that," he said. "Let's get this one out of my seat."

He stood, and Leilani unbelted the dead captain and pulled him loose while Kurt held the controls.

"You're flying the plane," she said as if she'd just realized it.

"Kind of."

"I thought you said you didn't know how to do that?"

"I should have been more precise," he said. "I can make it go side to side, up and down, fast and slow. I can probably point it in the right direction. What's going to be tougher is landing this thing without leaving a smoking crater in the ground or having it break into little pieces when it hits the water."

"Oh," she said, looking suddenly pale.

57913

"But I'm a quick study," he said, trying to boost her confidence. "And with those two dead I don't really have a choice."

Kurt had flown small planes before, never long enough to get any licenses or ratings, but he knew the basics. Most of it was instinct. Other than high-performance military aircraft, planes tended to fly themselves. They were designed to be stable and forgiving, although he found this Russian flying boat to be nose-heavy like a ship with a ballast problem.

"What about the LAPES thing?" she said. "Couldn't we drop out the back?"

"We might just try that when we get where we're going," he said.

He studied the instrument panel, spotting the controls for the rear door and tail ramp. He marked their location in his mind.

By now they'd climbed back up to five thousand feet and were back on the original course. Several miles ahead of them he saw the other two jets silhouetted against the brightening sky. They were still descending, but the nosedive and spin had brought Kurt and Leilani well below their altitude.

"They don't know what happened," Leilani said.

"No," Kurt replied. "Traveling on radio silence with no rear-view mirrors or aft radar coverage means they can't have seen a thing. More important, they won't see us turn away and head for the Seychelles."

"Is that where we're going?"

Kurt had found a navigation readout on a small computer screen. They were almost dead center of the Indian Ocean. The Seychelles were four hundred miles to the southwest, about an hour's flight away.

Kurt smiled. "Closest bit of civilization around," he said. "And by civilization, I mean somewhere that has a phone and a Coke machine and where people aren't trying to kill us."

Leilani smiled. "That sounds good to me."

Kurt found the smile endearing. It was kind and simple and uncomplicated. Somehow, uncomplicated seemed utterly perfect at the moment.

He began to turn the Russian jet to the west, figuring he'd be a hundred miles away by the time anyone even bothered to look around. But before he got too far off course, something caught his eye. A black dot on the silver sea.

Apparently Leilani saw it as well. "You think they're headed for that island?"

"We're a long way from the closest island," he said.

"Well, that's too big to be a ship," Leilani replied.

Kurt stared. The truth hit him as the light from the rising sun glinted off a series of tall triangular structures dotted around the perimeter of the floating monstrosity.

"That's because it's not a ship," he said. "It's a floating hulk of metal called Aqua-Terra."

A spike of adrenaline shot through Kurt's weary body. Three amphibious aircraft, filled with weapons, inflatable speedboats and Jinn's goons, did not qualify for the benefit of the doubt. They weren't coming for a tour of the facilities. They were an attack force, operating under radio silence, planning to hit and take over the island at the break of dawn.

"Strap yourself in," he said.

"Why?" Leilani asked. "What are we doing?"

Kurt reached over and shoved the throttles to the stops. "We're about to make our presence known."

CHAPTER 36

KURT SCANNED THE CONSOLE, LOOKING FOR THE RADIO. HIS eyes settled on a transceiver currently set to an odd frequency.

COM-1, he thought. "That's got to be Jinn's frequency," he said. "Can you find me one of those headsets?"

Leilani began to scrounge around on the floor for one of the dead pilots' headsets. She picked it up and handed it to him.

He plugged it in. He found a second transceiver and set the switches so he would still be able to hear anything coming over COM-1 but be broadcasting only over COM-2. He began to adjust the frequency to the one Nigel, the helicopter pilot, had used when they first approached Aqua-Terra.

"Can you please tell me what we're doing," Leilani asked. "I thought we were flying away from them, not getting closer."

"Several friends of mine from NUMA are down there. They've been trying to figure out what happened to your brother. They must be getting close to an answer because they're about to be attacked for it."

"Attacked?"

"I saw Jinn's men boarding the other aircraft," he said. "They're commandos. I'm pretty sure they're about to storm the island."

"I agree," she said. "We must warn them."

Kurt continued to flick through frequencies until he'd set 122.85 in the display window. "This is the one."

He listened for a second, heard nothing and then pressed the transmit switch. "Aqua-Terra, this is Kurt Austin. How do you read?"

Nothing.

As Kurt spoke, he kept his eyes on the descending transports. They seemed blissfully unaware.

"Aqua-Terra, come in."

"Try another frequency."

"No. This is the one." He pressed transmit again. "Aqua-Terra, do you copy? This is Kurt Austin. You're about to come under attack. Prepare to repel boarders."

He let go of the switch.

"Why don't they answer?" she asked.

Kurt could think of a number of reasons, the most sinister of which had to do with the impostor in their midst. She might have disabled the radio or done something worse.

The two aircraft were now dropping below two thousand feet. They'd be on the deck in a minute, probably discharging their boats using the LAPES parachutes. From the dimensions of the cargo hold he figured each plane might carry up to seventy commandos, but not with the boats and the equipment on board too. Thirty would be the max. That still meant sixty commandos against Marchetti's crew of twenty, plus Paul and Gamay. With the robots deactivated, they didn't stand a chance.

With no answer on the radio, Kurt realized the time for warnings had passed, it was time to make a move.

* * *

IN THE CENTER OF AQUA-TERRA's communications room, Zarrina stood with Otero and Matson, listening to Kurt Austin as he tried to warn his friends of the imminent attack.

Otero looked sick. "I thought Jinn said Austin and Zavala were dead?"

"Apparently he spoke too soon," Zarrina said.

"Where is it coming from?"

"It could be anywhere," she said, glancing out the window. She saw no boats on the horizon, but she did see the three aircraft approaching. One of them was well out of formation. It all but confirmed the worst of her fears.

"He's taken over on one of the jets," she said. "We need to warn Jinn. And we need leverage. Get the woman up here. Now!"

KURT PUSHED THE THROTTLES to full, and the one-hundred-and-ten-foot aircraft surged forward with surprising power.

As it accelerated, a plan formed in Kurt's mind. He watched the other jets slowing almost to stall speed as they dropped toward the water.

They'd be vulnerable as they flew along the deck, discharging their commandos, and Kurt could force them into the drink like a stock car racer wrecking his competition by putting them into the wall.

The two aircraft ahead were spaced a half mile apart at less than three hundred feet. Kurt and Leilani were closing in rapidly when suddenly Kurt heard shouting in Arabic over COM-1.

Both jets reacted instantly. Their pitch changed from nose

down to nose up, and the heat distortion trailing out behind their engines intensified rapidly.

"Damn," Kurt said. "So much for the element of surprise."

The jets began to accelerate, but Kurt was barreling down on them rapidly, moving at least a hundred knots faster. He chose the aircraft to the left and headed for it, pointing his nose down like a madman.

Kurt's aircraft charged like a hawk swooping in for the kill. The other jet was coming up, struggling to climb and pick up speed like a big, slow pigeon.

It grew larger and closer, filling the window and then disappearing from Kurt's view, flashing under them.

JINN SAT IN THE FLIGHT ENGINEER's chair in the lead aircraft, shouting instructions to the pilot. The throttles were at full, the aircraft was straining to climb and accelerate.

"Look out! He's right above you!" Zarrina shouted over the radio.

A wave of thunder and turbulence shook the aircraft. A shadow raced across the windshield, and the captain shoved the stick forward. Smoke, heat and exhaust from Kurt's engines blasted the cockpit, but the planes did not collide.

Kurt's pulling up at the last second gave them a few feet of precious space. On the other hand, the pilot's involuntary flinch and the wake turbulence from the thirty-five-thousand-pound jet roaring past sent them down and to the left, headed for the waves.

"Pull out!" Jinn shouted. "Pull out!"

The pilot rolled the wings level and pulled back on the yoke. The jet skimmed the water, touched it briefly, skipping like a stone, and then climbed skyward once again.

*   *   *

"THEY PULLED OUT," Leilani said, looking back through the side window. "Somehow, they pulled out."

Kurt thought of heading around for another run, but he was already lined up on the second plane. Plan A had failed, and with the second aircraft climbing above a thousand feet and accelerating it would have no effect this time. Still, he had to do something.

Kurt used the extra speed he'd carried to outclimb his quarry, gaining altitude faster than the other jet. Once he was above it, he angled toward the other plane and matched its course, closing in from the seven o'clock high position.

For a second he had no clue what he'd do next. But an idea came to him that felt so brilliant, he would have patted himself on the back if he could have.

He looked around the cockpit. Amid the myriad gauges and switches and screens he spotted what he was looking for.

"Grab that handle," he said, pointing.

Leilani put her hand on a thick metal bar lined with yellow-and-black warning chevrons.

"Get ready to pull it!"

As he closed in on his quarry, the plane began to shake. The slipstream coming off the other jet made him feel like a water-skier crossing a powerboat's wake. He pulled back and climbed above the turbulence and, after ten seconds, he pushed the nose forward again, knifing toward the other jet as if on a strafing run.

He raced over the top of the jet, higher than he'd been before. "Now!"

Leilani slammed the yellow-and-black down.

A great whooshing sound swept through the plane, and Kurt felt the nose pitch up and the plane all but leap skyward.

Out behind the aircraft a cloud of gray vapor had appeared, whipping backward, slamming into the second jet. Despite the vaporlike appearance, the central column of the dumped mixture was still together. Twelve thousand pounds of water and microbots hit the cockpit, shattering the windshield and crushing the pilots like a tidal wave.

The rest of the load swept over the aircraft, catching the starboard wing and engine. The turbofan exploded from the impact, compressor blades and other pieces flying outward through the cowling.

The weight of the water hammered the right wing more than the left, forcing it down and back, and the aircraft rolled over and dove seaward. It hit seconds later, cartwheeling across the ocean's surface. The impact tore the jet apart, sending people, cargo and metal shards in all directions.

Kurt realized he'd just dumped a bunch of Jinn's bots into the sea, but it was the only weapon he had at his disposal. He circled to the right, spotted the wreckage and immediately began looking for the surviving jet lest he and Leilani suffer a similar fate.

Suddenly, a voice came over the radio. Kurt recognized it as Gamay Trout's.

GAMAY TROUT SAT at the radioman's console in Aqua-Terra's communications room. The cold end of a pistol was pressed against the back of her head.

"Speak to him!" Zarrina's harsh voice demanded. "Tell him to surrender or I'll kill you all. Your husband dies first."

Paul had been forced to lie down on the floor. Matson stood

with a foot on the small of Paul's back. He pointed a Luger-style pistol toward the nape of his neck. Otero stood close by with another gun.

"Speak!"

Gamay grabbed the microphone they'd placed in front of her. She held the transmit switch. "Kurt, this is Gamay. Do you read me?"

It took a few seconds, but Kurt's voice came through in her headphones.

"Gamay, you're under attack. Take cover. Have Marchetti activate the robots."

"Tell him to surrender!" Zarrina ordered.

Gamay glanced out the window. She'd seen one of the jets go down, the other two were climbing and turning, one appearing to be stalking the other, but she had no idea which was which.

Zarrina shoved Gamay's head forward with the muzzle of the gun. "I won't ask again."

Gamay grabbed the microphone but still hesitated.

"Kill him!" Zarrina said to Otero.

"Wait!" Gamay shouted. She pressed and held the transmit switch.

"Kurt, this is Gamay," she said. "They have us already. They have us in the brig. They're going to kill us if you don't land the plane and surrender."

Silence followed. Gamay stared out the window. One of the planes had stopped maneuvering. She guessed that was Kurt. The other jet was closing in.

She watched for a second and then pressed the switch again. "Look out!" she shouted. "They're on your—"

She never finished the sentence because Zarrina knocked her from the chair. She tumbled into the wall, got up ready to throw a punch and took a kick to the stomach that knocked the wind out of her and dropped her to the ground.

Outside, she saw the two planes almost collide. They crossed paths, separated and then crossed paths again. A trail of dark smoke began to stream from one of them.

KURT REACTED TO GAMAY'S warning as fast as he could. He banked left and almost slammed into Jinn's plane. He shoved the yoke to the right, rolled the plane over and heard the sound of shells tearing into the fuselage.

Jinn's craft was matching his turn. Men were firing .50 caliber machine guns through an open cargo door.

Kurt cut back toward them. The two planes crossed paths and almost collided a third time. As Kurt peeled off and began to make a run for it, a bank of warning lights came on in the cockpit. He pointed the nose down to pick up speed, kept the throttles to the wall and retracted the flaps he'd never pulled in.

The plane accelerated, and Kurt turned to the southwest. Various warning lights continued to blink, but nothing seemed disastrous.

He juked to the left and then back to the right, remembering the rule he'd heard an old fighter pilot tell him once: *He who flies straight, dies.*

After several sets of these maneuvers, he still hadn't seen Jinn's plane.

He kept the jet on the deck and at full speed. He made a slight turn to the west. So far, so good. But still no sign of Jinn.

"Do you see him?"

Leilani was swinging her head around, doing everything she

could to spot the other craft. Kurt turned to the right, hoping to give her a wider view.

"No," she said. "Wait . . . yes. He's behind us," she said excitedly. "He seems to be falling back. He's heading lower."

That didn't sound right. "Are you sure?"

"Yes, we're leaving him behind. I think he's landing."

Kurt couldn't believe their luck. He wondered why Jinn would be letting him go.

Zarrina's voice came over the radio. "Kurt Austin, you will land and surrender or I will kill your friends."

The line stayed open, and the sound of someone grunting in pain and then screaming reached his ears.

"You harm them and you're a dead woman, Zarrina," he said, returning a threat with a threat.

Kurt had no choice but to run. Surrendering wouldn't stop them from murdering his friends. It would just mean there were no witnesses around to report it. But if he could escape, that turned the tables. It meant Zarrina and Jinn had to worry about being discovered and facing retribution. Sometimes those thoughts protected prisoners who were otherwise considered expendable.

"You harm them and there won't be anyplace in this world where I won't hunt you down."

Above him, more warning lights came on. Static and feedback came through the headphones.

"I look forward to it," Zarrina replied. A shot rang out, the transmission ended and the COM panel went dark. Kurt flipped the switch a few times and got nothing.

"Radio's down," he said.

"What are we going to do?" Leilani demanded.

"Head southwest and follow the original plan."

He hoped he hadn't just sacrificed the Trouts, but he had no choice. They had to make it to the Seychelles or at least to a vessel in the shipping lanes. They could signal a ship and ditch nearby, but either way they had to get away from Aqua-Terra.

THE FURY IN JINN AL-KHALIF'S eyes burned hot enough to melt steel. The distance between his aircraft and Austin's continued to grow. Austin was escaping, and carrying with him both a woman Jinn desired to have and, more important, the secret of his whereabouts, a secret he needed to maintain.

"Why are they faster than us?" Jinn demanded to know.

"He dumped the cargo," the pilot replied. "They're six tons lighter than us. Thirty knots faster at least. If you want to catch them, we have to jettison our cargo as well. Otherwise we lose a mile every two minutes."

Jinn considered this. He'd suffered a major defeat already. One plane down, another in the hands of an enemy he wanted to see dead. Two cargos gone, there was no telling what percentage of the microbots had survived either impact.

"Even if we dump the cargo," the pilot said, "we'll only be able to match his speed. We'll never catch him."

Jinn had a better idea. He unlatched his seat belt. "Land," he said. "Immediately."

CHAPTER 37

KURT HELD THE JET ON A COURSE DUE WEST FROM AQUA-
Terra. He pulled back on the stick slightly, bringing the aircraft
into a shallow climb, nursing every bit of speed he could from it.
He was bitter, angry and oblivious to any thought beyond escape
and informing the authorities of Jinn's actions. A stinging sensation in his eyes snapped him out of it.

"Smoke," Leilani said.

Kurt glanced around. The cockpit was filling with it. Banks of
new warnings lit up. The plane began to shake, the controls got
heavy. Kurt fought it for a while but it felt like the hydraulics
were going out.

Stall. Stall. Stall. The computer voice was talking again, this
time a warning instead of advice.

Kurt leveled off and the stall warning ceased, but the problems
did not end there.

In a moment it seemed like every device in the cockpit was
either flashing or beeping or chirping an alarm. Kurt had no idea
what any of it meant aside from the obvious.

"Time to go," he said.

He stabbed at the autopilot button and jumped from the seat. In a blink he and Leilani were down the ladder and racing through the cargo hold.

"Get in the boat!" Kurt yelled, pointing to the rigid inflatable near the tail end of the plane. With the plane shaking, he found a lever for the cargo hatch and threw it over. The ramp began to drop, the wind whistled in and around them. Smoke and kerosene fumes swirled in.

"Turn around," he shouted to Leilani. "Feet forward."

As Leilani turned, the plane began to shudder like it was encountering heavy turbulence, Kurt guessing the hydraulics were going and the autopilot was struggling to compensate.

He released the straps that held the boat to the floor and clambered in, landing on top of Leilani and, to his surprise, the guard he'd knocked cold an hour ago.

"Hold on!" he yelled, wrapping his arms around Leilani and latching onto a handhold in the transom with a death grip that left his knuckles white. With a flick of the wrist, he released the drogue chute.

A small "leader" chute was sucked out first. It yanked the others from their packs. The boat shot backward and then slammed to a stop a few inches from the edge of the ramp.

Kurt looked up. A third strap he hadn't seen led from the nose of the boat to a tie-down in the center of the cargo hold. It was stretched taut like the leash on an angry pit bull and it showed no signs of breaking.

BY THE TIME JINN'S AIRCRAFT touched down on the water, Jinn was already in the cargo bay, hoisting a rocket launcher onto his shoulder and aiming it at the small dot that was Kurt's aircraft.

He activated the sight. The system locked onto the heat coming from Austin's fleeing aircraft. A green light and a high-pitched tone confirmed that the target had been acquired.

"No!" the pilot warned.

Jinn pulled the trigger. The missile leapt from its case and shot out over the water. The propellant ignited and a streak of orange fire raced away from them. Jinn watched as the brilliant flare from the tail of the missile closed in on Austin's fleeing aircraft. He counted the seconds.

KURT'S PLANE WAS BURNING and coming apart around them. The renegade strap held them in place. A two-thousand-foot drop awaited, but the parachutes that might lower them down safely would be shredded in seconds if he didn't act.

He rose up, pulled the pistol from his belt and wedged his foot under the thug who was tied down. Holding tight to one of the boat's grab handles with his left hand, he fired the gun with his right.

The bullet pierced the nylon. The belt snapped in two and the boat was yanked backward again as if pulled from the plane by a giant hand.

For an instant they were in daylight, but the smoke that trailed the plane engulfed them, and then the flash and concussion wave of an explosion shook the sky. A billowing cloud of burning kerosene mushroomed in all directions ahead of them, filling the air with thick black smoke.

The boat—fortunately, still attached to the chutes—plunged into the smoke, traveling forward and down like an arrow.

*   *   *

JINN SAW THE MISSILE hit Austin's aircraft. The initial flare of impact was followed by two other explosions, each bigger than the last. Black clouds of smoke expanded in all directions. Flaming debris arced through it, curving downward like a series of falling comets, drawing smoke trails across the dark morning of the western sky.

The explosion was at least five miles off. Jinn's only regret was that he hadn't been able to see Austin burn up close where he could have watched his skin peel and blacken as the fire engulfed him. Still, it was a satisfying display, and one he was quite certain even Kurt Austin could not live through.

DESPITE JINN'S BELIEF, Kurt was alive. He'd felt the heat of the detonation and knew instantly that the plane had exploded, though he knew nothing about Jinn's missile. Nor did he care. His only concern was holding on as he, Leilani and their prisoner dropped through the air in the inflatable boat.

When first yanked out of the cargo hold, the small boat flew almost flat on its keel like a dart flung at its board. But the parachutes were attached at the back of the boat, designed to slow it as it launched from a few feet off the deck, not to drop it safely from a great height. As the speed and momentum of the boat slowed, the nose began to pitch down.

By the time they entered the cloud of smoke, they were pointed downward about fifteen degrees, with the chutes trailing out behind them like feathers on a dart. It felt nothing like the smooth drop of a normal skydive. It was more like riding a toboggan down a black-diamond ski slope.

The boat shook and shuddered and the angle grew steeper. Out behind them, one of the chutes seemed to have been hit with debris and was fraying in the middle. Up ahead Kurt saw only smoke and darkness.

Suddenly, the surface of the ocean appeared. The nose of the boat hit the water, submarined for a second and then burst free. Kurt was actually flung up into the air, but he gripped the handle like a bull rider in the rodeo and managed to land in the boat.

They skidded forward forty yards or more before slowing to a stop and the chutes settled on the water behind them.

They'd landed amid the debris field from the shattered aircraft. Smoke surrounded them. Flames flitted across the water, making pools of burning kerosene, while tiny flakes of debris and insulation from the plane fluttered down like confetti.

For several seconds neither he nor Leilani spoke. They just sat in the boat, still gripping the handholds. The prisoner, who could not possibly know what had just happened, was staring at them with eyes like saucers.

Finally Kurt let go and began to look around.

"I can't believe we're still alive," Leilani managed.

Kurt could hardly believe it either. He had the distinct sense of their luck changing for the better.

"Not only are we alive," he said, "but we're in a boat with an outboard motor on the back."

He moved toward it, checking for fuel. He thought of releasing the chutes but realized that once something was gone they couldn't retrieve it, and he considered the fact that the open boat offered no shade. He grabbed the lines and reeled them in hand over hand.

"Let's store these," he said to Leilani, "we might need them later. And see if you can find something to bail some of this water."

A good twenty gallons were sloshing around in the boat's interior.

As Leilani wrapped the nylon chutes in their cords and tucked them into a space near the front of the boat, Kurt primed the outboard. It started on the third try and was soon running smoothly.

He twisted the throttle and pointed the boat west, guiding it between the fires and through the smoke.

They came out on the other side of the smoke field, and the clear air felt glorious.

"Where are we going?" Leilani asked.

"Away from *them*," Kurt said. With the smoke and the burning wreckage between them and Aqua-Terra, he hoped they'd be invisible for a while.

"But we can't make it to Seychelles in this."

"No. But we might reach the shipping lanes and be able to flag down some help."

Kurt's check of the fuel level showed half a tank. By the smell of things, the rest had poured out on the way down. How far they could go was anybody's guess. Once they'd made some distance, he would ease back on the throttle to conserve fuel, but for now he held it wide open and the little boat ran like the wind on the flat gray sea.

All seemed well for about forty minutes until Kurt noticed Leilani squeezing the inflated sidewall like one might squeeze a melon at the supermarket.

"What's wrong?"

Her eyes remained on the inflated chamber. "We seem to have sprung a leak," she said.

"A leak?"

She nodded. "Not water coming in. Air . . . going out."

CHAPTER 38

KURT HELD THE BOAT ON A WESTERLY HEADING WHILE Leilani looked for the source of the leak and any way to fix it.

"What do you see?"

"Half a dozen little pinpricks," she said. "I can feel the air leaking through them."

He waved her to the back. "Drive the boat for a second."

She came back to the transom, and Kurt took a look at what she'd found. Eight little holes, some of which were so small he could press the rubber together and the air stopped escaping.

"What do you think happened?" Leilani asked.

The holes were spread out in a weird pattern, almost a spray pattern, running from front to back. "Shrapnel from the plane," he guessed, "or even tiny drops of burning kerosene. The rubber looks singed in a spot or two."

Kurt ran his hands along the other air chambers, which were basically inflated rubber tubes, eight feet long and seventeen inches in diameter. The boat had four total, two in the front that ran straight and then angled together to create the blunt nose of the boat, and two in the rear, one on each side. The back of the boat was a metal transom on which the outboard was mounted.

He found two more pinpricks, both in the front right chamber. Worse yet, he could see little dots here and there that looked like they might have been additional impact zones for shrapnel or fuel. He wondered how long until those opened up.

"How does it look?" Leilani asked.

The prisoner seemed anxious to know as well. He might have been gagged, but his ears weren't blocked.

"The port side seems okay," Kurt said. "But that's not going to help us if the whole starboard side goes flat."

Two small lockers rested in the deck near the front. He opened both, only to find a single life jacket, a couple of flares, a small anchor and some rope.

"Rubber boat without a pump or a repair kit," he mumbled. "Somebody's going to hear from my lawyer."

"Maybe we should turn around," Leilani said, "go back to that floating island and surrender."

"Not unless you want to be a prisoner again," he said.

"No," she said, "I don't want to drown either."

"We won't drown even if both of them go flat."

"But we'll be stuck clinging to the other side like shipwreck survivors," she said.

"Better than waiting for Jinn to shoot us," he said. "Besides, I have a bet to win. All we have to do is push on until we find some help."

"And if we don't find help?"

"We will," Kurt insisted, feeling confident.

He reached into the locker and pulled out the flares, which he stuffed into his breast pocket next to the binoculars. He grabbed the life jacket and handed it to Leilani.

"Put this on," he said. "Don't worry, it's just a precaution."

Next he pulled out the anchor—a fifteen-pound fluke anchor hooked to an anchor rope by a large carabiner. He detached the anchor from the rope and hooked it onto the cord that bound the prisoner's feet. The man looked up at Kurt in terror.

"Also just a precaution," Kurt told him.

The man's face showed little faith in that statement.

Kurt pulled the gag off the man's face. "I know you understand when we talk," he said. "Do you speak English as well?"

The man nodded. "I speak . . . some."

"I don't suppose you know the story of the little Dutch boy?"

The man stared at him blankly.

"This boat is sinking," Kurt explained, "losing air. I can either throw you overboard to lighten our load or you can help us."

"I'll help," the man said. "Yes, yes, I definite want to help."

"The anchor is on your feet to keep you from trying anything stupid," Kurt explained, and then he pointed to the forward section. "I need you to cover up these two holes and keep the air in."

The man nodded. "I can do that. Definite, big-time."

"Good," Kurt said. "'Cause if you don't, you're going to hit the bottom of the sea faster than the rest of us."

Kurt loosened the ropes around the man's wrists and pulled them free. "What's your name?"

"I am called Ishmael," the man said.

"Great," Kurt mumbled. "As if we didn't have enough to worry about. Let's hope we don't encounter an angry white whale."

With his legs still tied together and hooked to the anchor, Ishmael twisted and slithered a foot or so until he reached the prow of the boat. He placed his hands on the two leaks Kurt had pointed out.

"Press and hold," Kurt said.

Ishmael pressed his fingers on the two spots and held them down. After a few seconds, he looked back, smiling.

"Perfect."

"What about the other leaks?" Leilani asked.

"I'll take first shift," Kurt said, trying to spread his fingers like a piano player, "you keep us pointed west."

Kurt and Leilani switched positions twice in the next three hours, but the rear chamber continued to deflate and the boat began to list to starboard and the aft corner settled. From time to time seawater washed over the top, soaking whoever was trying to stem the leak and weighing them down even further.

Fortunately, the Indian Ocean was the calmest of the world's major seas and the swell was very small, only a foot at most. Kurt found that lower speeds kept the breaches to a minimum and he backed off the throttle just a bit.

As noon approached, they still hadn't encountered anything resembling help, not even a trail of smoke on the horizon. With the sun high overhead, the outboard began to sputter and Kurt had no choice but to shut it off.

"Out of gas," Leilani guessed.

"We have a gallon or so in the reserve tank," he said, pointing to a stopcock on the fuel line that could be turned to access the reserve. "But we need to save that."

"Save it for what?"

"Suppose we see a ship on the horizon," he said. "We'll need to intercept it, to get in front of it or at least alongside."

She nodded. "Sorry."

He smiled. "It's okay."

In the absence of the droning outboard, the silence felt oppressive and ominous, like a sign of their eventual doom. There was no wind. The only sound that could be heard was the light chop slapping against the sides of the boat.

Bathed in this silence, they bobbed up and down, wallowing in the low swells, three people aboard a sixteen-foot inflatable boat in a million square miles of ocean.

"Now what?" Leilani asked.

"Now we wait," Kurt said patiently. "And see what fortune holds for us."

CHAPTER 39

JOE ZAVALA HAD SPENT FIFTEEN HOURS IN THE CARGO HOLD of an unknown ship with only a group of trucks and untold billions of microbots for company. Another man might have gone stir-crazy and given himself up, banging on the doors just to get out. Joe had put the time to good use.

He'd searched each truck thoroughly. He'd found three bottles of water, drinking two of them and saving the third. He'd also discovered a plastic Ziploc-style bag filled with some type of jerky. Beef it wasn't, but goat or camel or lamb it might have been. He ate as much as he could and put the rest back.

He'd also measured out the confines, took a look under the hoods of the trucks and come up with several alternate plans of action. He'd even considered sabotaging the engines, pulling out distributor wires, tampering with the carburetors or attempting to loosen the oil plugs so the big rigs either wouldn't start or would break down shortly after they got going.

He chose not to. If the trucks couldn't go, he couldn't get off the ship. If they moved and then broke down twenty miles into whatever land they were heading to, Joe might be stuck some-where worse than Yemen—and surrounded by angry militants to boot.

He considered breaking out. The huge doors were still pinned shut, but Joe was pretty certain he could bash them open with all the horsepower he had available. But then what? Based on what he remembered about their entry into the freighter and the thick layer of tire marks on the floor, he figured he was near the back end of some kind of dedicated transport. Almost like an auto ferry.

It wasn't a roll on/roll off ship because there was no front exit, but it was definitely designed for vehicles. From the way it wal-lowed and swayed he didn't think it was all that large either, which meant they probably weren't taking him too far.

He decided not to break out. The only thing that would lead to was going overboard. Instead he waited, took a nap in the bed of the lead truck and woke to the sound of shouting on the decks above.

It felt as if the ship was slowing and maneuvering in smaller increments.

The sound of horns and whistles from other ships suggested they were near a port or harbor somewhere. Joe sensed the time for action approaching. If the ship docked in this mystery port, he was finding a way off even if this wasn't the truck's final destination.

Finally the sound of rattling came from the rear doors. Some-one was working a heavy padlock. Moments later light spilled into the hold as the doors began to slide open.

CHAPTER 40

It was late afternoon. The sun was setting in the western sky. Jinn had secured his ownership of the floating island, bringing on board thirty men, heavy machine guns, RPGs and even a dozen ground-to-air missiles, minus the one he'd used against Kurt Austin.

The flying boat sat, fueled and waiting, in the marina in case he had to leave quickly. He felt safe, he felt secure. He would not have to concern himself with Xhou or the other members of the consortium here, nor would he face any repercussions from the Americans who were still in the dark as to his methods and goals.

Such success had put him in a boasting mood. He stood on the observation deck that jutted out from Aqua-Terra's control room. The annoying Americans and the Italian billionaire stood near the edge, hands cuffed to the rail in front of them. Zarrina and a couple of Jinn's men stood behind them. Otero sat just inside the door of the control room, his fingers on the keys of a laptop.

"I suppose you're wondering why you're still alive," he said to his three most important prisoners.

"We're alive because you need us to keep up the façade," the tall man said, apparently speaking for the others. "To pretend everything is smooth as silk here if anyone calls in. Which will happen soon and which we're not going to help you to do."

A smirk crossed Jinn's face. They weren't stupid, but they were certainly not up on current events. Jinn approached the tall man from behind.

"Paul, is it?"

"That's right."

It bothered Jinn that this man Paul was so much taller than him. He remembered Sabah telling him that a king's throne was always the tallest chair in the room and that the Shah of Iran used to hold court in a room with only one chair, his. All others had to stand while he sat a full head higher than them.

Jinn swung his leg, bringing the pointed toe of his boot across the back of the American's knees, chopping him down.

The man let out a grunt of pain and surprise. He dropped straight down, hitting his chin on the rail as he fell. He bit a chunk from his lip, and blood filled his mouth.

"That's better," Jinn said, towering above the man now that he was on his knees. "Don't bother to get up."

"You bastard," the woman said.

"Ah, the loyal wife," Jinn said. "This is why I know you will do as I say. Because if either one of you disobeys, I will cause excruciating pain to the other."

"You don't need to do this," Marchetti begged. "I'll pay you for our release and the release of my crew. I can give you a fortune. I have millions, close to a hundred million in liquid assets, money that Matson and Otero don't have access to. Just let us leave."

"A long time ago I heard someone make a similar proposal," Jinn said. "*All that I have for one child.* I now realize why the offer was denied. Your bid is a drop in the bucket. It is meaningless to me."

Jinn turned back toward the control room, making eye contact with Otero. "The time has come. Signal the horde, bring it to the surface."

"Are you sure about this?" Zarrina asked.

Jinn had waited long enough already. "Our ability to affect the weather had been limited by keeping the horde beneath the surface. To fulfill our destiny, not to mention our promises, we need to cool the ocean more quickly."

"What about the American satellites? If the effect is noticed, we'll have bigger problems to deal with than these people from NUMA."

"Otero has plotted the paths, altitudes and transits of every spy and weather satellite that crosses this section of the ocean. By directing the horde from here, we can signal them to rise and drop back at far more precise intervals than we could from Yemen. They will appear when no one is watching. They will disappear again before the eyes of the world ever turn their way."

"Sounds complicated," she said.

"Less so than you would think," Jinn insisted. "This is the open ocean. Aside from the occasional warship, there's not much worth looking at. The world's spy satellites are aimed a thousand miles to the north, watching the armies and oil of the Middle East. They study Iran and Syria and Iraq, they count Russian tanks and aircraft near the Caspian Sea or American battle groups in the Persian Gulf."

He looked to Otero. "How long is the current window?"

Otero checked his computer. "We have fifty-three minutes before the next satellite comes in range."

"Then do as I command," Jinn ordered.

Otero nodded and brought up the control screen and typed in Jinn's nine-digit code. The line-of-sight transmission would be broadcast all the way to the horizon. From there the bots would signal one another like dominoes.

He hit the ENTER key. "Signal processing now."

Jinn stared out across the water, waiting to catch sight of the display. It took a minute before the first sign appeared, but then the ocean's surface began to change quickly.

There had been no wind to speak of throughout the day, and the sea was glassy around them. But as the bots surfaced, the smooth appearance took on a grainy look, like a secluded bay choked with algae.

Jinn watched as the effect spread in all directions, running into the distance. It soon reached the limits of his vision, but he knew it went far beyond, at least fifty miles in every direction. Thinner wisps of his creation stretching for a hundred miles beyond that, spreading forth like the arms of a galaxy.

"Direct them to spread their wings."

Otero began tapping away once again. "Order encoded," he said. "Transmitting . . . now."

Jinn slipped a pair of expensive sunglasses from his pocket. He expected the dark lenses would be necessary in a moment or two. He slid them over his eyes as the surface of the sea began to evolve once again.

A wave seemed to travel through it, almost like a tremor. The color went from a leaden gray to a dull gloss and then began to brighten until the sea around them shimmered with a mirrorlike finish. With the afternoon sun still high overhead, the effect was blinding even through the shield of polarized glass.

Jinn saw the prisoners staring in wonder and then turning away as the glare became painful to look at.

Jinn squinted and stared for just a moment, his chest swelling with pride.

Out on the surface of the sea, trillions upon trillions of his tiny machines had unfolded mirrored wings, hidden until then under shells like those on the back of a beetle. The act tripled the surface area of each microbot. The reflective surface of the wings quadrupled the amount of sunlight bounced back into the upper atmosphere and away from the ocean.

It was as if a reflective blanket had been pulled across five thousand square miles of the Indian Ocean.

Gamay made the connection first.

"The temperature change," she said. "This is how it's being done."

"Yes," Jinn said. "And the cooling trend will now accelerate. These waters are already four degrees colder than the coldest temperature ever measured here at this time of year. Based on my calculations, the surface temperature will drop another full degree by nightfall. Each day, the effect will deepen. Soon, a giant well of chilled water will occupy the center of this tropical ocean while in another section of the ocean the microbots are doing the exact opposite, absorbing heat, keeping the ocean warm. The temperature differential will create winds, for some it will bring storms, for others it will smash all hope of avoiding a monstrous famine."

"You're insane. You'll kill millions of people."

"The *famine* will kill them," he corrected.

She fell silent. Neither of the other two spoke. All three of them kept their eyes turned away from the blazing reflection.

Jinn bathed in the crystalline light as if it were glory itself.

Certainly it was vindication, and proof of the godlike powers he now held in the palm of his hand.

"You'll never get away with this," Paul said.

"And just who is going to stop me?"

"My government, for one," Paul added. "The Indian government, NATO, the UN. No one is going to let you starve half a continent. Your little force here won't last long against a squadron of F-18s."

Jinn stared at Paul. "You operate from a fundamental misunderstanding of power," he said. "True, I and my people are inconsequential in the global scheme. But power does not exist only in your nations. It exists in balance all around the world. Once the rainfall begins to feed Chinese mouths, the Chinese will not allow the UN or your government or the men in New Delhi to redirect their newfound bounty so quickly. They will veto any resolution to act, frustrating your desires to proceed. They will be joined by the countries of the Middle East and Pakistan and the Russians, all of whom will benefit from what I've wrought and who will pay me and protect me for what they receive. It will be an easy thing to play them against your nation. If you believe otherwise, you are hopelessly naive."

"You risk war," Gamay said. "Enough to engulf the whole world, you included."

"More likely, just a bidding war."

He relished the moment. In little over twenty-four hours he'd crushed his enemies, both internal and external. He'd proven his brilliance and now he would reap the rewards. Money would pour in from China and new partners he'd take on in Pakistan and Saudi Arabia. Counteroffers from India and other lands would follow and the bidding would rise.

"They'll still come after you and your vile creation," Paul said.

"Of course they will," Jinn replied. "But they will never find me, and they will prove to be no more capable of destroying what I have built than they are of eradicating the world's insects or bacteria. So they kill millions of the horde. The trillions that remain will continue to reproduce. It will be a simple matter for the microbots to take the remnants of their dead and use the same materials to build new ones. That's what they do. That's what Marchetti designed them to do."

Marchetti looked away, shaking his head in anguished regret.

"And there will be consequences if anyone challenges me," Jinn added. "The horde will spread to the far corners of the world. The seven seas will soon be under my control. If any nation is foolish enough to defy me or simply refuses to pay the tribute I will demand, they will suffer. Their fishing grounds will be destroyed, their food sources consumed before their very eyes, their ports will be overrun and blockaded, their ships attacked in transit."

"They'll come after you in person," snapped Paul. "You're the snake, all they have to do is cut off your head."

"They will be well advised to leave the snake alone," Jinn insisted. "For I have already programmed a doomsday code into the horde. Should I die or be forced to activate it for other reasons, the horde will go from a weapon wielded with precision to a scourge of unimaginable proportions, consuming and growing and attacking everything in its path. Like the locusts of the desert, it will leave nothing but death behind it."

The two Americans looked at each other. If Jinn measured the look right, it was one of defeat. The silence that followed confirmed this for him.

He wiped his brow. He was beginning to sweat as the air

temperature around the island began to rise with all the re-flected energy. A breeze began to blow across the deck, the first one in days, but it wasn't cool and refreshing. It was a hot wind caused by the differential heating. It marked the beginning of the storm.

CHAPTER 41

AFTER SEVERAL HOURS OF FLOATING, LUCK HAD SHOWN
Kurt nothing but contempt.

The sun beat down on them, blocked only by the makeshift
tarp of the parachutes. The rear air chamber was so far down now
that it made little sense trying to keep it from deflating further.
The boat was tilted over, awash in that right rear corner like a car
with a flat tire. And despite Ishmael's valiant effort, the right
front cylinder was looking weaker all the time.

Kurt gazed out through a small gash in the parachute the way
a child might look through holes cut in the bedsheet of a ghost's
costume.

"Anything?" Leilani asked.

"No," he said. The word came out hoarsely. Despite the water
he'd guzzled on the airplane, his throat was getting dry once again.

"Maybe we should start the engine," Leilani said. "We must
not be in the shipping lanes."

Kurt knew for certain that they weren't. Few ships passed

across the dead center of the Indian Ocean. His hope had been to get close enough to Africa to reach a north-south route from the Red Sea or a tanker route from the Gulf, plowed by ships too big to pass through the Suez and making their way for the Horn of Africa.

They'd fallen well short of those goals. By at least a hundred miles.

"We can't get there on the gas we have left."

"But we can't just stay here," she said.

"We have one gallon of fuel," he said. "We're not wasting it and then wishing we had it."

Leilani stared at him, her eyes filled with fear. She was trembling. "I don't want to die."

"Neither do I," Kurt said. "Neither does Ishmael. Right, Ishmael?"

"Right," Ishmael said. "Not ready for that. Not ready to die, big-time."

"And we're not going to die," Kurt said. "Just stay calm."

She nodded, still near the aft section, trying to keep the cylinder from completely deflating.

"Might as well move up front," he said. "That one's had it."

Leilani let go of the rubber fabric and moved to the front of the boat on the port side. With her weight up front, the rear corner rose a fraction and the boat wallowed a bit less.

Kurt looked out from under the makeshift tent again. From the position of the sun he guessed it was three o'clock or so. He was waiting for nightfall. Once the stars came out, he could determine more exactly where they were and they could make their plans accordingly.

Kurt let his gaze fall to the horizon and watched as a strange effect took hold. It was something like the shimmer of a mirage on an open road in the desert. He blinked twice as if his eyes were deceiving him, but the effect only intensified.

Without a sound the sea began to shimmer. It wasn't the dappled sun on the water that every mariner and amateur painter knows so well but an almost effervescent appearance.

It was brightest to the west, in line with the afternoon sun, but he could see the same thing looking to the east, north and south as well.

"Kurt!" Leilani shouted.

He looked back under the tarp.

"You're sparkling."

Kurt would have looked at himself, but he was too entranced by what he saw on her. She looked as if she'd been spritzed with stardust.

Ishmael wore a similar coating, but Leilani was covered the worst. It was as if they'd been coated with a fine spray of reflective highway paint.

"What is it?" she asked.

Kurt looked at his palms, rubbing his fingers across it. The reflective dust spread like wet powder, some of it coming off. The glittering effect was plainly visible, but no matter how hard he squinted the cause was impossible to see. Nor could he feel it, even when trying to rub it between his fingers. All of which meant one thing.

"Jinn's microbots," he said.

He explained what they were and pointed out how the sea was filled with them. Looking straight down, he saw that the concentration was like a spoonful of sugar thrown onto a black dinner plate. He felt the heat reflecting off it. He explained that some of the little machines had been found on the catamaran.

"Are they harmful to us?" Leilani asked.

"I don't think so," Kurt said. He left out the part about them consuming organic matter. Fortunately, the ones on their skin didn't appear to be in eating mode like the ones in Marchetti's lab. "All the same, I wouldn't mind stumbling across a boat with a good shower right about now."

Leilani tried to smile.

Kurt had no way of knowing that they were near the edge of Jinn's horde and that the concentration he was seeing and the reflective effect they were witnessing was nothing compared to what Paul, Gamay and Marchetti had seen from the balcony of Aqua-Terra's control room. Still, he found it hard to take his eyes off the sparkling sea.

As he stared, a breeze tugged at his sleeve and ruffled the parachute tarp. Without moving, Kurt looked toward the bow and watched as the tarp rose up, settled softly and then rose again.

The breeze grew stronger, and Kurt had to grab the lines to keep the big chute from billowing out. He turned to Leilani. "Tie this chute to those handles on the right and get the other one out."

Leilani was already moving, not even questioning him. The breeze was blowing in from behind them and slightly north. It was a hot wind like the Santa Anas of California or the siroccos of the Sahara. It felt like a hair dryer on his back, but Kurt didn't care.

He and Leilani worked rapidly. The boat was equipped with a half dozen separate handholds and a pair of cleat handles up front. In a minute, the lines of both parachutes were tied off to these eight points and were snapping taut as the chutes billowed out in front of the boat.

They filled like sails, and the boat began to move, pulled along by the two parachutes as if they were a pair of magical horses. As the chutes caught more and more wind, the boat picked up some speed. The deflated parts of the boat kept it from moving as fast as it had with the outboard running, but at least it was going.

Kurt had no idea where a wind in these doldrums had appeared from, but he didn't care. They were moving again and moving was better than sitting any day.

Gusts blew in, the lines snapped and strained, yanking the boat forward.

"Hang on!" Kurt shouted for at least the third or fourth time that day. "I have a feeling this is going to be a wild ride."

CHAPTER 42

AQUA-TERRA'S BRIG SAT ON THE LOWEST LEVEL OF THE island that was above the waterline. Now back in their luxury cell, Paul, Gamay and Marchetti were similarly at their absolute lowest. For exactly fifty-three minutes Jinn had kept them cuffed to the rail out in the blazing solar reflection, the swirling gusts and the heat.

Paul Trout had never seen the inside of a tanning booth in his life, but it felt like the observation deck had been turned into just that, with heat and blinding light added for good measure.

It had been a surreal experience as reflections danced across Aqua-Terra in a dizzying, almost hypnotic display. Because the tiny mirrors moved independently on the water, the light they reflected also moved independently, making it impossible to really study the effect. Paul could only get a sense of it, like being in a swirling fog and yet knowing that it was made up of billions of independent molecules of water vapor as opposed to being a single thing.

And as hard as it was to look at the decks and structures around them, it was impossible to look at the ocean for any length of time. To protect his eyes, Paul had kept them shut tight for most of the fifty-three minutes. As a result, his main impression of the ocean's surface was a glittering mass like an endless sea of diamonds. Low ripples ran through it, brought on by minor swells that hadn't been present an hour before. Wind currents stirred up by the reflected heat swept across the shimmering surface, making it appear almost like a living thing. It was breathing, moving, waiting. In a way, it was as beautiful as it was terrifying.

Eventually the time expired and Jinn had given the order, turning the sea of diamonds gray once again. The bots quickly submerged and the ocean looked like any other throughout the world.

"I feel like I fell asleep on the beach," Paul said, amazed at how taut and red his skin was.

Across from him, Marchetti paced and occasionally checked the view through the large windows while Gamay sat beside him and attempted to apply some sort of first-aid balm to his split lip and bloody tongue.

"At least we know how they've been able to tamper with the water temperature," Marchetti said.

"Please hold still," Gamay asked.

She held a swab and some antibacterial ointment from a first-aid kit at the ready, but each time she'd moved in Paul started to speak again.

"Fat lot of good it'll do us," he said.

"Paul."

"I am holding still."

"Not the part I'm trying to fix."

Paul nodded and held his mouth open like a patient at the dentist.

Marchetti stopped his pacing. "The question is, what will happen now that they've put their plan into overdrive?"

Paul hesitated, waiting as long as he could. "I can tell you exactly what's going to happen," he said finally.

Gamay exhaled sharply and pulled back.

"They're creating a massive column of cold water, with temperatures more at home in the North Atlantic than here in the middle of a tropical sea. Temperature gradients like that are known to intensify or even create storms and cyclones. Not just in the air but under the surface."

"And once they stop radiating the heat back into the air, the cold water will start absorbing heat from the air above it again," Marchetti said, "reversing the equation."

"If this plan continues," Paul added, "the ambient air temperature will drop rapidly, but only above the one area they've affected. The rest of the ocean will still be hot and humid. Have you ever seen what happens when hot and humid air combines with cold?"

"Storms," Marchetti said.

Paul nodded. "I was in Oklahoma several years back when a cold front blew through after three days of humidity. They had a hundred tornadoes touch down over a three-day period. I'm guessing out here we'll see one big storm: a tropical depression or a cyclone. We might see a hurricane form all around us."

Gamay had given up trying to dab Paul's lip. "But this is the dead zone," she said. "The storms don't usually form here. They form to the north and east, and they track toward India. That's where the monsoons come from."

Paul considering the implications. "We're almost on the equator. A storm forming here will track west and get swept up toward Somalia, Ethiopia and Egypt," he guessed.

"That's already happening," Marchetti said. "I read something about record rains in the Sudanese highlands and southern Egypt. The article said Lake Nasser had risen to a level not seen in thirty years."

Paul remembered hearing something similar. "And that's probably just the beginning."

Marchetti was pacing, rubbing his chin with one hand and looking very shaky. "What happens once the air is destabilized into a storm?"

Paul looked off toward the windows, facing southwest. He was recalling lectures on storm generation and the factors that built them. "Hurricanes in the Gulf intensify over hot spots. Jinn's storms will travel over nothing but that. They'll steal the heat, moisture and the energy that usually goes into the monsoon. They'll carry it off like thieves."

"Leaving India and Southeast Asia unusually dry at this time of year," Gamay said. "This madman has done what people have sought to do for all eternity: he's taken control of the weather, turning it away from its normal pattern."

Marchetti sat down awkwardly. He all but collapsed on the edge of the seat. "And he's used my design to do it," he said.

He looked over at them. The billionaire with overflowing confidence was gone, as was the proud designer with the bold ideas and even the rational engineer. All the different personas seemed to vanish before their eyes, leaving only a broken man behind.

"All those people," he whispered. "A billion people waiting for a monsoon that's never going to come. I'll be the worst mass murderer in history."

Gamay looked as if she were about to jump in and say something to buck Marchetti up. This was the moment when she usually did, but she couldn't seem to find the words.

Paul gave it a try. "Your legacy isn't written yet. Alfred Nobel invented dynamite and ran a company that built weapons and armaments, but nobody remembers him for that. And you still have a chance to change the direction of things."

"But we're alone," Marchetti said. "Your friends are gone. No one even knows what's happening out here."

Paul looked at Gamay because he shared her grief for their friends and because he loved her and wanted her to feel something more than despair. He squeezed her hands and looked into her eyes. "I know all that," he said to Marchetti. "But we'll find a way. First we have to get out of here."

Gamay smiled a bit. It was a hopeful look, not quite enough to replace all the doubt and pain, but it was a start.

"Any inkling as to how?" Marchetti asked.

Paul looked around. "I do have one idea," he said. "I'm just not sure you're going to like it much."

"At this point," Marchetti said, "we don't have much of a choice."

CHAPTER 43

THE SURPRISE WIND THAT HAD PULLED KURT, LEILANI AND Ishmael along gusted for the better part of two hours. At times it threatened to lift the boat out of the water. Halfway through the ride, the strange reflective effect vanished as quickly as it had come, both from the water around them and from their bodies.

"Do you think they're gone?" Leilani had asked.

"Doubt it," Kurt said. "Whatever made them shine seems to have passed, but I'm guessing they're still on us and in the sea."

The wind began to taper over the next hour. Wherever it came from, it blew itself out an hour before dusk. The starboard side of the boat sagged further and the three of them had no choice but to hug the port bolsters to keep the boat from tipping. As it was, every little wave that came up washed over the slanted deck.

Kurt reeled the chutes in, wrung them out and stored them. He was almost done when a shout from Ishmael startled him.

"Land!" Ishmael shouted. "Land ahead!"

Kurt looked up. Low on the horizon was a greenish blur. In

the failing light it could have been a cloud catching some weird reflection.

Kurt pulled the binoculars out, wiped the lenses and held them to his eyes.

"Please let it be land," Leilani said, clasping her hands together. "Please."

Kurt could see green and the tops of trees. "It's land all right," he said, slapping Ishmael on the shoulder. "It's land, big-time."

He put the binoculars away and moved to the tail end of the boat. He switched the fuel line to reserve and cranked up the outboard. It sputtered to life, and Kurt twisted the throttle.

With the prop going again, the half-deflated boat moved in a crablike fashion that soon had Kurt soaked to the bone in the surprisingly cold water.

After twenty minutes, he could see a central peak, maybe fifty feet high and covered in vegetation. Flat land ran out on both sides of it. He could see waves breaking on a reef that surrounded the island.

"Volcanic atoll," he said. "We're going to have to get over the reef to get on dry land. We might have to swim for it."

He looked at Ishmael and then to Leilani.

"You still have his gun?"

She nodded. "Yes, but—"

"Give it to me."

She handed him the pistol that both of them knew was empty. He held it at the ready. "She's going to untie you," Kurt said. "You cause any trouble, I'll fill you full of more holes than the boat."

"No trouble," Ishmael said.

Kurt nodded and Leilani disconnected the carabiner and heaved the anchor over the side. Next she untied his legs and threw the rope away.

Kurt waited for him to make some move, but all he did was stretch his legs and smile with relief.

By now they were closing in on the reef that surrounded the island. The waves weren't too bad, but it was pretty turbulent where there were gaps in the reef.

"Should we look for a calmer spot?" Leilani asked.

"Tank's got to be almost dry," Kurt replied.

He went for the first gap he saw. The floundering boat plowed toward it like a barge, shoving a low surge of water in front of it. The water around them changed from dark blue to turquoise, and the chop got worse where the submerged sections of the reef affected the wave dynamics.

One second they'd crest a two-foot wave and the next they'd be hit from the side by another and dropped into a trough that seemed to drag them backward. The hard spine of the boat ground across something solid, and the prop chewed into it.

Two waves from behind combined and shoved them forward and to port. They scraped over more coral as the foam from a third wave washed over them.

Kurt turned the outboard this way and that, gunning the throttle and backing off, using it as both a motor and rudder. The backwash through the gap fought against them, but with the next set of breakers they surged forward again. This time the port side hit hard and both the chambers were ripped open.

"We've taken a hit," Leilani shouted.

"Stay in the boat as long as you can," Kurt shouted.

He gunned the throttle once more. The outboard revved for ten seconds or so and then began to sputter. He backed off a little, but it was too late. The motor stalled, starved of fuel. Another wave smashed them sideways.

"Go!" Kurt shouted.

Ishmael clambered over the side. Leilani hesitated and then went in, diving forward. Another wave smacked the sinking boat, and Kurt also lunged forward into the surf.

He swam with everything he had. But twenty-four hours without food, a lack of water and the exertion of the past two days counted against him. Fatigue would not wait long to set in.

The undertow pushed him back and then a wave swept him forward. He scraped over some more coral, jammed his foot onto a solid piece and pushed off hard, again launching himself forward. The boots made it hard to swim, but they were worth their weight in gold each time he kicked off against the reef.

When the undertow returned, he wedged his feet into the coral and held his ground. The foam blinded him as the swells rose over him. Something soft crashed into him from the front.

It was Leilani.

He grabbed her and shoved her forward with the next wave, and they surged through into the calmer section of water inside the protective ring of the reef.

Kurt swam hard. Leilani did the same. When his feet hit the sand, he dug in and waded forward, one hand on Leilani's life jacket, dragging her with him.

They made it out of the surf and collapsed on the white sand, far enough down the beach that the waves still washed up against them.

Breathing was almost the limit of what he could handle at the moment, but he managed to say a few words: "You all right?"

She nodded, her chest heaving and falling, as his was.

Kurt looked around. They were alone. "Ishmael?"

He saw nothing, heard no response.

"Ishmael!"

"There!" Leilani said, pointing.

He lay facedown in the foam as the waves washed him up onto the sand and then dragged him backward.

Kurt got up, stumbled in Ishmael's direction and crashed back into the sea. He grabbed Ishmael and dragged him to shore.

Ishmael began coughing and choking and spitting up water. A brief look told Kurt he would survive.

Before he could celebrate, a pair of long shadows fell over Kurt from behind. He recognized the shapes of rifles and burly men in the surreal shadows painted on the sand.

He turned. Several men stood with the sun to their backs. They seemed to be wearing ragged uniforms and helmets and carrying heavy bolt-action rifles.

As they approached, he saw them better. They were dark-skinned men, looking almost like Aboriginal Australians but with Polynesian features as well. Their rifles were old M1 carbines with five-shot clips and their uniforms and helmets looked like U.S. Marines circa 1945. Several more of them stood among the trees at the top of the beach.

Kurt was too exhausted and too surprised to do much more than watch as one of the men approached him. The man held the long rifle casually but wore a look of utter seriousness on his face.

"Welcome to Pickett's Island," he said in deeply accented English. "In the name of Franklin Delano Roosevelt, I make you my prisoner."

CHAPTER 44

FROM JOE'S PERSPECTIVE EITHER THE DOCKING PROCEDURE for the ferry was overly complicated or the boat and its captain were ill suited to the task. A full hour after the bay doors had been opened and the ship had been shunted back and forth a dozen times, they finally bumped against a pier.

Joe remained huddled in the rear of the flatbed. The drivers and crewmen had clambered into their rigs long before the ship stopped and now began firing up the big trucks. For another few minutes they idled their engines, and despite the open doors Joe was sure he would pass out from the diesel fumes before they left.

At last, with a headache pounding inside his skull like a jackhammer, the trucks began to roll. One by one they pulled out of the cargo hold and onto the pier. Joe didn't risk a peek until he felt they were away from the waterfront. But he was surprised at how quickly they were moving only minutes after leaving the ferry.

He crept past the barrels to the back end of the truck. Since his truck had been the first into the hold, it became the last one out.

They were now the tail-end Charlie of the convoy, which meant he could look out without fear of being spotted.

He lifted the tarp a few inches, saw gray-weathered macadam flying out behind them as the trucks flew along a road at speeds they'd never come close to in Yemen.

It was almost night yet again after twenty hours on the boat. Joe saw desert terrain in all directions. It looked remarkably like he'd arrived back in Yemen.

"Didn't we just leave all this?" he mumbled.

There were differences of course, primarily the paved road. There was more vegetation and the occasional road sign. There had been none out in the deserts of Yemen. As signs whipped past, Joe tried to read them, but he could see only the back side of those on his side of the road, and those meant for drivers heading the opposite way were lit only by the big trailer's taillights. The dim red glow was not bright enough for Joe to see much before the sign went out of range.

All he noticed was the lettering. It was done in the swirling calligraphy of Arabic and also the block letters of English, the mere presence of which meant he was much closer to civilization than he'd been in days.

As Joe waited for more signs, the night grew darker and the landscape became monotonous. The only thing that changed was the scent. Joe began to smell dust and moisture and the desert wet with rain. It reminded him of Santa Fe, where he'd grown up, when the dry season ended. Looking up, he realized the sky was a curtain of starless black.

Moments later, rain began splattering the truck and the road around him. Joe heard thunder in the distance. As the trucks drove on, the shower intensified and the air grew cool and damp. To Joe's surprise it wasn't a passing shower but a steady soaking rain that continued to fall as the convoy pounded out the miles. Before long the tarp above him was soaked and dripping.

"Rain in the desert," Joe whispered to himself. "I wonder if this is good news or bad."

As the rain fell, they passed another group of signs. As luck would have it, a car was traveling in the opposite direction at almost the same instant. Its high beams cut through the rain and lit up a sign on the far side of the road long enough for Joe to read it.

The weathered blue placard was sandblasted and bent, but the words were clear enough.

"Marsa Alam," Joe said as he read the sign. "Fifty kilometers."

The name was familiar. Marsa Alam was the name of an Egyptian port on the Red Sea. It lay behind them. It must have been where the ferry tied up and the trucks disembarked. That meant they were three-quarters of the way from Cairo to the Sudanese border and only a couple of hours from Luxor.

"I'm in Egypt," Joe whispered, quickly realizing what that meant. "These guys are headed for the Aswan Dam."

CHAPTER 45

RAIN CONTINUED TO PELT THE CONVOY OF JINN'S TRUCKS as they rumbled west on the highway from Marsa Alam. With the moisture, the natural cooling of the desert at night and the wind swirling around the back of the truck as it raced along, Joe began to shiver.

At first he welcomed it as a relief from his time in Yemen and in the hot box of the ferry, but as the night wore on, the cold began to seep into his bones, and Joe pulled the flap shut to keep the wind and the mist from the truckbed.

It was four hours overland from Marsa Alam to Aswan, but after three hours the convoy began to slow as they came out of the open desert and into the swath of civilization that bordered the Nile.

The trucks crossed the Nile on a modern bridge and entered the town of Edfu on the west bank of the river. As Joe looked around, he saw multistory apartment blocks and storefronts and government buildings. It wasn't exactly the Beltway, more like a dusty version of East Berlin in the desert, but it was civilization.

The truck slowed further, and Joe hoped they'd come to a red light, but they found a roundabout instead, turning a three-quarter circle before heading north in a straight line once again.

"It had to be a roundabout," Joe mumbled.

He figured they might end up back on another highway at any moment and that he'd be in Aswan before he could get free. As the engine growled in low gear and the truck picked up speed, Joe decided the time to abandon ship had arrived.

He climbed under the flap and out onto the rear bumper. He glanced around the edge of the tarp, straining to see what was coming. No telephone poles or lights or signs. The coast was clear, and Joe leapt off the truck.

He hit the wet macadam, rolled and slid through an expansive puddle of muck where the rain had gathered as it soaked the street. He stayed down in it for a moment, watching the trucks for any sign the drivers had witnessed his stunt.

They rumbled north in the dark, never changing speed or even tapping the brakes.

Soaking and filthy, Joe pulled himself from the muck and looked around. He'd landed in an open area. Through the rain he could see a huge structure to the left lit by spotlights.

Ignoring new pains in his shoulder and hip and doing the best he could not to notice how badly his ankle hurt once again, he limped toward the lit-up area. It looked like a construction site and an ancient temple cross-pollinated, and only as Joe got close did he realize he was standing in front of the Temple of Horus, one of the best preserved ancient sites in all of Egypt.

The front wall had two huge wings that rose a hundred feet

into the night sky. Human figures carved into the wall were sixty feet tall, and gaps that allowed the light into its interior were spaced evenly up, down and across.

During the day the site would have been filled with tourists. But at night, in the pouring rain, it was empty. Except, Joe noticed, for a pair of security guards in a lit booth.

He ran toward it and rapped on the window. The guards just about died from shock, one of them literally jumping from his seat.

Joe pounded on the window again and eventually one of the guards opened it.

"I need your help," Joe said.

The still-startled guard appeared confused, but he recovered quickly. "Ah . . . of course," he said, "come in. Yes, come inside."

Joe moved to the door. Fortunately for him, guards at the site were picked partly for their ability to speak English, as many of the tourists were Americans and Europeans.

Joe stepped into the lighted booth as soon as the door opened. He was soaking wet, dripping muddy water all over the floor. One of the guards handed him a towel, which Joe used to dry his face.

"Thank you," Joe said.

"What are you doing out in the rain?" one guard asked.

"It's a long story," Joe replied. "I'm an American. I was a prisoner of sorts until I jumped out of a moving truck, and I really need to use your phone."

"An American," the guard repeated. "A tourist? Do you want us to call your hotel?"

"No," Joe said, "I'm not a tourist. I need to speak to the police.

Actually, I need to speak to the military. We're in danger here. We're all in danger."

"What kind of danger?" the guard asked suspiciously.

Joe looked him in the eye. "Terrorists are going to destroy the dam."

CHAPTER 46

THE FIVE TRUCKS IN JINN'S CONVOY RUMBLED NORTH, eventually pulling off the main road and onto a dirt track. They passed the dam and continued on, traveling a perimeter road that wound along the jagged shore of Lake Nasser.

A half mile up from the dam, they came to a gate left conspicuously open and went through it. Traveling in the cab of the lead truck, Sabah ordered the lights doused and had the drivers use night vision goggles.

Blacked out in this manner, the convoy reached a boat ramp at the edge of the lake.

"Turn the trucks around," Sabah ordered. "Back them in."

Sabah climbed out of the lead truck and directed traffic. The big rigs lined up side by side, the wide ramp large enough to accommodate all five at once like great crocodiles basking on the shore.

Because the lake was so high from all the rain, most of the ramp was submerged. Sabah estimated a hundred feet of concrete lay hidden beneath the water before the ramp intersected the natural lake bed.

On his signal, the trucks began to ease down the ramp. The drivers took it slow, checking their progress in mirrors and through open windows.

As the flatbeds began backing into the water, Sabah took a radio controller from his pocket. He extended the antenna, pressed the power switch and pressed the first of four red buttons.

In the back of the five trailers, magnetic seals around the yellow drums popped open. The pressurized lids popped up and slid off to the side.

A green light told Sabah the activation had been successful.

Unseen by anyone, the silver sand of the microbots came alive, stirring and swirling, as if there were snakes hidden beneath the top layer, and beginning to climb over the edges of the barrels.

Unaware of what was happening in the flatbeds behind them, the drivers continued backing down the ramp, allowing gravity to do the work. None of them had done this before and most felt like they were being pulled in.

Sabah judged their progress. Their caution pleased him. It meant they weren't paying attention to him.

"Good," he whispered as he pressed the second of the four red buttons.

Inside the cabs, the door locks slammed down, the windows slid up into a ninety-percent-closed position and froze. The noise and movement startled the drivers.

An instant later chloroform gas began pumping from tiny canisters and filling the cabins. The men lasted only a second or two, none managed to pry open a door. One got a window half down before passing out and slumping onto the seat.

Without waiting, Sabah pressed the third button. The truck engines revved. They began to accelerate backward, crashing through the water like a herd of thundering hippos.

The engines had been modified to include a secondary air intake, disguised as an exhaust stack rising high above the roof of the truck. When Sabah activated the chloroform, the primary intake had been sealed shut and this secondary intake had opened. In effect, it acted like a snorkel, allowing the engine to breathe and continue to rev even after the entire truck was submerged.

Because of that, the motors continued to run and the wheels continued to spin in reverse, pushing the trucks down the ramp and out across the submerged rocks and gravel beyond it.

The charging trucks fanned out like the fingers of a hand, burrowing beneath the water and vanishing from view.

Momentum and the slope of the stony lake bed allowed them to continue even after their engines were finally swamped. When the trucks finally settled, they were thirty feet below the surface, one hundred and fifty feet from shore.

The unconscious drivers soon drowned. If and when they were discovered, they would be identified as Egyptian radicals. Sabah and Jinn's connection to the incident would remain unknown, except to General Aziz, who would do well to keep silent and most likely have no choice but to return to the bargaining table.

As the waters settled, Sabah pressed the final button on his controller. A half mile away, on the wall of the dam, two separate devices began to issue homing signals.

The size of an average carry-on suitcase, but shaped something like mechanical crabs, the two devices had been placed there by a scuba diver forty-eight hours before. One was just below the waterline while the other clung to a spot on the sloping wall of the dam seventy feet below.

If the divers had done their jobs properly, ten-foot starter holes had already been bored through the outer wall and into the aggregate behind it. A batch of dedicated microbots from each crab would already be hard at work expanding those holes.

The large force now escaping from the trucks would home in on the signal and accelerate the process rapidly. In six hours a trickle of water would appear on the far side of the dam near the top. That trickle would scour out a channel, and the erosion that followed would quickly turn the flow into a torrent.

The first stage of the disaster would follow as the waters of Lake Nasser flooded over the top, widening the channel in an unstoppable flow, wreaking havoc on the Nile Valley below, but that was just the prelude.

The second tunnel, far deeper in the dam, would destabilize the core, scouring out a tunnel in the heart of the structure. Eventually it would give way and a huge V-shaped section would collapse backward all at once. The flood would become a tsunami.

In a way, General Aziz had done them a favor. Between the message about to be sent at Aswan and the actions Jinn was taking in the Indian Ocean, Sabah doubted any nation of the world would refuse their demands or dare to threaten them.

Would the Americans be willing to see the Hoover Dam crumble, Las Vegas flooded off the map and their southwestern states deprived of power and water at the same time? Would China allow the Three Gorges Dam a similar fate? Sabah thought not.

He flung the remote into the lake and began walking away. A half mile off, a camel waited for him. He would climb on, pull the kaffiyeh around his face and disappear into the desert like the Bedouin had done for a thousand years or more.

CHAPTER 47

KURT AUSTIN AWOKE IN A QUONSET HUT SEVERAL HOURS after being made a prisoner on Pickett's Island. Imprisoned, exhausted and thinking he would need the rest later, Kurt had lain down on the floor almost as soon as they'd been locked up. He'd fallen asleep in moments. Upon waking, he was upset to find the whole thing hadn't been a dream.

The men in fatigues dragged him from the hut to another hidden beneath the trees. Inside he found a distinctly military setting that seemed like a tribunal of some kind. Leilani and Ishmael stood beside him.

From behind a desk at the end of the hut another islander of Aboriginal and Polynesian appearance stood and was presiding over the hearing as one of the judges. He was taller and leaner than the man who'd found them on the beach and a fair bit older, Kurt thought. He had a tousle of gray in his black hair.

"I am the eighteenth Roosevelt of Pickett's Island," the man said.

"The eighteenth Roosevelt?" Kurt repeated.

"That is correct," the judge said. "And who am I addressing? You will state your names for the record."

"I'm the first Kurt Austin of the United States of America," Kurt said. "At least the first one I know of."

The judges and the others around them took a collective breath, and Kurt tried to make sense of what he was seeing and hearing.

On the march from the beach to the huts hidden in the trees they'd encountered fortifications, trenches, emplacements of heavy machine guns and then an area of ramshackle buildings, including the old Quonset huts with roofs patched and repaired with thatch and woven palm fronds.

Men in green Army fatigues stood around them. Their uniforms were in no better shape than the huts. In fact, some of them looked like badly sewn replicas. The M1 rifles they carried looked authentic enough, Kurt had several in his collection at home, but they hadn't been used by any soldiers he knew of since the Korean War.

Beside him, Leilani gave her name, as did Ishmael. Neither did so in the manner Kurt had. Nor did they list their countries of origin.

The eighteenth Roosevelt spoke again. "You are charged with trespassing, possession of weapons and espionage. You will be held as enemy combatants and prisoners of war. Tell us how you plead."

"Plead?" Leilani blurted out.

"Yes," the judge said. "Are you members of the Axis forces or not?"

Leilani tugged on Kurt's sleeve. "What's going on? What are they talking about?"

Kurt felt like he was playing catch-up. An idea began to form in his head.

"I think this is a cargo cult," he whispered.

"A what?"

"In the Pacific, during World War Two, islands with tribal societies were suddenly caught in the middle of the largest war ever fought. Any island of strategic value was claimed and used for one purpose or another, often times for storage of supplies that came off ships in endless quantities. Stuff the soldiers and sailors called cargo."

He nodded at the soldiers surrounding them. "For the people in the tribal societies the sudden appearance of men from the sky or out of great ships from the sea, bringing what seemed like endless amounts of food and manufactured goods, it was like the arrival of minor gods."

"You have to be kidding me," she said.

"I'm not. To garner the support of those on the islands, a great deal of stuff got handed over to the islanders like manna from heaven. But when the war ended and the soldiers left, it was a huge shock. No more stuff. No more cargo coming off the ships and planes. No more big silver birds dropping out of the sky.

"In most places life went back to normal, but on some islands the tribes started looking for ways to encourage the return of the soldiers and their cargo. They became known as cargo cults."

A second judge, who seemed lower in the pecking order than the eighteenth Roosevelt, grew impatient with Kurt's whispering.

"The defendants will answer!" he demanded.

"We're discussing our plea," Kurt replied.

Kurt finished his explanation. "One common practice was mimicking what they'd seen on the American bases. Some of the cults were known to drill like soldiers in boot camp. Dressing like these guys. Carrying fake guns carved from wood. They did morning reveille, had flag-raising ceremonies, they even had ranks and medals and military-style burials. The most famous group I can recall was the John Frum cult on Vanuatu. Rumor had it, the cult got its name because the Americans would introduce themselves by saying, *'Hi, I'm John from so-and-so.'* So the cult named themselves the John Frummers."

"That's just great," Leilani said sarcastically, "but we're not in the Pacific. And these guys aren't carrying fake wooden guns."

"No," Kurt said. "Something's different here."

He noticed other items around the room. Charts lay spread across a desk, a compass, a barometer and a sextant were nearby. He spotted an antique gray life vest and a pair of dog tags in a spot of honor on the eighteenth Roosevelt's desk. A faded Yankees baseball cap that had to be seventy years old sat nearby.

"The time for discussion is ended," the eighteenth Roosevelt said. "You will make your plea or we will enter one for you."

"Not guilty," Kurt said. "We're Americans like you. Well, at least two of us are."

The judges looked them over. "How can you prove it?" one of them said. "She could be a Japanese spy."

The statement riled Leilani. "How dare you call me a spy! Even if I was part Japanese, there's nothing wrong with that."

"Are you?"

"No. I'm an American, from the state of Hawaii."

"She means the territory of Hawaii," Kurt interjected.

"No, I don't."

"Yes, you do," Kurt insisted. "It didn't become a state until 'fifty-nine!"

Leilani gazed at him with big chestnut-colored eyes. There was trust in that gaze, along with hope and confusion.

"Just let me do the talking," Kurt whispered, and then turned back to the first judge. "What she means is, she grew up near Pearl

Harbor. She's been there many times to visit the *Arizona* memorial and pay respects to those who died on December seventh."

The judge seemed to accept this. "And what about you?" he asked Kurt.

"I work for the National Underwater and Marine Agency. Which is an ocean research section of the U.S. government. It was founded by Admiral James Sandecker."

"Sandecker?" the second judge said.

"Never heard of him," a third judge said.

"He's a real admiral," Kurt insisted. "He's a good friend of mine. I've been to his house many times. He's now the Vice President of the United States."

The judges' collective eyebrows went up. "The Vice President is a good friend of yours?" one of them asked.

The others started to laugh.

The eighteenth Roosevelt shook his head. "It does not seem possible that the new Harry Truman would be a friend of such a dirty-looking man."

Kurt considered his appearance. He was battered and bruised with four days of stubble on his face. The stolen uniform fit a little large and was torn in places. At the moment he was just thankful not to be sparkling.

"You're not exactly seeing me at my best," he said.

Leilani leaned close. "The new Harry Truman?"

"I have a feeling they've mixed up names and titles," Kurt said. "Whoever came here must have told them the leader of the country was Roosevelt, the Vice President was Truman."

"Is that why this guy is the eighteenth Roosevelt of Pickett's Island?"

"I think so."

"I feel like I'm in the twilight zone," Leilani said.

So did Kurt. But he figured there were some advantages to the setup, and with his friend's lives still hanging in the balance, he had no choice but to take advantage of them.

"What I've said is true," Kurt insisted. "And I'm here on Pickett's Island, looking as I do, because I've just escaped the grasp of some enemies of the United States."

The men seemed impressed and began to whisper among themselves.

"How can we be sure he's an American?" the second judge said.

"He looks a lot like Pickett," the eighteenth Roosevelt said.

"He could be German. His name is Kurt."

The eighteenth Roosevelt seemed to take this as a fair question, he turned to Austin. "You must prove it to us."

"Tell me how?"

"I will ask you some questions," he said. "If you answer as an American would, we will believe your story. If you speak wrongly, you will be held guilty."

"Go ahead," Kurt said confidently, "ask away."

"What is the capital of New York State?" the judge asked.

"Albany," Kurt said.

"Very good. But that was an easy one."

"So ask a harder one."

The judge knitted his dark brows together, squinting at Kurt, before asking the next question. "What is meant by the term *the pitcher balked*?"

Kurt was surprised. He'd expected another geography question or a history question, but in retrospect it made sense. History and geography were easy to learn, obscure rules of national sports were not. As it happened, Kurt had played baseball all his young life.

"A balk occurs many different ways," he said, "but usually it's when the pitcher doesn't come to a complete stop before throwing the pitch to home base."

The judges nodded in unison.

"Correct," one said.

"Yes, yes," another said, still nodding.

"Third question: Who was the sixteenth Roosevelt of the United States?"

Kurt assumed he meant the sixteenth President. "Abraham Lincoln."

"And where was he born?"

Another good question, Lincoln so widely known as being from Illinois that most assumed he was born there. "Lincoln was born in Kentucky," Kurt replied. "In a cabin made of logs."

The judges nodded to one another. It seemed he was making progress.

"I feel like we're on a bad game show," Leilani mumbled.

"Too bad we don't get any lifelines," Kurt said, "I'd love to make a call right about now."

"One more question," the eighteenth Roosevelt said. "Tell us what is meant by The House That Ruth Built?"

Kurt smiled. His eyes fell on the old-style Yankees cap. Someone who'd influenced these men had loved baseball and had obviously been from New York.

"The House That Ruth Built is Yankee Stadium. It's in the Bronx," he said, and then added, to the judges hearty approval, "It was named for Babe Ruth, the greatest baseball player of all time."

"He is correct," the eighteenth Roosevelt said excitedly. "Only a true American would know these things."

"Yes, yes," the others agreed. "Now, what about the woman?"

"She's with me," Kurt said.

"And the man?"

Kurt hesitated. "He's my prisoner."

"Then he will be our prisoner," one of the judges said.

"Our first prisoner," the eighteenth Roosevelt proclaimed to the great excitement of those around the room. "Take him away."

Ishmael looked shocked as two men with carbines rushed forward and grabbed him.

"He must be treated according to the Geneva convention," Kurt said sternly.

"Yes, of course. He will be cared for. But he will be guarded night and day. We have never lost a prisoner on Pickett's Island. Then again, we have never had one before. He will not escape."

Without a chance to defend himself, Ishmael was dragged off. Kurt figured he would be okay. As the room emptied around him, he approached the bench.

The eighteenth Roosevelt extended a hand. "My apologies for your treatment," he said. "I had to be sure."

Kurt shook the hand. "Understandable," he said. "May I ask your name?"

"I'm Tautog," the judge said.

"And you're the eighteenth Roosevelt of the island," Kurt confirmed.

"Yes," Tautog said. "Every four years, a new leader is chosen. I am the eighteenth. I have served for two years, defending the island and the Constitution of the United States of America."

Kurt calculated backward. If each term lasted four years and Tautog had only served for two, that meant the first Roosevelt was chosen seventy years ago, in 1942.

World War Two. These islanders had come into contact with someone during World War Two and been turned into a small fighting force. It seemed like no one had bothered to tell them the war was over.

Kurt's eyes traveled over the nautical equipment and the life vest. A faded name on it was impossible to read. "A ship landed here?" he said.

"Yes," Tautog said. "A great ship of fire and steel. The S.S. *John Bury.*"

"What happened to it?" Kurt asked.

"The keel is buried in the sand on the east side of the island. The rest we took apart and used to build shelters and defenses."

"Defenses?" Leilani asked. "Against what?"

"Against the Imperial Japanese Navy and the banzai charge," Tautog said as if it were obvious.

Kurt caught her before she spoke. Tautog and his fellow islanders were extremely isolated and not just geographically. He didn't know how they would respond to hearing that the war they and their fathers and their grandfathers had been hunkering down to fight had been over for six and a half decades.

"Who trained you?" Kurt asked.

"Captain Pickett and Sergeant First Class Arthur Watkins of the United States Marine Corps. They taught us the drills, how to fight, how to hide, how to spot the enemy."

"Who was the Yankees fan?" Kurt asked.

"Captain Pickett loved the Yankees. He called them the Bronx Bombers."

Kurt nodded. "And what happened when they left?"

Tautog looked as if he didn't understand the question. "They did not leave," he said. "Both men are buried here along with their crew."

"They died here?"

"Captain Pickett died from his injuries eight months after the *John Bury* ran aground. The sergeant was badly injured as well. He could not walk, but he survived for eleven months and taught us how to fight."

Kurt found the story amazing and intriguing. He'd never heard of a cargo cult where the Americans had stayed behind. He only wished he could reach St. Julien Perlmutter and access his extensive history of naval warfare. The cargo ship had to be listed somewhere, probably labeled *missing and presumed sunk*, just another footnote to the huge war.

"I don't understand," Leilani said. "Why would you need to fight? I understand about the war and the Japanese, but this island is so small. It's so far out of the way. I don't think the Japanese were—I mean are—interested in taking it over."

"It is not the island itself that we protect," Tautog said. "It is the machine Captain Pickett entrusted to us."

Kurt's eyebrows went up. "The machine?"

"Yes," Tautog said. "The great machine. The Pain Maker."

CHAPTER 48

KURT AUSTIN HAD NO IDEA WHAT THE PAIN MAKER WAS, but with a name like that he had to find out. But first he had to deal with being a celebrity.

In a far cry from their initial reception, he and Leilani had become honored guests on Pickett's Island. The fact that he was their first American visitor in seventy years was one thing, the fact that he knew the current Harry Truman had the tribesmen in their military fatigues treating him like MacArthur returning to the Philippines.

After giving Leilani and him fresh water to drink and allowing them to shower and change into fatigues like the other islanders wore, the men of Pickett's Island treated them to a meal of fresh-caught fish along with mangoes, bananas and coconut milk from the trees that grew in abundance on the island.

While they ate, Tautog and three others regaled them with stories, explaining how all that they had and all that they knew had come from Captain Pickett and Sergeant Watkins. They didn't say it in so many words, but it seemed like Pickett and

Watkins had created their civilization out of thin air and were regarded almost like mythical spirits.

With dinner finished, Kurt and Leilani were taken on a tour of the island.

Kurt saw remarkable ingenuity in the setup. Structures built of rusting steel plate hid everywhere among the trees. Trenches and tunnels linked the supply-filled cave, lookout posts and areas with cisterns dug to catch rainwater. He saw material from every part of the ship in use somewhere: old boilers, piping and steel beams. Even the *John Bury*'s bell had been moved to a high point on the island where it could be rung to warn others of an emergency or in case of attack by the Japanese.

"I can't believe no one's told them," Leilani whispered as they walked beneath the palm trees a few paces behind their guides.

"I don't think they get a lot of visitors," Kurt said.

"Shouldn't *we* say something?"

Kurt shook his head. "I think they don't want to know."

"How could they not want to know?"

"They're hiding from the world," Kurt said. "It must have been part of Pickett's strategy to keep this Pain Maker machine safe."

She nodded, seeming to understand that. "How about we get out of here and let them keep hiding," she said. "This is an island, after all. These people have to have boats. Maybe we could borrow one."

Kurt knew they had boats because Tautog had said the camp actually included two other islands, which could be seen only from the high point of the central peak. He figured that meant a range of at least fifteen, maybe twenty miles. If a boat could handle that, it could get to the shipping lanes. If that's where one planned to go.

"They do have boats," Kurt said. "But *we're* not going any-where, just me."

Leilani looked as though she'd been jabbed with a pin or some-thing, her eyebrows shot up, her posture stiffened, she stopped in her tracks. "Excuse me?"

"You're safe here," he said.

"That doesn't mean I want to stay. This place is the bizarro version of *Gilligan's Island* and I'm not about to become Ginger."

"Trust me," Kurt said, "you're more of a Mary Ann. But that's not why you're sticking around. I need you out of harm's way while I try to reach Aqua-Terra."

Now she paused as if trying to process what he'd said. "You're going back? Didn't we almost drown trying to get away from there?"

"And we landed here," Kurt said. "Things are looking up."

"Don't you think going back to the floating island controlled by terrorists will reverse that trend?"

"Not if I go with rifles and the element of surprise."

She studied him for a second, seeming to pick up on his thoughts. "Your friends on the island?"

He nodded.

"Not only that," Kurt said, "Jinn is there. And he's up to something bigger than terrorism or gunrunning or money laun-dering."

"Like what?"

"This whole thing started with an investigation of the water temps. The weather pattern over India has become unstable. They're dealing with two years of decreasing rains, and this year's looking to be the driest yet. Your brother was studying the current and temperature patterns because we believed the cause might lie there, in a previously undiscovered El Niño/La Niña effect."

She nodded. "And he found those little machines of Jinn's spread out through the ocean."

"Exactly," Kurt said. "And when they started reflecting the sunlight, I could feel heat coming off the water. The two things have to be connected. I'm not sure why but Jinn's messing around with the temperature gradient, and the butterfly effect is producing horrible results down the road."

By now they'd arrived at the eastern side of the island on a low bluff no more than twenty feet high. Ahead of them was a wide stretch of sand with a far more accommodating approach through the reef than the one Kurt had taken from the north.

He hoped they'd finally arrived at the one thing he wanted to see.

Tautog waved his hand across the open beach. "Captain Pickett told us if the Japs come, they would attack here."

That made sense to Kurt. It looked like an easy beach to hit.

"So he had us bring the Pain Maker to this side of the island."

Tautog motioned to a group of his men and they moved a fence made of thatch to one side. Behind it, recessed into a cave, was a strange-looking device. It reminded Kurt of a speaker system. Four feet wide and perhaps a foot tall, the rectangular shape was divided into rows of hexagonal pods, four rows of ten. There was a ceramic quality to the pods.

"Apply the power," Tautog said. Behind him two of his men started pulling back and forth on a lever-type system. They looked like lumberjacks working a log with a large two-handed saw, but they were actually accelerating a flywheel. The flywheel was attached to generator coils, and in a few seconds both the wheel and the dynamo in the generator were spinning rapidly.

A crackling buzz began to emanate from hexagonal pods in the speaker box. Out on the water, a hundred feet away, a ripple began to form, and in moments a fifty-foot swath of water was shaking and splattering as if it was being boiled or agitated somehow.

Tautog waved another hand. Along the wall of the bluff seven additional fences of the camouflaging material were removed. As the generators in these units were cranked up, the whole beachfront entered a similar state of agitation.

Kurt noticed fish fleeing the onslaught, launching themselves over one another like salmon racing up a ladder. A pair of night birds dove after them, thinking them easy prey, but turned away suddenly as if they'd hit a force field.

Some kind of vibration was definitely issuing from the speaker boxes, though all Kurt heard was a crackling buzz like high-voltage lines carrying too much power. "Sound waves."

"Yes," Tautog said. "If the Japanese come, they will never get off the beach."

Kurt noticed the birds and fish were okay. "It doesn't appear to be lethal."

"No. But the causing of pain will bring them to their knees. They will make easy targets."

"A weapon made out of sound," Leilani said. "It almost seems crazy, but you see it in nature already. On dives with Kimo I've seen dolphins use their echo-location to stun fish into a stupor before snatching them in their jaws."

Kurt had heard of that but never witnessed it. He knew of sound weapons from another angle. "The military has been working on systems like this over the past few decades. The plan is to use them as nonlethal crowd-control devices, saving the need for all those rubber bullets and tear gas canisters. But I didn't know the concept went as far back as the Second World War."

"Any idea how it works?" Leilani asked.

"Just a guess," Kurt said. "Simple harmonic vibration. The sound waves travel at slightly different speeds and slightly different angles. They converge in the zone where the water is jumping, amplifying the effect. Almost like a beam of sound."

"I'm glad you didn't use it on us," Leilani said to Tautog.

"You landed on the wrong beach," Tautog replied matter-of-factly.

Kurt was glad for that. "One point for hasty navigation."

As he watched the water buzzing, a new idea began to form in his mind, but to risk it he first needed to know how effective the Pain Maker really was.

"I want to test it."

"We can demonstrate on the prisoner if you like."

"No," Kurt said, "not on the prisoner. On me."

Tautog regarded him strangely. "You are a curious person, Kurt Austin."

"I do what I have to in order to survive and get the job done," Kurt said. "Other than that, I'm not interested in seeing anyone suffer. Even a former enemy."

Tautog pondered this, but he voiced neither agreement nor disagreement. He flipped a switch, the speaker box near them shut off and a gap in the wall of sound appeared over the beach and out onto the bay.

Leilani grabbed his arm. "Are you nuts?"

"Probably," Kurt said, "but I need to know."

"I warn you," Tautog said, "the impact will hurt a great deal."

"Strange as it sounds," Kurt replied, "I honestly hope it does."

A minute later Kurt was on the sand at the water's edge. He noticed a few fish floating motionless in the waves. Apparently they hadn't all escaped unscathed.

Around him, the sound waves from the other speakers reverberated and continued to vibrate the air and water, but most of the energy was in a range beyond human hearing. What he could hear were ghostly and ethereal sounds.

Kurt looked back up the beach to the bluff. He saw Leilani with her hands clasped in front of her mouth. Tautog stood proudly, and Kurt steeled himself like a gladiator about to do battle.

"Okay," Kurt said.

Tautog threw the switch. Kurt felt an instant wave of pain through every fiber of his body as if all his muscles were cramping up at the same time. His head rang, his eyes hurt, the ethereal buzz he'd heard before was now a wailing sound he felt through his jaw and into his skull. He thought his eardrums would burst, and maybe his eyeballs too.

With all the considerable strength and willpower he possessed, Kurt stayed on his feet and tried to fight his way forward. It felt like he was pulling a great stone block behind him or pushing one up the beach. He could barely move.

He made it one step and then another, and then the pain became unbearable and he collapsed in the sand, covering his ears and head.

"Turn it off!" he heard Leilani shout. "You're killing him."

At another time and place Kurt might have chalked those words up to female hysterics, but as the waves of pain racked every millimeter of his body he thought she might be right.

The speaker shut down and the agony vanished like a rubber band breaking—one instant it was everywhere, the next it was gone.

It left behind fatigue and a feeling of complete and utter exhaustion. Kurt lay on the sand unable to do any more than breathe.

Leilani ran to him and dropped down in the sand beside him.

"Are you okay?" she asked, rolling him over onto his side. "Are you all right?"

He nodded.

"Are you sure?"

"Don't I look it?" he managed.

"Not really," she said.

"I am," he insisted. "I swear."

"I haven't known you very long," she said, helping him to a sitting position, "but you're really not normal. Are you?"

Even through the exhaustion Kurt had to laugh. He was hoping for something like *I don't want to lose you* or *I've started to care for you* or a similar sentiment along those lines.

"What's so funny?" she asked.

"I really thought you were going somewhere else with that," he said. "But that doesn't make you wrong."

She smiled.

"How far did I get?" It felt like he'd climbed Mount Everest with a heavy pack on his shoulders.

"All of two feet," she said.

"That's it?"

She nodded. "The whole thing lasted only a couple of seconds."

It had seemed like an eternity.

Around them the other beams shut down. Tautog came to see them, arriving as the first undisturbed wave lapped the beach.

"I agree with her," he said. "You are not even close to normal."

Kurt felt his strength returning. "Well, as long as we've settled that question, my next request shouldn't come as any surprise."

Kurt put out his hand. Tautog grabbed it and pulled Kurt up to his feet.

"And what request would that be?"

"I need a boat," Kurt said, "a dozen rifles and one of these machines."

"You are planning to rescue your friends," Tautog guessed.

"Yes," Kurt said.

Tautog smiled. "Do you really think we will let you go alone?"

CHAPTER 49

Since finding the guard shack at the Temple of Horus, Joe Zavala's luck had turned decidedly sour.

First, it proved an epic undertaking to get anyone from the military out in the pouring rain to speak with him. When they did come, they arrived with no interpreter, forcing the temple's part-time security guard to act as the go-between. Despite his valiant effort, Joe was certain that important details were being lost in translation.

With each attempt at clarification, the military men went from looking perplexed to incredulous to annoyed.

When Joe insisted that their delay was only increasing the danger, they began shouting at him and pointing fingers as if he was making threats instead of bringing a warning.

Maybe this was how messengers get themselves shot, Joe thought.

And with that, he'd been hauled out of the guard shack at gunpoint, thrown in the back of a van and driven to a military compound of some kind, where he ended up in the stir Egyptian military style.

The filthy holding cell would have given any germaphobe nightmares. And Joe found little solace in the fact that sooner or later ten trillion gallons of water from behind the shattered dam would sweep in and wash the cell clean.

His luck began to change when the new shift arrived at four a.m. With them came an officer who spoke better English.

Major Hassan Edo wore tawny military fatigues with only a few adornments beyond his name. He was in his mid-fifties, with close-cropped hair, a hawklike nose and a thin mustache that might have been at home on Clark Gable's face.

He leaned back in his chair, propped his boots up on the enormous desk in front of him and lit a cigarette that he proceeded to hold between two fingers as he spoke, never actually taking a puff.

"Let me get this straight," the major said. "Your name is Joseph Zavala. You claim to be an American—which isn't the best thing to be around here these days—but even then you have no proof. You say you've entered Egypt without a passport, a visa or any other kind of documentation. You do not even have a driver's license or a credit card."

"Without trying to sound overly defensive," Joe began, "*entered Egypt* kind of makes it sound voluntary. I was a prisoner, held by terrorists who are intent on severely damaging your country. I escaped, came here to warn you and so far have been treated like some kind of rabble-rouser."

Receiving a blank stare from the major, Joe paused. "You guys know what a rabble-rouser is, right?"

Major Edo pulled his feet off the desk, landing them on the wooden floor with a heavy clump. He pulled the cigarette from the ashtray, where he'd put it, threatened to actually smoke it for a second and then leaned toward Joe instead.

"You come to warn us of trouble?" he said as if Joe had been hiding that fact.

"Yes," Joe said. "Terrorists from Yemen are going to destroy the dam."

"The dam?" Edo repeated with a tone of disbelief. "Aswan High Dam?"

"Yes," Joe said.

"Have you seen the dam?"

"Only in pictures," Joe admitted.

"The dam is made of stone, rocks and concrete," the major said with fervor. "It weighs millions of tons. It's two thousand feet thick at the base. These men—if they exist—could hit it with fifty thousand pounds of dynamite and they would only take a small chunk out of one side."

With every phrase, the major waved the cigarette around. Ash flew here and fell there, the thin line of smoke danced, but still the cigarette didn't go to his lips. He sat back, utterly convinced of himself. "I tell you," he finished, "the dam cannot be breached."

"No one said anything about blowing it up from the bottom," Joe replied. "They're going to cut a channel across the top, just below the waterline where the dam is narrowest."

"How?" the major asked.

"How?"

"Yes," the major said, "tell me how? Are they going to drive backhoes and diggers up on the top and begin an excavation without us noticing?"

"Of course not," Joe said.

"Then tell me how it is to be done."

Joe went to speak but stopped with his mouth wide open before uttering a word.

"Yes?" the major said expectantly. "Go on."

Joe closed his mouth. The way he saw it, he could explain what he knew, telling the major that the dam would be brought down by machines so small no one could see them, and expect only laughter and utter dismissal. Or he could make something up and do nothing but muddy the waters and send the major off looking for a threat different than the one that actually existed.

"Can I make a phone call?" he said finally.

If he could reach the American Embassy or NUMA, he could at least warn someone else of the danger in Aswan and also of the impostor's presence on the floating island.

"This is not America, Mr. Zavala. You have no entitlement to a phone call or to an attorney or to anything I choose not to give you."

Joe tried another tactic. "How about this," he said. "There are five trucks out there. Identical flatbeds, with tarps over the top. They were heading north, carrying yellow barrels in the back, drums filled with a silvery sandlike substance. Find them and detain them, question the drivers. I'm sure you'll discover they have no visas, passports or credit cards either."

"Ah yes," the major said scornfully. He picked up a notepad and scanned it under the harsh lighting.

"The five mystical trucks from Yemen," he said. "We have been looking for them since you first gave us your story. By air, by car, on foot. There are no trucks out there to be found. Not here. Not in any warehouse large enough to hide them. Not near the dam or on the shore of the lake. Not even on the road back to Marsa Alam. They do not exist except, I think, in your imagination."

Joe sighed in frustration. He had no idea where the flatbeds could have gone. Edo's men had to have missed something.

The major tossed the notepad aside. "Why don't you tell us what you're really up to?"

"I'm just trying to help," Joe said, as close to surrendering out of frustration as he'd ever been. "Can you at least inspect the dam?"

"Inspect it?"

"Yeah," Joe said. "Look for leaks, look for damage. Anything that might be out of the ordinary."

The major considered this for a second, sitting up straighter and nodding. "An excellent idea."

"It is?"

"Yes. That's just what we'll do."

"*We?*"

"Of course," the major said, standing and mercifully stubbing the cigarette out at last. "How will I know what to look for if I don't bring you along?"

Joe wasn't sure he liked this idea.

"Guards," the major shouted.

The door opened. Two Egyptian MPs came in.

"Shackle him appropriately and deliver him to the dock. I'm taking our guest on a tour."

As the men began to bind Joe in irons, the major spoke. "You will see that the dam is impregnable, and then we can end this charade and talk about your true purpose, whatever that might be."

CHAPTER 50

TWENTY MINUTES LATER JOE FOUND HIMSELF IN A PATROL boat motoring quietly up the Nile in the dark. The Egyptian major gave orders while another soldier piloted the craft and a third man stood by with an assault rifle.

The night air was cool, but fortunately the rain had passed. The stars had come back out as the sky cleared. There was little traffic on the river at this hour, but the valley was lit up. Hotels and other buildings on the banks of the river virtually glowed with the illumination, as did the dam, awash in the glare of flood-lights like a football stadium at night.

Because Aswan was an embankment dam made of aggregate, it blended better into the background than dams like the Hoover. Instead of a towering gray wall at one end of a narrow valley, Joe saw a huge sloping structure like a giant ramp almost the color of the desert around it.

The outside of the structure was a thin layer of concrete de-signed to prevent erosion. Beneath that shell lay compacted rock and sand and, in the center, a watertight clay core that led down to a concrete structure known as a cutoff curtain.

Behind the dam sat a wall of water over three hundred feet tall.

"Do we have to be on this side?" Joe mumbled.

"What was that?" the major asked.

"Couldn't we inspect the dam from the other side or even from the top?"

The major shook his head. "We are looking for a leak, no? How do you expect to see a problem on the high side? Everything is underwater."

"I was hoping you had some cameras or an ROV or something."

"We have nothing like that," the major said.

"I know a few people," Joe mentioned, "I could probably get you one cheap."

"No thank you, Mr. Zavala," the major said. "We will inspect the face of the dam from here and I will show you that it is secure, and then we will discuss your lengthy incarceration for wasting my time."

"Great," Joe mumbled. "Just make sure my cell is far away from here."

The patrol boat continued forward, easing into the restricted zone that stretched a half mile down river from the base of the dam.

Constructed in the sixties with Soviet help, the dam was built in two distinct sections. The western side, on Joe's right, presented the broad sloping face. On the eastern side, past a triangular peninsula of rock and sand covered with high-tension lines and transformers, stood a vertical wall of concrete with gaps in it for the spillways. It was set back on a narrow outlet known as a tailrace, where the high-speed water that flushed through and spun the turbines reentered the river and slowed.

Joe noticed that the water in the tailrace was relatively calm at the moment. "Aren't you generating power?"

"The spillways are open to a bare minimum," the major said. "Maximum power isn't needed at night. Peak demand is in the afternoon, for air conditioners and commercial lighting."

They continued to move closer, bearing to the right-hand side and the sloping portion of the structure.

The closer they got, the easier it was for Joe to appreciate the enormity of the dam. The massive segmented ramp was wider and flatter than he'd expected. It seemed more like a mountain dropped into the river than a structure built by men.

"How thick is it again?"

"Nine hundred and eighty meters at the base."

Nearly a full kilometer, Joe thought. Over half a mile. He began to see why the major was so confident. But Joe also knew a little about hydro engineering and he knew what he'd seen in the tank in Yemen.

The breach on the model had started up high and the collapse had proceeded from there, like a levy overtopped on the banks of the Mississippi.

"We're not going to see anything from down here," he said. "We need to inspect the top. We need to get teams out onto the dam itself and look for leakage."

The major seemed exasperated.

"I had thought this would show you how foolish your efforts at wasting our time are," he said. "I have no plans to imprison you. I was merely 'yanking your chain,' as you Americans like to say. But if you continue to try my patience, I will grow angry and have no choice but to . . ."

The major's voice trailed off. He was looking past Joe, staring at the sloped wall of the dam. They were fifty feet away.

Joe turned. A trickle of phosphorescence could be seen where the water met the dam, turbulence where there shouldn't be any. Water was running down the face of the dam and into the river. Not a flood, more like someone had left a spigot open somewhere high above, but there should not have been any.

"Oh no," Joe mumbled.

"Take us closer," the major ordered, stepping up to the front of the boat.

The driver nudged the throttles, and the patrol boat surged forward. A few seconds later they were right up against the face of the dam, two spotlights on the patrol boat's light bar trained on the flowing water.

"It's picking up speed," Joe noted.

He stared upward along the sloping face as the major tilted one of the lights. An elongated snaking path led up and away from them.

"Can this be true?" Major Edo mumbled to himself. "Can this be happening?"

"I swear to you," Joe said, "we're in danger. The whole valley is in danger."

The major continued to stare as if in shock. "But this is not that much," he said.

"It'll get worse," Joe insisted, still looking up. "Can you see where it's coming from?"

The major manipulated the spotlights to follow the path of the trickling water, but the trail disappeared where the lights faded.

"No," the major said, all airs of superiority gone.

"You need to get a warning out," Joe urged. "Get everyone away from the river."

"It will cause a panic," the major said. "What if you're wrong?"

"I'm not."

The major was paralyzed. He didn't seem able to act.

"Unchain me," Joe shouted. "I'll help you look. Once we find the source, maybe we can do something about it, but at least you'll know for sure."

All the time they waited, the flow increased steadily. Two spigots' worth now, turned wide open.

"Please, Major."

The major snapped out of it. He grabbed the keys from one of the guards, unlocked Joe's cuffs first and then the shackles around his feet.

"Come with me," the major said, grabbing a walkie-talkie.

Joe climbed off the boat and onto the angled surface of the dam. He ran alongside the major, clambering upward and following the trail of water.

The slope of Aswan is only thirteen degrees, relatively mild unless one is running up it at full speed. After covering seven hundred feet horizontally and ninety-one feet vertically, the major was winded, and they still hadn't found the breach.

"The flow is getting worse," he said, pausing near the stream.

Joe saw fine sand and other sediments in the flow. The scouring had begun already.

"We have to go higher," Joe said.

The major nodded, and they resumed their climb. By the time they were within fifty feet of the top, the flow of water was a six-foot-wide stream, surging with foam and small rocks. Suddenly, a section of the wall gave way and the flow doubled instantly, rushing toward them.

"Look out," Joe shouted, pulling the major aside.

He and Joe backed away from the flow. There could be no denying it now.

The major brought the radio to his mouth and keyed the talk switch.

"This is Major Edo," he said. "I report a level 1 emergency. Sound all alarms and begin a full evacuation. The dam has been compromised."

Something unintelligible came back through the radio, and the major responded instantly. "No, this isn't a drill or a false alarm! The dam is in danger! I repeat: The dam is in danger of imminent collapse!"

Another small section of the upper rim gave way, and the foaming water poured down the slope in turbulent fashion. If anyone doubted the major's warning, all they had to do was look out the window and see for themselves.

In the distance the sound of alarms rose forth in the dark. They sounded like air-raid sirens wailing.

Down below, the patrol boat raced off to the south.

"Cowards!" the major yelled.

Joe couldn't honestly blame them, but it left him and the major in a bad predicament. The dam began to tremble underfoot. The structure might have been massive and the breach only fifteen feet wide at the moment, but Joe and the major were far too close for it to be safe.

"Come on," Joe said, grabbing the major by the shoulder and racing toward the crest of the dam. "We have to get to the top, it's our only chance."

CHAPTER 51

THE SAME DARKNESS THAT RULED OVER EGYPT HAD ALREADY
settled across the Arabian Sea and the Indian Ocean, with one
minor difference. The skies had cleared over Egypt but were
clouding up over the ocean. Enough so, that two hours before dawn Kurt Austin could no longer see the stars.

That concerned him more than usual as he was standing on a
fifteen-foot raft in the middle of the sea, navigating with a seventy-
year-old sextant and a set of yellowed, moth-eaten charts left over
from World War Two.

The boat was an outrigger-style craft. It resembled a cross between the famous Kon-Tiki raft and a Hawaiian five-man canoe.
It had a raised bow, a wider central section and a squared-off
stern. Its propulsion came from oars or, more preferably, a strange-
looking triangular sail known as a crab claw that stuck out to
one side.

The crab claw was an ancient sail, used for over a thousand
years and very effective at propelling small boats without being

ungainly. Ahead of it Kurt's addition to the raft billowed in a ten-foot arc. The more modern-looking sail was a makeshift version of a spinnaker. It acted something like a wing and allowed the raft to sail closer to the wind.

Behind him, four similar rafts followed them. A flotilla from Pickett's Island.

The plan was to sneak aboard and take over the floating island. With eighteen men plus Leilani and himself, five of the Pain Makers and forty rifles—the extras being brought along to arm the prisoners Kurt hoped to set free—it would almost be a fair fight, providing Kurt could lead them to the battleground.

He lowered the sextant.

"Any luck?" Leilani asked.

"No," he said. "We're sailing blind."

Kurt stepped back from the bow and put the sextant away. He turned to Tautog. "Let's stay on this heading for now."

Tautog nodded. He and his nephew Varu were guiding the boat.

The fleet had been sailing for five hours. They'd been making good time because the winds had reversed direction, the way sea and land breezes alternated as day turned to night on the coast. The pattern was helpful, though it shouldn't have been occurring in the open ocean. Kurt put it down to Jinn's weather manipulation.

"You're worried," Leilani said, moving closer to him.

"I may have just sailed us all into oblivion."

Kurt turned his gaze back to the *John Bury*'s old charts. Pickett had determined the island's exact position and marked it on the map where there had been nothing but blue ocean. He'd also marked the other two islands and drawn a circle around them. *The Bury Archipelago* was scribbled in faded pen along with the letters *U.S.* It seemed Pickett had claimed them for America.

Leilani looked over his shoulder. "Where are we?"

"Roughly here," Kurt said, pointing to a spot on the map.

"And where's Aqua-Terra?"

"That's a very good question," he said.

After discovering the Pain Maker, Kurt had immediately gone to the charts. After a series of estimations and calculations, he'd guessed at Aqua-Terra's location, assuming, perhaps foolishly, that it would remain in the same general area. Judging from the wind and the distance from Pickett's Island, he calculated that they could just about reach Aqua-Terra before dawn if they left right away.

Any real delay would have made it impossible and meant waiting until the next night, since approaching the island in daylight would have been suicide. And that twenty-four-hour hold meant leaving Paul, Gamay and the others in Jinn's clutches. It meant another day for Jinn's scheme to play out or for him to leave the island behind and disappear. Kurt considered those possibilities unacceptable, and the fleet had moved out with great haste.

As it turned out, the small boats had sailed better than Kurt thought they would, enjoying more favorable winds along the way. They were well ahead of his schedule, but also it seemed on the verge of being lost.

"When we last saw Aqua-Terra, it was sitting idle right here," he said. "If it stayed that way, we should be right on top of it."

"I see light," Varu said. "Light off the port bow."

All eyes swung to port. There, perhaps three miles away, was a dimly glowing apparition. It almost looked like a ghost ship floating in the fog, but it was Marchetti's island. It was running dark, with only a few lights turned on here and there.

Leilani smiled. "You were saying?"

Kurt grinned. "Let's turn to the northeast," he said to Tautog and then pointed. "That way."

Tautog and Varu shifted the rudder and the sails. The boat came around to a northeasterly heading. The rest of the fleet matched the turn.

"Why not sail toward it?" Leilani asked.

Kurt kept an eye on his bearings and began counting. "A half mile to the northeast and we can turn and run almost straight downwind toward the island. It'll give us more speed and better maneuverability."

"What if they spot us?" she asked.

"The island is two thousand feet long and twenty stories high in places and we almost missed it. We're on a dark raft, with dark sails and coming at them in the middle of a foggy night. Even a lookout won't be able to see us until we're right on top of them. And according to Ishmael, Jinn has no more than thirty men on board, at least half of them have to be asleep. The chances of anyone noticing us are slim."

KURT WAS THREE-QUARTERS CORRECT. Twenty of Jinn's thirty men were asleep. A few others manned the brig and still others worked on the damaged engine room with the traitors from Marchetti's crew. Only two lookouts were posted. They patrolled the island, but there was no way they could adequately watch what was essentially a mile of shoreline and a dozen acres of deck.

It was a lost cause. The men made their rounds with all the enthusiasm of underpaid security guards.

One guard who was lucky enough to avoid the long, boring walks found himself stationed in Aqua-Terra's control room monitoring radar.

So far, not a single image had appeared on the screen. The quiet had lasted so long that when a couple of targets did appear for a moment, the guard didn't see them. He wasn't even really looking anymore, just trying to fight off the need for sleep.

The images vanished quickly and then appeared for the second time minutes later. Diagonal lines were drawn to them, indicating ranging mode had been activated. At this point the guard became confused. By the time he traced the lines to the targets, the return had disappeared again, replaced by a pop-up box that read CONTACT LOST.

The guard straightened in his seat.

A wave of suspicion flowed through him.

Had he just seen something? If so, where had it gone? How had it disappeared? The thought of American Stealth fighters ran through his head.

He looked out the window into the darkness, saw nothing and then returned his eyes to the set.

When the targets failed to reappear, he grew even more suspicious.

He grabbed a pair of large binoculars and stepped out onto the observation wing. Trying to focus in the misty gloom was difficult, and he didn't see anything. Partly because he spent most of his time scanning the sky for aircraft or helicopters, but also because, even powered down for the night, the lights from the island put a soft glow out into the mist that made anything beyond the reach of the lights impossible to see. Had he looked directly toward the five bamboo rafts, he would not have seen anything but the white veil of the mist.

Frustrated, he went back to the radar and crouched over it, watching it closely like a cat guarding a hole in the wall where a mouse lives.

CHAPTER 52

As Kurt approached the colossal island of Aqua-Terra with his fleet of matchstick rafts, it loomed out of the mist like the Rock of Gibraltar. He felt like an ant attacking an elephant.

"It is gigantic," Tautog said.

"Mostly empty," Kurt reminded himself.

"What if they brought more people in since we left?" Leilani asked.

He turned to her with pursed lips, not exactly needing the voice of reason at this point. "You really have to meet Joe," he said. "I think you two were separated at birth."

Knowing that Marchetti's brig lay near the aft end of the island, Kurt decided to make for it. He stepped to the bow, easing around the lower spar of the sail and unlashing a tarp from the Pain Maker's sound box.

"Leilani," he said quietly, "you and Varu start powering this up."

She moved to the generator and flywheel near the aft end of the boat. It was a little ungainly to operate the hand-powered generator on the small craft, but once they got the flywheel up to speed the weight of the heavy disc spinning would provide most of the power.

Kurt heard the dynamo begin turning and saw the power needle edge up. They were almost within a hundred yards. He set the range dial, and the aperture of the speakers changed.

They were close enough now that the bulk of the island hid them from the two main towers and the control room and any radar beams. The only thing they had to worry about were guards on patrol. If Kurt spotted any, he would have to hit them with the blast. If that failed, a rifle he'd tested lay close by.

The windows of the lower deck began to appear more clearly. He counted. The last five windows belonged to the brig.

Kurt took out the old binoculars and stared through them. The five windows were dimly backlit. He couldn't see any activity inside.

He thought about making for the ladder and the gangways near the aft, then changed his mind. If a permanent guard was posted anywhere, that might be a prime spot for it. Instead he'd try something else.

He held up a hand for the other boats to follow, and they angled toward the fifth window. At thirty-five yards, roughly the distance he'd been at when hit with the sound wave on the beach, Kurt flipped the switch to STAND BY, aimed the speaker box using a lever and locked onto the window.

With Leilani and Varu still providing the elbow grease to give it power, Kurt changed the range setting to thirty-five and flipped the switch from STAND BY to ACTIVE. Instantly, the ethereal waves of noise began to issue forth.

With the Pain Maker aimed at the fifth window, Kurt saw the heavy glass begin to vibrate.

"More power," he said.

Tautog took over for Leilani, and the power needle came up into the red. Kurt kept the beam focused on the target.

"What are you doing?" Leilani asked.

"Ever see the old Memorex commercial?"

She shook her head.

"Just watch that window."

The window was vibrating, shaking back and forth with the sound waves like the skin of a drum. He could see the ripples catching the light. A strange noise began echoing out over the water like the ringing of a Tibetan Singing Bowl. Kurt worried it would give them away, but it was too late to stop, they were committed now.

"More power," he whispered again, and then, realizing Varu was sweating and exhausted, he took the young man's spot and put his own muscle into the effort. The boat drifted, but Leilani kept the Pain Maker focused on the glass.

It looked like they were going to fail, as if the hurricane-proof window was going to hold up against the vibration, when all of a sudden two of the other boats snapped their systems on and focused them on the same window.

The three combined beams of sound shattered the glass instantly. It exploded inward, an effect Kurt hadn't counted on. He only hoped Marchetti and the Trouts were in the room and had been smart enough to back away from the vibrating windowpane.

INSIDE THEIR CELL, Gamay heard the sound first: a strange resonance that initially seemed only like her ears were ringing.

* * *

"WHAT'S THAT?" Paul asked.

Apparently it wasn't her imagination.

"I have no idea," she said.

Gamay stood, leaving her post at the door and poking about the dark quarters like a suburbanite looking through a quiet house for a chirping cricket.

The noise grew slowly in intensity, if not volume. Had there been a dog present, it would have been howling at the top of its lungs.

"Maybe we're being abducted by aliens," Marchetti suggested.

Gamay ignored him. The noise had brought her to the large window overlooking the ocean. She pressed her face against it. Out in the dark, barely illuminated by the few lights Aqua-Terra was running, she saw a collection of native-looking rafts. She recognized a figure on the lead boat.

"It's Kurt," she said.

Paul and Marchetti ran over.

"What on earth is he doing?" Paul asked, gazing at the strange goings-on. "And who are those people with him?"

"I haven't the foggiest idea," Gamay said.

As they watched, two of the other rafts aligned themselves with Kurt's, and the strange resonance spiked an octave or two. A crash of shattering glass rang out somewhere to their left.

"I believe he's trying to rescue us," Marchetti said.

"Yes," Gamay replied, proud and sad all at the same time. "Unfortunately, he's breaking into the wrong room."

OUT IN THE HALL, the men charged with guarding the prisoners heard the vibration for a moment, but it sounded to them like the massage chair on full tilt once again. The shattering glass was a different story.

They jumped to their feet.

"Check the prisoners," the lead guard ordered.

Two of his men grabbed their weapons and ran down the hall. As they vanished, he picked up the phone and dialed up to the control room. After four rings, no one had answered.

"Pick up, already," he grumbled.

The tinkling of more glass falling caught his attention. It was coming from the room across from him, not from down the hall.

He considered the possibility that the prisoners had escaped or the even wilder possibility that someone had broken in through the window. It occurred to him that he'd better check it out before he reported. He hung up the phone and stepped cautiously from the desk, drawing out his pistol as he approached the door.

He doused the lights in the hall and pushed the door open, swinging the gun forward.

He saw nothing but darkness. Then a breeze wafted across the room, and he saw the illuminated mist outside the shattered window.

He checked all around but saw nothing odd, and definitely no intruders. Still, something had to have broken the window.

He eased toward it, the glass crunching under his feet. Something was floating next to the hull. He stepped closer and saw a strange-looking sailboat. Another floated next to it. Neither looked like something the American Special Forces might use. He took another step, heard a strange buzzing noise and then felt his whole body tense up as if he'd been shocked with a high-voltage line.

Pain ran up and down his arms and torso. His neck stiffened, and he bit his tongue as his jaw clamped down on it. He fell to his knees, collapsing on the glass and dropping the pistol. The pain vanished as he hit the floor but the effect lingered.

A figure vaulted over the sill of the busted window, landing beside him.

The guard reached around for the gun he'd dropped, and then felt a heavy boot come down on his hand, crushing his fingers. He yanked his hand back, grunting, and then was knocked cold by the butt of a rifle that hit him in the side of the head.

FROM THEIR CELL GAMAY, Paul and Marchetti watched as Kurt and a couple of others tossed up grappling hooks and began climbing. They couldn't see the broken window from their viewpoint, but Marchetti had no doubt it was one or two doors aft of where they were.

"Doesn't mean they can't get here," he said. "All they have to do is get rid of the goons at the post and we're home free."

Commotion outside their door drew Gamay's attention away. "Could it be them?"

"Too soon," Paul said.

"Then it's the guards."

Gamay sprinted back toward her post beside the door. She heard the guard's card key in the lock, heard the lock buzz and release. She dove across the floor and slid into the wall next to the power outlet just as the door began to swing open.

Paul's plan to use the massage chair as a weapon depended on timing. As Gamay hit the wall, she grabbed the cord and jammed the plug into the outlet, hoping she wasn't too late.

A shower of sparks blew out from the wall, while others snapped from the metal door. The guard, who still had his hand on the frame, received a heavy jolt and was knocked backward. The leads they'd pulled out of the chair and hooked to the door sparked and smoked, and a fuse blew somewhere.

Paul pounced on the guard and grabbed for the gun. A scuffle ensued, but Paul's knee hitting the man's groin was enough to end it quickly. He and Marchetti dragged the man back in, and Gamay unplugged the cord and grabbed the door, keeping it from shutting. A quick look told her the hall was empty.

"Let's go," she said.

Paul and Marchetti left the writhing guard on the floor, tied up with a bedsheet. They slipped out and went to the right.

KURT HAD REACHED the guard post in front of Marchetti's brig. It resembled a spa's reception area more than a post. A computer sat on one side of the stark white counter, a multiline phone on the other.

Tautog and Varu came in. Kurt pointed to a few secluded spots from which the hallway could be defended. "Watch for trouble," he said.

He turned to run down the curving hall but spotted three figures shuffling up it toward him. To his surprise and relief, he recognized Gamay, Paul and Marchetti.

"Boy, are we glad to see you," Gamay said. "We thought you were dead."

Kurt pulled them behind the desk. "I was worried that you guys might be dead as well. What are you doing out of your cage?"

"We escaped," Gamay said. "Just now."

"And after I came all this way to rescue you," Kurt said, smiling.

"Is Joe with you?"

"No," Kurt said. "I put him on a truck in Yemen two days ago."

"A truck to where?"

"That's a good question," Kurt said. The fact that Paul, Gamay and Marchetti had remained under lock and key rather than being rescued by some American Special Forces team told Kurt Joe wasn't out of the woods yet. He knew Joe could take care of himself and though he'd feel better when he knew for certain that Joe was okay, there was little he could do about it now.

"What's our situation?" he asked, focusing on the present.

"We took one guard out," Paul said. "He's locked in our cell now."

"We took out the guy up here," Kurt said.

"Who are your friends?" Gamay asked.

"I'm Leilani Tanner," Leilani said. "The real one."

Gamay smiled. "And the rest of the cavalry?"

"Pleased to meet you," Tautog said. "I am the eighteenth Roosevelt of—"

"Save it for later," he said. "Someone's coming."

The footsteps approached more casually this time. It was another guard, who Kurt realized must have been sent to check on the other prisoners. The guard rounded the corner, came face-to-face with several rifles and froze.

Kurt grabbed the man's card key and his pistol.

"What now?" Paul asked. "Do we leave?"

"No," Kurt said. "When the moment of victory appears, it must be seized."

They stared at him.

"Sun Tzu," Leilani told them as if she were an old hand.

"So what does that mean in English?" Gamay asked.

"It means now that we're on board, we're not going anywhere except to find Jinn, Zarrina and Otero. Once we have them, this thing is over."

He turned to Marchetti. "Are your crewmen down here?"

"Most of them."

"You and Paul take this guy and get your crew out. Lock him in the cell when you come out."

Paul nodded and went to work.

Kurt turned to Tautog. "Let's tie up the boats, get the rest of your men aboard. At this point we need all hands on deck."

Moments later, with the prisoners and guards having traded places and the small flotilla tied up to a water pipe in the cabin with the broken window, Kurt commanded a force of thirty-seven armed men and women—Marchetti's men knowing the island, Tautog's trained in using the rifles and the Pain Makers.

Kurt had two of the machines brought aboard and found a pair of dollies to mount them on. One went with the group who was heading for the crew quarters, the other stayed with Kurt, Leilani and the Trouts. The four of them, along with Tautog and Varu, wheeled the bulky machine into the elevator like roadies moving amps backstage.

As the bulk of their force headed for the crew quarters, Kurt planned to find Jinn al-Khalif.

"Which floor for the Presidential Suite?" he asked.

"You mean my quarters?" Marchetti said.

"If yours are the most luxurious on the island, then yes, that's exactly what I mean."

"Top floor of course," Marchetti said, pressing the button.

As the elevator doors closed, Kurt patted the sound box and smiled a roughish grin.

"Time to wake the neighbors," he said.

CHAPTER 53

JOE ZAVALA WAS RUNNING FOR HIS LIFE. BAD ANKLE AND all, he was charging diagonally across the wet slope of the Aswan Dam in search of higher and safer ground. The major lagged behind, seemingly still awed by what was going on.

"I wouldn't keep looking back if I were you."

The major got the message and pressed forward, catching up with Joe.

Joe's plan was to get to the top, away from the widening breach, and survey the damage.

Upon reaching the crest, Joe stood on the road that crossed the dam. A thirty-foot-deep V had already been gouged out. Water from Lake Nasser was pouring through it and down over the side.

In the garish illumination of the floodlights, Joe could see water scouring away the rocks and sand like a flash flood shooting through a narrow mountain canyon.

As this effect took hold, the damage spread sideways in both directions, and the V widened toward each side of the dam.

As the flood removed the aggregate underneath it, the asphalt of the road held out for a moment, forming a jetty of sorts over the rushing water. But the supporting ground washed away quickly and large chunks of the blacktop collapsed and went tumbling over the side.

Looking back to the lake, Joe noticed something. "The water's so high."

"The highest it's ever been," the major admitted. "Two years of record storms."

Joe knew nothing about General Aziz and his dealings with Jinn, but it was these record rains that made Aziz bold enough to break his contract. These same rains would now devastate his country.

"Where's the control room?" Joe shouted.

The major pointed to the east side of the dam and a new building that sat near the dead center, about even with the peninsula. "The new control room is by the power plant."

"Let's go."

Joe took off running once again and this time the major kept up with him. Behind them, the breach in the top of the dam continued widening by a foot or more every fifteen seconds.

Reaching the control room, the major threw open the door and he and Joe rushed inside. They found the command center in utter chaos. Half the posts were empty. The brave men and women who remained were trying to get a handle on what was happening.

A supervisor spotted the major. "Have we been attacked?" he asked. "We saw no explosions."

"You have to open all the floodgates," Joe shouted, not waiting for the major to reply. "Even the emergency spillways."

"Who are you?" the man asked. There was no real malice in

the man's words, just shock that the scruffy-looking man with the major was giving orders.

"I'm an American engineer. I've worked on levees and river projects once or twice in my life and I'm telling you open all your spillways if you want one chance in ten of surviving this."

"But—"

"There's a thirty-foot break in the top of the dam," Joe said, cutting the supervisor off. "It's just below water level, halfway between here and the west bank. If you get the level down below this break, you might survive. If you don't, the whole dam will wash away."

The supervisor stared at Joe for a moment and then at the major, who nodded and shouted, "Trust him!"

Done wondering, the supervisor turned and shouted across the room. "Open all the spillways! Open all gates to full!"

The workers began throwing switches and levers.

"Floodgates opening!" one of them replied. "Blocks One and Two filling. Blocks Three and Four also responding."

On a wall-sized display known as a mimic board, the indicators turned from red to green. Twelve blue channels in the display represented the twelve generator channels beneath the dam.

"What about the emergency spillways?" Joe asked.

All major dams have emergency spillways around them just in case of such an event. These high-volume bypass channels were rarely used.

"Coming open now," the supervisor said. He watched and counted: ". . . twenty-eight, twenty-nine, thirty. All gates are open. Also the Toshka Canal. Within ten seconds, we will be discharging maximum water volume. Four hundred thousand cubic feet per second."

Joe heard and felt a great reverberation shaking the building from within. He looked out over the Nile down below. The water in the tailrace was churning like world-class rapids.

Thrown wide open, the spillways were dumping enough water to fill a supertanker every fifteen seconds. Maybe twice that amount was already flowing over the breach. Joe had a bad feeling it wouldn't be enough. If Lake Nasser was full to the rim, it would take hours or even days to lower the water below the level of the breach. In that time, the gap would deepen and the process would continue. Joe feared they would never catch up.

As the flood raged, the multimillion-ton structure shook like a city in the grips of an earthquake. But instead of passing, the tremors held steady and grew worse.

Another huge section of the dam broke off and rumbled down the slope like an avalanche. In minutes the rushing water had swept it away, and now the breach stood two hundred feet wide. The outflow from it had to be ten times greater than all the other spillways combined. It looked like Niagara Falls.

Downriver, the flood swept onward, dragging boats and docks and anything in its path along for the ride. Barges and riverboats that took tourists on Nile cruises were torn from their moorings and flung downstream like children's toys in the bath.

The water raced along the banks of the Nile, scouring out the walls in places, undercutting the rock and sandstone and causing landslides and collapses reminiscent of glaciers calving in the arctic.

It surged up over the banks and swept around the hotels and other buildings. Smaller buildings were obliterated as if they were made of toothpicks. One moment they were there, the next they were gone, replaced by rushing water. And this was only the beginning.

The supervisor stood silent. The major stood silent. Even

Joe Zavala stood silent. They were powerless to do anything but watch.

Ninety percent of Egypt's population lived within twelve miles of the Nile. If the whole dam gave way, Joe could see a disaster counting its victims in the millions. Even as the water spread out over the valley, sparing victims downstream from the destructive force, the aftermath might be worse than the flood.

Millions would be homeless. Half of Egypt's farmable land would be flooded and at least temporarily destroyed. Dysentery, cholera and all the diseases that come with unsanitary conditions, and those spread by mosquitoes and other insects, would become epidemic.

It would only add insult to injury that the dam provided fifteen percent of Egypt's electricity. But when piled on top of the nation's other problems and its precarious political state, Joe feared a governmental implosion. He could see a nation of eighty million people falling into anarchy in one fell swoop.

"How long before total collapse?" he asked.

"Difficult to say," the supervisor replied. "It depends on whether the core can hold."

Joe noticed how the topside breach had widened substantially but hardly deepened at all. It was no longer a V shape, more like an extremely elongated U.

"What's the core made of?" he asked, remembering how it had appeared to be a different material in the cross section of the model.

"Semiplastic, impermeable clay," the supervisor said. "Concrete down below."

If Joe was right the rushing water had scoured down through the aggregate and reached the core. The erosion rate had almost stopped. "Does it run the whole width of the dam?"

The supervisor nodded. "It's dug into the rock on either side."

"Can it hold the lake back?"

The supervisor thought about that for a moment. "The core won't erode like the aggregate does, but as the back side of the slope is scoured away the amount of rock and stone keeping the core in place will be reduced steadily. At some point the weight of Lake Nasser will simply shove the core aside like a bus might push a small car."

Joe looked out past the breach. The water was cascading over the top, plummeting and spreading. But the gentle thirteen-degree slope and the stone covering seemed to be helping, the covering was holding its own at least for now.

"I think the surface lining is holding up," he said. "If the water level drops far enough, the core might save the day. And with the breach as wide as it is, that shouldn't take more than a few hours."

The supervisor nodded. "It's possible," he said, sounding like he didn't want to get ahead of himself.

Major Edo pointed to something else, something Joe hadn't seen before. A small geyser farther down below. All but lost in the greater flood, it was blasting outward like a water feature in some ornate garden. The spray soared and fanned into a fine mist that caught the illumination from the floodlights.

"What about that?" Major Edo asked.

Joe's heart dropped. He remembered the mock-up in Yemen. The higher flood had come first, but the lower tunnel had caused the core to fail and the entire dam along with it.

"That's a bigger problem," Joe said.

"How did this happen?" the supervisor asked.

Joe tried to explain about the microbots and how they burrowed through things, including concrete and clay. No one questioned him this time.

"Could they still be down there?"

"Possibly," Joe said. "Maybe burrowing into the clay to widen the tunnel in ways the water can't."

"If it widens too much . . ." the supervisor began. He didn't need to finish.

"Do you have any way to seal something like this?" Joe asked.

The supervisor rubbed his chin. "There may be one way," he said. "We have a compound known as Ultra-Set. It's a polymer that bonds with clay, expands many times over to fill small gaps. It becomes impervious in a matter of seconds. If we could pump it into the tunnel that those things you're talking about have drilled, it might block it up. If the topside holds and the water level drops fast enough, we might avert a total failure."

A new wave of tremors shook the building.

"What's the drawback?" Joe asked.

"There's only one way to get the Ultra-Set into the tunnel," the supervisor said. "We have to pump it in under high pressure. To do that, someone has to find the entry point on the lake side of the dam."

Joe looked at the supervisor and the few others who remained at their posts in the shuddering control room. "You need a diver," he guessed, finding it hard to believe his fate. He smiled anyway. "How lucky for me."

CHAPTER 54

THE ELEVATOR DOORS OPENED TO REVEAL THE TOP FLOOR of Marchetti's pyramid and a luxurious foyer. Three of Jinn's men were stationed there and they turned at the sound of the elevator's ping.

It was a natural reaction. They had no reason to suspect any trouble. In fact, it looked to Kurt as if they were snapping to attention as the sound wave from the Pain Maker hit them and dropped them to their knees.

One let out a grunt, another stumbled backward and knocked over a table with a vase on it that smashed to the ground, the third man just fell straight down.

Kurt let go of the handle that powered the system as Paul, Gamay, Tautog and Varu bound the men in cuffs from the brig. The men looked dazed and confused.

"I feel your pain," Kurt said. "Or at least I did about ten hours ago."

The men were gagged with duct tape and stuffed in a janitor's closet.

"This way," Marchetti said, heading to the right. They made it to the corner, where the foyer intersected the hall. Poking his head around it, Kurt saw it was empty.

"Let's go."

Halfway down the hall they came to a large set of double doors. Marchetti went to a keypad. As he pressed in his code, the sound of shooting broke out far below them. Little pops that sounded like cap guns going off.

"Some of Jinn's men must be resisting," Gamay said.

Kurt nodded. "Hurry."

Marchetti punched in the code as Paul and Tautog charged up the Pain Maker.

Kurt kicked the doors open and flipped the switch. There was no one there.

"Wrong room?" Gamay asked.

Kurt shut the machine off and stepped inside, looking around. The bed had been slept in. He smelled the scent of jasmine. The same perfume Zarrina had worn. Apparently she was closer to Jinn than they thought.

"Right room," he said. "We just missed them."

As he stormed back past Marchetti, he mumbled, "Might want to change your sheets."

"Or burn the whole bed," Marchetti said.

Kurt was moving down the hall as more gunfire rang out. The others were rushing to catch up with him.

"That explains why his men were snapping to attention," Paul suggested. "They thought someone was coming back."

"So where did they go?" Leilani asked.

"I can only think of one place," Kurt said.

* * *

JINN STOOD IN AQUA-TERRA'S control room shocked by what had occurred. Zarrina, Otero and Matson surrounded him, along with the radar operator and another one of his men. The rest were scattered, perhaps ten or less now, fighting Marchetti's crew and what looked like U.S. Marines.

"How? How is this possible?" he asked. "There are no patrol boats or helicopters here. Where did they come from?"

"We have video from the detention level," Otero said, studying a laptop. "I hate to say this, but it's Austin."

"It can't be," Jinn said. "He's dead. I've killed him twice."

"Then he's come back from the dead," Otero said, turning the laptop toward Jinn. "Look."

It was Austin. Jinn could not imagine how. It was as if Austin had appeared in his midst like a ghost. An appropriate thought as Jinn had been certain he'd been sent to perdition.

The shooting was growing closer. From the observation deck a few of Jinn's men could be seen running toward Marchetti's central park. They didn't make it.

"We have to get out of here," Zarrina said. "This battle is lost."

Jinn studied the layout. They would never make it to the dry dock, where the flying boat was moored. Even if they did, a few well-placed bullets or the missiles he'd brought in would take them down.

"We can't run," he said.

"And we can't win this fight," Zarrina replied sharply. "There are only five of us."

"Silence," Jinn snapped.

He was trying to think, trying desperately to come up with a way to turn the tables. He looked to Otero. "Access the horde and energize the transmitter."

Otero began tapping away on his laptop and then pushed it across the table to Jinn.

"You have access."

"What are you going to do?" Matson asked.

Jinn ignored him. He began typing. Slowly at first, making sure he was in the right area of the system, and then faster.

Gunfire in the hall spurred him on.

He selected a command from the menu and hit ENTER.

The door to the room flew open and shots were exchanged, with shells ricocheting around the room.

Jinn took cover as Matson and the radar operator were cut down. A few seconds later Jinn's other guard was killed as he tried to get off a shot.

"Give it up, Jinn!" Austin's voice called out.

Jinn found himself behind an island in the center of the control room with many of the vital controls on its surface. Otero and Zarrina crowded in behind with him. "And if we do?"

"I'll put you in chains, deliver you to the proper authorities."

"You expect me to believe you won't kill us?"

"Much as I'd like to," Austin replied, "that's not my choice to make. Don't count on going back to Yemen, though. I'm thinking the World Court or some American military base."

"I will not be put in such hands!" Jinn shouted.

"Then show yourself and let's finish this man-to-man."

Jinn could see Austin in a reflection. He was hidden around the corner of the steel bulkhead. Jinn had no shot. If he stood, Austin would cut him down. If he hid, Austin or some member of Austin's team would soon flank his position.

"I have a better idea," Jinn said. "I will now teach you a lesson about power and its proper use."

He glanced at the laptop. A blinking green box on the screen told him his instructions had been sent and received. He could now take action.

He slipped the pistol from his holster, pressed the safety with his thumb until it clicked and held it tight to his chest.

"Time's about up," Austin informed him.

Jinn knew it was.

He placed the barrel of the pistol against the back of Otero's skull and pulled the trigger. The muffled explosion blasted the computer programmer and what was left of his head out into the open space of the floor. Jinn's second shot shattered the laptop, sending bits of plastic and microchips in all directions. He fired again just for good measure, destroying the laptop's screen.

He tossed the weapon away. "I surrender," he said, putting his hands up.

SHIELDED BY THE BULKHEAD, Kurt watched Jinn in the same reflection that Jinn had caught sight of him. Something didn't add up. He'd seen Jinn pull the weapon and expected the man to go down swinging, but the bullet to Otero's head and tossing the gun aside were suspicious actions to say the least.

Zarrina tossed out her weapon and put her hands up. She and Jinn stood slowly and Kurt leveled the M1 carbine at Jinn's chest.

"You flinch, you die."

Kurt stepped in the room. Paul and Tautog came in next. They fanned out.

Kurt sensed a trap. With his rifle still leveled at Jinn, he checked the dead men: Jinn's guard, Matson, what was left of Otero and the radar operator.

He found nothing out of the ordinary, but the smug look remained on Jinn's face. Like he'd just palmed a card or gotten away with something.

"What did you do?" Kurt whispered, waiting for a booby trap to spring or an explosion to go off. "What did you do?"

Jinn said nothing. Kurt noticed the shattered laptop. He realized that Jinn had just executed Otero, the programmer. The two things had to be connected.

Shouts drifted in through the open door from down below. They came from Tautog's men on the zero deck.

"Something's happening," one of them called out. "The sea has come to life!"

Kurt stepped outside. Through the fog of the night he could see the water churning.

"Marchetti, get the lights on!"

Marchetti ran to the control panel and started throwing a bank of switches. All around the island, sections of the ocean lit up as Marchetti switched on floodlights both above and below water. Instantly, Kurt saw what was happening.

The water was stirring almost as if it was boiling over. The horde surrounding them had come to the surface and was surging toward the island.

"He's called them in," Marchetti whispered fearfully. "He's called them home."

Jinn began to laugh, a deep laugh that was sinister, sadistic and utterly filled with an egomaniac's pride.

"You will now understand what I mean by power," he said. "Unless you release me, the horde will consume you all."

CHAPTER 55

KURT AUSTIN HAD KNOWN THEY WERE IN DOUBLE TROUBLE as soon as he heard the madman laugh. He stormed back into the control room and jammed the barrel of the carbine against Jinn's face right between the eyes.

"Call them off!"

"Let us go," Jinn said, "and I'll do as you wish."

"Call them off or I'll splatter your brains all over the wall."

"And what will that get you, Mr. Austin?"

Kurt pulled back. "Marchetti, find a computer, you're going to have to do your code-breaking thing again."

Marchetti raced over to another laptop, docked on the main console.

"He'll never break it," Jinn insisted. "He'll never even get in."

Marchetti looked up. "He's right. I was able to reverse Otero's last trick because I could access the files, but we're locked out of everything."

"Can't you hack it?"

"It's a nine-digit code protected with top-level encryption. A supercomputer couldn't break it without a month or so to work on it."

"You've got to be able to do something."

"I can't even log on."

Now Kurt understood why Jinn had blasted Otero and the laptop. It was Otero's code. No chance he would give it up lying dead on the floor and no chance Marchetti could check the laptop for any type of keystroke memory or temp file.

Leilani eased up beside Kurt. "What's happening?"

"Those things that made us sparkle, they're all around the island, a lot thicker than they were when we saw them. Jinn's sent them into a frenzy. They'll come on board like a horde of locusts and eat everything in sight, including us."

"What are we going to do?" Leilani asked.

"Is there any way to stop them?" Kurt asked Marchetti.

Marchetti shook his head. "There are too many, fifty miles' worth in every direction."

"Then we have to get off the island. Where are those airships of yours?"

"In the hangar bay by the helipad."

"Take that laptop and get everyone to meet us there," Kurt said. He looked at Tautog. "Get your men up here. We're leaving by air."

"Not to the boats?" Tautog asked.

"The boats won't help us now."

Tautog went to the balcony and began yelling to his men, waving for them to come up. Marchetti grabbed a microphone and began an island-wide broadcast through a series of loudspeakers.

Kurt noticed two small radios on the flat part of the control console. He grabbed them and then shoved Jinn toward the elevator doors. "Let's go."

Moments later Kurt and his growing entourage stood on the lighted helipad suspended between the two pyramid buildings. From this vantage point the sea around Aqua-Terra looked more like solid ground covered with millions of beetles. They reflected the glare of Aqua-Terra's floodlights in a smoky charcoal color. Streams of them could be seen coming inland like long, probing fingers.

"They look thick enough to walk on," Paul mentioned.

"I wouldn't try it," Kurt said.

A hangar door opened in the side of the starboard pyramid, and Marchetti's men began rolling one of the airships out. Two others waited behind it.

"How many people can each one hold?" Kurt asked.

"Eight. Nine at most," Marchetti said.

"Dump out everything you don't need," Kurt said. "See if you can lighten the loads."

Marchetti went to supervise. Paul and Gamay went with him. Leilani stepped over to Zarrina, who was standing against the edge of the helipad with Jinn.

"So you pretended to be me," she said.

"I wouldn't get too close," Kurt warned.

"You're a weak little woman," Zarrina said. "That was the hardest part to play."

Kurt grabbed Leilani as she went to slap Zarrina, pulling her away a safe distance.

"She's baiting you," Kurt said. "Go help the others."

Leilani pouted but did as he asked.

"It's too bad you didn't try more to comfort me," Zarrina said. "You might have enjoyed it."

"Don't flatter yourself," Kurt said.

Beside her, Jinn fumed.

Tautog greeted the last of his men and shepherded them toward the hangar. "What about the prisoners?" one of them asked.

Kurt looked at the sadistic leader. "What's it going to be, Jinn? Are you going to leave your men to be eaten alive?"

"Whether they live or die means nothing to me," he said. "But perhaps you'd like to go get them since you care for them so much."

"No," Kurt said, "I'm not sending anyone down for them."

"Then you are as ruthless as me."

Kurt glared at Jinn. The man disgusted him. But Kurt wouldn't risk one good person for the lives of those down below.

"This is what's going to happen," Kurt said. "We're going to get on those airships and fly away and you're going to be left behind to die in a manner you justly deserve. Your power play does nothing but murder your own men and take the two of you with them in a slow-motion suicide."

He took the laptop, placed it on the rough surface of the helipad and shoved it toward Jinn.

Jinn stared at it but did nothing more.

Zarrina seemed nervous. She bit her lip, hesitated and then spoke. "Type in the code," she said to Jinn.

Behind them the first two airships were ready, their pods inflated to full volume, their fans powering up. The third was right behind them.

"What's the word?" Kurt asked Marchetti without turning.

"If we deploy the air anchors and get up to speed before we go off the edge, I think we can carry eleven," Marchetti said. "I think."

"Put twelve on each."

"But I'm not sure—"

Kurt silenced him with a glance and looked Marchetti in the

eye. "I'm going to need your help," he said, handing him one of the small radios. "Now, what's the word?"

"Twelve," Marchetti said. "We can do twelve . . . I hope."

"That's only thirty-six," Gamay said, calculating quickly. "There are thirty-seven of us."

Jinn smiled at the numbers. "I suppose someone is staying behind to die."

Kurt replied without blinking. "I am."

CHAPTER 56

JOE WENT INTO THE WATER OF LAKE NASSER IN AN OLD-school diving getup. It wasn't exactly the old brass helmeted, Mark V salvage gear the U.S. had stopped using shortly after World War Two, but it came close.

A thirty-pound helmet of stainless steel fit over his head and onto the shoulders of the suit. A fifty-pound belt strapped around his waist and heavy, weighted boots made taking a few steps a Frankenstein-like walk.

An air hose, a steel cable and a high-pressure line for pumping the Ultra-Set were attached to the shoulder mounts. They made him feel like a marionette, but once he hit the water Joe was glad for every ounce of weight and the security of the steel cable.

The weight kept him balanced in the swirling current. The cable, which was attached to a dive boat above him, was the only way to ascend with so much weight on. If it snapped, he would sink to the bottom like a stone and probably be excavated in a thousand years or so, only to baffle future archaeologists.

Joe had no desire to be part of the Valley of the Dead. All he wanted to do was to stop the dam from being washed away.

If he and the supervisor were right, the main breach was containable, and while disastrous, especially for those close to the dam, it was not cataclysmic. It would widen, perhaps to the full width of the dam, but the clay core and the gentle slope of the structure would keep it from eroding any deeper.

Eventually, like water spilling out of an overflowing bathtub, the water level in the lake would drop to a level matching the depth of the breach and the flow would slow and eventually stop.

But if the microbots were burrowing into the clay core from the tunnel, the incredible pressure of the water would weaken the core itself. It would eventually fail. A bigger, deeper, more jagged breach would form and there would be nothing to keep the dam from total collapse.

As Joe's feet touched down on the sloping surface below, the speaker in his helmet crackled.

"Diver, can you hear me?" It was the supervisor. He was up above, risking his life on the dive boat, along with the major and another technician.

"Barely," Joe said.

"We're just over a hundred feet from the breach," the supervisor said. *"It continues to widen at a rate of three feet per minute. You have less than thirty minutes to find the entry point or we'll be caught in the outflow and dragged over the top of the dam."*

Joe figured differently. Within twenty minutes, the breach would be too close for either he or the boat to fight the effects of the current.

"I never wanted to go over the falls in a barrel," he said, "and I still don't. Let's get this done. Start pumping the dye."

A pump above on the dive boat began to rumble, and a secondary line attached to the Ultra-Set hose pressurized.

Down below, a high-pressure spray of fluorescent orange particles began to jet out of the hose. Joe switched on a black light attached to his helmet. The particles lit up like fireflies as they swirled in the murky water washing slowly to Joe's left.

At the limit of his vision, Joe saw them quicken and speed toward the surface headed for the breach in the dam. That was the death zone. When that high-speed current reached him, there would be no escape.

Joe moved across the wall, hopping side to side like a spaceman on the moon. He washed the dye up and back across the area where the tunnel's entry point was suspected to be. It flowed oddly over the uneven surface of the boulders and stones.

Ten minutes and twenty swaths later, they were still without luck.

"We need to go deeper," Joe said. "Pull us back away from the dam."

"The farther out we go, the stronger the drag from the break in the dam," the supervisor said.

"It's either that or call it a day," Joe said.

"Hang on."

A second later Joe felt the steel cable lift him off the slope. From there he was dragged backward perhaps another thirty or forty feet and dropped down again.

As he landed, he could feel the sideways pull of the current tugging at his feet. He pulled the trigger on the fluorescent spray and saw it catch in the crosscurrent to the left. At first it looked no different than the other marking attempts, but this time Joe noticed an eddy swirling in the pattern.

"Ten feet left," he said.

"Closer to the breach?"

"Yes."

Joe began to walk. High above, the dive boat moved with him. He pulled the trigger again, aiming the reflective stream of particles right at the center of the eddy.

The glowing particles swirled and the majority of the spray was sucked into a gap between two railroad tie–sized beams of concrete, vanishing in a blink like fish disappearing into coral at the sight of a predator. It happened so quick, Joe had to trigger a second burst of the spray just to be sure.

"I've found it," he said. "The gap is between two concrete pylons in the riprap. I can feel the suction from it."

As Joe got closer, he felt himself being pulled into the gap. He could see sand and gravel disappearing from around the edges of the beams. A crater was widening beneath them, he could see what looked like a twenty-inch-diameter hole.

He wedged a foot against one of the concrete beams to keep from getting sucked in. As much as he wanted to block the hole, he personally didn't want to be the plug.

"I'm ready for the mud."

"Mud?"

"The Ultra-Set," Joe clarified, awkwardly holding himself back.

"Starting the pumps now," the supervisor said.

Careful to maintain his balance, Joe managed to jam the front end of the hose into the opening. As the pressure came up, he pulled the trigger.

The Ultra-Set began flowing out at high pressure, some of it escaped into the water, looking like magenta-colored whipped cream as it expanded and hardened. Most of it funneled into the breach drawn down by the suction of the unwanted tunnel.

"How much does this stuff expand?" Joe asked.

"Twenty times its original volume," the supervisor said. *"And then it hardens."*

Joe hoped it would. And if there were any microbots left in the core, trying to widen and expand the breach, he hoped they would be caught in it and frozen in place like insects in amber.

The current tugged him to the left and he heard the rumble of the falls over the motor of the boat and the pump above him.

"Anything?" Joe asked after about thirty seconds.

"Control reports orange dye from the lower geyser," the supervisor said. *"The water flow is unchanged."*

"How much of this stuff do we have?"

"The tank holds five hundred gallons," the supervisor told him. *"It pumps two hundred gallons per minute."*

Joe hoped it would be enough. He held the nozzle and reset his feet to fight the crosscurrent.

The major came on the radio next.

"Mr. Zavala, we're awfully close to the breach. We're running full power just to keep ourselves out of the fray. If you could hurry . . ."

Joe looked up through the window in the top of the huge helmet. He could see the lights on the underside of the boat and the swirling turbulence where the propeller was churning full speed.

"I'm not exactly taking a lunch break down here," he said.

Joe shut the nozzle off for a moment, climbed up on the boulder field and, using the leverage of his feet, pushed a boulder down the slope and into the gap. It plugged somewhat, leaving a much smaller fissure.

Joe jammed the hose back into place and pulled the trigger again. "Go to full pressure on the hose," he said. "We either fill it or we don't."

Joe held the trigger down and the Ultra-Set surged forward.

As it did, he felt the current changing around him. The pull from the opening in front of him was lessening, but the side load dragging him toward the breach was picking up steam.

"Control reports the flow lessening. Ultra-Set spewing from the geyser!"

Joe's left foot slipped out from under him as the side current intensified and suddenly he was surrounded by red foam. The tunnel was packed and the Ultra-Set was spewing out of the now blocked hole like a bottle of carbonated soda that had been shaken and then opened.

Joe caught himself and then stumbled again. He shut off the valve.

"Bring me up!" he shouted.

The steel cord yanked him off the slope and then dropped him back down again, but it wasn't a vertical tug, it was a sideways one that almost tipped him off his feet. For a second Joe was confused. Why was he being pulled sideways?

A call from above straightened it out. *"We're caught in the current!"* the major shouted. *"We're getting pulled into the breach!"*

CHAPTER 57

GAMAY TROUT STARED AT KURT AUSTIN ON THE DARK, COLD bridge of the helipad. Nothing in the air could have chilled her like the words he'd just spoken.

"You're not staying here," Gamay said.

"Those things are overloaded with twelve of you," he said. "Another one hundred and ninety pounds will put one of them in the drink."

Down below, the lights had begun to blow as the horde of metal sand crawled over them and covered them up. All of zero deck had gone dark, central park no doubt being stripped bare.

A strange sound, like concrete blocks being dragged over metal, seemed to resonate from all directions as trillions of the microbots slid across one another, filling the nooks and crannies of the island and beginning to climb vertically.

"But you'll die here!" Leilani cried out.

"I'm not going to die," Kurt insisted.

Gamay noticed he never took his eyes off Jinn. "He's going to give us the code and shut these things down before they eat us alive."

"I would not count on that," Jinn said.

To their left, the first airship accelerated forward, picking up speed and rolling off the edge of the platform before dropping . . . dropping . . . dropping toward the zero deck. As its speed came up, the descent slowed and then finally at thirty feet or so it began to climb.

"You two get on the airships and get out of here," Kurt said.

Leilani stared at Kurt with her mouth agape. Gamay understood him better. Kurt was locked in a test of wills with Jinn.

"Come with me," she said to Leilani. They walked along the edge of the platform as the second airship launched. Marchetti and the last ride out waited.

"What is he doing?" Leilani asked.

"He thinks he can break Jinn and force him to countermand the doomsday order."

"But that's insane," Leilani said.

"Maybe," Gamay said. "But if what Jinn told us yesterday is true, his doomsday command will take a lot of lives and cause years of worldwide misery. If he dies, it'll never be countermanded, but to take him with us means two or three of our people have to stay behind and die. Kurt would never give in to that and I can't blame him. The only way we can help him is to get off the island. Give him one less thing to worry about."

Marchetti hustled them aboard the airship as the fans cranked up to full speed.

"Ready," she said.

A few pairs of boots were thrown out and the rifles the men carried, even some of the heavy jackets, anything to lighten the load a few more pounds.

Paul grasped her hand tight as they picked up speed.

Gamay held her breath as they went over the edge. It felt like they were cresting a ridge on a roller coaster. Her knees went weak and her stomach seemed to float for several seconds as the nose pitched down and the airship dropped and accelerated.

Rising up toward them, she saw the flat area of the central park teaming with masses of the microbots. The descent didn't seem to be slowing fast enough.

"Marchetti?"

"Hang on," he said.

They were still descending way too fast. Marchetti was pulling back on the controls, and the horrible sound of untold numbers of metal machines eating rang in her ears. The descent began to slow, the craft leveled and skimmed across the park, narrowly missing a tree covered top to bottom with the invading horde.

Finally they began to rise, climbing slowly as they crossed the island's threshold and moved out over the ocean.

"Fly the airship," Marchetti said to his chief. "Keep our speed up. Keep us close enough for a signal lock on Wi-Fi."

"What are you going to do?" Gamay asked.

"I have to set up the computer," he said.

"The computer?"

He nodded. "Just in case your friend actually knows what he's doing."

CHAPTER 58

THE HORRIBLE FEELING OF EVENTS SPIRALING BEYOND HIS control filled Joe Zavala with dread. The dive boat above was being pulled toward the breach where it would go over the falls in a fatal manner. And since he was attached to that boat by a steel cable and an air hose, Joe would soon follow.

Cutting the cable and the hose wouldn't help. He couldn't swim to the surface. Even if he dumped the weight belt, he had fifty pounds of gear on his shoulders and feet.

His feet touched down, he tried to set them but was picked up and pulled sideways once again.

"Give me more line!" he shouted. "Quick!"

He saw the boat high above, saw the phosphorescent wake behind the boat as it fought the current, angling this way and that as the pilot tried to keep its nose aimed upstream. Any side turn would be the end of them as they'd be swept away in a matter of seconds.

Finally Joe felt some slack in the line. He dropped onto the slope and began to scramble over it. He found a large boulder, half the size of a VW or even a VV.

Marching around it, he wrapped the steel cable against its bulk. "Tighten the cable!" he said.

The cable pulled taut, constricted around the boulder and all but sung in the depths as the slack was used up. The boat up above locked into place.

"We're holding," the major called down. *"What happened?"*

"I made you an anchor," Joe said. "Now, tell me someone up there knows what centripetal force is?"

Joe was holding tight. The cable was looped around the boulder but threatening to break.

"Yes," the major said, *"the supervisor knows."*

"Point the boat toward the rocks, take a forty-five-degree angle if the cable holds, then you should slingshot to safety. Beach the boat, and don't forget to reel me in."

"Okay," the major said, *"we'll try."*

Joe held the cable tight, putting his steel boots up against the boulder.

The boat above changed course and began to move sideways. Like the Earth's gravity directing the moon, the steel cable caused the boat's path to curve and accelerate. The boat cut through the current and was flung forward.

A twang sounded through the water. Joe felt himself tumbling backward.

The cable had snapped in two.

At first he was dragged by the current toward the topside breach, but then the lines and hoses connecting him to the dive boat pulled him the other way.

As the boat raced into the shallows and beached on the rocks, Joe was dragged into the boulder field down below. Each blow felt like being in a car crash and Joe was suddenly thankful for the hard stainless steel helmet.

When the ride stopped, Joe was thirty feet under, the suit was filling with water and the air hose was either severed or kinked because no air was coming through. Joe knew he couldn't swim, but he could climb. Up he went, crawling across the concrete pylons and boulders like a raccoon in a garbage dump.

He shed the weight belt and the task got easier. As he went higher, the light from the bottom of the boat grew brighter. With his air running out, Joe pulled himself to the surface, emerging like the Creature from the Black Lagoon.

He collapsed between two of the boulders, unable to hold up the helmet and shoulder harness without the buoyancy of the water. He struggled to lift it off, but it wouldn't budge until two sets of helping hands pulled it off for him.

"Did we do it?" Joe asked.

"You did it," the major said, hugging Joe and lifting him up. "You did it."

CHAPTER 59

HIGH UP ON THE HELIPAD, THE EERIE, OMNIPRESENT SOUND of the microbots continued to grow louder. It came everywhere at the same time like demented electromagnetic cicadas, chirping by the billions and moving closer with every passing moment.

The noise was grating to Kurt Austin, but it seemed to be affecting Zarrina and Jinn more than him.

Zarrina looked over the edge and ran her gaze upward along the sides of the buildings between which the helipad rested. The stain of the approaching horde was now three-quarters of the way up the pyramids, the white structures becoming covered in dark gray and black.

"Give him the code," she said.

"Never," Jinn replied.

"You should listen to her, Jinn," Kurt said. "She's not a good woman, but she's not an idiot either."

"We have people, money, lawyers," she reminded him. "We don't have to die."

"Do not speak!" Jinn demanded.

She grabbed him. "Please, Jinn," she begged.

Jinn slapped her hand away and grabbed her by the collar of her shirt. He glared at her in fury. "You weaken me, woman!"

Before she could reply he shoved her backward, sending her over the edge.

Zarrina fell, screaming as she dropped. She hit what was now a six-inch layer of microbots ten stories below, blasting them in all directions like a cloud of dust. She lay there uncovered for all of a few seconds and then the swarm converged on her, covered her up and began to feed.

Jinn stared for a moment, anger, not pity, etched on his face. But Kurt thought he detected a little bit of fear. The speed with which the microbots devoured things was unsettling. Jinn knew that better than anyone else.

"Take a good hard look, Jinn. That's how you're going to die," Kurt said. "Ready to go out like that?"

It continued to grow darker around them. The bots were only one story below, cutting off all light that shone upward. Only the few halogen lamps on the side of the hangar and the red post lights at the edges of the helipad illuminated them now.

Jinn looked slightly less sure of himself. "You're going to die with me," he reminded Kurt.

"For my friends. For my country. For people around the world who would suffer if you win. I don't have a problem with that. What are you dying for?"

Jinn stared, his face flush with anger, his lip curling into a snarl as his eyes narrowed. He knew his bluff had been called. Dying got him nothing. No wealth, no power, no legacy. His whole world was his own being, his own arrogance, his own greatness. When his existence ended, even the doomsday actions of the microbots would bring him no satisfaction.

At that moment he hated Kurt with every fiber of his being. Hated him enough to lose all sense of balance.

He charged toward Kurt like a wrestler going in for the kill.

Instead of shooting Jinn, Kurt turned the rifle sideways, using it as a bar. He took Jinn's momentum and used it against him. Falling backward, Kurt kicked a boot into Jinn's solar plexus and flipped him. The move sent Jinn flying through the air and tumbling hard.

Kurt popped back up to his feet in time to see Jinn crash squarely on his back. Jinn got up a little slowly, more stunned than injured.

"Not used to fighting much, are you?" Kurt baited Jinn.

Jinn grabbed some type of pipe that had been tossed out of one of the airships. He came at Kurt, swinging it like a sword.

Still holding the rifle in both hands, Kurt blocked the pipe and jabbed the butt of the rifle into Jinn's face. The blow opened a gash that bled profusely.

Jinn stumbled back, dropping the pole, putting his hands to his bloody face. Kurt stepped forward and kicked the pole off the platform.

It fell into the dark, trailing a strange whistling sound from its hollow ends.

By now the rising stain of the horde had reached the edge of the helipad, its first probing fingers curling up and onto the flat surface, converging toward the middle from all sides.

Kurt was running out of time.

Through a mask of blood Jinn shouted, "If you didn't have that rifle, I would kill you with my bare hands!"

Kurt pointed the rifle at him and then flung it off the deck. "You can't beat me, Jinn!" he yelled. "I'm better than you. I'm fighting for something that matters, all you're doing is playing out the string. You don't want to die. You're afraid to die. I can see it in your eyes."

Jinn charged again, the rage distorting his face. This time Kurt set his feet and dropped his shoulder, slamming it into Jinn's gut. He wrapped his arms around Jinn's torso, picked him up and body-slammed him to the deck.

From out of nowhere Jinn produced a knife. It sliced Kurt's arm before he could grab Jinn's wrist. Blood flowed, pain surged through him, but Kurt's strength and determination prevailed. He slammed Jinn's hand down on the deck, smashing it three times before Jinn released the knife.

Kurt swatted it away and it skipped into the approaching tide of microbots.

It was now or never. Jinn tried to get up, but Kurt elbowed him in the face and then slammed his head to the deck. Gripping Jinn's hair, he twisted the man's face to the side, forcing Jinn to look at the horde that was approaching.

"Look at them!" Kurt shouted, holding Jinn's cheek to the deck. "Look at them!"

Jinn had given up fighting now. He stared at the advancing horde. The line was getting closer, the circle around them getting smaller.

They reached a trail of blood and swarmed into it like ants crawling all over one another. They glistened beneath the overhead lights, and the sound of their movement was overwhelming, like a monstrous swarm of bees and fingernails on chalkboard mixed together.

"Give me the code!" Kurt demanded.

The laptop sat a few feet away, the horde had already encircled it. It was literally floating on the sea of microbots.

"What good will it do you now?"

"Just give it to me!"

Kurt held him down, Jinn pushed back into him, trying to keep his face out of the approaching line of bots. His lips trembled as they crawled onto him, moving into the cut on his cheek. He spat them from his mouth, but some got into his eyes, they stung like acid.

"Now, Jinn! Before it's too late!"

"221-798-615," Jinn shouted.

Kurt yanked Jinn to his feet. "Did you hear that, Marchetti?"

A tinny voice came from Kurt's pocket. *"Transmitting now!"*

The scraping sound continued. Kurt pulled Jinn back, but the circle of safe ground had shrunk to the size of a kitchen table and then to a manhole cover.

"Marchetti?!"

Suddenly, the horde went still. The sound of their chewing and crawling and scratching dissipated in a wave, flowing outward in all directions like a giant wave of dominoes falling.

They dropped from the sides of the buildings in huge sheets, flowing down and piling up dunes of gray and black with their bodies. A cloud of them drifted like dust across the zero deck below.

In the wake of all that terrible noise came normal sounds, the creaking of the huge metal island and the soft fans of the airships circling it.

"Good work, Marchetti," he said. "Now, come back down here and help me clean up this mess."

CHAPTER 60

KURT AUSTIN WAITED IN THE DARK AS THE AIRSHIPS CIR-
cled and finally began to approach. Standing at the edge of the
helipad, he watched as the lead ship floated in, slowly sinking
toward the pad. With the fans tilted down in a vertical position
to slow the descent like retro-rockets on a moon lander, the microbots were blasted around like ash from a volcano.

They swirled into the air, a cloud of metallic dust, drifting and
falling toward the zero deck below.

A few feet away, down on his knees, Jinn watched the cloud
fall but otherwise made no movement. He was a beaten man, a
broken man. He looked different, Kurt thought.

"You'll send me to prison," he mumbled.

"For ten times your natural life span," Kurt replied.

"Can you see a man like me surviving in prison?" Jinn asked,
looking up.

"Only long enough to go insane," Kurt replied.

Jinn looked toward the edge. The darkness beckoned. "Let
me go."

Kurt could see what he had in mind. "Why should I?"

"As a kindness to a vanquished enemy," Jinn mumbled.

Kurt stared at Jinn for a long moment. Without a word, he stepped back.

Jinn came up off his knees and glanced at Kurt. "Thank you," he said and then turned away.

He took three steps and was gone.

CHAPTER 61

By high noon in Egypt the danger at Aswan had nearly passed. The water level in Lake Nasser had dropped twenty feet. A six-foot wave continued to pour across the crest and through the four-hundred-foot-wide gap, but it was a smoother, more controlled flow now. With the spillways, turbine gates and the diversion canal remaining wide open, it was hoped that a point of equilibrium would be reached by the middle of the next day.

Still, tragedy had not been completely averted.

As Joe stared downstream, it looked entirely different than what he'd seen the night before. The buildings were gone—not damaged, not flooded out, just gone. So were the docks and the boats and even some of the sandstone cliffs. The banks of the river remained flooded and instead of looking like a narrow river, it looked like a lake.

Above that lake, helicopters circled by the dozens like dragon-flies over a pond. Small boats had been brought in and were zipping here and there. Power remained on at the dam, though there was nowhere to send it as all the transmission lines had been swept away.

Joe turned and slumped down by an Army trailer. At Major Edo's insistence, a nurse checked on him. He could have used an IV, but he refused it. Medical supplies would run short rather quickly, he guessed, and others would need them more than him.

She handed him a bottle of water, threw a blanket over his shoulders and moved away.

Major Edo sat down and offered him a cigarette. Joe refused it, and the major stuffed them back in his pocket. "Dirty habit," he said, trying to smile.

"How many?" Joe asked.

"At least ten thousand," the major said sadly. "Probably twice that when we're done looking."

Joe felt like he'd gone twelve rounds with a heavyweight, survived, thinking he'd won, only to find out the judges had scored it the other way.

"It could have been millions," the major said firmly. He put a hand on Joe's shoulder. "Do you understand?"

Joe looked up at him and nodded.

A helicopter landed nearby. A private ran up to the major. "We're loaded with wounded."

"Where are you taking them?" the major asked.

"Luxor. It's the nearest hospital that has power."

"Take him with you," the major said.

"Who is he?" the private asked.

"His name is Joseph Zavala. He is a hero of the Egyptian people."

CHAPTER 62

ONE WEEK LATER PAUL AND GAMAY TROUT WERE SITTING around a large circular table in the luxurious Citronelle restaurant in Washington, D.C. They were joined by Rudi Gunn and Elwood Marchetti. They ordered cocktails and traded stories while waiting for the other guests to arrive.

"What's going to become of your island?" Paul asked Marchetti.

The inventive genius shrugged. "It's ruined beyond repair. And no one can step aboard until we're sure all the bots are cleaned out. It may take years. By then the Indian Ocean will have battered Aqua-Terra until it sinks down to the seabed."

"That's dreadful," Gamay said. "All those years of effort gone forever."

Marchetti smiled slyly. "That's what the insurance company is going to say when I put in a claim for irreversible infestation."

Paul glanced over at two empty chairs. "Where are our honored friends?"

"Not to mention our dinner benefactors," added Rudi Gunn.

Kurt and Joe's bet had been ruled a tie. They were glad to agree to split the tab and just thankful they were alive to host the party. Though no one had heard from them yet this evening.

"What's the latest on the Pickett's Islander's Pain Machine?" Gamay asked.

"Our computer division scoured it out of long-missing files," Gunn answered. "It was described as a secret World War Two project created to stop Japanese banzai missions. In those days, the Japanese believed it was a glorious thing to die for the Emperor. When they couldn't attack using normal flanking maneuvers, they would make suicidal charges in human waves, shouting, 'Banzai!' or 'Tenno Heika Banzai!' which meant 'Ten thousand years of rule to the Emperor!'

"The Pain Maker was designed to incapacitate the attacking force and allow the Americans to capture and interrogate valuable prisoners while stopping wholesale slaughter the Japanese were intent on causing themselves."

"Why wasn't the machine used during the war?" asked Paul.

"Soon after the *John Bury* went missing, the War Department determined that the machine was too easy to replicate if captured and could be used against our island assault forces."

"And now the machines from Pickett's Island sit in some obscure military warehouse, gathering dust," added Gamay.

"That's the size of it," replied Gunn.

At that moment their attention became focused on a tall, craggy figure with dark hair and sharp green eyes who entered the private dining room.

"Please don't get up," Dirk Pitt said with a broad smile. He held up a small card in his hand. "One of the Agency's credit cards. This one is on Uncle Sam."

Gamay laughed. "Kurt and Joe will be happy."

"Where are they?" asked Paul.

"Right behind me," Dirk said, motioning toward the arched doorway.

They all turned toward the doorway as Kurt walked in with Joe, and Leilani a step behind. The women embraced. The men shook hands, hugged one another and kissed the ladies on the cheek.

"We have a head start on you," Paul said, motioning a waiter to the table. "What will be your pleasure?"

Dirk ordered a Don Julio Blanco Tequila on the rocks with lime and salt. Joe took a Jack Daniel's on the rocks. Leilani preferred a Kettle One Cosmopolitan while Kurt asked for a Bombay Sapphire Gin Gibson straight up—a martini with onions instead of olives.

"Well, now," Dirk said to Joe. "Since you're the man of the hour, with a gold star on your chart, show us your Egyptian medal."

Joe flushed with embarrassment. "It's been seen for the last time."

"What did you do with it?"

"It's in my sock drawer."

Gamay laughed. "Now, *there's* a modest man."

Paul held out a newspaper. It was pink. *The Financial Times*, printed in the UK.

He read a list of possible consequences had the tragedy not been averted. It included a million dead, starvation, anarchy and even all-out war in the Middle East had the blame mistakenly been foisted on Israel instead of being traced back to Jinn and his group in Yemen.

At this point he almost looked chagrinned. "But Joe is not going to like this part," he said, then read on. "*All of this* and more was averted due to heroic efforts of the dam's operations team, the military force, including Major Edo and an unnamed American who is now being hailed as an Egyptian hero and who will receive the coveted Order of the Nile medal."

Gamay shook her head. "That's not fair."

"At least he got a medal for it," Dirk said grinning.

"That's the best the government could do for Joe saving a million lives?"

Leilani joined in. "I know him well enough now to have learned Joe doesn't like being the center of attention unless of course he's surrounded by a bevy of gorgeous women."

Joe laughed. "You've just given me a reason to return to Egypt."

"All joking aside," said Dirk, "if not for Joe risking his own life on an intrepid mission to stop the flow coming through Aswan Dam, a million lives along the river would have been lost."

"Do they have a count?" Rudi Gunn asked.

"At least ten thousand," Pitt replied slowly.

Joe looked like he'd crawled into a shell of embarrassment. "I'd like another Jack Daniel's on the rocks. A double this time."

For a few moments they sipped their drinks in a silence that was finally broken by Paul. "How do we stand with Jinn's underground factory?"

Dirk checked the orange dial of his Doxa dive watch. "It was blown into a scrap yard forty minutes ago, allowing for the time differential."

"Would bombs from the air penetrate deep enough into the mountain to destroy the factory?" Gamay inquired.

"They can and they did," revealed Pitt. "A heavy drone fired two missiles. An initial impulse invisible from the ground accelerated them to three hundred miles per hour straight down. Their main boosters erupted and they accelerated to well over two thousand miles per hour. Crashing and blasting a twenty-foot crater, but not strong enough to burst into Jinn's vast subterranean factory.

"So five minutes later a different kind of ordinance was launched at the deep caverns. Four B-2 bombers flew over Yemen carrying what were known as MOPs, a military acronym for Massive Ordinance Penetrators. Thirty-thousand-pound GPU-57s, the most powerful nonnuclear bunker-busting weapon in the world. The bombs carry over five thousand pounds of explosives packed in a twenty-five-thousand-pound metal casing. They strike with such momentum, they can punch through four hundred feet of dirt and rock. When the dust settled, the entire mountain was gone. All that remained was a pile of sand and rubble. The equipment and material for creating the microbots are gone."

"What about Jinn's right-hand man, Sabah?" Kurt asked, checking his own watch and glad to have it back, even at the cost of a new, top-of-the-line scooter.

"Blown to the size of microbots," Pitt said caustically.

Dinner was finally served in a festivity directed by the executive chef, beginning with Black Sea spiced King Olaf salmon. The next course was smoked sturgeon, followed by goose foie gras and a selection of pork pâtés and duck terrine.

The main course was St. Louis–style baby back ribs accompanied with lobster ravioli and braised leeks with fried eggs.

Dessert was a crepe stuffed with guava and mascarpone. The red wine was Purple Angel Carménère and the white Duckhorn Sauvignon Blanc.

Sated with good food, delightful wine, and exhilarating company, they all bid their farewells and began drifting from the restaurant, eventually congregating in a stretch limousine Dirk had provided for his friends so they would all reach their homes safely.

Leilani was staying in the city at a hotel and Kurt promised to see her home.

Dirk looked at him for a long moment. "You may hold your booze, but if a cop stops you, it's the slam with a DUI. I strongly suggest you take a cab."

"I shall do so," said Kurt.

After the rest had left in the limo, a cab pulled up to the restaurant. Kurt and Leilani settled into the backseat on the way to her hotel.

"Have you decided on taking the job at NUMA that Dirk offered you in the marine biology department?" he asked.

She almost looked sad. "Washington isn't for me. I'm going back to Hawaii and the biological institute on Maui."

Kurt squeezed her hand. "I'll miss you."

"I'll miss you too," she said. "I hope you understand."

Kurt smiled. "What's his name?"

Her eyes widened for a moment and then she smiled back. "His name is Kale Luka."

Kurt smiled again. "I'm glad you won't be alone."

The cab arrived at her hotel. She opened the door and paused.

"Good-bye, Leilani," Kurt spoke softly. "I'll think of you often."

"And I of you." She leaned over and gave him a light kiss on the lips. Then the door closed and she was gone.